The Red Icon

SAM EASTLAND

FABER & FABER

First published in 2015
by Faber & Faber Ltd
Bloomsbury House
74–77 Great Russell Street
London WC1B 3DA

Typeset by Faber and Faber Ltd
Printed and bound by CPI Group (UK) Ltd, Croydon CR0 4YY

A CIP record for this book
is available from the British Library

ISBN 978–0–571–31228–3

FSC
www.fsc.org
MIX
Paper from
responsible sources
FSC® C101712

2 4 6 8 10 9 7 5 3 1

For Deb

2 February 1945

Ahlborn, Germany, near the River Oder, 70 km from Berlin

'You can always tell when a man's luck has run out.'

Captain Antonin Proskuryakov of the Red Army's Kantemirovskaya Armoured Division, was fond of saying this. He would often use the expression in the presence of young officers newly arrived at the front and he greatly enjoyed the effect it had upon them. As the longest surviving tank commander in the Division, Proskuryakov's words took on the weight of prophecy.

'You can see it in his eyes,' Proskuryakov told these newly minted lieutenants, who would glance nervously at one another, wondering whether the curse of lucklessness might already be upon them.

But now, as Captain Proskuryakov surveyed the blazing ruins of his T34 tank, he was forced to consider the possibility that his own run of good fortune might finally have stumbled to a halt.

It was Proskuryakov's father, a former officer in the Tsar's Nizhegorodsky Cavalry Regiment, who had explained to him that luck, good or bad, always travelled in threes. In the Nizhegorodsky Regiment, that was the number of horses a person could have shot out from under him, after which work would be found for the soldier as something other than a rider.

It didn't matter that the death of the three animals might not have been the man's fault. What mattered was that it had happened.

This was the third T34 under Proskuryakov's command to have been reduced to uselessness, and he knew that it would almost certainly be his last.

The first tank, an early model A, had gone through the ice of a lake near Cheropovets in the winter of 1941. Although he had expected either to be executed for gross negligence or, at the very least, transferred to a penal battalion, Proskuryakov was stunned to learn, soon afterwards, that a new tank had been found for him and that he would suffer no disciplinary action. He was even awarded the Distinguished Tanker badge and a Combat Service Medal in Silver, both of which he immediately fastened to his combat jacket.

His second tank, a model C, lasted him almost a year before it was hit by a Stuka dive-bomber on the outskirts of Stalingrad. Proskuryakov had been sleeping in a foxhole a short distance from his tank when he woke to the shriek of the bomber as it plunged towards its target. Already folded almost double in his primitive shelter, he curled into an even tighter ball and clenched his teeth. There was nothing else he could do. Just when it seemed that the sound itself would shatter Proskuryakov's bones, he felt a stunning crash as a bomb landed squarely on the turret of his tank not twenty yards away. A wave of heat passed over him. Through one of the buttonholes of his cape, he saw the grass catch fire at the edge of his foxhole.

By the time Proskuryakov made it to his feet, the Stuka was nothing more than a black, smoky stain on the horizon.

He and the rest of the crew, who had been cowering in

their own shelters during the attack, now stared in amazement at the ruin of their 26-ton machine. The turret, which itself weighed more than four tons, had been lifted from the chassis and now lay upside down beside the tank. On closer inspection, Proskuryakov observed that the bomb had not only wrenched away the turret but had blown a hole the size of a bathtub in the floor of the driving compartment.

In spite of the grim predictions Proskuryakov made, loudly and to anyone who would listen, regarding his future, he received no reprimand. In fact, he was commended for having the forethought to evacuate his crew as a safety precaution in the night. This earned him two more medals; the Order of Glory (Second Class) and a coveted Order of the Red Banner, as well as command of a new tank.

In addition to the impressive row of medals that he wore even when riding into combat, Proskuryakov had now begun to exhibit some of the quirks of those whose longevity had earned them a place more meaningful than any rank or decoration. One such eccentricity was a heavy leather jacket, which he had peeled from the back of a Hungarian tank man whom he found sitting cross-legged against a tree, dead and frozen solid, back in the winter of 1942.

There was no way to remove this jacket from the ice-bound man, so Proskuryakov picked up the corpse and tied it to the back of the tank. There, the Hungarian sat for days, his eyes filled with snow and hands folded like a Buddha in his lap, until a warm snap in the weather thawed him out and Proskuryakov was at last able to claim the trophy, which he had been wearing ever since – along with his medals, of course.

The night before he lost his third tank, Proskuryakov's

machine had developed a leaky fuel pump and he had received permission to make his way to the nearest repair depot, ten kilometres away in the village of Eberfelden.

'Looks like you'll be walking to Berlin,' remarked a fellow tank officer.

'I will ride through the streets of that city,' Proskuryakov had replied indignantly, 'and I will do so in this beautiful machine!'

With poppy-coloured flames pouring from the open hatches of his T34, Proskuryakov remembered his boast about riding into Berlin.

At first light, he had set off for the depot, bringing with him only his driver, Sergeant Ovchinikov. Proskuryakov was determined that this trip should take as little time as possible since he had just been granted leave, his first in over two years. His plan was to get the monstrous vehicle repaired, hand over temporary command to Sergeant Ovchinikov and then get on the first truck headed east towards his home in Noginsk, just outside of Moscow.

'Soon,' Proskuryakov told his sergeant, resting his hand lovingly upon the dull green metal of the tank, 'soon all of this will be yours.'

Ovchinikov turned and scowled at him, his wind-burned face contrasting starkly with the pale and unwashed skin beneath his oil-stained blue overalls. 'That's what the devil said to Jesus!'

'I know,' replied Proskuryakov.

Sergeant Ovchinikov was a deeply religious man, and given to begging for God's mercy at every possible occasion.

All this devotion irritated Proskuryakov, to the point where he felt he must either go insane or else shoot his driver and let Ovchinikov's God decide what to do about it. After what he had seen in this war, the idea of a compassionate deity struck him as darkly comical. As far as Proskuryakov was concerned, the universe was not ruled over by some capricious, bearded ancient, hand cupped to his withered ear to catch faint murmurings of adoration from his worshippers below, but rather by a vast, unfeeling mechanism, as infallible as a mathematical equation, whose intricate calculations were responsible for holding the world in balance. It was this mechanism, see-sawing endlessly back and forth with the untiring precision of a metronome, which his father had primitively referred to as luck and to which Sergeant Ovchinikov prayed, loudly and annoyingly, several times a day. The only thing which prevented Captain Proskuryakov from murdering the little driver was the off-chance that he might actually be right.

With only two kilometres to go before reaching the depot, Proskuryakov and Ovchinikov arrived at the outskirts of a village called Ahlborn. The winter snow had thawed, briefly, and the streets of this tiny settlement were thick with mud. No sooner had they entered the village than it felt to Proskuryakov as if the whole right side of the tank had been picked up by an angry giant and thrown down to the ground. He realised at once that they had run over a mine.

The T34 slewed around and then stopped.

Proskuryakov immediately threw open the top turret hatch, climbed out of the tank and jumped down to the ground, followed by Sergeant Ovchinikov.

Together, they inspected the damage.

It had not been one of the large Teller mines, which would

probably have penetrated the main compartment, chopping the interior to pieces, along with anyone who happened to get in the way. More likely, it was one of the smaller Schu mines, which were designed to blow off a man's leg at the knee. The explosion had sheared through one of the holding pins, causing the tread to break, and the forward momentum had carried it right off its track.

Now the track lay like a huge dead snake in the ditch at the side of the trail. If it had been on the road, they might have been able to reverse the tank back on to the track and attach it again with a new pin, but it would take more than the strength of two men to heave the tread out of the ditch.

'We'll have to walk the rest of the way to the depot,' said Ovchinikov. 'They can send another tank to tow us out.'

Proskuryakov hoped it would not be one commanded by the officer to whom he had boasted about driving into Berlin.

Setting out on foot, they had just reached the main street running through the centre of the village when Proskuryakov heard a sound like someone shaking out a rug, and turned to see flames pouring from the open hatch of his tank. Speechless, he stared at the inferno.

There was any number of ways in which the fire could have started. A piece of shrapnel may have ruptured a fuel line. The engine might have overheated as a result of the damage they had been on their way to fix. Whatever the cause, nothing could be done about it now. Once a tank started burning, it usually didn't stop until only a husk of iron remained.

Over the sound of machine-gun bullets exploding inside the T34, with a noise like a string of Chinese firecrackers, both men heard the rumble of a vehicle approaching.

'At least we won't have to walk to Eberfelden,' remarked Ovchinikov. He stepped out into the middle of the road and waved his arms back and forth.

Soon afterwards, they saw a truck enter the outskirts of the village. It was preceded by a small staff car. Probably one of those American lend-lease Jeeps, thought Proskuryakov.

Ovchinikov was still waving his arms when he noticed the large white cross painted on the bonnet of the car, and he realised it wasn't a Jeep after all. It was a German Kübelwagen, and the truck that followed it was a five-ton Hanomag filled with enemy soldiers.

'Run, you idiot!' shouted Proskuryakov.

The two men sprinted for their lives.

After a short sprint in their heavy tanker's clothing, both men were so out of breath that they were forced to take shelter in a small church at the edge of the village. Finding the front door bolted shut, they had forced their way in through a window at the side, only to discover that the roof of the church had collapsed and the interior was a shambles of old pews, roof beams and plaster dust. To the side of the main altar, they came across a doorway leading to a narrow staircase which spiralled down into the earth. At the bottom of this staircase, on the other side of an unlocked iron gate, the two men made their way into a crypt, where pinewood coffins rested in alcoves chipped from the crumbly, sand-coloured rock. There, the Russians huddled silently, freezing in the meat-locker cold.

An hour went by.

'Surely they have gone by now,' whispered Ovchinikov.

Proskuryakov had been thinking the same thing. All he could hear was the murmur of wind blowing through the shattered rafters of the church and the patter of rain, which made its way down through a hole in the floorboards and dripped on to the dusty surface of the crypt. Perhaps they never even saw us, thought Proskuryakov, but he was not yet confident enough to abandon the safety of their hiding place. 'I'll take a look through that gap in the floorboards,' he said, 'but I need something to stand on.'

The two men lifted a coffin from its alcove and heaved it into the middle of the room.

Proskuryakov removed his leather coat and placed it in the corner, out of the way. Then, very carefully, he stepped up on to the coffin and looked out on to the main floor of the church. All he could make out were smashed wooden pews and prayer books lying scattered on the ground. 'There's no one,' he said with a sigh. Even for a man as stubbornly faithless as Proskuryakov, it was hard not to feel as if fate had intervened on their behalf.

What happened next took place so quickly that it was over before Proskuryakov even realised what had occurred. With a loud, dry crack, the lid of the coffin collapsed. One of the captain's heavy boots dropped through the splintered wood, while the other slid off the end of the plank. The whole coffin tipped over and Proskuryakov landed heavily upon the floor.

For a few seconds, he only lay there, too dazed by the fall to react. He swatted at the wreckage which lay on top of him and as his hands tore through old and rotten fabric, he felt his fingernails scrape against what he now realised was frozen human flesh. With a cry Proskuryakov scrambled to his feet, slapping his face and chest as if bees were swarming around him.

'It's all right, Captain,' Ovchinikov assured him as he

attempted to brush the dust out of the captain's hair. 'There's nothing to worry about.'

'I'm not worried!' barked the captain, 'and stop pawing at me, for pity's sake!'

Ovchinikov lit the stump of a candle which he carried in his pocket and the two men turned their attention to the contents of the coffin, which now lay strewn across the floor.

'It's just another dead man,' remarked Proskuryakov, determined to show that he had regained his composure, 'and it looks like he's been that way for quite a while.'

'No,' Sergeant Ovchinikov pointed to an object clutched between the withered, ice-rimed fingers of the corpse. 'There's something else.'

'What is it?' asked Proskuryakov, squinting as he leaned forward to get a better look.

The light of the candle flickered in the sergeant's trembling hand. 'Mother of God,' he whispered.

2 August 1914

St George's Hall, the Winter Palace, St Petersburg, Russia

Inspector Pekkala felt a drop of sweat moving slowly down his neck. It meandered along the trench of his spine, pausing at the knot of each vertebra before continuing its journey. The passage of that droplet filled Pekkala's mind, until he could focus on nothing else. He shrank away from it inside his coat, as if, by some contortion of his body, he might separate his flesh from any contact with his clothes.

Pekkala was a tall, broad-shouldered man. His dark hair, greying at the temples, was swept straight back upon his head. His eyes, a deep, shadowy brown, contained a peculiar silveriness, which people only noticed when he was looking straight at them.

The Great Hall of St George, in which he stood, was filled to capacity. Lining the walls, some in chairs but most of them having remained on their feet, was the entire Russian court, decked out in their formal tailcoats, starched white collars gripping at their throats. Among them waited representatives from all branches of the Russian military. Like exotic birds among the dreary black of politicians stood hussars in scarab-beetle-green tunics, generals of Artillery in strawberry red and men of the elite Chevalier Guard in close-fitting dove-grey uniforms. Present were admirals of the Tsar's Navy, their midnight-blue tunics bisected by the white sashes of the Pacific Fleet at Vladivostok, the pale blue sashes of the Baltic Fleet and the red sashes of the Black Sea Flotilla. The silver-buttoned jackets worn by members of the State Police, known as the Gendarmerie, winked in bolts of sunlight which flooded into the room through the tall window frames, causing the bone-white walls to shimmer like the inside of an abalone shell. And there were a few, like Pekkala himself, who wore no uniform but that which they had chosen for themselves in carrying out their secret duties for the Tsar. These were the men of the Okhrana. They lived in the shadows of the Romanov Empire, hunting its enemies one by one through back alleys where the bomb builders, the contract killers, the anarchists, the poison makers and the forgers plied their trade. For the most deadly of these, the Tsar would always call upon Pekkala. No one else had earned such sacred trust.

Ever since the Tsar had picked him out of a group of military cadets, newly arrived from Finland, which at that time was still a colony of Russia, Pekkala had been trained for one task only – to be the Tsar's personal investigator, answerable to Nicholas II alone, and with no rank or badge of service other than a gold medallion, as wide across as the length of his little finger. Across the centre was a stripe of white enamel inlay, which began at a point, widened until it took up half the disc and narrowed again to a point on the other side. Embedded in the middle of the white enamel was a large, round emerald. Together, the white enamel, the gold and the emerald formed the unmistakable shape of an eye. And it was from this that Pekkala had earned the name by which he was now known across the length and breadth of Russia – the Emerald Eye.

Pekkala shifted uncomfortably in his heavy boots, rocking slowly back and forth from his heels to the balls of his feet. The leather creaked with a sound that reminded him of a wooden boat rolling with the tide. Although the windows had been opened, there was no breeze but that which slithered from the rooftops of St Petersburg, heated on the snake-like scales of slate until it felt like the breath of an oven. Inside hung rows of golden chandeliers, each one of which could burn more than a hundred candles simultaneously. At winter gatherings, these chandeliers would fill the hall with soft light and the soothing smell of beeswax. But now they were extinguished and their presence seemed more menacing, suspended above the bowed and unprotected heads as if they were the blades of guillotines.

Nobody spoke. The only sound came from the clearing of parched throats and the involuntary sighs of those who wondered how long they could last without fainting in a heap upon the polished marble floor.

At the far end of the hall, on a platform raised waist high above the crowd and reached by a series of long, shallow and difficult-to-negotiate steps, knelt the Tsar. He wore a white military tunic and dark trousers tucked into knee-length boots.

Normally, he would have been facing the gathered assembly of dignitaries, seated on a red-and-gold throne, which was sheltered from above by a red velvet canopy, trimmed with yellow brocade and embroidered in gold bullion thread with the double-headed eagle of the Romanovs. On this occasion, however, the throne had been put to one side, making way for a wooden easel as tall as a man and covered with several layers of gold paint, on which rested a small, but vividly painted icon known simply as *The Shepherd*.

The painting showed a man in a white robe, standing beside a large stone. Leaning up against the stone was a stylised version of a shepherd's crook. The man stood at the edge of a lake, on which there were many small islands, all of them crowded with sheep.

Set against the hall's bewildering array of pillars, and the thousands of embellishments growing like moss from every corner, the icon appeared almost too crude to have deserved such a place of honour in the room. Only those who knew its history could understand the reason why the Tsar of all the Russias knelt before it.

The icon had been painted by an unknown artist in Constantinople, sometime in the eleventh century. From there, it had been carried by Crusaders to the city of Kazan, where it was placed for safekeeping in a monastery. In the year 1209, Kazan was overrun by the Tartars, who held it for the next 350 years. It was during this time that *The Shepherd* disappeared and, for generations afterwards, was presumed to have been destroyed. In 1579, as a fire raged across the city, many of Kazan's inhabitants were forced to flee into the surrounding countryside. According to legend, a boy named Nestor, whose family had joined this flood of refugees, received a vision. Jesus appeared before him, wearing the robe of a shepherd, and ordered the boy to return to the house they had recently abandoned. There, the vision told him, something of great value had been hidden. He appealed to his parents, who refused to help, knowing that by now their home had been reduced to ashes. The next night, the vision appeared again. Once more Nestor begged his parents to return and for a second time they refused. When the vision appeared a third time, the parents finally relented. They retraced their steps to the smouldering remains of what had been their house, where, beneath the charred floorboards of his room, Nestor discovered the icon, wrapped in oilcloth and undamaged by the flames.

The following year, the family entrusted *The Shepherd* to Tsar Ivan IV, known as 'Ivan the Terrible', who promised that he, and those who came after him, would keep it safe for all eternity. From then on, the icon was established as the spiritual guardian of the Tsars. Jealously guarded by generations of rulers, it was eventually brought to a secret chamber in the Church of the Resurrection, private chapel of the Tsars on their summer estate at Tsarskoye Selo, just outside St Petersburg. Only in moments of supreme importance was *The Shepherd* brought out from its hiding place and shown to the people of Russia as proof of God's blessing upon the Tsar and his safe-guarding of the country.

Now the Tsar rose slowly to his feet. His face was flushed and, for the first time, the others who waited in the hall could see that he too was suffering in this oppressive August heat.

Unsteadily, he walked down the steps to the floor of the hall, where he was joined by his wife of twenty years, the Tsarina Alexandra, formerly the Grand Duchess of the German State of Hesse, against whose native country Russia was about to declare war. She wore a floor-length dress made of a wispy, off-white fabric, with a white ruffled shirt that covered her entire neck. Her wide-brimmed hat was decorated at the front with a spray of feathers and she carried a white parasol in her right hand. For a moment, their hands touched, his right against her left, and then the Tsar reached into the pocket of his tunic and withdrew a neatly folded sheet of paper.

The silence in the room grew more intense. The crowd watched, leaning forward so as not to miss a word of what was spoken. Even the faint, persistent rhythm of their breathing had been hushed.

The paper trembled in the Tsar's hand as he began to read.

There was no mystery to what he had to say. Those who had filed into the hall two hours before to await the arrival of the Romanovs could have guessed, some of them syllable for syllable, the exact words the Tsar would use to unleash the Russian war machine upon Germany and the crumbling Habsburg Empire.

Barely a month before, on 28 June, a sickly-looking, narrow-shouldered man named Gavrilo Princip had stepped up on to the running board of a Model 1911 Gräf & Stift Double Phaeton saloon transporting the Austrian Archduke Franz Ferdinand, and fired a bullet into his neck, severing the jugular vein, before putting another bullet into his wife, Sophie, Duchess of Hohenberg. In the last seconds of his life, Ferdinand turned to her and, with blood pouring from his mouth on to his powder-blue tunic, begged her not to die. But it was already too late for the Duchess, and the Archduke himself perished before he reached the hospital.

Princip had been part of a small group of anarchists in Serbia who called themselves the Black Hand and had sworn to strike at the Habsburgs on behalf of their Bosnian brothers, whose country had long ago been swallowed up by Austro-Hungarians. They chose, as the date of their attack, the anniversary of Bosnia's inclusion in the Empire and, as their target, the man who had been sent there to commemorate the day.

Armed with hand grenades and Browning automatic pistols supplied to them by a Serbian Intelligence officer, Dragutin Dimitrijević, who went by the code name 'Apis', members of the Black Hand stationed themselves along the route that had been planned for the Archduke's tour of Sarajevo.

As the Archduke's motorcade made its way across the city, one of the assassins, a man named Nedeljko Čabrinović, threw a hand grenade under the car. The grenade had a ten-second fuse and, by the time it exploded, the Archduke's saloon had already passed by. The bomb detonated beneath a car which was travelling behind the Archduke, injuring several of his retinue and a number of nearby civilians.

Čabrinović ran for his life, chased by police and outraged members of the public. Unable to outpace his pursuers, he swallowed a vial of poison and jumped off a bridge into the Miljacka River. The poison failed to work. Čabrinović was hauled out of the water, which was less than a foot deep at that time of year, and nearly beaten to death by the crowd.

Although he was advised against it, the Archduke decided to continue his tour of the city, during which time his motorcade passed by several other members of the band who had sworn to kill him. But confronted by the physical presence of a man and a woman who had, until that moment, been only symbols to them, the assassins hesitated, one after the other, and the moment for action was lost.

An hour later, by which time he had covered most of his planned tour, the Archduke ordered his chauffeur, Leopold Lojka, to proceed to the hospital where those who had been injured earlier in the day were being treated.

Princip, considered by the other members of the Black

Hand to be the least reliable of their number, was standing outside Moritz Schiller's restaurant when the Archduke's car drove past on its way to the hospital.

It was 10.55 a.m.

The street was bustling with pedestrians, slowing the Archduke's progress, and a local governor, Oskar Potiorek, shouted to the chauffeur that he should have taken a different route instead.

The chauffeur, who was unfamiliar with the city, became confused and attempted to back up, but stalled the car when putting it into reverse, almost directly in front of where Princip was waiting.

Faced with this opportunity, and contrary to the expectations of his fellow assassins, Princip decided to carry out his sworn duty.

Believing that he lacked the courage to shoot the couple in cold blood, Princip initially made up his mind to throw a hand grenade, but there were so many people crowding the sidewalk that Princip doubted he would have enough room to throw the bomb and still escape the blast. Instead, he drew his pistol, stepped out into the street, and leapt on to the running board, which acted as a step for passengers climbing in and out of the vehicle. Princip fired the gun without aiming. He was even seen to close his eyes, turning his head to the side as he pulled the trigger twice. Before he could fire a third shot, Princip was dragged to the ground by a guard of the local militia named Smail Spahović.

Hauled away to prison, Princip would die there four years later, wasted away from the effects of tuberculosis.

Within days of the assassinations, Austria had delivered a

series of ultimatums to Serbia, a country only a fraction the size of the Habsburg Empire. When Serbia attempted to negotiate the details of the ultimatum, Austria responded by sending troops across the border to occupy the country.

The incursion by the Habsburgs into what Russia considered a 'buffer state' between itself and the potential threat of invasion by a western army forced the Tsar to begin mobilising his troops. It was no secret, to the Russians or anyone else, that at least six weeks would be required for Russia to bring its army into full preparedness for war. In that length of time, Germany and Austria-Hungary could not only mobilise their troops but could have launched a full-scale invasion. It was vital to the Russians, therefore, that they began mobilising first, if they were to have any hope of defending their country.

But Germany had plans of its own.

If Russia began to mobilise, Germany military policy dictated that the Kaiser must order his own troops to prepare for battle.

With such inflexible strategies in place, the outbreak of war became a foregone conclusion. Long-standing alliances between Britain, France and Russia on one hand, and Germany, Turkey and Austria-Hungary on the other, assured that hostilities would spread.

Too late, the Tsar came to understand that his cousin, Kaiser Wilhelm, had wanted this war all along. Surrounded by the weak and sagging Empires of the Ottomans and Habsburgs, and with only a fraction of the colonies possessed by France and Britain, Wilhelm felt that it was time for Germany to claim an empire for itself. The murder of the Archduke Ferdinand provided him with exactly the catalyst he needed to set in motion the Schlieffen Plan, by which the German Army could strike first at France and the West, before swinging east to devastate the Army of the Tsar. The Tsar appealed to the Kaiser to act as an intermediary between Russia and the Austrians, but Wilhelm had no intention of brokering a peace deal. Nicholas's attempts to avoid hostilities were simply viewed as weakness by his German cousin, who responded by demanding that Russia demobilise its army, even as his own prepared to fight. To this, the Tsar could not agree. Doing so would have left his borders unprotected against two nations, whose armies were already deployed. Reluctantly, the Tsar instructed his Foreign Minister, Sergei Sazonov, that Russia would be going to war.

'I solemnly swear,' announced the Tsar, as he drew his declaration to a close, 'that I will never make peace so long as one of the enemy is on the soil of the fatherland.' This was the same oath Tsar Alexander I had taken when Napoleon's troops invaded in 1812 and, months later, froze to a halt at Borodino, only a few days' march from Moscow.

Carefully, the Tsar folded the piece of paper and returned it to his pocket. Then, with his wife at his side, he began the long walk to the end of the hall, where a balcony looked out over Palace Square, in which thousands of Russians had been waiting for this moment.

As Nicholas and Alexandra passed between the ranks of courtiers, those standing on either side began to applaud. At first, the clapping was uncertain and sporadic. No one seemed sure of what to do. But now the applause began to spread, until it echoed like thunder in the room. Encouraged, the Tsar quickened his pace. The weight of this monumental decision, which had hung on him for days while he tried hopelessly to negotiate a way out of hostilities, now seemed to rise from him and dissipate among the chandeliers.

Pekkala stood beside the balcony, just inside the hall. He had positioned himself there at the beginning of the ceremony, in the hope that it might be more bearable than sweltering in the centre of the room. He did not care for crowded places, and would gladly have stayed away, even from such an historic occasion, if the Tsar had not demanded his presence.

Now, as the Tsar stepped out on to the balcony, he turned and caught Pekkala's eye. Immediately, the creases vanished from his forehead and the clenched muscles of his jaw relaxed. The only time he ever felt truly safe was in the presence of the Emerald Eye.

As soon as the Tsar stepped out on to the balcony, a roar went up from the square which drowned out even the hammering of palms inside the hall. If the Tsar had planned to speak a few words to the crowd, he soon thought better of it. To those below, no voice on earth could have been heard above that roar of celebration.

The Tsar stood beside a huge stone pillar, dwarfed by a shield bearing the Imperial crest which hung from the white metal railings. Unnerved by the long drop to the flagstoned street below, he gripped the railing firmly with one hand and, with the other, saluted the crowd. Glimpsing the pale moon of his palm, the cheering of the masses doubled and redoubled, until Pekkala could feel its vibration in his bones, as if he were standing on a platform as a train raced past the station.

And then the Tsar was calling his name.

Pekkala leaned around the corner. 'Majesty?'

The Tsar beckoned to him. 'Come,' he said. 'You will never see the likes of this again.'

The Tsarina, who had been greeting the throng with both hands raised above her head, saw a movement from the corner of her eye and turned, just as Pekkala stepped cautiously out on to the balcony. 'What are you doing here?' she snapped. 'Get back inside with the others. Get back where you belong!'

'He is not one of the others,' said the Tsar, 'and he is here because I asked him to be.'

For a moment, the Tsarina stared angrily at her husband. Then she turned abruptly and resumed waving to the people below. Pekkala looked out at the thousands of faces, like pink cat licks dappling a summer-clothing sea of browns and reds and blues and whites. Then his gaze wandered to the Tsarina.

He wondered how she must feel, being forced to celebrate this declaration of war against her own people and knowing that, no matter what happened in the months ahead, all allegiance to her adopted Russia would be doubted and dismissed.

The Tsar, by now, was completely swept up in the exhilaration of the moment. 'Do you see, Pekkala?' he shouted, struggling to make himself heard over the crowd, which had pressed forward against a line of policemen, whose linked arms strained to hold them back. 'The spirit of the Russian people is unconquerable! With their faith in me and mine in them, we will bring a peace to this country that will last a thousand years! Nothing can defeat us! Not while we are guided by *The Shepherd*!' He leaned across, resting his hand upon Pekkala's. 'And while the icon is looking after Russia, you will be looking after me!'

For a young man named Stefan Kohl, far to the east of
Petrograd in a tiny village called Rosenheim, a war had already
begun.

His family came from a long line of German farmers who
had been invited by Catherine the Great, herself originally a
German, to settle on the rich farmland near the river Volga.
Beginning in the late 1700s, many such families arrived and
were soon planting crops of wheat and rye in the Volga region's
black and fertile soil. They prospered and, although they were
subjects of Russia, the Volga Germans kept their heritage
intact.

But not all of the inhabitants of Rosenheim considered this
cultural stubbornness to be a good idea.

Instead of the local school, where only German was spoken
and the classes were so small that students of all ages were
lumped together in the same rooms, Stefan's father, Viktor
Kohl, a Lutheran minister, sent his sons to the Russian school
in the nearby town of Krasnoyar.

In Krasnoyar, the Kohl brothers were singled out for bul-
lying, the result not only of their refusal to abandon their
heritage but also of the lingering memory of the preferential
treatment they had received when they first immigrated to
Russia.

Stefan's older brother, Emil, survived at the school by making himself as inconspicuous as possible, and by submitting so
completely to the ridicule and torment of the bullies that they
could find no sport in it, and eventually left him alone. Lacking
the same instincts of self-preservation, Stefan was beaten so

frequently that it became a rite of passage for Russian boys at the school to pick a fight with him.

The last of these scraps occurred between Stefan and a boy named Vyachyslav Konovalov. He was a slight and inoffensive young man, who would never have gone looking for trouble, least of all with the tall and powerful German, if he had not been goaded into it by his Russian classmates. Anxious to prove himself, Konovalov simply walked up to Stefan in the playground and took a swing at him.

Stefan, by now so used to these unprovoked attacks that nothing ever caught him by surprise, stepped back as Konovalov's fist swept harmlessly past his face. Then, using the momentum of Konovalov's swing to set him off balance, Stefan took hold of the boy's arm, turned him sideways and landed a punch of his own. Stefan had been aiming to hit Konovalov in the jaw but as Konovalov spun around he lost his footing and began to fall. Stefan's blow missed Konovalov's jaw and struck him in the throat, causing a haemorrhage of the occipital vein. Konovalov dropped to the ground and immediately began coughing up blood. He was rushed to the hospital and, for a while, his life hung in the balance. Even though Konovalov eventually recovered from his injury, the sight of him retching up gore in the playground was too much for the school and Stefan was expelled.

Viktor Kohl, who had been anxious to improve ties with the nearby Russian community, was so shamed by his son's dismissal that he refused to transfer Stefan to the local school in Rosenheim. Instead, he handed the boy, then aged fifteen, over to the local butcher, a leviathan of a man named Werner Grob, to be trained in a profession in which, he felt, the boy's inherent violence might find some respectable outlet.

Emil, meanwhile, graduated from the school at Krasnoyar and won a scholarship to study at the University of Kiev. Although he did not bear the scars of the beatings which his brother had endured, Emil had not escaped unscathed. The time he spent at school in Krasnoyar had left him deeply troubled from having lived so long in constant fear. Emil found it difficult, if not impossible, to set aside his mental barricades. As a result, he made few friends and retreated increasingly into the world of his studies, where numbers and equations became the only things on which he felt he could truly rely.

His parents understood very little of Emil's work, or of the effect it was having on him. In their eyes, as the first university-educated member of the family, Emil could do no wrong.

Meanwhile, Stefan continued his apprenticeship with Werner Grob, the butcher. Grob was a sensible, competent and monosyllabic man. He proved a good mentor to the boy, who had been all but disowned by his family.

Once a week, Stefan and Grob loaded up their butcher's cart and rode to the marketplace at Krasnoyar, where Grob had a good reputation.

At first, Stefan had been nervous about returning to Krasnoyar, but he was surprised, and profoundly relieved, to hear none of the jeering or the angry voices which had followed him through his schooling. Instead, customers barely looked him in the eye as he stood among the hanging carcasses of pigs, chickens and sheep, blood-smeared hands heaving severed hearts, tongues and kidneys on to the scale to be weighed.

What Stefan did not realise was that people were afraid of him. He was no longer someone to be picked on with impunity by anyone who wished to try their luck. The boy they had once known was quickly growing into a man who, the inhabitants of Krasnoyar were quick to realise, would be unlikely to forget the cruelty they had shown to him.

In the months that followed, as Stefan learned his trade, he began to resign himself to the possibility that he belonged in the bloody apron of a butcher. But he was lonely, and frustrated by the way that his life was turning out. Some nights, as he lay in bed, listening to his father snoring down the hall and knowing he was barely welcome in his parents' house, a gaping emptiness would open in his heart.

After a year as the butcher's apprentice, Stefan was sometimes allowed to go alone to Krasnoyar on market day. On that same hot August afternoon that the Tsar declared war against Germany, a fact of which no one in Rosenheim was yet aware, Stefan was returning home when his horse shied away from something lying in the ditch. Bringing the cart to a halt, Stefan set the brake and climbed down to see what had startled the animal. What he found was a man, clothed in little more than rags and so bruised about the face that at first he appeared to be dead. But as Stefan dragged the body from the ditch, ready to bring it to the undertaker, the stranger opened his eyes.

'Don't hit me again,' he pleaded deliriously, his lips split and teeth stained red.

'There is nothing to fear,' Stefan assured him as he wiped the man's face with a handkerchief. 'Who are you?' he asked. 'Who did this to you?'

The man said his name was Anatoli Bolotov and that he was a pilgrim from the village of Markha, near the city of Irkutsk in Siberia. Judging from the state of his clothes and the fact that his only possession was a Bible, Stefan had little reason to doubt that the pilgrim was telling the truth. After two years of wandering the country, Bolotov had just begun his journey home when he walked into the town of Krasnoyar.

There, while begging for food, he had been set upon, beaten senseless and heaved into a ditch on the outskirts of the town by some of the same people who had made a sport of beating Stefan Kohl.

Recalling the times he had stopped on this same road to wipe the blood from his own face, Stefan lifted Bolotov on to the cart, since the man was too weak to climb aboard himself. Then he brought the pilgrim into Rosenheim and presented the man to his father.

After hearing Bolotov's story, and seeing the Bible he clutched against his chest, Viktor Kohl warily agreed to feed him and put a roof over his head for the night. 'But only one night!' he decreed.

At the table, while they ate, Bolotov spoke of his travels across Russia.

At first, Viktor Kohl seemed to warm to the man, impressed by his ability to quote so freely from the Scriptures, but there came a point in the evening, as Bolotov began to speak about the details of his faith, that the look in Viktor's eyes began to change.

'It is on our own flesh,' said Bolotov, 'that we must inscribe our dedication to the Lord.'

'And what is meant by that?' demanded Viktor Kohl.

'The end is near,' explained Bolotov, 'and we must abandon not only the consolations of the flesh, but the things that make such consolation possible.'

Viktor Kohl set down his knife and fork. Slowly, he pushed his plate away and rose to his feet, watched by his wife, Christiana, and his son, neither of whom had yet fathomed the meaning of those words.

'I know you now,' whispered Viktor Kohl. 'I know what group of outlaws you belong to and I will not foul the air in this house by even mentioning their name.'

'I will not deny it to a fellow man of God,' replied Bolotov.

'There is no fellowship between a man like me,' said Viktor, his lip curling in disgust, 'and one who does what you have done in the name of Jesus Christ.'

'These are they,' Bolotov answered defiantly, 'who follow the Lamb wheresoever he goeth. These alone are redeemed.'

'Do not obscure your deeds with holy words!' shouted Viktor, aiming a finger at the door. 'Now get out!'

'You promised to take him in,' argued Stefan. 'What has he done to offend you, except to speak his mind?'

But Bolotov was already on his feet, a look of tired resignation on his face. He turned to Christiana, who by now could only stare at him in uncomprehending fear. 'I thank you for the meal,' he told her quietly.

'You can't just throw him out into the night!' Stefan protested.

'He is no stranger to the darkness, I assure you,' answered Viktor.

As Bolotov left the house, Stefan followed him out.

It was raining and the air was raw and cold, although Bolotov barely seemed to notice.

'Forgive my father, please,' begged Stefan.

'Do not blame him,' replied Bolotov. 'It is my fault for

thinking that I could speak as one man of God to another.'

'What was it in your words that angered him?' Stefan asked, confused. 'I've never seen him act like this before.'

'I simply told him a truth which he did not want to hear.'

'And what truth is that?'

They had been standing side by side under the eaves of the house, where they were partially sheltered from the rain. But now Bolotov turned to Stefan, and his gaze burned into the young man. 'The truth is that only by freeing yourself of earthly chains can you enter the kingdom of heaven.'

'That happens to us all when we die,' said Stefan, 'and it seems to me that he is well aware of that already.'

'But what he does not know, or chooses not to see, is that the only way to prove yourself worthy of heaven is to cut through those chains while we still live. Only those who separate themselves from the flock will be saved.'

'And the rest?' asked Stefan. 'What will happen to them?'

'They will be swept away in a tide of blood.' Gently, Bolotov took hold of Stefan's arm. 'Do not be afraid of what I'm saying. We all have a chance to prove our worth. But it takes courage. More courage than most men and women possess. It is not enough simply to acknowledge the suffering of Christ. Anyone can do that. What we must do is test the mettle of our faith by showing that we, too, are capable of suffering for what we believe. It requires setting out on a new path, instead of the one which has been chosen for us by those who think they know us better than we know ourselves.'

Stefan thought of the day his father had handed him over to the butcher. There had been no discussion. No words of comfort. Not even a hand on his shoulder to offer consolation. 'I learned to accept it,' he muttered, as much to himself as to the pilgrim.

'But why should you?' exclaimed Bolotov. 'Why spend your life trying to meet the expectations of those who cannot even meet those same demands themselves? Why not begin a journey which only the bravest can make? No man is free until he has proven himself to himself.'

At almost any other time, Bolotov's words might have rung hollow to Stefan Kohl but, in that moment, they struck him so profoundly that he felt as if he had been sleeping all his life and had only now awakened.

As they stood there, watching the rain pour from the roof like threads of mercury, and Bolotov went on to explain exactly what he meant by the severing of earthly chains, Stefan was appalled by his description of the bloody rituals, but also fascinated by such a brutal gesture of commitment. No one had ever asked him to sacrifice anything before, as if nothing he had was worth consigning to his faith. To his amazement, Stefan realised that he was not afraid, even if that sacrifice was to be paid in his own flesh. For the first time in his life, he glimpsed the possibility of a life filled with a purpose that was greater than the one for which he had been taught to settle.

'Come with me,' said Bolotov.

Those words seemed to snatch the air from Stefan's lungs. 'Now?' he gasped.

'Now or never!' exclaimed Bolotov. 'Your chance may never come again. Everywhere I go I hear talk of war with Germany. It may already be too late. The heritage of your forefathers, which you have struggled so hard to maintain, will be the doom of this place. Soon the Russians will drive you from this land and send you back where you came from.'

'But this *is* where I am from!' Stefan protested. 'I have never known anything else.'

'They don't care about that,' Bolotov told him. 'In their eyes, you have already been tried and convicted. All that remains now is for the sentence to be served. But you should consider yourself lucky.'

'And why is that?' he asked.

'Unlike them,' Bolotov waved his hand out into the dark, where chinks of light shone through the shuttered windows of houses, 'you have a choice. One way or another, you are about to become an exile, but which kind you become is up to you.'

Bolotov promised to wait until sunrise, in order to give the young man a chance to make up his mind.

'You will have your answer before then,' Stefan assured him.

As soon as he stepped back inside the house, he was confronted by his father. 'Did you speak with him?'

'Yes,' replied the son.

'Don't believe a word he spoke,' warned Viktor. 'His people are a poison on this earth.'

'What he said made sense to me,' answered Stefan.

'What?' Viktor laughed angrily. 'Then perhaps you should go with him when he leaves!'

'Maybe I will,' said Stefan.

Viktor had only been trying to scare him, but now he paused as he realised that his son was serious. 'I cannot stop you,' he said. 'You are old enough now to make your own decisions. Choose that beggar or choose your family, but know that you cannot have both.'

At that moment, Stefan's mother entered the room. She had

been listening, as afraid of her husband's anger as she was of her son's unyielding temperament. 'Why must you always be so cruel?' she shouted at Viktor.

The man stared at his wife, amazed that she would take any side but his.

She made a fist and struck him on the chest. 'You cannot abandon your son!'

'It's all right,' Stefan told his mother. 'He did that a long time ago.'

'Stay,' she begged him.

But it was already too late. Until the moment when his father had laughed in his face, Stefan's mind had still been clouded with doubt. But his father's mockery brought back to him the memory of every insult he had endured at the school in Krasnoyar, and the echoing pain of the beatings which had accompanied them. The sound of that laughter clarified his mind. There are times in a person's life when they cannot know if they have made the right decision until after that decision has already been made. And now he knew.

'Remain with us,' pleaded his mother, 'here where you know you are safe.'

Stefan shook his head. 'No one is safe any more,' he replied.

The next day, just as Bolotov had predicted, Russian soldiers arrived from the barracks at Krasnoyar. With them came a rabble of self-appointed militia, armed with old shotguns, sledgehammers and kitchen knives.

The inhabitants of Rosenheim were given an hour to pack one suitcase each. Then, clutching their bags, they were marched to a barge, which waited for them on the banks of the Volga at Pokrovsk. After being ferried across the Volga to the railhead at Saratov they were put aboard cattle cars and transported to the German border, a journey which lasted several days. At the border, the Kohl family were met by their eldest son, Emil. By Imperial decree, he had been dismissed from the University of Kiev, along with all the other students of German or Austro-Hungarian extraction.

As the people of Rosenheim crossed over into a country they had never seen before, Stefan Kohl was not among them. Even before the soldiers had arrived in Rosenheim, Stefan had set out in the company of Bolotov on the long journey to Siberia.

1 June 1915

Tsarskoye Selo, summer estate of the Imperial Family

On the outskirts of the estate stood a small, flat-roofed cottage, flanked on either side by single-storey additions which gave to the structure the impression of a military bunker, with tall and narrow windows where gun slits might have been. The stonework of the house had been painted a warm orange yellow which, in the afternoon sun, glowed like the flesh of a ripe apricot.

Inside the house, whose rooms were small and crammed with mismatched furniture, sat the Tsarina Alexandra and her closest friend, Anna Vyroubova, to whom this cottage had been given as a gift, in order that she might be always close at hand.

For some minutes, there had been no other sound but the faint clink as their tea cups were lowered into saucers. Of the biscuits which Vyroubova had laid out on the small table that stood between them, only one remained. In what had become an almost daily ritual, there was always a single biscuit left untouched, as if by unspoken agreement.

It was the Tsarina who broke the silence. 'I have just heard,' she said, 'that General Brusilov will soon begin a full retreat from Galicia. For all I know, it has already begun. Meanwhile, the Austrians are advancing.'

'Can they be stopped?' asked Vyroubova. She was a short, stout woman with a round face and heavy jaw. She wore her thick dark hair piled high upon her head. Her dress, with its simple, embroidered collar, had been carefully chosen not to outshine that of her benefactor, whose white feathered boa draped extravagantly across her shoulders and down into her lap.

'Or could they even be slowed down?' she added, glancing at the two walking sticks which leaned against her chair. Following injuries sustained in a train crash earlier that year, Vyroubova could barely move without those ugly canes and she hated the fact that she was now dependent on them. Even before the crash, there had been too many things on which she was dependent, including the woman who sat before her now.

'Slowed down?' echoed the Tsarina. 'I doubt it. I have read in the official reports that, for every ten thousand of our wounded, we can provide only a single doctor. No wonder the men are dying in such numbers.'

'But is it not true,' Vyroubova offered, 'that we have more men to lose? Surely, for every enemy soldier who dies in battle,' she said encouragingly, 'we can spare ten, perhaps even twenty men!'

'We cannot afford to lose *any*!' shouted the Tsarina.

Vyroubova flinched, as if she had received an electric shock. The Tsarina seldom raised her voice during these afternoon meetings and now Vyroubova felt a sudden sense of panic that she had finally said something which would lose her the use of this cottage, along with all the privileges to which she had become accustomed in her years of friendship with the Tsarina.

'What good is our numerical superiority,' continued the

Tsarina, 'when the enemy has thirty-six heavy machine guns for each battalion, and ours must manage with only two? And what hope do our sixty artillery battalions have against the three hundred and eighty battalions of those who now wage war against us?'

Vyroubova stared at her blankly. She did not know what a heavy machine gun was. She imagined that all machine guns must be heavy. And she had no idea what an artillery battalion consisted of. One gun? Ten? Ten thousand? 'Our dear friend was right,' she muttered. This friend, whom they rarely referred to by his full name, was Grigori Rasputin. His influence over the Romanovs, and the shrinking numbers of those who remained loyal to the family, was now so powerful that questions had been raised, even by members of the Russian parliament, as to whether the Tsar, or Rasputin, was truly in control of the country.

Fearing that the privacy of their correspondence had been compromised, Nicholas and Alexandra had taken to using code names to describe those in the inner circle of the Romanovs.

Their son Alexei was known as 'Sunbeam', while their youngest daughter Anastasia, had earned for herself the nickname of 'Imp'. The Tsar himself had been christened 'Blue Boy', after a character in a children's fairy tale. Vyroubova had been dubbed 'the friend', whereas Rasputin had become the 'dear friend'.

But the enemies of the Romanovs had coined names of their own for the Tsarina and her chosen band of followers. They called her 'Nemka', 'the German', refusing to believe that her loyalties could lie anywhere but with her blood relations who were killing Russian soldiers in their tens of thousands every month. Despising Vyroubova almost as much as the Tsarina herself, they dismissed her as 'La Vache', and, among the Okhrana agents who shadowed Rasputin on his nightly visits to the bars, he was quietly referred to as 'The Dark One'.

Rasputin was not the first mystic to have been welcomed into the gilded halls of the Romanovs. First there was the Blessed Mitya, hobbling on bowed legs and hiding his acne-scarred face beneath a hooded cloak. Next came Matryona the Barefoot, who howled like a dog and prophesied in languages which no one understood. Matryona's place was soon taken by a carnival side-show hypnotist named Monsieur Philippe. In time, all were dismissed or else retreated into obscurity.

Only Rasputin had endured.

'Russia will drown in blood,' said the Tsarina. 'Those were Grigori's words to me before this war ever began. He tried to warn us.'

'He tried,' agreed Vyroubova.

'He begged us not to wander down this path,' continued the Tsarina, 'and now it is too late to turn back, so we must press on regardless of the losses. The Germans have a word for this predicament, you know. *Ausharren*. Strange that no such way exists in Russian to sum up our misfortunes so precisely.'

Vyroubova, struggling to pay attention, set down her tea, picked up the pot, and refilled their cups. She added precisely the same amount of milk and sugar to each one. Vyroubova had taken great care to tailor her own habits to those of the Tsarina, to whom she handed one cup before settling the other in her lap. For a moment, they resumed their gloomy silence.

If, at that moment, Vyroubova could have spoken honestly

to the Tsarina, she would have said that she was weary of the war, and weary of talking so incessantly about it, and that she would have liked nothing more than to return to the days when such topics were far from their minds as they sat down to tea in this cosy little parlour. The whole purpose of their meetings, at least as far as Vyroubova was concerned, was to shut out the world, even if only for a while, usually by whispering of the intrigues of the court. For topics like these, Vyroubova had inexhaustible amounts of energy. But this chatter of the war fatigued her. Perhaps it was the psychological effects of the train crash, and the extraordinary pain it had brought to her daily existence, which left her without the necessary reservoirs of sympathy to dwell upon the suffering of others. Mostly, though, it was that she simply couldn't imagine it. One death, she could imagine. Five deaths. Ten. But a thousand? Ten thousand? A million? Faced with such staggering numbers, Vyroubova simply went blank, and her mind would wander aimlessly about the room, like a bird that had flown down the chimney and was now searching for an open window to escape.

Anna Vyroubova studied the framed photographs hanging on her wall. Many were of herself in the company of the Tsarina. The best of these had been hung where the Tsarina could see them. Her most recent addition, a large, oval photograph in a gold-painted frame, had been taken in this very room. It showed the Tsarina sitting in her usual chair and Vyroubova herself kneeling beside her, hands resting upon the Tsarina's knee. Both women faced the camera. Vyroubova was smiling. Indeed, from the moment she had received the Tsarina's blessing to engage a photographer for their portrait, she had practised that smile for hours in the mirror. It was only two weeks later, when the printed picture arrived in its frame from the studio, that Vyroubova glimpsed the expression the Tsarina had worn at the moment when the shutter clicked. Vyroubova had not expected her to smile. The Tsarina seldom smiled, because her teeth were bad. Predictably, her lips had remained tightly pressed together. But it was the look in the Tsarina's eyes which dismayed Vyroubova. In the dull haughtiness of her stare, the Tsarina had failed to convey their sacred pact of comradeship, from which, Vyroubova believed, the Tsarina drew the strength to defy the angry voices of a country which did not love her, and never had. Instead, the Tsarina looked bored and intolerant, like someone doing a favour for which no excuse to decline had been available at the moment of its asking. The reason, Vyroubova knew, was quite simple. It had not been the Tsarina's idea to take the photo, and even by suggesting it, Vyroubova had tangled the cat's cradle in which their friendship hung suspended. Her role was not to lead. Only to follow. To approve. The photograph had been Vyroubova's attempt to bring this lopsided acquaintance into balance. For Vyroubova, it was to have been a declaration of equality in their feelings towards each other, in spite of the abyss of social rank which lay between them. The eyes in the photograph put an end to that; bluntly, silently and permanently. It would never be spoken of. It would never be attempted again. Neither, in Vyroubova's mind, would it ever be forgiven, and that was why she hung the photo where the Tsarina could not help but see the portrait every time she came to visit.

'I have come to a conclusion,' the Tsarina said slowly, and then she paused, as if suddenly unwilling to give voice to her thoughts.

'What conclusion, Majesty?' asked Vyroubova. Is this about us? she wondered. Does she mean to throw me out into the street?

With her voice barely above a whisper, as if afraid the portraits on the walls might lean their frozen faces from the frames and overhear, the Tsarina began to speak again. 'Russia cannot survive this war against Germany. Not without a miracle.'

Vyroubova's first reaction was one of relief. It is not about us, after all, she thought to herself. But her next thought was that, if anyone else had said such a thing, with the possible exception of Rasputin, the Tsarina would have accused them of treason.

'It's in God's hands,' said Vyroubova, not so much because she believed it but because she knew it was what the Tsarina wanted to hear. 'There is nothing to be done, Majesty.'

The Tsarina's mouth remained open for a second, her teeth turned glassy yellow by the tincture of Sweet Vernal, which had been prescribed to her as a heart medicine and which she now took regularly, along with numerous other powerful tonics to combat stress. 'It so happens,' said the Tsarina, 'that something is being done. Even as we speak. Something that may bring an end to this slaughter.'

Vyroubova blinked in astonishment. 'But what is it, Majesty?'

The Tsarina reached out and rested her fingertips upon Vyroubova's knee. 'All you can know for now is that it has the full support of our dear friend, and therefore the blessing of God.'

5 June 1915

The Forest of Malevinsk, west of Stavka
Headquarters at Mogilev

Pekkala stood on the train tracks, hands in the pockets of his coat. A breeze rustled the coin-shaped leaves of the poplars that grew beside the tracks, keeping the blackfly temporarily at bay. He smelled the sun-heated creosote of the heavy wooden sleepers, laid out like the rungs of a ladder beneath the shining steel of the rails.

At two o'clock that morning, Pekkala had been wakened at his cottage near the stables on the Tsarskoye Estate. The visitor, a member of the Tsar's Household Guard, was a humourless Cossack named Ostrogorsky, whose long moustache and drooping, bloodhound eyes gave him a permanently melancholy expression. He handed over a telegram, from which Pekkala learned that his presence had been requested by the Tsar.

He knew at once that this was not to be a short drive across the Estate. These days, the Tsar was seldom to be found among the comforts of Petrograd, renamed after St Petersburg was found to be too Germanic for wartime Russian tastes. Instead, he had moved to the remote settlement of Mogilev, home of Russian Army Headquarters, known as STAVKA.

In an attempt to rally the country's flagging support for the war, the Tsar had taken over direct control of the military, replacing his uncle, the bearded and imposing Grand Duke Nikolai Nikolaevich, who stood almost seven foot tall, so dwarfing the five-foot-six-inch Tsar that, on those rare occasions when they were photographed together, the Grand Duke was stooped almost double, so as to speak face to face with his nephew.

Assuming control of Russia's war effort was a noble gesture for the Tsar, but one whose futility had immediately become apparent. The early victories of 1914, which halted German advances at Tannenberg, albeit with extraordinary losses, had been quickly overshadowed by defeats on a once unimaginable scale. By the end of that year, Russia had lost over a million troops. The entire Russian Second Army had surrendered. In addition, Lithuania, Latvia and parts of Poland previously under Russian control had all been lost.

By the time the Tsar took charge, three-quarters of a million soldiers had already deserted and Russian officers in the front line stood an 85 per cent chance of being killed. In some areas, their life expectancy was less than four days. In fighting south of the Masurian Lakes, German Spandau crews had been seen leaving their trenches in order to push aside Russian bodies which had fallen so thickly before the German barbed wire that they obscured the gunners' field of fire.

Against such overwhelming portents of defeat, there was little the Tsar could do to stem the tide.

'You have five minutes to get ready,' said Ostrogorsky. Then he turned on his heel and walked back to his car, whose engine puttered quietly on the gravel path that ran by Pekkala's house.

Quite apart from the midnight summons, Pekkala knew that something very unusual must be taking place. Neither the driver, nor the car, a Serex Landau normally reserved for use by the wardens on the Tsarskoye Selo estate, were what the Tsar would normally have sent to collect him.

In the past, Ostrogorsky had patrolled the estate of Tsarskoye Selo, on the back of his Kabardin horse, riding in a particular jerky, short-gaited style which would have shaken loose the spine of anyone besides a Cossack. Then, one day, having spotted an intruder on the grounds, Ostrogorsky drew his *shashka* sword, with its long, gently curved blade and a pommel which hooked at the end, like the beak of a large hunting bird, and gave chase to the trespasser, who appeared to be making off with a ladder. As he closed in on the thief, Ostrogorsky raised the fearsome weapon and gave a terrible shout as he prepared to hew down the intruder.

Only now did the stranger understand that he was being pursued. He turned, dropped the ladder and screamed.

At that instant, Ostrogorsky realised it was not a thief at all, but rather the twelve-year-old son of the gardener, Stefanov, who had spent the morning cleaning windows at the Catherine Palace.

Ostrogorsky reined in his horse so sharply that the animal reared up on its hind legs and fell backwards. The Cossack, unable to extricate himself from the stirrups, went down beneath the horse. The blade of the sword passed through the animal's ribs and reappeared above its left shoulder, slicing through the Kabardin's heart and killing it instantly. Ostrogorsky's hip was fractured by the weight of the horse falling on top of him and the doctors determined that he would never be able to ride again. Having learned the news, Ostrogorsky decided to hang himself.

He was standing on a chair in his hospital room with a bed sheet twisted about his neck and attached to the beam of a ceiling above his head when the Tsar himself appeared, having stopped by to check on Ostrogorsky's progress.

Both men were so surprised that, at first, neither of them could speak.

It was Ostrogorsky who found his tongue first. 'I am a Cossack,' he announced defiantly, 'and I will not walk through life like some ordinary man.'

'You know,' said the Tsar, 'I have been looking for a driver.'

'I am no wagon slave!' blurted Ostrogorsky. 'No horse and cart for me.'

'I meant the driver of an automobile,' explained the Tsar.

Ostrogorsky mouthed the word 'automobile'. He struggled to imagine himself behind the wheel of a machine. For a moment, his life hung in the balance as he contemplated such an occupation, and whether it was dignified enough to justify a change of plan.

'Well,' asked the Tsar, 'what do you say?'

'I say,' replied Ostrogorsky, his hands rising to the makeshift noose around his neck, 'please get me down from here before I hang my stupid self!'

Ostrogorsky's reputation as a chauffeur, namely that he operated his car with the same merciless disregard for human comfort that he had shown when riding his horse, ensured that he was a driver of last resort, although his propensity for silence guaranteed discretion. And the Serex was a car which almost never left the grounds of the estate, which meant that it would not be recognised as belonging to the Tsar's stable of vehicles.

Whatever the Tsar wants from me, thought Pekkala, he means to keep it secret.

They drove all night, arriving at the outskirts of the Malevinsk Forest just before dawn. Here, they turned off the main highway. In spite of its name, this was still only a dirt track, heavily rutted by the passing of military wagons, whose steel-rimmed wooden wheels had scored the earth to ribbons. They found themselves upon a nameless, muddy path barely wide enough to fit the car. After getting bogged down twice, Ostrogorsky turned to Pekkala, who sat patiently in the back seat, awaiting the inevitable conclusion.

'You will have to continue on foot,' said Ostrogorsky, his long dark moustache twitching as he spoke.

'Where to?' asked Pekkala.

'To the railroad tracks,' Ostrogorsky gestured vaguely down the road. 'And there you are to wait.'

'For what? For how long?'

The Cossack stared at him blankly.

Knowing it was useless to question him any further, Pekkala climbed out and buttoned his coat. He wondered how far he had to go. The Cossack's breezy flip of the hand had seemed to indicate that he had no more idea than Pekkala.

By keeping to the edge of the path, Pekkala managed to avoid the worst of the mud and, as long as he kept moving, the blackfly did not swarm.

For the next hour, Pekkala saw neither people nor houses. There was only the green labyrinth of the forest, and the sound of unfamiliar birdcalls echoing among the trees.

Finally, he arrived at the tracks. He hoped there might be someone there to meet him, but no such luck. Now that he had stopped, the sweat began to cool upon his back and insects spun in crazy pirouettes about his head. The time was fast approaching when the blackfly would rise in their millions for their annual feast upon every warm-blooded creature in their reach. These blackfly were not much bigger than the head of a pin, but each one that found its way behind an ear or down the collar of a shirt or underneath the band of a wristwatch left a tiny red dot of blood from the microscopic toll of flesh torn from their victims' hides. Pekkala recalled times from his childhood when his father had returned home after a day of foraging in the woods with trails of blood streaming down his face, as if a crown of thorns had been jammed on to his head.

It was almost noon. The sun beat down squarely on the tracks, raising phantoms of heat haze from the iron. Pekkala retreated among the shadows of the forest, where he sat on a fallen birch trunk, picking at the hard black scab of a chaga mushroom which had sprouted from the dying tree. He let the crumbs fall into his pocket. Later, he would use them to make tea. On his way to the tracks, he had eaten some asparagus that he found growing by the path, as well as some fiddlehead ferns and wild strawberries, the largest of them no bigger than the last joint of his little finger. In amongst the trees, he had found a shallow puddle, lined with old pine needles. Skimming his palm across the surface, he scooped up several handfuls, tasting the bitterness of tannins in the corners of his mouth.

Pekkala was just beginning to wonder if he might be the victim of some elaborate practical joke when a faint, metallic ringing reached his ears. He waited. The sound came again, as if one of the rails had been struck with a tuning fork. Leaving his place in the shadows, Pekkala walked out on to the tracks.

Shielding his eyes, he looked to the north and then to the south and it was then that he spotted a light in the distance. It was indistinct at first, and shifted in the heat haze as if it were a ball of fire rolling unevenly down the skittle alley of the railroad. Slowly, the train began to take shape. Where his foot rested on the track, he felt the vibration of its thundering approach.

As the huge machine drew close Pekkala recognised the Imperial Train, the deep green paint of its engine piped with gold and red. The train, ten carriages long, came to a shuddering halt beside Pekkala. A door opened and a man leaned out.

It was the Tsar. He grinned and beckoned to Pekkala.

Pekkala climbed up into the carriage and found himself in a richly decorated space. The walls were upholstered with quilted green silk from which electric lights leaned out, their opaque glass shades as delicate as jellyfish. Carpeting, woven with elaborate red and gold floral designs, covered the floor. Thick velvet curtains had been drawn over the windows. There were no seats as in an ordinary train. Instead, there were chairs and round tables and Pekkala wondered what would happen to anyone sitting in them if the train were ever in an accident, as had happened at Borki Station, near Kharkov, back in October 1888.

'Majesty, why have you sent for me?' asked Pekkala. 'And why are we meeting here?'

The Tsar did not answer directly. He sat down and gestured to a seat on the other side of the small table. 'Make yourself comfortable,' he said.

Pekkala settled himself cautiously into one of the thin-legged chairs, as if uncertain it would hold him. He had an instinctive mistrust of the fussy trappings that so beguiled the Romanovs.

On the table beside the Tsar lay a letter with a Petrograd postmark. From the even spacing of the letters and the carefully formed Russian of someone who was neither a native speaker, nor a writer of the language, Pekkala recognised the handwriting of the Tsarina.

The Tsar's hand rested on the letter, as if he expected a gust of wind to blow it out through the window. Unconsciously, his fingers drummed upon the envelope.

From this slight and barely conscious gesture, Pekkala realised that, no matter how much the Tsar loved his wife, he was hesitant to read what she had written.

'Pekkala,' the Tsar began. But before another word could leave his mouth, a steward arrived, bearing a tray of the Tsar's favourite oolong tea, and the Tsar's mouth snapped shut like a trap.

The steward, wearing a short, silver-buttoned black tunic over a collarless white shirt, looked neither at Pekkala, nor at the Tsar as he set before them two glasses in ornate brass holders. Wisps of steam curved sensually from the surface of the black, smoky-tasting tea.

Nobody spoke.

The only sound was of the patient stamping of the steam engine.

The Tsar waited until the steward had left the carriage. Then he leaned forward, resting his hands upon his knees and fixed Pekkala with his pale blue eyes. 'How much do you know about icons?' he asked.

'Enough to know one when I see one,' replied Pekkala. 'Beyond that . . .' he let his words trail off.

'I am thinking of one icon in particular,' continued the Tsar. 'It is called *The Shepherd*.'

'That one I do know,' said Pekkala. 'It was on display in the Hall of St George the day you declared war on Germany.'

The Tsar nodded. 'And it was there with good reason, Pekkala. For the faithful of this country, that icon represents the surest guarantee that God is on our side.'

'What does this have to do with me?' replied Pekkala.

The Tsar smiled at Pekkala's impatience. 'Normally, I would have said that it has very little to do with a heathen like yourself.'

'I am not without faith, Majesty.'

'But yours and mine are not the same, Pekkala. What spirits guide you live out there,' he gestured at the wilderness that lay beyond the cushioned walls, 'and their names are hidden from all but the savages who gave them life.'

'Savages?' He thought about his mother, a Sami from the tundra of northern Finland, and the parallel worlds she inhabited, shifting from one to the other like the steam which drifted off their tea.

'Yes,' replied the Tsar, 'and I mean it as a compliment. It is why I have chosen you for this particular task, Pekkala. You are not bound by the same attachments as we who must struggle with the trappings of our Orthodox religion. The very thing that separates us is the basis for my trust in you. You may not care for this icon, Pekkala, but to millions of Russians, its safety is as important as the safety of Russia itself.'

'Has something happened to *The Shepherd*?' asked Pekkala.

'No,' replied the Tsar. 'For the moment, it is safe in its usual place at the Church of the Resurrection at Tsarskoye Selo.' He paused as he hooked a finger through the brass loop handle of the glass and drank a mouthful of the tea, breathing in sharply as he sipped. 'And if I had my way,' he continued, 'that's exactly where it would remain. But my wife has decided that the icon should be placed in the care of Rasputin.'

An image of the Siberian flashed behind Pekkala's eyes. The unwashed hair combed down about his ears, the lower part of his face hidden behind an unkempt beard and the stare of his sledge-dog-grey eyes.

'You know how much he is despised,' said the Tsar. 'If it were not for the lengths to which my wife and I have gone to protect him, he would have been thrown in a dungeon long ago.'

And if it were not for your own fascination with the man, thought Pekkala, no one would have cared enough to hate him in the first place.

There were many reasons why the Romanovs protected Rasputin, but the most important reason was one that most people didn't know about. Their only son, Alexei, had been born with haemophilia, what Russians referred to as 'The English Disease' because of the fact that it had been passed down through several generations of British royalty, and put at risk the children of anyone whose bloodline, which included that of both the Tsar and the Tsarina, intersected with the British kings and queens. The disease could not be cured, and it almost always proved fatal. His blood unable to clot, Alexei could have bled to death from the kind of nicks or scrapes a normal boy might expect to receive every day. This frailty had required him to live as a person might if they were made of glass.

Even Alexei's friends were hand selected by the parents for their ability to play gently. Pekkala remembered the soft-spoken Makarov brothers – thin and nervous boys whose ears stuck out and who carried their shoulders in a perpetual hunch, like boys do when they are waiting for a firework to explode. In spite of his fragility, Alexei had already outlived them, since both boys perished in battle.

No matter what precautions they took with their son, the parents seemed always to be waiting for that moment when Alexei would simply fade away. In doing so, it was as if the Tsar, and the Tsarina Alexandra in particular, had absorbed the disease into their own bodies.

Fearing that news of this disease might be interpreted as some kind of curse by the superstitious masses, who were only too ready to find the hand of God, or of the devil, in every deviation from the norm, the haemophilia was kept secret from all but the Romanovs' doctors, and the closest associates of their family.

The secrecy surrounding Alexei's illness forced the Tsar and the Tsarina to bear the burden of their son's terrifying fragility in silence.

It was Rasputin, and Rasputin alone, who had proved capable of alleviating the symptoms of Alexei's illness.

Sceptical as Pekkala was about the Siberian monk's ability to work miracles, there could be no denying that the Tsar's own doctors had on several occasions informed the parents that there was nothing to be done for the boy, and that they should begin preparations for his funeral. At moments like these, Rasputin would be summoned to the boy's bedside. There, with nothing more than the sound of his voice and the gentle laying of his hand upon Alexei's forehead, the boy's symptoms would immediately begin to lessen. Within a matter of hours, the boy whom the best medical experts in Russia had given up for dead would be walking around his room. On one occasion, when Alexei had fallen while getting out of a rowing boat at the Romanovs' hunting lodge at Spala in Poland, Rasputin happened to be on the other side of the country and it was feared that he would never reach Alexei before the boy succumbed to his injuries. Instead, Rasputin sent a telegram, assuring the parents that the boy would soon recover. And he did, in spite of all predictions from Alexei's attending physicians.

No one had been able to scientifically explain this phenomenon. In their search for answers, the Tsar and the Tsarina chose to see it as a divine miracle, a conclusion with which Rasputin, wisely choosing not to claim the credit for himself, was happy to agree.

Rasputin became, for the Tsar and the Tsarina, their son's only assurance of survival. Their faith in him, and in his abilities, was absolute. He had become, in the minds of these terrified parents, the most valuable person in the world, more important than the country over which they ruled, more important than the fortunes of the Russian people, more important even than their own lives.

The Russian people knew nothing of this, and they quickly drew their own conclusions about the Tsarina's seeming appetite for the dirty, coarse and ill-mannered Siberian. In their ignorance, they came to loathe Rasputin as completely as he was adored by the Tsar and the Tsarina.

In Pekkala's opinion, Rasputin was a man who understood his limitations. It was the Tsar, and even more so the Tsarina, who had increasingly demanded from Rasputin a wisdom he never claimed to possess. He had been called upon to judge matters of state, as well as the conduct of the war. The best he could do, in such situations, was to offer vague words of comfort. But the Romanovs had fastened on those words, stripping them of vagueness and turning them to prophesy. It was no wonder Rasputin had become so despised by those who sought the favour of the Tsar.

But the Romanovs could not shelter Rasputin forever. Sooner or later, the hatred of the Russian people, peasants and nobles alike, was bound to turn deadly. The child and the man who was able to cure him had become as horribly fragile as each other. The only difference between them was that Rasputin had long since come to understand the meaning of this terminal equation.

'If word gets out,' continued the Tsar, 'that Grigori has taken possession of *The Shepherd*, those whose faith has already been shaken by recent setbacks on the battlefield will fasten on it as the reason for every misfortune we have suffered in this war. That is why I chose this meeting place, where my absence from headquarters would only be hours, not the days it would take if I had come to you.'

'I could have come to Mogilev.'

'Not without raising suspicions. No, Pekkala, it was too risky. No one can know that the subject has even been raised, or the results would be disastrous!'

'Have you explained this to the Tsarina?'

'Of course!' exclaimed the Tsar. 'But you know how she is. She has become fixated on the idea that only in the hands of this holy man can the true power of the icon be unleashed.'

'And you expect me to convince her otherwise?' asked Pekkala.

The Tsar laughed. 'I have given you many difficult tasks

before, Pekkala, but none as impossible as that! No, I do not expect you to persuade her. It's Rasputin I need you to convince!'

Now the Tsar's plan was becoming clear. Pekkala had met with Rasputin many times in the past, often at the special annexe of a club known as the Villa Roda, which had been built on the orders of the Tsarina for Rasputin's private use. The reason for this structure's existence was that Rasputin had been banned from almost every other club in the city.

'He will listen to you,' said the Tsar.

'He might,' agreed Pekkala, 'but you he will obey, if you only command him to do so.'

'Impossible!' The Tsar waved a hand in front of his face, as if shooing away an insect. 'If the Tsarina finds out that I have had a hand in this, she will dig in her heels even further.'

'But even if I can talk Rasputin into this, it is the Tsarina who must be convinced.'

'Exactly,' the Tsar wagged a finger at Pekkala, 'and the only one who can do that is Rasputin! She will follow his advice as if God himself had whispered in her ear.'

Pekkala could not deny the Tsar's reasoning. 'I will do my best, Majesty.'

The Tsar nodded, satisfied. He reached in to the pocket of his waistcoat. He removed his pocket watch, which was an 18-carat gold Patek Philippe, commissioned by his wife from Tiffany and finished with diamonds by the Tsar's own jeweller, Carl Fabergé. Glancing at the time, he sighed. 'I must get back to running the war.'

A few minutes later, Pekkala stepped down from the carriage.

With a jolt like the slamming of a huge door, the engine's wheels began to move.

Pekkala watched the train pull out, his gaze fixed upon a guard who stood on the platform at the back of the caboose. The long, cruciform bayonet glinted at the end of his Mosin-Nagant rifle. The guard stared down along the empty tracks. Like the steward who had brought him tea, the man seemed oblivious to Pekkala's presence. It was as if the Inspector had been a ghost, visible only to the Tsar. And then Pekkala realised that the Tsar had wanted it that way all along. He had never been here. This meeting had never taken place.

Pekkala turned and walked back down the road, his boots swishing through fragile globes of dandelions which had sprouted from cracks in the earth.

He found the car just where he had left it, Ostrogorsky leaning on the bonnet, puffing away on a long-stemmed pipe and humming an old Cossack tune. His deep, sad voice drifted on the still air as the smoke smoothed out the ragged edges of his mind. As they travelled back towards Tsarskoye Selo, Pekkala looked out at the dense ranks of pine and white birch trees which crowded down to the road, separated on either side of them by ditches overgrown with daisies, their white petals almost hidden under a coating of the grey road dust. The sun was already low in the sky, and beams of tannic-tinted light flickered down through the branches. He thought of his childhood in Finland and, in spite of the good fortune which the Tsar had bestowed upon him here in Russia, there were times when he longed to disappear back into the wilderness of his native country, where the brutal simplicity of life and death was not obscured by the lies men told to make themselves believe that they were masters of their fate.

*

Meanwhile, as the Imperial train headed south towards Mogilev, the Tsar opened the letter from his wife.

Unfolding the neatly creased page, he breathed in the dry sweet smell of his wife's White Rose perfume, a tiny drop of which she always dabbed on to the paper.

Alexandra wrote to him almost every day, often interspersing her Russian with English or French, although seldom with the language of her birth. The Tsar always read the letters, sometimes more than once, but it had lately begun to seem as if the letters weren't really written to him. He could not escape the feeling that his wife was pouring out her heart to another man – someone who looked like him, who sounded like him, who behaved like him – but who was not him. It was as if she had created an illusion more in keeping with the man she wanted for a husband, in whom the failings of reality had all been scrubbed away. As the Tsar read his wife's most recent tirade against the members of the Russian parliament, who had begun to loudly criticise the handling of the war, he knew she was appealing to a mirage of his true self, a man who might sweep aside all opposition to his will in a wave of rage and ruthlessness. 'Be Peter the Great!' she pleaded. 'Be Ivan the Terrible. Crush them all!' In Alexandra's mind, nothing less would restore the love and confidence of ordinary Russians. Rage equals love. Ruthlessness demands respect. The man she had invented would understand these things, and the world she had invented

55

for him to live in would obey such contradictions. But here he was, the ruler of an Empire, knowing in his heart that all the raging in the world would not bring back the millions who had been killed in the fighting, or the millions more who would die before this war was over.

6 June 1915

Petrograd

Rasputin's apartment, located in a quiet section of the Gorokhovaya Ulitsa in Petrograd, did not belong to him. It was on permanent loan from one of his many benefactors, most of whom cared less for Rasputin than they did for his influence over the Tsar.

The power of Rasputin's opinions, particularly with the Tsarina, had never been publicly acknowledged. It was, nevertheless, the worst-kept secret in Russia. Each week, Rasputin received dozens of visitors, who trudged up the stairs to his apartment, their pockets stuffed with cash, hoping for the Siberian monk's help in currying favour with the Romanovs. Sometimes it was the matter of a military contract, supplying saddles for the cavalry or hobnails for a million pairs of marching boots. Other times, it concerned an unfavourable ruling of the court which could, with a few words from the Tsar, be overturned. The visitors pleaded their cases, while Rasputin lounged upon a threadbare couch, sighing and staring at the ceiling. As they departed, the visitors emptied their pockets, heaping stacks of money in a large blue-and-white washbasin, secure in their minds that their generosity would not go unrewarded. But the names of these people, along with their long-winded and carefully rehearsed appeals, were forgotten even before they reached the bottom of the stairs. And the money, with which Rasputin could have retired a wealthy man, would usually be given away to the next person he saw who looked as if they didn't have enough.

Pekkala entered the courtyard, which was damp and gloomy and smelled of the mildew which clung to the painted stone. Shards of broken green glass lay on the cobblestones, the remains of bottles, pitched out of the window high above, which had once contained the sweet Georgian wine that was Rasputin's favourite.

Rasputin had not always been a heavy drinker. This came only after the attempt on his life, when an insane woman named Khioniya Guseva, who had become convinced he was the anti-Christ, found him in the street and stabbed him with a butcher's knife. Although Rasputin recovered physically from the attack, inwardly he was never the same. It was as if, in that moment when the knife blade pierced his flesh, he glimpsed the horrors that awaited him on New Year's Eve of 1916, in the halls of the Yusupov Palace.

As Pekkala began to climb the stairs, a woman passed him on the way down. She was in her late forties, with a high fore-head and small, deep-set eyes which she averted from Pekkala as she clattered down the steps in patent leather shoes. With a passing glance, Pekkala noticed that the buttons on her shirt had not been fastened correctly, and that loose strands of her auburn hair, spliced with threads of grey, hung down over her neck where it had been hastily bundled into place.

He knew at once that she was not one of those who had come to curry favour with the Tsar. She was one of Rasputin's other guests, who were equally numerous, who sought absolution for their sins. Pekkala knew of highly ranked ladies in Petrograd society who had knelt at Rasputin's feet for the privilege of cutting his toenails. These women saved the clippings and sewed them into ribbons of silk, which they used to line the necklines of their dresses.

Arriving at Rasputin's apartment, Pekkala found the door open. He walked in just as Rasputin emerged from a back room, wearing only a long shirt and a pair of slippers. His face wore its usual scowl but, at the sight of Pekkala, he broke into a wide grin, showing his strong, white and unusually long teeth. 'Inspector!' he shouted, spreading his arms as if to embrace Pekkala, although the two men remained several paces apart. 'Come in! Come in!' he commanded, even though Pekkala had already entered the room. 'Sit down!'

'Where?' asked Pekkala, looking around him. Every seat in the room was heaped with clothes and unwashed crockery.

'Any chair will do,' replied Rasputin, tipping a heap of laundry on to the floor and dusting off the cushion with his hands. 'Here!'

For now at least, Pekkala remained on his feet. 'That woman on the staircase. One of yours?'

Rasputin nodded as he gathered up a handful of olives discarded on a plate by the windowsill. 'Irina Krupskaya,' he confirmed, tossing an olive into his mouth.

'The wife of the Finance Minister?' asked Pekkala, unable to mask his surprise.

Rasputin held up a finger, begging for patience as he rolled the olive around between his teeth, peeling away the meat, before spitting the stone out of the open window. 'Deputy Finance Minister.'

Pekkala nodded towards the back room. 'And this is how you wash away their sins?'

'Only God can grant her clemency,' argued Rasputin. 'What you, and the rest of this spiritually bankrupt city, fail to grasp is that only by sinning can one drive out the devil of sin. Without it, there can be no focus for her repentance and without repentance, there can be no remission of guilt. I have brought her soul to the edge of a great precipice, and now she must throw herself off. Her choice is clear now, in a way it never was before.'

Pekkala shook his head, marvelling at the contortions of Rasputin's logic. 'How selfless of you, Grigori.'

'Irina Krupskaya thinks so,' Rasputin waved at the doorway, through which the woman had departed, 'and if she believes it, who's to say it isn't true? Trust me, Inspector. You and I are not so different.'

'We are what time and circumstance have made us,' answered Pekkala.

'All the more reason why you should learn to trust me better than you do.' With those words, Rasputin flopped down on the couch and swung his bare feet on to the coffee table. 'Sit, for pity's sake, Inspector! You are making me nervous, standing there as if you have come to make an arrest.' Then he narrowed his eyes. 'I take it that's not why you're here.'

'The Tsarina has decided to loan you some artwork.'

'She has indeed, Pekkala.'

'Do not accept it.'

'Too late!' Rasputin boomed with laughter. 'See for yourself.'

Pekkala turned in the direction of Rasputin's stare. There,

on the wall behind him, was the icon. Pekkala had never studied *The Shepherd* up close before, and was shocked at the intensity of the colours. He could not deny that there was something unearthly about this little painting.

'It arrived this morning,' Rasputin said cheerfully. 'Seems as if this was a wasted trip for you.'

'Not if I can persuade you to give it back.'

'And this on account of your deep and abiding love of Russian icons,' Rasputin remarked sarcastically. 'The Tsar sent you, didn't he?'

Pekkala nodded. There was no point in denying it.

'That coward!' hissed Rasputin.

'He is a realist,' replied Pekkala, 'at least when it comes to his wife.'

'Curious, don't you think,' sneered Rasputin, 'that a man who would gamble the safety of his country on the power of an icon would not trust that same power to protect the icon itself? But if that is what the Tsar wants, he should come here and ask me himself.'

'You know what will happen if word gets out that this country's most sacred object is hanging on your wall like some old family portrait, and that the Tsarina herself ordered it to be delivered to your door.'

'You think I haven't considered this?' demanded Rasputin. 'I know exactly how much damage this could do.'

'Then make her see reason, Grigori! You are the only one who can.'

Rasputin breathed in deeply, then exhaled in a long and melancholy sigh. 'Don't you see, Pekkala? I can only convince the Tsarina here,' he tapped a bony finger against his chest, 'if she is already convinced in here.' He shifted the finger to his temple, drilling his long fingernail into the skin. 'My power, if you want to call it that, lies in being able to predict what the Tsarina wants, before she knows herself what it is that she desires. I cannot change her mind once it has been made up. All I can do is convince her she is right. And that,' grinned Rasputin, 'is one of the reasons she loves me.' As suddenly as it had appeared, the playful smile slid away from his face. 'Go back to your master, the Tsar. Tell him I refused to yield. Tell him it is the will of God. Tell him whatever you like, but make him understand that there is nothing to be done.'

'What have you got yourself into this time?' asked Pekkala.

'Trust me when I tell you,' answered Rasputin, 'that even for a man as curious as you, some things are better left unknown.'

*

Two weeks later, Pekkala was summoned again, only this time, it was not by the Tsar.

The old gardener, Stefanov, whose son Ostrogorsky had almost cleaved in half, knocked on the door of Pekkala's cottage. Then, unsure at what distance to wait, he retreated to the road.

By the time Pekkala came to the door, Stefanov was standing on the other side of the garden gate, cap in hand, his thatch of long grey hair matted down on his head.

'Yes?' asked Pekkala. It was a Sunday morning, the time when Pekkala would polish his boots, mend tears in his clothes and oil his Webley revolver. He always looked forward to this time. They were the only few hours of the week when his mind was not focused on his work.

There was something meditative in the threading of needles, in the rustle of the horsehair brush over the toe caps of his boots and in the precise click of metal parts as he carefully disassembled the gun.

Now the Webley lay in pieces on the bare pine of his kitchen table and Pekkala's fingertips were smudged dark brown, since he did not use a brush to work the polish into his heavy, double-soled boots. He wore a tattered pair of corduroys, the lines partially rubbed out above the knee so that they seemed to spell out Morse-code messages. He also had on a collarless grey wool shirt with buttons made of antler bone, the cloth so worn down that even he, who wore his clothes until they all but vaporised, had consigned it for use only when doing his chores.

'A message for you, Inspector,' mumbled Stefanov. He shifted uneasily from foot to foot, his dark eyes darting about.

'Is everything all right, Stefanov?'

'Oh, yes,' lied the gardener. In truth, he was terrified of Pekkala. He was a superstitious old man, and had heard so many stories about the mysterious Finn that he no longer considered Pekkala to be human, but rather some creature conjured into being by the black arts of some arctic shaman.

'You said something about a message.' Pekkala wiped the polish from his fingers on to an old dish towel he carried as a handkerchief.

'Ah, yes. The message is that you should come at once.'

'Come where, Stefanov?'

'To Madame Vyroubova's house.'

'Is she all right?'

'Seemed so to me. I was passing by her house when she called to me out of a window. Said to fetch you right away.'

Pekkala nodded. 'Very well.'

Stefanov replaced his cap and stepped back into the road, heels scuffing in the sandy yellow gravel. 'That is all I have to say,' he announced solemnly. Then he paused for a moment, as if to reconsider. 'No,' he reassured himself. 'That's all of it.'

'Thank you, Stefanov.'

'Thank you, sir!' The gardener smiled, revealing the grey stumps of long-neglected teeth. He raised one finger in a farewell salute, like a man testing the direction of the wind, then set off down the road.

Pekkala did not bother to change. Quickly, he reassembled the revolver, his movements so practised that they required no conscious thought. After loading the gun, he put on his leather shoulder holster, a pattern of his own invention which held the revolver almost horizontally across his chest. With the familiar weight of the Webley resting on his solar plexus, he put on his heavy, double-breasted coat, laced up his boots and set out towards Vyroubova's.

Her house stood at the opposite end of the Tsarskoye Selo estate. Pekkala neither rode a horse, nor owned a car or bicycle. He preferred, whenever possible, to travel on his own two feet. In spite of Vyroubova's command to come at once, Pekkala did not hurry. He knew from experience that when Vyroubova wanted something, no matter how trivial, it was always a matter of urgency, requiring that everyone around her drop everything until the task had been completed to her satisfaction. So he took his time, strolling with his hands behind his back, while dust from the path settled on his freshly polished boots, and it was some time before he arrived at the squat stone building which Vyroubova called home.

The door opened just as he was reaching for the brass ring that served as a knocker. Vyroubova, in a lavender-coloured dress with white ruffles at the throat, gazed down her nose at him, eyebrows crooked into chevrons of indignation. 'I sent for you to come at once! If my house had been on fire . . .'

'You would not have called on me, Vyroubova, nor sent the gardener to do it.'

She flashed him a humourless smile and stood aside to let him pass. As Pekkala stepped inside, he smelled the cloying fragrance of perfume, mixed with the sharp odour of carbolic soap and cigarette smoke sunk into the curtains and upholstered chairs. Turning the corner into the sitting room, he realised that Vyroubova already had a guest.

It was the Tsarina.

Although Pekkala had not expected this, seeing the Tsarina here did not catch him entirely by surprise. She was often to be found in the company of Vyroubova. This cottage served as her refuge from life at the Alexander Palace, the Romanovs' own residence on the Tsarskoye Selo estate, where the Tsarina could seldom find a moment to herself. Vyroubova's house doubled as a meeting place for guests, such as Rasputin, whose presence at the palace might cause complications.

Now Pekkala knew who had really called him to this rendezvous. The only thing he didn't know was why.

'Kind of you to join us, Inspector,' said the Tsarina. She sat straight-backed in a chair by the window. Sunlight through the gauzy day curtains made it difficult to see her face. She wore the long grey dress of an army nurse, with a red cross emblazoned upon the off-white apron which covered her chest and extended the full length of the dress itself. On the Tsarina's orders, a portion of the Catherine Palace, also located on the estate, had recently been converted into a hospital for wounded officers. Not only the Tsarina, but her daughters, and even Vyroubova, had been working there as medical attendants. Many times, on his walks in the dove-grey twilight, Pekkala had seen men, their faces pinched with pain, hobbling on crutches across the palace grounds.

Pekkala bowed, suddenly aware of his threadbare corduroys, his dusty boots and unbuttoned coat.

'You must be wondering why you're here,' said the Tsarina.

'I am now, Majesty,' he replied.

'I thought that you should be the first to know,' continued the Tsarina. 'A robbery has taken place. The icon of *The Shepherd* has been stolen from the house of Grigori Rasputin.'

Pekkala's first instinct was to doubt what he had just been told. As far as he knew, nothing had ever been stolen from Rasputin. There was no need to rob a man who gladly made a gift of everything he owned. In fact, thought Pekkala, that's probably what happened. Rasputin got drunk and gave it away and now that he has sobered up he can't remember who he gave it to. But, for now at least, he kept his suspicions to himself. 'Has the Tsar been informed?' he asked.

'He will be, in due course.'

Pekkala heard a floorboard creak and turned to see Vyroubova waiting in the doorway.

Her small eyes glittered.

'Do not stand behind the Inspector,' cautioned the Tsarina. 'He is liable to shoot you with that English cannon which he carries beneath his coat. Perhaps you would be kind enough to bring the Inspector some refreshment.'

Mechanically, Vyroubova stepped back into the hall. A moment later came the sound of her clattering about in the kitchen.

'The Tsar should be notified at once,' said Pekkala. 'The loss of that icon . . .'

'The Tsar is very busy with affairs at Mogilev,' snapped the Tsarina, 'and I know perfectly well what the loss of *The Shepherd* means to this country.'

'I'll go to Rasputin,' said Pekkala, 'and find out exactly what took place.'

'I have just told you what happened,' snapped the Tsarina, 'and as for you bothering Grigori, I have a better idea.'

'And what is that, Majesty?'

The Tsarina lifted her hand from where it balanced on her knee. With a careless gesture, she twisted her fingers in the air. 'Do nothing,' she told him.

Pekkala's eyes widened. 'Nothing?'

'An investigation now would only draw attention to its loss.'

'Not as much as if it became known that we had taken no steps to recover the icon.'

'That is why,' continued the Tsarina, 'we will inform the public that the icon is being restored, and that this work is likely to take some time. No one would find it unusual.'

'That is a lie which will not hold for long, Majesty. The icon could surface again at any time.'

'Agreed, but by then the war may be over and the country will have turned its attention to other things.'

'I really should speak with Rasputin,' insisted Pekkala.

The Tsarina breathed in slowly, the air whistling faintly through her nose. 'Leave him be, Pekkala. He had no role in this.'

'Forgive me, Majesty, but you have just told me that the icon was stolen from his house!' exclaimed Pekkala.

'So you think our dear friend is the one who stole it?' The Tsarina smiled faintly at the absurdity of this idea, her expression almost hidden in the flare of sunlight through the curtains.

'No,' answered Pekkala, 'but others will. He is very much a part of this, whether he intended to be or not. Surely you would want me to prove his innocence.'

The Tsarina sighed. 'Very well. Go then, if you insist. But be careful, Pekkala. These days, there is danger everywhere.'

At that moment, Vyroubova reappeared from the kitchen. In her hand, she held a glass of water. 'Your refreshment, Inspector,' she said quietly.

'Some other time perhaps,' he told her as he walked out through the door.

Vyroubova watched him fade away among the trees, until all that remained was the sound of his footsteps crunching on the gravel path.

'I warned him,' said the Tsarina.

'He listened but he did not understand,' remarked Vyroubova.

'Oh, he understood me perfectly,' replied the Tsarina. 'He is simply doing what he has often done before.'

'And what is that, Majesty?'

'Whatever he chooses,' answered the Tsarina, 'only this time he will regret it.'

*

Later that same day, as Pekkala entered the gloomy courtyard of Rasputin's house in Petrograd, he noticed several newly smashed bottles on the cobblestones. The vinegary reek of spilled wine drilled into his senses. Glancing up, he caught sight of a figure staring down at him from one of the windows at the top. That was Rasputin's floor, and Pekkala recognised the figure as Grigori himself, wearing only a sleeveless white undershirt, his bare arms sinewy with muscle. Although he rarely used it, Rasputin was a man of great physical strength. With a rustle of the curtains, he disappeared back into the room.

Once more, Pekkala trudged up the stairs. At each of the three floors leading up to Rasputin's apartment, he studied the closed doors which led to the rooms of the building's other inhabitants. He wondered what they thought of the constant tramp of visitors to the apartment on the top floor. Whatever their suspicions, they had doubtless learned to keep their opinions to themselves. News of any confrontation with Rasputin would soon find its way to the ears of the Tsarina, to be followed swiftly by a visit from special agents of the Tsar's Secret Service, whose task it was to smooth over, with bribes if possible, by force if necessary, Rasputin's increasingly difficult reputation. Rasputin himself seemed barely aware of these gun-toting guardian angels, who often delivered him senseless to his lodgings after a night at the Villa Roda. Waking fully clothed upon his unmade bed, in the early afternoon of the following day, with no idea of how he came to be there, the Siberian would simply consign the missing hours to oblivion and throw open his door to the next group of guests in search of salvation or cash.

This time, however, when Pekkala arrived on the landing, he found the door locked. Gently, he bounced his knuckles off the wood, then, when no one answered, less gently, and finally, he pounded with his fist so that the hinges rattled on their pins.

Eventually, there came the creak of footsteps on the other side, the clunk of a lock being turned, and the door creaked open, just wide enough to show one of Rasputin's eyes, peering nervously out into the hall. 'Inspector!' he said through gritted teeth. 'What a pleasant surprise.'

'You knew it was me,' replied Pekkala.

Rasputin cleared his throat. 'Well, it so happens I was just on my way out. You'll have to come back some other time.'

'Then I'll walk you down to the street, Grigori, and keep you company wherever you are going.'

'No,' muttered Rasputin. 'I am very busy. There is no time for talk.'

Pekkala set his toe upon the door and pushed.

At first, Rasputin tried to hold him back, but then, with a growl of surrender, he let go.

In the time it had taken Pekkala to climb the stairs, Rasputin had changed from his white undershirt into a red tunic with black trousers and knee-length, calfskin boots. He was in the process of fastening around his waist a woven horsehair belt with an intricate, silver buckle, fashioned in the Cossack style, like two halves of a scallop shell split open end to end.

The walls, Pekkala noted, had been freshly painted in a particular shade of mauve which was the choice of the Tsarina for her own rooms in the Alexander Palace. 'An interesting colour choice,' he remarked.

'You know perfectly well it wasn't my idea,' Rasputin mumbled into his beard.

'Why did she want it done?'

Rasputin shrugged, rolling his shoulders as if he were in pain. 'She didn't want the icon hanging on a dirty wall.'

'What did the owners of the apartment have to say about that?'

To this, Rasputin laughed. 'What could they say, except to thank her for her generosity? Now, perhaps we can talk about all this at a later time.' He moved to push past the Inspector.

Pekkala held out his arm and set his thumb and first two fingers, like the spear tips of a trident, against the Siberian's chest. 'Grigori,' he said, 'it can't wait.'

At this, Rasputin's resolve seemed to fail him. 'You should not have come here,' he whispered. 'I told her to keep you away.'

'She tried,' answered Pekkala.

'I asked her to keep it a secret!'

'She knew I would find out eventually. That's why she told me herself.'

With a sigh, Rasputin turned and stared at the empty space on the wall, marked only by a nail driven into the surface. 'Well,' he said, 'this is the scene of the crime.'

'When was the icon stolen, Grigori?'

'It disappeared last night, while I was out.'

'Out where?'

'Here and there.'

'Grigori,' said Pekkala, his voice growing cold with impatience, 'I need you to be specific.'

'Well,' began Rasputin, scratching his head with his long fingernails as he struggled to recall, 'first I went to Yar, the gypsy restaurant in Petrovsky Park. The Lebedevs were playing. I stayed until they closed and then I went over to the Bear Café.'

'I thought you were thrown out of there,' said Pekkala.

'Oh, I was,' agreed Rasputin. 'I am always thrown out of the Bear. I walked home from there and that's when I noticed it was gone.'

Pekkala turned towards the door. Carefully, he brushed his fingers over the latch mechanism. 'It shows no sign of being forced.'

'I may not have locked it,' answered Rasputin. 'Sometimes I forget.'

Now Pekkala began to look around the room. He noticed the blue-and-white washbowl, decorated with scenes of pagodas and men fishing from spindly boats. It was half full of money. 'Strange,' he said, 'that this should have been left by the thieves.'

'Perhaps they just came for one thing,' offered Rasputin. 'They found it, they took it and that's that.'

'So what you are telling me,' continued Pekkala, 'is that whoever robbed you knew the icon was here.'

'They must have.'

'And which of your recent visitors expressed an interest in the icon?'

'Don't drag them into this!' Rasputin began pacing about the room. 'I assure you they had nothing to do with it.'

'So let us say, for the sake of argument, that none of your guests were involved.'

'That's more like it!' Rasputin clapped his hands. 'Now we are seeing eye to eye.'

But Pekkala wasn't finished with him yet. 'And yet you maintain that the thieves came with only one object in mind. Or else, surely, they would have taken other things of value, such as this bowl of cash.'

'Yes, that's what I'm saying.' Sensing that he was being led into a snare, Rasputin screwed up his face. 'At least, I think I am,' he added.

'But whoever stole the icon knew that it had been moved from the Church of the Resurrection to your home. And if it wasn't one of your guests, then who else besides the Romanovs knew it was here?'

Rasputin twisted a finger in his beard. 'I didn't tell anyone.'

'Why not, Grigori?' asked Pekkala. 'Certainly, it would have been an interesting topic of conversation.'

'You think I have nothing else to talk about?' snapped Rasputin. 'Besides, you know perfectly well what would happen if the wrong people found out. They hate me enough as it is.'

'So you didn't tell anyone.'

'I just told you I didn't!'

'Then who is left?' asked Pekkala. 'Surely you don't mean to implicate the Tsarina herself?'

Rasputin clasped the Inspector's arms and shook him gently. 'Stay away from those thoughts, my old friend!' he hissed. 'Don't even dare to think them! Instead, just ask yourself what matters more – the things that give us peace or peace itself?'

'Do you really believe that this icon can bring an end to the war?'

'Perhaps.' Rasputin nodded. 'But if we are not careful it could be the end of us as well.'

'I don't see how,' replied Pekkala. 'I have seen that icon and it's just a picture of a man and some sheep, which does not strike me as particularly worrisome.'

'It's what lies behind the picture that should worry you. You cannot see it, Pekkala, but this picture is dripping with blood.' And when Rasputin next began to speak, quoting from the Gospel of St Matthew, his voice turned low and steady, like that of a man in a trance. '*And before him shall be gathered all nations, and he shall separate them one from another, as a shepherd divideth his sheep from the goats. And he shall set his sheep on his right hand and his goats upon the left. Then shall the King say unto them on his right hand – Come ye who are blessed of my Father, inherit the kingdom prepared for you from the foundation of the world.*'

'And what happens to the goats?' Pekkala wondered aloud.

'What do you think?' demanded Rasputin. 'They are slaughtered and their bodies are cast into the fire. There is nothing gentle about *The Shepherd*, Inspector. Quite the contrary. Contained within that image is all the fury of the Last Judgement. And as far as the rulers of this country were concerned, that is exactly what this icon could deliver – not just protection for themselves but oblivion for their enemies. Whoever possesses this image holds the key to Armageddon. That is why you must turn around now, Pekkala, and walk away from this while you still can.'

Pekkala slowly shook his head. 'It's too late now, Grigori.'

'I see there's no convincing you.' Rasputin's hands slipped away from their grasp upon Pekkala's coat sleeves. 'Perhaps you're right. Maybe it is just a painting, and one day all that will be left are the ghosts who once adored it.'

After leaving Rasputin's apartment, Pekkala descended the stairs and strode across the uneven cobblestones of the courtyard, boots crunching on shards of broken wine bottles. He emerged into the street, turned right, and began to make his way to the station, where a short train ride would bring him back to Tsarskoye Selo. He had travelled that route many times, and knew each sway of the carriages as they clattered towards their destination. Even at night, he could tell by the pitch of the engine exactly where they were upon the journey.

Pekkala paused to watch a car speeding down the street. It was a beautiful, open-topped Opel saloon car, belonging to the Grand Duke Pavel Alexandrovich, a career cavalry officer and commander of the Garde du Corps. Although his rank and position dictated that he should be driven by a chauffeur, the Grand Duke preferred to do his own driving and would often make his chauffeur sit in the back while Alexandrovich, with the chauffeur's cap wedged on to his head, would steer the car at high speed through the busy streets of Petrograd. Pekkala recognised the stiff moustache of the Grand Duke, wearing the high-necked tunic of a Grodno Hussar. In the back, with arms folded and staring sullenly into space, sat the bare-headed chauffeur.

It was late in the day now and even though the sun had not yet set, shadows filled the streets and the horse-drawn droshky carriages making their way along the road had already lit their lanterns.

At that moment, from the corner of his eye, Pekkala caught a glimpse of somebody following behind him in the exact spot where a person would be if they wanted to remain unnoticed. It could simply have been a coincidence. The streets were busy, after all, but Pekkala had an inkling that something was not right. To make sure, one way or the other, he slowed and then knelt down, pretending to tie one of his bootlaces. If the man walked past, the chances were that Pekkala was not being followed. But the man hung back, and Pekkala's suspicions grew. Standing, he crossed the street and as he stepped from the pavement, he glanced casually to his left. He saw a tall, heavyset man with a lumbering gait, his face almost hidden beneath a long-brimmed wool cap of the type worn by newsboys who sold late editions of the *Ryetch* newspaper at street corners during the evening rush hour. His long coat was unbuttoned and the hem flapped around his calves as he walked. He also wore a pair of greyish-white suede gloves, which struck Pekkala as unusual for the time of year.

The man did not appear to be carrying a gun. Certainly, there was no shoulder holster and the open coat revealed no weapon tucked into his belt.

Pekkala made no effort to confront the stranger, or to lose him in the crowds of commuters who had begun to fill the streets. Instead, he allowed the man to track him. Every few minutes, he paused at a shop window, pretending to examine things for sale. In fact, he was studying the man's reflection in the glass.

Each time, the man would slow his pace, lower his head and turn, seemingly preoccupied, like someone who has just remembered something he forgot at home.

From his observations, Pekkala concluded that the man's clothing was of Russian make, but not that of a city dweller. By the way he carefully hid his face, as well as maintaining a precise distance, not too close but never so far as to risk losing sight of his target, it was clear to Pekkala that the man did not desire an immediate confrontation.

Pekkala guessed that this man was not on his own errand, but was likely working for somebody else, and that this probably had less to do with him than it did with some transgression of Rasputin. Having no wish to become involved in one of Rasputin's intrigues, Pekkala might normally have waited until he reached the station, busy at this time of day, before losing the man in the crowd.

But the conversation with Rasputin, combined with the theft of the icon, had unsettled him. Rasputin had been hiding something, and Pekkala knew that there would be much work ahead if he was to unravel the reason for the icon's disappearance, let alone restore it to its rightful place in the cathedral. And there was a chance, however slim, that this man had something to do with it.

Pekkala decided to double back on the man. If he had to, he would make an arrest, but he hoped it would not come to that. If this lumbering giant was simply doing his job, as Pekkala suspected, it might be possible to learn all he needed to know with a few whispered words and a glimpse of the Emerald Eye.

There was an alleyway that ran parallel to the Gosciny Dvor, the main road to the station. The alley, known as St Christopher's Way, was used primarily by tradesmen delivering goods to shops whose storefronts opened out on to the Gosciny. It was also where rubbish was placed, sometimes in large galvanised bins, but just as often dumped in the narrow thoroughfare, blocking the way for anyone who did not feel like kicking his way through the heaps of cardboard boxes and prickly bundles of hay used to cushion fragile objects on their journey from factory to store.

Pekkala ducked into the Watkins Bookshop, which had for many years kept Petrograd supplied with French and English and, until recently, German editions of novels not yet available in translation. He strode through the store, breathing in the dry and comforting smell of new books, and passing the alcoves where customers lounged in comfortable chairs, sometimes reading entire books in one sitting, or else falling completely asleep. Rather than evicting them, the staff would coax the sleepers back to consciousness with cups of sweet Kusmichov tea, and, whether from embarrassment or gratitude, they would usually end up buying more than they had planned to when they came in.

Pekkala exited the book shop into St Christopher's Way, pushing past several splintery shipping crates. His plan was to run the length of the alley, turn back on to the Gosciny Dvor and catch the man as he waited outside the shop for Pekkala to emerge. He knew there was little danger of the man actually going inside. Even an untrained tracker knew better than to follow his quarry into a confined space where he would immediately give up the advantage of his anonymity.

Pekkala set off at a sprint down the alleyway, dodging past rubbish bins, bundled stacks of old newspapers and broken pieces of furniture. The sun had angled to the west and only at the very top of the alley could its coppery light be seen upon the brickwork and the windows of the garrets where bachelors and students lived in attic rooms whose angled ceilings made life miserable for anyone who dared to stand up straight.

He was just rounding the corner on to a side street, which would take him, with a dozen steps, to the crowded thorough-fare of the Gosciny, when he ploughed into someone coming from the other way.

As Pekkala staggered back, a muttered apology on his lips, he realised it was the man who had been following him. He had no time to contemplate the fact that he had misjudged both the man's skill as a tracker and also his speed. From the corner of his eye, he saw a flash, as if the light from a lantern on a passing droshky had winked off a shop window out on the main street. Then he felt something brush across his chest. He heard a dull click and one of his coat buttons went flying off over his shoulder. Now he understood that the flash had come from a blade, and that the man's first swing with the cutting edge had sliced through the wool of his coat, glancing off the Webley in its holster on his chest.

The man brought his arm back, a long, strange knife gripped in his hand. It was about the same length as from the tip of a man's fingers to his elbow, the end squared off and the back edge of the blade unusually thick, as if the knife was meant for wielding like an axe.

Pekkala saw that the man's greyish-white suede gloves were not gloves at all but the actual colour of his skin. The man's face, too, was pale and waxy, his features abnormally rounded and his eyes little more than slits in the puffy skin. He ap-peared, at first glance, to have no eyebrows, nor any facial hair at all and what there might have been on his head was hidden by the newsboy's cap. He reminded Pekkala of a drowned fish-erman he had once found washed up on the beach as a child, on the tiny Finnish island of Kovasin.

The man reached out to grab Pekkala's coat. In his other hand, he held the knife.

Pekkala knew that if the man succeeded in getting a hold on his lapel, he would be knocked off balance, in which case he was as good as dead. There was no time, nor room enough to draw his gun. He jumped back, just as the man swung again with the knife and this time Pekkala felt a sharp stinging pain on the left side of his forehead. He stepped to the side as the man was carried forward by the momentum of his swing. Pekkala lunged, grabbing the wrist of the hand which held the knife. He twisted the man's arm straight, forcing his shoulder to drop. Then, Pekkala smashed the heel of his left hand into the man's elbow. He heard a faint crunch as one of the man's tendons gave way. The man cried out through clenched teeth as the knife fell from his grasp and fell with a clatter into the alley.

By now, blood was pouring from the gash on Pekkala's forehead. He could see nothing at all from his left eye. As yet, there was no pain, and he had no idea how badly he'd been cut.

With both hands still gripping the man's arm, Pekkala swung him head first into the brick wall, then stepped back, giving himself enough space to finally reach for his gun. But his hand slipped instead into the lining of the coat, which had been torn open by the first swipe of the blade. By the time he had withdrawn his hand, ready to try again, it was too late.

The man had turned to face him. He was breathing heavily. His right hand hung useless at his side and his skin was scored with bloody creases where it had scraped against the wall.

For a moment, the two men remained motionless, only an arm's length apart.

Pekkala had no idea where the knife had fallen. The alley was in darkness now and he knew it must have come to rest somewhere behind him. Perhaps the man could see it from where he stood. Pekkala wasn't certain he could get to his revolver, or if his hand would once more become tangled in the lining of his coat. At this distance, it would have been foolish even to try.

For the first time, the man spoke. 'Stay away,' he whispered. Then he lunged at Pekkala, knocking him off balance.

Pekkala tripped backwards, his back striking hard against the ground. He gasped from the pain of his landing. With his consciousness flickering, he reached once more for his gun and this time his hand closed around the brass handle of the Webley. But it was no use. By the time he had drawn the weapon, the man was already gone.

Dazed by loss of blood, Pekkala lay there in the alley, his gaze fixed upon the silhouettes of pedestrians strolling past out on the Gosciny Dvor, completely unaware of what had happened only a few feet away. Then he slowly clambered to his feet. Half blind and groping about in the dirt, he searched for the knife until he found it lodged beneath a drainpipe. He tore a page from a stack of old newspapers, rolled it around the weapon and used another page to wipe some of the blood from his face. With gritted teeth, he touched his fingertips to the puckered wound. It wasn't as bad as he had thought. The cut was deep but it hadn't gone down to the bone.

An hour later, he was sitting in the office of Chief Inspector Vassileyev, head of the Petrograd Okhrana, wincing while a medic named Isaac Blaustein, hastily summoned from his dental practice across the street, stitched up the cut on Pekkala's forehead.

'This isn't my line of work!' protested the dentist.

'Well, it was either you or me,' replied Vassileyev. 'We have a doctor on our staff, but he went home early today.'

'Believe me,' Pekkala said to Blaustein, 'between you and Chief Inspector Vassileyev is no choice at all.'

'I am glad to hear it,' answered the dentist, 'but now will you please hold steady, Inspector!'

Vassileyev paced about the room, steadily making his way through several of the sixty Markov cigarettes he smoked each day. Stacks of red boxes, each one emblazoned in gold with the brand name, lined the Chief Inspector's windowsill.

He had one wooden leg, having lost his right limb in an assassination attempt several years before. The prosthetic was heavy and caused him a great deal of pain and he could often be found with the leg laid out on his desk while he hollowed it out with a chisel, trying to reduce its weight. Now his footsteps marked uneven time upon the creaking floorboards.

It was Vassileyev himself who had trained Pekkala for his work as the Tsar's personal investigator. As soon as he learned that Pekkala's attacker had been tailing him before the fight in the alley, he immediately began to quiz his former student. 'Did you stop to tie your shoes in order to see if he would pass you?'

'Yes.'

'Did you cross the road and glance back?'

'Yes,' answered Pekkala.

'And did you stop in front of shop windows to study him in the reflection?'

'Yes!'

Vassileyev patted Pekkala on the shoulder. 'Good boy,' he said quietly. 'And don't you worry. We'll get him. This man was just a common crook.'

'I wouldn't be too sure,' replied Pekkala. 'Take a look at this.' He held out the blood-stained scroll of newspaper, in which he had bundled the knife.

The Chief Inspector carefully unrolled the paper, then lifted up the weapon. He gave a low whistle. 'The bastard went after you with this? What is it, anyway? I've never seen a blade like this before.'

'I'll tell you what it is,' said the dentist. He had finished the stitches, sixteen of them in all, and now he was pouring rubbing alcohol over his hands, which he then dried with a handkerchief. 'It's a halal knife.'

'A what?' Vassileyev and Pekkala chimed in unison.

'Halal,' repeated Blaustein. 'For the ritual slaughter of animals. That's why it is so sharp.'

Vassileyev lifted a piece of writing paper from his desk and drew the knife vertically down the page. With a faint rustle, the blade cleaved it neatly in half. 'My word, Pekkala,' he muttered, 'you don't have many enemies, but those you do have certainly mean business!'

'He told me to stay away,' remarked Pekkala. 'Those were the only words he spoke.'

'If I were you,' said the dentist, 'I'd be tempted to take his advice.'

'But stay away from what?' Pekkala wondered out loud. 'He was the one following me!'

'Well, obviously,' remarked Vassileyev, 'he thought you'd understand.'

'How do you know about this knife?' Pekkala asked the dentist.

'My father was a kosher butcher,' answered Blaustein, 'and a halal is the only blade that can be used to kill an animal for food. May I see it, please?'

Vassileyev turned the weapon and held it out, handle first, to the doctor.

Blaustein gripped the halal with the ease of someone who was used to handling knives. He studied the metal, lifting his small round glasses and placing them on top of his head.

'What are you looking for?' asked Vassileyev.

'A maker's mark,' replied Blaustein. 'Here.' With the tip of his little finger, he indicated a small square, over-stamped with a cross. 'This is the mark of the knife-smith Adi Melzer. His shop is on the Savodskaya Prospekt. My father used to buy from him.'

'That's a start,' said Vassileyev. 'I'll send over one of my men, first thing in the morning.'

'I'd rather handle this myself, Chief Inspector,' replied Pekkala. 'There is more to this than just a knife attack.' He went on to explain about the missing icon.

'By all means hunt for that picture,' blustered Vassileyev. 'My quarrel is with the man who owns this!' He brandished the weapon, causing both Pekkala and the dentist to duck. 'Nobody cuts up my students!' he declared. 'I'll hunt the bastard down myself, and then beat him to death with this leg!' He rapped his knuckles on the wooden thigh.

'Take the Chief Inspector up on his kind offer,' Blaustein advised Pekkala, as he put away his instruments in a black leather bag. 'You should be resting while this heals. Besides, you don't want to run into that man again any time soon.'

'He kissed you good and proper,' laughed Vassileyev, pointing to the row of x-shaped stitch marks on Pekkala's forehead.

'Now then, Inspector Pekkala,' said Dr Blaustein, 'if you wouldn't mind opening your mouth.'

'What for?' demanded Pekkala.

'Now that I'm here,' answered the dentist, 'I may as well look at your teeth!'

*

Late that night, Pekkala stood before the Tsar.

Thanks to a call from Vassileyev, news of the attack had preceded Pekkala's return to Tsarskoye Selo, and a car was waiting for him at the station. It brought him straight to the Alexander Palace.

Unknown to Pekkala, the Tsar had travelled up from Mogilev earlier that day. By the time Pekkala arrived, the rest of the household had already gone to bed. In spite of the size of the palace, voices often carried down the hallways, so the two men retreated to the Tsar's study, where they could talk without the risk of waking anyone.

'That is a nasty cut,' remarked the Tsar, grimacing at the crescent-shaped line of sutures.

'It will heal,' replied Pekkala. 'I am more concerned about the news I learned today when I paid a visit to Rasputin.'

'Yes,' whispered the Tsar. 'I have already heard. The icon is missing.'

With a deep sigh, he sat down at his desk, a solid slab of walnut supported by two heavy, engraved posts which ran the full width of the desk and which were joined by a foot rail carved in a spiral like the tusk of a narwhal. Towering behind him stood a grey stone fireplace, with a screen placed in front of the hearth since no fires were lit in summer time. 'Alexandra informed me as soon as I arrived. When I sent you to persuade Rasputin to have the icon returned to the cathedral, I was only thinking about what would happen if people knew it had been entrusted to his safekeeping. I never thought someone would actually dare to steal it!'

'I must tell you, Majesty, the Empress seemed anxious that I not pursue this case.'

The Tsar brushed his fingers along the line of his jaw, rustling his thumb through his moustache. 'She doesn't want Grigori dragged into it, but I told her it was too late for that now.'

'Do you intend to keep the theft a secret?' asked Pekkala.

'No,' the Tsar said abruptly. 'I know that is what Alexandra would like, but the truth would come out sooner or later. What if the icon surfaces in the hands of some unscrupulous art dealer, or on some auction block outside the country? How would we explain that to the people of Russia? I told the Empress it was better just to tell the truth, and to let the world know that the Emerald Eye is now on the trail of the thief. From this moment on, *The Shepherd*'s safe recovery is to be your primary concern.'

'Yes, Majesty,' replied Pekkala.

'Good evening, Inspector,' said a woman's voice.

Both men turned to see the Empress standing in the doorway. She wore a lavender silk robe over her nightdress. Stripped of its daytime mask of cosmetics, the features of her face looked small and blurred.

'Did we wake you, my dear?' asked the Tsar, rising to his feet.

'It appears that you have had a narrow escape,' she remarked to Pekkala, ignoring the Tsar's question.

'Not for the first time,' he replied.

'The Inspector was just making his report,' said the Tsar.

'I know why he is here!' said the Tsarina as she levelled a finger at Pekkala. 'I warned you before to be careful, and I will warn you once again. If your inquiries bring harm to Grigori, you shall answer for that before God and, as you yourself have learned this night, the angels he sends to wreak his vengeance will not show mercy, even to the favourite of the Tsar!'

'Majesty, you may be right,' answered Pekkala, 'but I have yet to see an angel with a butcher's knife.'

*

On the morning of 21 June 1915, Pekkala entered the shop of Melzer, the knife-maker, and was perplexed to find that there wasn't a knife in sight.

Aside from several different blocks of wood for making knife handles, as well as a pile of oblong metal bars, from which the blades themselves would be fashioned, the shop was devoid of anything which might have been for sale.

Melzer himself stood behind the counter on which the bars and blocks of wood lay neatly stacked. He was a short, aggressive-looking man, with a redness to his face which made his skin appear as if it had been scoured with a wire brush. There was no hair to speak of on his head and, for a man who specialised in blades, he had made a poor job of shaving his chin. This contradiction did not catch Pekkala by surprise. He had known cobblers who shuffled about their workshops in shoes so ragged and worn down that, if those shoes had been brought in for repair, they themselves would have refused to work on them. Likewise, the tailor Linsky, who provided Pekkala with his eccentrically heavy clothes, sometimes greeted customers wearing only a nightshirt.

'I do custom work,' explained Melzer, as if reading Pekkala's mind. 'By the time a knife has been made, it already belongs to someone else, so, in effect, there is nothing to display.'

'So how do people know to come to you?' asked Pekkala.

'My family has been making knives for generations,' said Melzer. 'There has never been a need to advertise.'

Pekkala wondered what this artisan would think of the battered old lock-knife, with its cracked stag-horn grips and dingy iron blade, which he always carried with him. It was made by a company called Geck in Brussels, and he had come across it one cheerful autumn afternoon some years ago while wandering through the Sukharevka market in Moscow. He had carried it with him ever since and, in spite of the length of its menacing edge, the knife had mostly been employed for sharpening pencils, peeling apples and for jemmying open the lock on his apartment door whenever he misplaced his keys.

Now Pekkala laid the halal, wrapped in a fresh piece of brown paper, upon the counter. 'I am told that you might have made this.'

Melzer unwrapped the knife and laid it on the unfolded paper. At first, he did not touch it, but only studied the implement, in a way which reminded Pekkala of the way his mother used to inspect the fish she bought at the market every week in Lappeenranta. Then he slowly closed his hand around the handle and raised the blade.

Seeing the long, razor-sharp edge, Pekkala couldn't help flinching as he thought of the fight in the alley, and how close he had come to being carved up like a sacrificial lamb.

'This is the work of my father,' said Melzer, 'from whom I inherited the business when he died ten years ago.'

'How can you tell the difference between one knife and another?'

'Here is his mark,' replied Melzer, indicating the square and cross stamp along the top edge of the tang. 'My own stamp is a triangle and cross. My son, who, God willing, will one day inherit the business from me, has a circle and a cross as his brand. Otherwise, indeed, it might be difficult to tell.'

'So that knife,' Pekkala nodded to the halal, 'is at least ten years old.'

'At the very least,' answered Melzer. 'The handle is made of arctic birch. You can tell by the closeness of the grain and by the way it seems to shimmer in the light.'

Pekkala had seen cups made from this wood, which were used by his mother's family in Lapland. 'But does this tell you anything about the person for whom your father made it?'

'Not who,' replied Melzer, 'but it does tell me when. This knife was made in Siberia, where my father learned his trade, in the city of Kurgan. He moved to St Petersburg almost forty years ago and our family has been here ever since. I never saw him work with arctic birch while he was here in St Petersburg.'

'Did your father keep a ledger with the names of his customers?' asked Pekkala.

'Unfortunately not.' Melzer smiled apologetically. 'He was a knife-smith, not a bureaucrat.'

At that moment, the door to the shop swung open.

'There you are!' said a voice.

Pekkala turned to see Vassileyev, cheerful and sweating from the exertion of walking on his wooden leg.

'I thought I'd find you here,' said Vassileyev.

'Is everything all right?' asked Pekkala.

'Better than all right, I'd say,' remarked Vassileyev. 'Some priest who worked at the Church of the Resurrection, where the icon is normally kept, just walked into Okhrana headquarters and confessed to stealing it!'

'A priest?' asked Pekkala.

Vassileyev shrugged. 'That's what he said he was, and he looked like one to me.'

'Have you spoken to him?'

'No. He's in a holding cell at headquarters, which is where he will stay until you decide what to do with him. This is your case, Pekkala. The Tsar himself instructed me to tell you that. He also told me that, as soon as you have interrogated the suspect, you are to report your findings to him at the Alexander Palace.'

'I can tell you one thing for certain,' Melzer said, as Pekkala was walking out the door. 'My father did not make this knife for any priest!'

*

Following the guard who was on duty at the Okhrana holding cells, Pekkala made his way down a long corridor to a room that had been set aside for interrogations.

There was total silence in the corridor, which was lined with steel doors, each one with a deadbolt and a small opening, covered by a sliding metal plate, through which food was delivered twice a day in metal bowls made of metal so soft that the bowls could be folded in half with a man's bare hands. No cutlery was provided, so the prisoners ate with their fingers. Once a week, if inmates were held that long at headquarters before being transferred to one of the larger prisons in the city, each man would put his head through the opening. In this uncomfortable position, he would wait to be shaved by the prison barber, a sombre, thoughtful man named Budny who, in spite of these harsh surroundings, was a gentle and accomplished practitioner of his trade.

Arriving at the interrogation cell, the guard slid back a deadbolt and pushed the door open with his other hand.

'I might be a while,' whispered Pekkala.

The guard nodded and set off down the corridor towards the guardroom, which was furnished with an assortment of couches with threadbare upholstery, wing-backed chairs and even a rocker, all scrounged by the industrious Vassileyev from the many noble patrons of his service. Unaware that Pekkala was still watching from the doorway of the cell, the guard held his arms out to the side, as if gliding through the sky like an albatross, fingertips brushing past the doors.

Pekkala stepped into the room and closed the door.

The interrogation cell contained no windows, only an air vent in the ceiling. A single lamp, hooded by a metal shade, hung over a table in the centre of the room. There were two chairs, one on either side of the table. Otherwise, the room was completely empty, and the dark grey walls, as grim as thunderclouds, combined with the cone of light above the table to give the impression of a raft floating in the middle of a stormy sea.

The priest had already been brought in. One of his legs had been shackled to a ring anchored in the floor beside the chair, and his hands were fastened with a set of heavy cuffs. He was a small man in his late thirties, with thinning hair and a sallow, puffy complexion. He wore the simple black robe of an Orthodox priest, which fastened down the left side of his body with hidden hooks, rather than buttons. Those being held at Okhrana headquarters were not issued the coarse grey-and-black-striped clothing of convicts. That would come later, for those who moved on into the long-term prison system.

The first thing Pekkala did was to fetch a small key from his pocket, lean across the table and unfasten the cuffs. With a heavy rattle, they slipped from the man's wrists on to the table and lay there like a pair of iron crab claws. Without undoing the chain which shackled the priest's right leg to the floor, Pekkala took his seat.

The prisoner watched with great curiosity as Pekkala removed a small notebook from the chest pocket of his waistcoat, and then a black fountain pen with a gold clip. He unscrewed the cap, revealing the long and graceful nib, pushed the cap on to the end of the pen and scribbled the day's date at the top of a page in his notebook. Only then did he raise his head and look the prisoner in the eye. 'What is your name?' asked Pekkala.

'Detlev,' replied the man. 'Alexander Nikolaevich Detlev.'

Pekkala wrote it down, the pen rustling across the page. 'Father Detlev, I understand that you have confessed to stealing the icon known as *The Shepherd* from the house of Grigori Rasputin.'

'Yes,' he answered readily.

'And where is the icon now?' asked Pekkala.

'It has been destroyed,' Detlev said, matter-of-factly.

Pekkala looked up sharply from his notebook. 'Destroyed?'

'That's what I said.'

'And who destroyed it?'

'I did,' answered Detlev.

'How?'

'I burned it. If you don't believe me, go to the pavilion on the island of the Lamskie pond at Tsarskoye Selo. There you will find what is left.'

'Why did you destroy it?' he asked.

'It was my sacred duty.'

'What do you mean by that?'

'No more than I have already said,' Detlev answered vaguely.

'And having done this thing...'

'Why did I turn myself in?'

'Precisely.'

'Because I do not consider what I have done to be a crime.'

'But surely you realise that those who stand in judgement of you now will never be persuaded of this?'

Detlev nodded, his lips pressed tightly together. 'It is not my intention to try.'

'Then why throw yourself at their mercy, since you know they will not show you any?'

'The judgement I await will not be passed by any mortal man.'

'In the meantime, however, you will simply be thought of as a fool.'

'A holy fool, perhaps. That does not trouble me.' Smiling, Detlev held out his hands, palms up and side by side. 'I've told you all you're going to learn from me, Inspector, so go ahead and put those chains back on.'

'Very well,' said Pekkala. 'You have already told me more than you realise, and it is all I need to know for now.' With those words, he replaced the handcuffs and headed for the door.

'It was a pleasure to have met you,' said the priest, before Pekkala left the room, 'and I regret that our acquaintance was so brief.'

'We will meet again, Father Detlev,' Pekkala answered. 'I am not finished with you yet.'

'It sounds as if you are threatening me, Inspector.'

'I am making you a promise,' said Pekkala.

*

Before making his report to the Tsar, as Vassileyev had instructed him, Pekkala paid a visit to the headquarters of the Petrograd Metropolitan Police, to check whether Detlev had a criminal past, but they had no record of the man. Next, Pekkala tried the State Police, the Gendarmerie, but they had nothing on him either. There was only one place left to look – back at the offices of the Tsar's Secret Police; although Pekkala doubted that he would find anything there. If Detlev had not shown up in the files of the local and national law enforcement, it was un-likely he would have come to the attention of the Okhrana.

In the bustling foyer of Okhrana headquarters, Pekkala asked the clerk at the records office if there was any information on file about Detlev.

'I'll take a look, Inspector,' said the clerk. The man turned smartly on his heel and marched back into his musty-smelling world of filing cabinets and manila envelopes.

While he waited, Pekkala took in the many sounds and smells of the headquarters building, separating each strand like a man unbraiding rope – the gasp of the main door as it opened from the street and the way the brush seal along the bottom edge shushed across the tiled floor of the entrance-way; the splashing gurgle of a toilet flushing in the guards' off-duty room; the voice of Chief Inspector Vassileyev berating some unfortunate agent, his curses suddenly muffled as his secretary rushed to close the door; the smell of hair tonic and stale tobacco smoke as an officer of the Gendarmerie strode past in his dark blue, silver-buttoned uniform, carrying a sheaf of documents: the scowl on his face showed how uncomfortable he felt to be among the secret-loving agents of the Okhrana.

'I found what you were looking for, Inspector,' said the clerk, returning to the metal grille window which separated the records office from the main hallway. 'At least, I thought I had,' said the clerk.

'What do you mean?' asked Pekkala.

The clerk slid the file through the opening beneath the grille.

Even before Pekkala picked up the envelope, he could already tell that it was empty. 'What happened to the contents?' he demanded.

Nervously, the clerk sucked at his teeth. 'They appear to have been misplaced.'

Pekkala let out a long sigh.

'These things do happen, I'm afraid,' added the clerk.

'But the existence of this file does prove that he had a criminal record,' said Pekkala.

'That is correct,' confirmed the clerk. 'You can tell from the dates on the envelope that the case was opened in June of 1910, five years ago, and closed only one month later. There's nothing current. Whatever business he had with the Okhrana it was finished a long time ago.'

'The fact that Detlev is on file here with the Okhrana, but not at the police or Gendarmerie . . .'

'Would imply,' said the clerk, finishing Pekkala's thought, 'that Detlev's crime was considered to be a matter of some delicacy. He was no common thief, you can be sure, but whatever brought him to the attention of the Okhrana, it was apparently resolved very quickly.'

'What he did exactly,' said Pekkala, 'and who worked on the case would all have been contained in the report.'

The clerk nodded. He mouthed the word yes, but no sound came out.

'And you have no idea where it could be?' asked Pekkala.

The clerk looked back at the labyrinth of filing cabinets, then turned and glanced pitifully at Pekkala. 'If you have time . . .'

'No,' Pekkala told him. 'The man I work for is not celebrated for his patience.'

*

Immediately after leaving Okhrana headquarters, he boarded the train for the short trip to Tsarskoye Selo, where he knew that the Tsar would be waiting.

Before making his report to the Tsar, Pekkala rowed out to the island on the Lamskie pond. There, among a heap of ashes, he discovered the remnants of a jewel-studded wooden frame belonging to *The Shepherd*. Unfortunately, it looked as if Father Detlev had been telling the truth.

It was early in the evening when Pekkala entered the Tsar's study at the Alexander Palace. The moment he entered the room, he knew it would be a difficult meeting. The Tsar was very regular in his habits, from his bland choice of meals (he could eat chicken cutlets and boiled potatoes for days in a row), to the number of cigarettes he smoked (six a day, and always at exactly the same interval), to the way he received visitors in his private office. Pekkala had learned that if the Tsar was sitting down when he entered the room, all would be well. But today the Tsar stood by the window, looking out over the leafy shades of green on the estate, a clear sign that there was trouble brewing in his mind.

In a few words, Pekkala delivered the sad news.

While Pekkala spoke, the Tsar continued to stare out the window. Only when the Inspector had finished did he turn and make his way over to his desk. 'What's done is done, Inspector, and I am glad, at least, that you were able to resolve the matter so quickly.'

'I'm not convinced that it is resolved,' replied Pekkala. 'It turns out that Detlev has a prior criminal record. There's a file on him at Okhrana headquarters.

'Indeed? And what does it say?'

'Nothing, Majesty. The file was empty.'

'Empty,' repeated the Tsar. Reaching out across the desk, he let his fingertips drift above the neatly organised sheaves of parliamentary reports, those ready for his review and those already annotated with the blue pencils he used for this purpose. The pencils themselves, sharpened into hypodermic points, lay in their silver tray, always within easy reach. The Tsar was a man who liked to keep everything in order; from the strict timetable of his days to his clothing, to his food, to the whereabouts of everything around him, people as well as property. The thought of something going missing, however small, filled him with a deep uneasiness, which he found himself unable to disguise.

'What I'm trying to tell you, Majesty,' said Pekkala, 'is that there's still more work to be done. This man is nowhere near as mad as he pretends to be. It is simply a mask he has chosen to wear in order to protect others who are responsible, perhaps even more than himself.'

The Tsar cleared his throat. 'I don't see it that way, Pekkala.'

'Majesty?'

'There's no evidence of anyone else being involved. You have your crime. You have your criminal. You even have your confession. All that remains is for justice to be served. That you can leave to the courts, and I assure you that he will be in prison for a very long time! Your work is done, and I congratulate you.'

'And then there is the matter of the man who followed me from Rasputin's place, and who attacked me in St Christopher's Way.'

'Then leave this to the regular police,' stated the Tsar. 'Men like us must learn to live with enemies. There will be others, Pekkala. Just be glad that this one did not finish what he started.'

'I believe it might be connected to the theft of the icon.' Pekkala tried again to reason with the Tsar.

'And you have proof of this?'

'Not yet, but . . .'

'The case is closed,' the Tsar announced abruptly, 'and that is by Imperial Decree. Is there anything else you wish to say, Inspector?' There was an unaccustomed formality in the Tsar's voice, as if he were speaking to a stranger, and not a man whom he had trusted with his life for many years.

Knowing that it would be dangerous to argue the point any further, Pekkala bowed his head, took three steps back, turned sharply on his heel and headed for the door.

'Wait!' the Tsar called to him.

Pekkala stopped and turned.

The Tsar held up his hands in a gesture of conciliation. 'Forget about all this,' he said with a smile. 'If it helps, I will make that an order.'

Pekkala tried, but he was not accustomed to forgetting.

In the weeks ahead, which spread to months and then to years, the image of *The Shepherd* would shimmer to life in his mind, as if brought back from the cinders of its miniature funeral pyre. Pekkala would see again the brilliance of its colours and the curiously hypnotic shapes which seemed to tell only half of the story contained within that simply painted narrative.

But that was not the only thing which haunted him. Many times, late at night, as Pekkala's mind swept towards the precipice of sleep, the man in the alley would lunge once more from the shadows. Again and again, Pekkala would fight for his life, dodging and ducking the terrible blade. Once in a while, he survived without a scratch. Other times, he would escape with nothing more than the gash whose pale scar still snaked across his forehead. And sometimes he would feel the plunging sting as the knife sank deep into his flesh. In that parallel life, which at those times would seem more real than any waking thought, Pekkala would lie there in the alley among the empty crates and tufts of blood-soaked packing straw, waiting for his heart to run dry.

There are some things from which a man does not recover. There is no hiding place deep enough inside the catacombs of his brain where he can hide the memories. They will always find their way out, baying like wolves in the black tunnels of his mind until they reach the light again. The only thing that he can do is to let them come, fighting the nightmares until even the demons which brought them grow sick of the carnage.

As much as Pekkala had ever prayed for anything, he prayed for that day to arrive. Until then, however, he lay down to sleep each night with the relentless dread of a man condemned to the gallows.

5 July 1915

Nyirbator, Hungary

It was raining. In the muggy darkness of an early summer night, a horse-drawn carriage rattled along the road, wheels splashing through potholes and jostling the four men who sat inside. None of them spoke.

From the distance came a sound of thunder.

With a hooked finger, one of the men moved aside a blind which had been pulled down over the windows and peered through the mud-flecked windows at the devastated landscape beyond.

The driver of the carriage, rain shining on his oilskin coat, whipped the horses onward through the ruins of a village. Not a single house remained intact. Skewed tiles lay like scattered playing cards upon the broken frames of rooftops. Of some buildings, only the chimneys remained; smoke-blackened pillars propping up the clouds.

Rounding a corner, the carriage swayed precariously on its springs and the passengers felt their stomachs lurch. A moment later, they heard the driver calling to his horses and there was a jangling of brass as the carriage slowed to a halt.

The passengers glanced nervously at each other.

One of them drew a pistol and placed it on the seat beside him, covered by the hem of his long coat.

They had arrived at a roadblock, constructed of three military wagons tipped on their sides in such a way that anyone hoping to pass through would have to weave between the obstacles, a task which could only be achieved at a vulnerably slow pace.

A man appeared from the shadows, waving a lantern from side to side. He wore the blue-grey uniform, short-brimmed cap and insignia of an Austro-Hungarian soldier from Landwehr Regiment Number 6, the three stars embroidered on his collar indicating that he carried the rank of Zugführer – a sergeant. On the heavy brass buckle of his belt, the crest of the Habsburg Empire lay almost hidden behind a layer of apple-green paint.

Behind him, from the ruins of a basement which served as their bunker, emerged two more men carrying Steyr-Mannlicher rifles. One of them hurriedly sucked in the last breath of a cigarette, which he held covered in his palm against the rain, before flicking the stub away into the dark.

The sergeant held up the lantern, illuminating the ghostly white face of the driver and, in the soft guttural German of a Viennese, demanded his papers of transit.

The coachman nodded sharply and, reaching into the folds of his rain slicker, pulled out a bundle of documents wrapped in a leather cover. He handed them down to the sergeant.

While the soldier struggled to read through the well-thumbed travel documents, road-use permits and coachman's licence, its details almost obliterated beneath official military stamps, his two comrades peered in through the carriage windows at the passengers huddled inside. With one callused knuckle, one of the Austrians rapped against the glass.

The window was raised, and a smell of garlic and vinegar wafted out into the rainy night. A moment later, a hand emerged holding an open jar of pickles.

The two soldiers exchanged glances, then looked at their sergeant, who was still struggling to decipher the documents, then each man in turn snatched a pickle from the jar and crammed them into their mouths. With salty juice dripping from their chins, they nodded thanks and stepped back, to show that their inspection of the carriage was complete.

The sergeant, who in fact could barely read and had only made a show of studying the papers, returned them to the coachman and waved him past the barricade.

As the carriage rode on into the night, one of the passengers struck a match and, by its quivering light, glanced at his pocket watch. He was General Yagelsky, a veteran of the recent campaign at Tannenberg. Before the match burned out, Yagelsky took a moment to admire the double-headed eagle of the Romanovs, emblazoned in blue enamel on the solid gold watch-case, which had been presented to its owner by none other than the Tsar himself, in gratitude for his many years of service. But Yagelsky knew that if he had been captured at that dreary roadblock, miles behind enemy lines, any knowledge of his mission, and that of his three colleagues, would have been denied by those same rulers of the Empire who had ordered this journey to be made. The gun he had drawn was not for use against those poor, soaked Austrian soldiers, but for himself and for his fellow passengers; Lutukin and Briulov, both career politicians, as well as Naval Commodore Asikritov of the Tsar's Pacific Fleet in Vladivostok. He would rather have shot them all than take the risk that, through bribery, torture or despair, the truth behind their plan might be revealed.

As Yagelsky blew out the match and settled back into his seat, his thoughts drifted back to an article he had read recently, by the British writer H. G. Wells, in which the author had said that this conflict was being fought at such terrible cost to human life that it must surely mark the end of warfare. From what the general had seen of it himself – the tens of thousands of unburied corpses rotting in the Masurian swamps and, in the foothills of the Carpathian mountains, many thousands more lying heaped where they fell before the Austrian machine guns – he was inclined to agree.

They had not gone far beyond the ruins of the town when the sky behind them lit up with a series of blinding flashes, which was followed a few seconds later by the whine of incoming artillery.

The shells passed over the wagon and exploded in geysers of poppy-red flame.

The horses skittered in their traces and the driver cracked his whip to urge them on.

The men inside the wagon glanced at each other nervously, as their faces were illuminated by another blast of cannon fire.

Once more, the shells tore past above their heads, with a shrieking, metallic sound like a train with its brakes on full skidding to a stop on the rails. A line of explosions straddled the road, closer now, since the wagon was heading straight towards them.

'It's a barrage,' said Yagelsky. 'They are preparing to attack.'

'Who is?' asked the gaunt and squinting man who sat across from him. This was Lutukin, a serving member of the Russian parliament, known as the Duma. In spite of the fact that Lutukin was a politician, and not a military man, he had brought along a silver-handled sabre, with which he liked to be seen in public.

'It's our own side!' came the answer from Yagelsky. 'I happen to know that those are the guns of General Tovash's 3rd Artillery Regiment.'

'Wasn't he told about our mission?' asked Briulov, a nervous, jowly man who had served as Russia's Minister of Education. Now Commodore Asikritov spoke up. He was a gruff career officer with an impressive moustache and tangled, bushy eyebrows. 'Of course General Tovash doesn't know,' he barked at Briulov. 'Do you honestly believe they would have told him what we're doing?'

'Ask the driver to stop!' shouted Lutukin. 'He is taking us straight into the line of fire. We must face the fact that we'll never make it to the rendezvous, and the German delegation will not wait. If we turn back now, at least we'll escape with our lives.' Without waiting for an answer from his colleagues, he took his sabre and banged its silver hilt against the roof of the carriage.

A moment later, they heard the driver call out to his horses. The rhythmic jangle of their hooves slowed and then stopped, just as another shell careened past and exploded close enough for it to rock the carriage on its springs.

The driver jumped down from his seat. A moment later, he appeared at the window.

Startled by the man's ghoulish face, Lutukin gasped, but he quickly regained his composure. 'You've got to turn back,' he told the driver. 'This whole area is about to come under attack.

If our own cannon fire doesn't get us, the Austrian infantry certainly will.'

'It's your choice which way we go,' said the man, 'but my price is still the same.'

'Yes, yes!' Lutukin replied impatiently. 'Now hurry up and get us out of here!'

The man turned away into the dark and the carriage creaked when he climbed back up into his seat. The air cracked again as he whipped his horses into motion. In order to turn the carriage around, he steered it off the road and they set off across a stubble field, the carriage springs groaning over the uneven ground.

The sound of the shelling receded into the distance as they left the line of fire. Before long, the carriage reached another path. The driver lashed the reins and his horses began to trot. The sound of their hooves clattered reassuringly upon the hard-packed ground.

Now that they were out of danger, Briulov opened up a silver cigarette case and passed it around. The contents were quickly emptied and the carriage was soon filled with the perfumed reek of high-quality Balkan tobacco.

'It couldn't be helped,' said Lutukin.

'We did our best,' agreed Briulov.

'Listen to yourselves!' Yagelsky barked at the politicians. 'This is no cause for self-congratulation. Our mission was the last, best hope for peace without surrender.' He paused to fill his lungs, then exhaled in two jets through his nostrils. The tide of grey rolled back over the window, condensing into droplets on the glass. 'Gentlemen,' he said, 'we're going to lose the last war ever fought.'

2 February 1945

Ahlborn, Germany

In the crypt of the little church where they had taken refuge from the enemy, the two Red Army tank men examined the contents of the coffin, which now lay emptied out on to the floor.

The stone-cold corpse still wore the black robes of a priest. A fine layer of ice crystals glinted on the flesh and wisps of hair hung down over the sunken, withered eyes. The hands, entwined with a crucifix on a small chain, had been crossed over the chest.

But it was what lay beneath those hands which had caught the attention of Sergeant Ovchinikov.

The small rectangular object was partially wrapped in dark brown oilcloth that had originally been tied with string. The string had broken when the coffin fell to the ground and the oilcloth had come unwrapped, revealing a layer of gauzy, muslin fabric, through which the men could make out splashes of colour. Greens and blues and whites seemed to radiate out of the misty fabric.

'It can't be,' whispered the sergeant.

'Can't be what?' demanded Captain Proskuryakov. 'Do you mean that you know what this is?'

'I think so,' replied Ovchinikov, 'but I still can't see it clearly.'

Proskuryakov nodded at the bundle. 'Well, pick it up and take a better look.'

Ovchinikov glanced at him. 'And desecrate the body of a priest?'

'I just put my boot through his coffin!' said Proskuryakov. 'I think we're past that point. Now pick it up! That's an order.'

With a grunt, Ovchinikov crouched down and slipped the oilcloth from the dead priest's grip. The sergeant's fingers trembled as he tore away the gauze. 'Yes,' he whispered. 'Yes, I was right!'

By the light of a candle, Proskuryakov found himself staring at a strange little painting, the likes of which he had never seen before. 'What a curious picture,' he muttered.

'This,' said Ovchinikov, 'is the icon of *The Shepherd*. But . . .' his voice trailed off.

'But what?' demanded Proskuryakov. 'Speak up, man!'

'*The Shepherd* was destroyed long ago, burned to ashes by a demented priest. At least, that's what I'd been told.'

'Well, whoever whispered that story in your ear must have told you all the other bits of rubbish in your head as well, because there it is!' Although he was unable to resist a sarcastic comment at the expense of Ovchinikov's faith, Proskuryakov found he could not take his eyes off the painting. The more he looked at the icon, the more bewildering he found it. He wondered what kind of man would ever wear a robe like that; and the sheep marooned on their little islands confused him.

Seeing the bewilderment on his captain's face, Ovchinikov tried to explain the meaning of the icon to him. 'This is life,' he explained, pointing at the islands in their sea of blue.

'And that is death?' asked Proskuryakov, nodding at the top of the picture.

'No,' replied Ovchinikov. 'That is the afterlife. There is a difference.'

'As far as I'm concerned,' Proskuryakov said, 'you're either alive or you're dead, and nothing I have ever seen has led me to think otherwise.'

'This icon is the proof that you are wrong,' Ovchinikov told him.

'I see no proof,' snapped Proskuryakov.

'You don't understand,' Ovchinikov told him. 'There are many who believed that the loss of this holy picture, while under the protection of the Tsar, is what caused him to be cast down from his throne.'

'I wonder what they'd say about it now,' muttered Proskuryakov as he tossed the painting back on to the corpse.

'Show some respect, you old fool!' barked Ovchinikov, carefully retrieving the icon.

It occurred to Proskuryakov to remind the sergeant that he was speaking to an officer, but it seemed, in the past few seconds, as if the balance of power had shifted and it was he, Proskuryakov, who must suffer the same abuse which he had, for so long, heaped without regret upon this dirty, boiler-suited man.

Gently, Ovchinikov began to wrap the icon back inside its cocoon of gauze and oilcloth. 'We must be careful with it,' he said, 'so that our heavenly Father will reward us in the world to come.'

'It's all very well getting prizes in the afterlife,' said Proskuryakov, 'but as long as I'm in this one, I'd settle for a T34.'

Carrying the picture, the two men left the church and made their way east towards the Russian lines.

They had gone some distance beyond the village when Proskuryakov suddenly stopped. 'My leather jacket! I left it behind.' He turned and looked back towards Ahlborn. 'My pass book and leave papers are in the pocket.'

'It's too late now,' said the sergeant. 'Besides, when we turn this icon over to Comrade Stalin, he'll get you a new jacket, and a handful of medals as well!'

'Medals, eh?' muttered Proskuryakov.

But Ovchinikov didn't reply. He was already running ahead, dodging like a rabbit from one evening shadow to another.

Maybe there's a God, after all, Proskuryakov thought to himself, as he ran to catch up with the sergeant.

9 February 1945

Sokolnika District, Moscow

In a dusty-windowed office on the fifth floor of 22 Pitnikov Street Inspector Pekkala was waiting for his supper.

It was Friday – the one day of the week when Pekkala would eat a proper meal, and the person who would cook that meal was Major Kirov. Prior to his instatement as a commissar in the Red Army, and his subsequent appointment as Pekkala's assistant, Kirov had trained as a chef at the prestigious Moscow Culinary Institute. If the Institute had not been closed down and its buildings taken over by the Factory Apprentice Technical Facility, Kirov's life might have turned out very differently. But he had never lost his love of cooking, and Pekkala's office had grown into a menagerie of earthenware pots and vases, in which grew rosemary, sage, mint, cherry tomatoes and the crooked branches of what might have been the only kumquat tree in Moscow.

The meals Kirov cooked for him were the only decent food Pekkala ate. The rest of the time, he boiled potatoes in a battered aluminium pan, fried sausages and ate baked beans out of the can. For variety, he wandered across the street to the Café Tilsit, its dingy space so clogged with smoke that the grey clouds seemed to take on human forms, making it appear as if the customers were dining among ghosts.

Pekkala hadn't always been this way. Before the Revolution, he had loved the restaurants in St Petersburg – the Strelnya, the English Tavern and late-night meals at the bar of the Hotel Davidov. But his years as an inmate of the Gulag of Borodok had cancelled the pleasure of good food. As Pekkala struggled to survive in the Siberian wilderness, it had simply become the fuel that kept him alive.

Major Kirov had set out to change that. With the help of his new wife Elizaveta, he embarked upon this sacred weekly mission.

Their office would fill with the smells of roast *tetereva* wood pigeon served with warm Smetana cream, Anton apples stewed in brandy, or *tsiplyata* chicken in ripe gooseberry sauce, which Kirov cooked on the temperamental stove.

Pekkala, installed in a comfortable chair, would tend the wheezy samovar while the meal was being prepared. When at last the food was ready, and Major Kirov laid these tiny miracles before him, his senses would be overwhelmed by cognac sauce, or the barely describable complexity of truffles, or the electric sourness of Kirov's beloved kumquats.

'Almost done!' announced Kirov. From the stove, he lifted a cast-iron pan, its handle wrapped with a red-and-white cloth to stop it from burning his palm. In the pan lay a handful of chanterelle mushrooms, their flesh the colour of ripe apricots, which he shook back and forth in a foam of sizzling butter. Then he tipped the mushrooms out on to a plate. Pinching up one of the hot chanterelles, he popped it quickly in his mouth.

'Don't eat them now!' scolded Elizaveta. She was slight, with freckled cheeks, a round chin and dark, inquisitive eyes. The two had met at the records office of NKVD headquarters, where Elizaveta worked as a clerk for Comrade Sergeant Gatkina, a woman of legendary ferocity. They had not been married long, and had reached that stage in their relationship where they had passed beyond the dreamlike early days into the hard work of actually creating a life together.

'Delicious,' muttered Kirov, puffing steam as he devoured the chanterelle.

Elizaveta threw a napkin at her husband, which landed neatly on his head.

Kirov peered out from beneath the folds of napkin, and Elizaveta was reminded of a picture of an Algerian Bedouin which she had seen in a book as a child. But instead of making her smile at this unintended costume, it troubled her how unfamiliar it made him appear. In the blink of an eye, her new husband had become a stranger.

This was not the first time since their marriage that Elizaveta had felt this way. She had been struck by the same unnerving sensation only the day before, when the two of them had travelled to a small farm north of the city to purchase the mushrooms that would soon be a part of their dinner. The farmer grew the chanterelles in earthenware pots high up on the rafters of his barn. The damp heat rising from his cows allowed the mushrooms to flourish, even in winter. Whenever a customer appeared, he would send his daughter tiptoeing across the narrow beams to gather the delicate chanterelles. As the newlyweds waited shivering in the farmyard for the young woman to emerge from her latest tightrope walk across the rafters, Elizaveta glanced at her husband and was shocked to see that he had been transformed by the dove-grey light of that February afternoon into a man she barely recognised.

'But you have only been married for a month!' exclaimed Sergeant Gatkina, under whom she served in the NKVD records office at the Lubyanka building, and to whom she had unwisely confided her fears. 'Do you expect to know everything about him?'

The answer, although Elizaveta did not give it, was yes. Kirov was not a man who handed out surprises, nor did he care to be surprised himself. But there was something behind the agile, bony frame, the perpetual youthfulness of those rosy cheeks and the calm honesty in his gaze which made her worry. Something cold and dangerous lurked just beneath the skin. Elizaveta did not know exactly what this thing was, and she suspected that even if she had known, there might be no name for it. But she did know where it came from. Elizaveta had sensed it at her first meeting with Pekkala, and she knew instinctively to keep her distance from it. But now it appeared to have spread, as she had always worried that it might, into the very soul of the man with whom she planned to spend her life.

Elizaveta had warned Kirov about Pekkala. Death follows in his path, she had said, but Kirov had taken no notice.

In spite of these misgivings, she could not help but marvel at the awkward but strangely functional way in which these two men muddled through their work. They were both brilliant, each in his own way, but the genius in them seemed to have come at the cost of things which normal people took for granted. Pekkala, for example, lived a life of such spartan self-neglect that it appeared as if someone had forgotten to inform him he was no longer a prisoner in the Gulag. And Kirov, at once so innocent and effortlessly lethal, on most days could not even pluck up enough courage to look Sergeant Gatkina in the eye.

Elizaveta was a newcomer in this curious little world. No matter how welcome Pekkala and her husband tried to make her feel, she knew that she would never fit in. And at no time did she feel it more strongly than at these Friday afternoon meals, with the old stove wheezing in the corner and sunset pouring through the dusty windows.

'Remember to save some for Zolkin,' said Pekkala, as he fetched a handful of battered knives and forks from a tin on the mantelpiece and began to set the table, which was made from two desks pulled together for the occasion.

Zolkin, their driver, was a loud and cheerful man with a thick neck and a wide, smooth forehead that looked strong enough to be used as a battering ram. His narrowed eyes gave him an air of hostility, which vanished as soon as he smiled. In that moment, all the harshness vanished from his face and he could be seen for what he really was: kind, ingenious and loyal.

A recent transplant from the wilds of western Ukraine, Zolkin had settled quickly into the frantic pace of Moscow life. At that moment, he was on his way back from a junkyard in Vorobjevo, where he had spent the day scrounging up parts for their Emka saloon. After his initial dismay at learning that he would not be the driver of an American lend-lease Packard or perhaps a Mercedes newly requisitioned from the reconquered territories, but rather a battered old Emka Mark I, Zolkin had thrown himself into rebuilding the carburettor, replacing the exhaust system and changing the oil, a task which Kirov had neglected to perform for over a year and which Pekkala had not realised was necessary at all.

'There'll be enough for him too,' Kirov told his wife. Breaking eggs two at a time and using only one hand, Kirov prepared the omelettes into which the chanterelle mushrooms would be mixed. The eggs came from a henhouse on the roof maintained by the enterprising caretaker of their building. With their windows open in the summer, they could hear the clucking of the chickens and glimpse the occasional feather carried by a breeze above the chimney pots of Moscow.

'We have just enough time to eat before we head over to the Kremlin,' said Pekkala.

'Do you know what this is about?' asked Elizaveta.

Kirov shook his head.

The call from Poskrebychev, Stalin's shrill-voiced secretary, had come in a short time before. Poskrebychev seemed to take a perverse enjoyment in the abruptness of his messages. 'You are to appear before Comrade Stalin at 6 p.m. today!' he announced, and had hung up again before Kirov, who answered the phone, had time to ask the reason for their visit.

Half an hour later, the meal finished and desks put back where they belonged, Pekkala, Kirov and Elizaveta descended to the street.

Zolkin, meanwhile, had returned from Vorobjevo, the Emka weighed down by spare parts wrenched from a graveyard of vehicles. Pekkala and Kirov waited patiently on the kerb while Zolkin wolfed his omelette off a tin plate, using a spoon which he carried, with the old habit of a front-line soldier, tucked inside his boot. 'Done!' he announced, his mouth still full but still managing to smile. After licking the spoon clean, he slid it back into his boot. He handed the empty plate to Elizaveta. Then, overcome by a burst of enthusiasm, he grasped her by the shoulders and kissed her on both cheeks before climbing in behind the wheel.

Entering the central Kremlin complex after a short drive across town, Zolkin brought the Emka to a stop outside a small, narrow alleyway, at the end of which was an unmarked door. In front of the door stood a guard in a long greatcoat, a Mosin-Nagant rifle at his side.

'Wait here,' Kirov ordered Zolkin. Then he reached into his pocket and tossed the driver a cardboard box of cigarettes. 'We might be a while,' he added.

Zolkin nodded thanks, already reaching for his lighter.

As Kirov and Pekkala approached the door, the guard cracked his iron-shod heels together. There was no need for them to show their papers. The guard knew both men by sight and stepped aside to let them pass.

Inside, Pekkala and Kirov ascended a narrow, poorly lit staircase to the third floor, emerging on to a marble-floored hallway, at the end of which they could see the white double doors which led to Stalin's office, flanked on either side by two more guards, each with a submachine gun slung across his chest.

Arriving at the outer doors, Kirov and Pekkala stopped and, with movements so practised as to be unconscious, reached into their chest pockets and withdrew their pass books, the red canvas covers worn down along the spines to the white threads beneath the dye. Although there had been no need to show their passes at the entrance to the Kremlin building, here that task was necessary. Nobody, no matter how well known, could enter Stalin's inner chambers without the necessary paperwork.

The doors were opened for them and they passed through

into the waiting room, which was Poskrebychev's private domain. Only with his permission could those who had come this far continue their journey into Stalin's office. This made him, although not a man of any high official rank, one of the most powerful people in Russia. He sat at a desk which was dominated by a large black intercom box that connected him personally with Stalin. Poskrebychev had long ago discovered that, by switching the intercom button off and then halfway back to on again, the green 'connected' light would not be triggered and he could still listen in on anything said in Stalin's chambers. As a result of his eavesdropping, Poskrebychev knew almost every secret worth keeping in the country. Sometimes, he would lie awake at night, in the tiny, dingy apartment where he had lived for more than a quarter of a century without a touch of fresh paint on the walls, terrorised by the vastness and the horror of his own forbidden knowledge.

'Poskrebychev,' said Pekkala.

The secretary nodded in greeting, but his face remained unchanged. Although Poskrebychev was a great admirer of the Emerald Eye, he worked hard to conceal his emotions. 'You are to go straight in,' he told them, and returned to rubber-stamping a pile of documents with a facsimile of Stalin's signature. No sooner had the men entered Stalin's office than Poskrebychev set aside the rubber stamp, fiddled with the intercom and leaned towards the black mesh of the speaker so as not to miss a word of what was said.

Stalin sat at his desk, arms stretched out and hands laid flat upon the red, leather-padded surface. Directly in front of him lay a rectangular object wrapped in a dirty piece of oilcloth. He smiled as the two men walked in, the gesture almost hidden behind his thick moustache, since his eyes reflected no emotion. 'Gentlemen!' he growled affectionately.

Kirov approached the desk and brought his heels together. 'You sent for us, Comrade Stalin.'

'I did indeed,' replied Stalin, folding his arms across his chest. The moisture imprint of his hand remained upon the desk, evaporating from the edges like a leaf curling in upon itself. 'What do you make of this?' He nodded towards the package.

Carefully, Kirov took up the bundle and began to unwrap it.

As Pekkala waited for the contents to be revealed, he noted a smell, faint but unmistakable, almost lost among the fragrances of Stalin's pipe tobacco. Initially, he could not place the odour but, whatever it was, it did not belong here, and its strangeness confused him at first. It was something sweet and musty which stuck in the back of Pekkala's throat as if his body were trying to prevent it being drawn into his lungs. And then he knew what it was. It was the odour of human decay, which he knew well from those corpses, sometimes it seemed almost too many to count, whose murders he had pieced together fragment by fragment until the killers had been caught. But those were not the ones which bobbed to the surface of Pekkala's thoughts. It was the killers who hadn't been found, whose victims called out to him in his sleep. And when he woke to the sound of their cries, his lungs would be filled with the stench of cadavers.

Letting the oilcloth fall to the floor with a rustle, Kirov held up the strange picture, with the sheep adrift on their tiny islands and the white-robed man peering out at them with pinprick eyes.

Pekkala shuddered when he saw what it was.

'What am I looking at?' asked Kirov.

'*The Shepherd*,' said Pekkala, and as he spoke the name, his thoughts tumbled into the past, like a man being swept away down the tunnels of an underground river, back to a winter's evening in 1917. He was crossing that same square where crowds had cheered the Tsar on the day that war was declared. But that had been more than two years before. Since then, millions of Russians had died on the battlefield and hundreds of thousands of wounded, who might have been saved with adequate medical treatment, had perished from neglect. With his coat turned up against a bitter wind blowing in off the Baltic Sea, Pekkala glanced up through frost-covered eyelashes towards the empty balcony where he and the Tsar had stood what seemed like a lifetime ago. Icicles hung from the metal railings and driven snow had pasted itself against the west-facing pillars. In one corner of the square, a few crippled soldiers, discharged from the army and with nowhere else to go, huddled by an oil-drum fire. They teetered on their crutches as they passed a bottle of vodka, marked with the red diamond of the State Monopoly of Alcohol, from one man to another. A lone carriage rattled past, the driver whipping savagely at the old black horse. As it passed, the horse's eyes locked with Pekkala's, and in them he saw nothing but fear, as if it knew exactly what was coming. One week later, soldiers stormed the Winter Palace. The Revolution had begun.

'You look as if you've seen a ghost,' laughed Stalin.

'Either a ghost or a copy,' replied Pekkala, nodding towards the icon, 'since the original icon no longer exists.'

'That remains to be seen,' replied Stalin.

'Would somebody please tell me what I'm looking at,' asked Kirov, 'and why I should care one way or another?'

'In your hands,' explained Pekkala, 'is one of the most sacred icons in all of Russia.'

'At least it was,' said Stalin, 'until a mad priest destroyed it, apparently.'

'I see you are familiar with the case, Comrade Stalin.'

'I am now, thanks to this.' Stalin lifted a grey file, crammed with tattered notes, and let it fall again upon his desk, raising a faint cloud of dust. 'It took Poskrebychev nearly a week to dig this out of Archive 17.'

Archive 17 was the graveyard of Soviet Internal Security documents as well as those which had been salvaged from the desks, sledge-hammered strongboxes and the dynamited safes of those who had been swept away by Revolution. Files on deceased criminals, mislabelled reports, unsolved cases and any other orphaned scrap of paper churned out by the Cheka, the GPU, the OGPU, the NKVD and the Bureau of Special Operations eventually found their way to a warehouse at the edge of Moscow where, before the Revolution shut them down, sculptors had once fashioned bronze statues of admirals, generals and other sanctioned heroes of the Empire. Pieces of those sculptures, some of them too big or too heavy to move, still lay scattered among the endless rows of filing cabinets which filled the warehouse.

'Then you will know, Comrade Stalin, that the case was closed by order of the Tsar himself.'

Stalin nodded. 'Which tells me, if I read between the lines, that you were not happy with its outcome.'

'Not entirely,' answered Pekkala.

'But what does any of this matter now?' demanded Kirov. 'Even if, by some miracle, it wasn't destroyed, who cares if it exists? Until today I'd never even heard of it!'

'That's because you were little more than a child when this icon was lost,' answered Pekkala.

'And its story had no place in the new country that emerged from our Revolution,' added Stalin.

Kirov looked from one man to the other. 'But surely you don't believe any of this antiquated fairy tale!'

'Maybe not,' answered Pekkala, 'but others did believe, and their trust in its miraculous powers made that power real.'

'And behold another miracle,' said Stalin. 'The icon has survived.' Now he rose to his feet. For a moment, he stood there in silence, fingertips resting on the surface of the desk. Then, slowly, he began to speak. 'Our forces are poised along the banks of the river Oder, ready to launch a final assault against Berlin. We have brought the war to the enemy's own soil, and he will fight for it more fiercely than he has ever done before. Who knows what terrible weapons he has saved for this final duel between our nations? The days ahead may test our resolve in ways we cannot even imagine. We face the greatest challenge of our age, perhaps the greatest that the world has ever seen. You know where I stand on religion,' he went on, 'but I am not so foolish as to disregard the faith I know exists beneath the surface of this land. Such faith can work against us if we fail to harness its potential. That is why I have opened the churches again. That is why services can once more be held without fear of reprisal. And now this icon has reappeared. If people wish to see it as a miracle, so be it, as long as we control the power of its message.'

'Who knows about the discovery?' asked Pekkala.

'Other than the two men who found it, and their commanding officer, all of whom have been sworn to secrecy, the only people who know of it are standing in this room.'

Just beyond the door, his ear pressed to the black mesh of the intercom, Poskrebychev bared his teeth in a smile.

'When do you plan on making it public, Comrade Stalin?' asked Kirov.

'When I am certain that the story of this little painting has not been tarnished by some unspeakable misfortune during its long absence. That story, whatever it might be, could quickly become more important than the discovery of the icon itself. All too quickly, a miracle can turn into an omen. That is why I want you to find out how this picture survived, whose hands it has passed through and how it ended up in a coffin in some country church in Germany!' For a moment, Stalin lapsed into silence. 'I must admit,' he said at last, 'I don't understand why they would have thought so much of such a poorly executed painting.' He brandished his hand towards the icon, which Kirov held against his chest in a gesture which could have been mistaken for reverence.

'Poorly executed?' echoed Pekkala.

'I mean, just look at it!' exclaimed Stalin. 'What are those sheep doing floating about on those islands? What is that man doing, standing around in a nightshirt? It makes no sense. Not like my Repin!' He pointed towards the far wall.

There, between the two main windows looking out over Red Square, hung a painting by Ilya Repin, Stalin's favourite artist. The painting was titled *What Freedom!* and showed a couple, dressed in clothing which clearly dated from before the Revolution. On a blustery winter's day, they stood holding hands at the edge of the Neva River. The man held his arms out in a gesture of defiance to the wildness of the storm, and the woman, her head turned from the wind, clutched his hand tightly and smiled nervously at his exuberance. The glassy green waves of the Neva, sea spray curling from their crests, seemed to chill the very air around the painting.

Stalin had a habit of removing paintings from various galleries in museums, and hanging them in that space where he could see them from his desk. The flare of light coming in from the windows on either side would often mask the painting from the view of people coming into the room, who naturally turned towards Stalin's desk as they entered. This rendered the painting invisible to anyone but Stalin himself.

A number of Repin's paintings had found their way to Stalin's private chambers. Until only a few weeks before, this particular work had been stored in a bunker, safe from bombing raids, in the city of Leningrad.

'I like it because it makes sense,' explained Stalin. 'There is that idiot, standing too close to the river, and his fool of a girlfriend . . .'

'It could be his wife,' suggested Kirov.

'No!' growled Stalin. 'No wife would do that. If she was married, she would have nothing to prove by risking her life for the amusement of her husband. She'd tell him to back away from the water and stop being such a bloody fool. No, Kirov.' Stalin raised a stubby finger. 'It's a girlfriend. I'm sure of it. She has to prove that she is willing to follow him anywhere.' Now Stalin aimed the finger at the man. 'You would never catch me taking such a risk.'

That much was true. Stalin rarely even walked the streets of the city where he lived. He seldom appeared in public and then usually only at military parades, at a considerable distance from the crowds who came to hear him speak. He drove everywhere in an armoured limousine, whose two-inch-thick reinforced windows were capable of withstanding a direct burst of machine-gun fire.

'Yes,' said Stalin, agreeing with himself. 'I like that artist Repin. You can always tell exactly what he wants to say. Not like that thing.' This time, he did not even point towards the icon but only jerked his chin in its direction. 'To me, that's just a waste of paint.' Then he sighed. 'Nevertheless, it's worth a king's ransom to others.'

*

'Where to?' asked Zolkin, when the two men had returned to the car, which by now was filled with a cloud of Papirossi smoke.

'The museum of the Kremlin,' answered Pekkala, rolling down the window in order to let the swirling grey cloud escape.

Minutes later, the Emka pulled up outside the museum, whose oak doors were as thick as a man's fist, and strapped with heavy iron bands.

Since the beginning of the war, the museum had been opened only a few days a month, and the timing of these openings was so irregular that most people had stopped visiting the building. In addition, many of the more valuable artefacts had been transported to Siberia back in 1941, when the advance of General Kleist's Army Group Centre had come close to invading the city. As yet, none of these works of art had been returned, and the space left behind for them on the walls gave a melancholy feel to the museum.

When the curator, Fabian Golyakovsky, answered the persistent knocking at the entrance, he opened a small door set into the larger double doors and peered out, squinting into the brassy evening sunlight, like the gatekeeper of a medieval fortress.

Golyakovsky was a tall, stooped man with a tangle of curly reddish hair. As he did most days, Golyakovsky wore a dark blue suit and a cream-coloured shirt with a rumpled collar and no tie. In earlier times, the suit would have been cleaned and pressed, but such luxuries were hard to come by now and instead of looking dapper, as he used to, he gave the appearance of a man who had been sleeping in his clothes.

The museum had closed half an hour before, but Golyakovsky and the few curators he had been allowed to keep on staff had not yet departed for home. Although Golyakovsky was annoyed by this rude pounding on his door, he was also curious. During the hours when the museum was open, he practically had to drag people in off the street to see what remained of his exhibits. Now here was someone, ill-mannered though they might be, who actually wanted to visit.

He opened the door, caught sight of Pekkala, and let out a squawk of alarm. It was all he could do not to slam the door in the Inspector's face and bolt himself inside. He thought of the staff of the Hermitage Museum in Leningrad who had walled themselves up in the museum, rather than risk seeing it looted for firewood by the cold and starving population of the city. Even though, according to rumours, the Hermitage staff had subsisted for more than a year on a diet of wallpaper paste, at this precise moment, Golyakovsky wished he had followed their example and bricked himself inside the museum.

The last time the Emerald Eye had paid a visit, he had left with one of the museum's most valuable remaining artefacts: a priceless fourteenth-century portrait from the Balkans, originally located in the Cathedral of the Assumption and known as *The Saviour of the Fiery Eye*.

When Golyakovsky had realised that these two men planned to take the painting with them, he pleaded with Pekkala, cradling the portrait in his arms, as if the Inspector had somehow awoken the man in the painting and now he meant to lull the Saviour back into his sleep of centuries.

It did no good at all, and when Golyakovsky watched Pekkala walk out with the priceless work of art wrapped in brown paper and tied with a piece of string as if he had bought it from the museum gift shop, Golyakovsky was sure he would never see the portrait again.

Even though the icon was returned soon afterwards, Golyakovsky's fragile nerves had never quite recovered from the shock.

'I trust,' said Golyakovsky, his voice thick with indignation as he stood aside to let them pass, 'that you have not come to make another withdrawal from our collection!' But as he spoke, Golyakovsky noticed that, this time, Pekkala had brought something with him. His expression changed immediately. 'Ah, Inspector!' he crooned. 'What treasure have you unearthed for me?' With those words, he reached out to take the package.

'Actually,' said Pekkala, 'I'm here to see Semykin.'

Golyakovsky's long-fingered hands curled in upon themselves, like snails withdrawing into their shells. 'But I am the senior curator here!' he protested. 'If anything is to be examined, I should be the one to do it.'

'Inspector!' a loud voice echoed down the cold and musty-smelling hallway, and all three men turned to see a figure advancing towards them.

The last time Pekkala had seen Semykin, it was in a small, windowless cell at Lubyanka, where Semykin had been sentenced to five years of solitary confinement. The charges against Semykin stemmed from his involvement with a certain People's Commissar of the State Railway named Viktor Bakhturin, a proud, vindictive, petty man, whose name had come up in connection with several murders. Each case presented a clear triangulation between the victim, the killer and Bakhturin, but there was never enough proof to convict him of actual involvement in the crime. He had also been tied to political denunciations of government officials, which had ended either with the execution of these officials, or else their deportation to Siberia.

The previous People's Commissar of the State Railways had been turned over to NKVD by his own wife for travelling in a railway carriage set aside for transportation of officials on government business in order to travel back and forth from Moscow to his holiday dacha on the Black Sea. Although the practice was widespread and usually ignored by NKVD, the fact that the commissar's own wife had denounced him caused an embarrassment which could not be overlooked. The commissar received a twelve-year sentence in a Gulag on the border of Mongolia.

The reason the commissar's wife had turned in her own husband was that she suspected him of having an affair. The source of this rumour, which turned out to be false, was believed to be Viktor Bakhturin. At the time, Bakhturin had been a junior commissar of State Railways, but he quickly rose to take the place of the man now in Siberia.

Semykin's own troubles with Bakhturin began with a painting by the Polish artist Stanislaw Wyspianski, which the People's Commissar had personally removed from the house of a railway official in Poland after the invasion of 1939.

After showing a photograph of the painting to Semykin, Bakhturin had asked if he would sell it for him. Initially, Semykin had agreed to broker the sale, but on receiving the actual painting, he realised that it was, in fact, a copy. When Semykin informed Bakhturin of this, the commissar ordered him to keep his mouth shut and to sell the painting as an original. Semykin refused, and Bakhturin had him arrested on the charge of attempting to sell forged works of art. Semykin's explanation that he was, in fact, trying *not* to sell a fake was lost upon the court and he was sentenced to five years in prison.

For a man used to being surrounded by works of art, the bare walls of Semykin's prison cell soon became an unrelenting torture. Unable to endure the terrible blankness any longer, Semykin had used blood from his own fingertips to reconstruct, from memory, Seurat's pointillist masterpiece known as *Une Baignade*.

In exchange for Semykin's help with deciphering a coded message in a painting found in the briefcase of an SS officer whose scout plane was forced down behind the Russian lines, Pekkala handed him the portrait he had just taken from the wall of the museum. Although it was in his possession for only a few minutes, the chance to reacquaint himself with the kind of beauty to which he had dedicated his life was enough to keep him sane until Pekkala could secure his release and, with some gentle persuasion, coax Stalin into granting Semykin a job on the permanent staff of the museum.

Semykin's face was framed by dark eyebrows, fleshy lips and a studiously unkempt beard. During his time at Lubyanka, the sudden loss of weight had caused his skin to hang loosely on his frame and his face had the look of a bloodhound stripped of its fur. But now he had regained his former portliness, and the colour had returned to his cheeks. He wore a thick, hand-knitted sweater with wooden toggle buttons down the front which was almost old enough to be a part of the museum's collection. Few civilians could afford new clothes these days. As the war dragged on, and clothing wore out, people reached deeper into their wardrobes for things to wear. The result was that the fashions in Moscow seemed to be travelling backwards in time.

'The man who saved my life!' announced Semykin, and as he spoke he wrapped his arms around Pekkala, who patiently endured the rough embrace.

Kirov could not help noticing the white scar tissue on Semykin's fingertips, which had puckered the skin like that of someone who had lingered too long in a bath.

'We have brought you a present,' said Pekkala, handing the cloth-wrapped bundle to Semykin.

'Let's go to the glass room and see what we've got,' replied Semykin.

'The glass room?' asked Kirov.

'You will see,' Semykin answered cryptically.

A few minutes later, the strange procession arrived at the centre of a gallery, and entered a room whose walls were made of glass. In the middle of this space stood an oval conference table and a dozen stiff-backed chairs.

'I feel like a goldfish in a bowl,' said Kirov, looking around him uncomfortably.

'This is where we bring the visiting dignitaries,' explained Golyakovsky. 'The people who like to be seen.'

'But not recently, I see,' remarked Pekkala, as he drew his finger through the dust that had collected on the table.

Semykin sighed and nodded. 'Only the art of war can draw a crowd these days.' With that pronouncement, he unwrapped the parcel. As soon as his gaze fell upon *The Shepherd*, he placed the icon down at once upon the table, as if it had suddenly grown hot to the touch. 'Is this some kind of joke?' he spluttered.

'It is no joke,' answered Kirov.

Semykin raised his head and stared at them in disbelief. 'But I thought . . .'

'So did I,' said Pekkala, and he went on to explain the circumstances under which the icon had been found.

As he listened, Golyakovsky removed a crumpled handkerchief from his pocket and dabbed it against his forehead. 'Impossible,' he whispered. 'It must be some kind of illusion.'

'An illusion or a copy,' remarked Pekkala. 'That's why I have brought it here, for Semykin to decide if it's one or the other.'

For a long time, Semykin studied the image, lost in thought. Then suddenly he picked up the icon, turned it over and began to examine the back.

'Why are you doing that?' asked Kirov.

'If a forger has been at work here,' answered Semykin, 'he is likely to have confined his efforts to the painting itself. It is here, amongst the scaffolding of art, that we can usually tell if we are dealing with a fake. Occasionally, a forger will get hold of an old canvas or wooden panel and simply paint over it. That way, the actual structure on which the image is created adds to the illusion of antiquity. But in this case,' he raised himself upright and breathed in deeply, 'I see no sign of foul play.' Turning the painting right side up again, Semykin bent down and studied the surface, his nose almost touching the image. For a long time, he gazed at the panel on which *The Shepherd* had been painted.

Kirov peered over his shoulder. 'What exactly are you looking for?'

'Traces of titanium oxide. Forgers sometimes use it, although this compound would not have been available at the time the original was painted. Occasionally, the canvas has been artificially aged, by rubbing it with stale bread.'

'Stale bread?' echoed Kirov.

Semykin nodded. 'It gives the canvas the appearance of having been handled many times, without actually damaging the paint. Forgers can be extremely inventive. I once knew a forger who used ground-up tobacco to simulate moisture damage on the backs of canvases.'

'So is it real?' asked Pekkala.

'Oh, it is real enough,' Semykin assured him. 'The question is whether it's the true *Shepherd*.'

'Does it really matter?' asked Kirov. 'Isn't one picture of the Shepherd as sacred as another?'

Semykin smiled gently. 'Not at all, Major. You see, this icon is not merely a representation of the divine. The icon *itself* is divine. For those who believe in it, this painting is a doorway to a spiritual realm. Copy the image, and all you'd have is a picture of that door. Only the real portal will grant you access to that other world and the power it commands.'

'Then which is it?' demanded Pekkala.

For a moment, Semykin did not reply. Keeping his focus on the back of the picture, he tilted it back and forth, squinting as he hunted for a clue. Then he brought it over to the edge of the room, where the light was marginally brighter. 'Here!' he said at last. 'Yes!' He turned to face the other men, who watched him expectantly. 'I don't know how or why it has survived,' he told them, 'but I am convinced that this icon is the true *Shepherd*.'

'What makes you so certain?' asked Kirov.

Slowly, Semykin traced one finger along a faint black mark at the very edge of the panel. 'Here is your proof.'

'That little smudge?' asked Golyakovsky.

Kirov bent closer to see. 'What is it?'

'This is where the icon really was burned,' replied Semykin, 'although only slightly, when the private chapel of the Romanovs was damaged by fire back in the winter of 1908.'

'I remember that!' exclaimed Pekkala. 'A votive candle was left burning after a service. It fell from its pedestal and the curtain behind the altar caught fire. But I heard nothing about this icon being damaged.'

'That's because it was kept secret.'

'Then how do you know about it?' asked Kirov.

'I was summoned by the Tsar to examine *The Shepherd*, which had been rescued from the blaze, but not without suffering some damage to the outer frame.'

'But why did he call upon you?' This time it was Golyakovsky who asked the question. 'Why not consult with one of the experts at the Hermitage?'

'The Tsar was well aware to what extent the art world thrives on gossip. I had brokered the sale of several paintings for the Romanovs, for which absolute discretion was required. In short, Comrade Golyakovsky, he called on me because he knew I could keep my mouth shut. Otherwise, the Tsar knew, rumours might begin to spread that he was not taking proper care of the icon. Or worse, that God has also come to that conclusion.'

'What did you find when you examined *The Shepherd*?' asked Kirov.

'Although there were no visible burn marks on the painting itself, the Tsar was concerned that the icon might have been damaged in more subtle ways, such as the paint becoming brittle in the heat, in which case it would rapidly begin to flake off. In a matter of years, the entire image could have been obliterated.'

'What did you tell him?'

'That the frame was ruined and that it should be replaced as soon as possible, but that the icon itself had not been compromised. The only trace that it had been touched by fire was this mark, right at the edge. They were lucky not to lose the whole thing. The paints used to create this icon are highly volatile. One spark could have reduced it to a pile of ashes. In due course a new frame was constructed using jewels from the original and the burn mark was cleverly hidden beneath the new frame.'

'And no one else knew about this?'

'No one,' confirmed Semykin, 'aside from the Tsar and his immediate family.'

'Which means you are the only one left alive who could identify that burn mark,' said Kirov.

Semykin nodded. 'That's why I am so certain.'

'Even if it is real,' said Kirov, 'I don't see what makes this icon any more important than the thousands of others in this country.'

'Even from an artistic standpoint, and leaving aside its historical significance,' explained Semykin, '*The Shepherd* is a most unusual painting. It is what we refer to as a reneg-ade icon. Its subject matter violates the edicts of the 82nd Canon, which dates back to AD 692, when the Quinisext Council in Constantinople forbade any representation of the Lamb of God.'

'And does that law still stand?' asked Kirov.

'Indeed it does,' answered Semykin, 'and, as you can see, whoever created this icon did not merely disobey the law, but flaunted it. This is an icon of rebellion. Who worshipped this was bound upon a different journey from those who stayed within the confines of the Orthodox Church.'

The next question came from Pekkala. 'Then why did the Tsars value it so greatly?' he asked.

'Because whether or not it conformed to the edicts of the Church, the Tsars still believed in its power,' said Semykin, 'and to the rulers of this country, then and now, power is the most sacred thing of all.'

*

Back at the office, Kirov and Pekkala slumped down into a pair of haggard-looking chairs which had once graced the lounge of the old Hotel Metropol. Driving through town one winter's day, Pekkala had spotted the chairs dumped on the pavement, ready to be collected by the municipal garbage collectors. He had immediately ordered Kirov, who used to double as chauffeur before the arrival of Sergeant Zolkin, to stop the car. In spite of Kirov's objections, Pekkala had loaded the chairs into the boot of the Emka, brought them back and, with Kirov's grudging assistance, carried them up the five flights of stairs to the office.

Kirov, who had been carrying the icon all this time, placed it on the floor in the narrow space between the wall and the stove.

'Don't leave it there!' warned Pekkala. 'You heard what Semykin said about the icon being flammable. One spark from the stove and the whole thing could catch fire.'

With a grunt, Kirov reached down, unwilling to leave the comfort of his chair. Twisting around, he slid the icon up on to the windowsill. 'Will that do?' he asked.

'For now,' answered Pekkala.

'If Semykin is right,' said Kirov, 'there is only one possibility.'

Pekkala had been thinking the same thing. 'That priest did not destroy the icon, after all.'

'But why would he confess to having done such a thing,' asked Kirov, 'when it got him thrown in prison, probably for the rest of his life?'

'Perhaps he will tell us himself,' said Pekkala. 'Tomorrow, get in touch with the authorities at Karaganda Prison and find out if he's still alive.'

10 February 1945

Karaganda

Prison Warder Feodor Turkov was asleep with his feet up on his desk. His hands, which rested on his lap, clutched an alarm clock with two large bells like mouse ears perched above its face. He wore a heavy grey coat lined with goat fur which smelled rancid when it was wet. In spite of this, Turkov almost never took it off, except in the middle of the summer. It always seemed cold in his dark, little office, as if the ghost of winter lingered in the shadows.

When the alarm clock sounded, as it would in a matter of minutes, Turkov would be forced to leave the relative luxury of his office and walk around his sector of the prison, a journey he was obliged to make three times a day, no matter what the weather.

He had worked at Karaganda for more than twenty-five years. In his early days, he had earned a reputation as one of the strictest, most short-tempered and feared warders at the prison. He despised all the inmates on principle, even when it was clear to him, from looking at their files, that they had been unjustly convicted. He did not care what had brought them to Karaganda, only that they were there now and would remain, in most cases, for a very long time. It was not their pasts that Turkov loathed, but the people they became while in captivity.

In recent years, however, the fierceness of his youth had mellowed greatly. He no longer had the stamina to maintain such a fortress of hate. It simply became too exhausting to be so angry all the time.

It was not long before Turkov's superiors noticed his flagging sense of rage. Had he been a younger man, the authorities at Karaganda might have dismissed him on the spot, but they took into account his decades of service and, instead, made him warder of the geriatric wing, where prisoners lucky enough to have survived into old age were left in peace to grow their own food, to raise their own chickens and pigs, and to be left alone except for the brief, daily visits of Warder Turkov.

The younger Turkov would have seen this as an insult even worse than dismissal, and many of his colleagues offered consolation at such an undignified posting, but Turkov was secretly relieved.

Since taking up the post, Turkov had discovered a peace of mind he'd never known before, nor ever thought was possible. He worked hard to reinvent himself and if the ancient prisoners of the geriatric wing still remembered bitterly the man he used to be, still they could not deny that he was better than before.

Turkov's duties were not strenuous, leaving him plenty of time to rest in his office, or to read or to play cards in the warders' canteen. Most days, he did not mind his strolls across the prison grounds, but the season of mud, known as the *rasputitsa*, had come early this year, making every footstep through the gluey mess a time-consuming and unpleasant task.

A metallic clatter startled Turkov awake. He sat up sharply, placed the alarm clock on his desk and tapped his fingers on the button which silenced the bell.

But the bell did not stop ringing and, still half asleep, Turkov stared in confusion at the clock. It was only after several seconds that he realised the sound was not coming from the clock but from the phone on the wall.

No one had rung that number in months. He had almost forgotten that the phone was there at all.

Turkov launched himself out of his chair and snatched up the receiver. 'Hello?' he shouted. 'Hello?'

A voice, calling faintly through the breaking waves of static, replied, 'This is Major Kirov of Special Operations in Moscow.'

Turkov let out a snort. 'Well, you must have the wrong number, Major Kirov! You've called the geriatric compound of the Karaganda Prison.'

'That is correct, Comrade Turkov.'

'Oh,' said Turkov, his voice filled with foreboding. What does Special Operations want with me, he wondered. 'And what is it you want, Comrade Major?' He listened while Kirov explained. 'Detlev? Father Detlev? He's the one you want?' Turkov heaved a sigh of relief. 'Yes, he's very much alive. In fact, I am looking at him now.' Through the dirty window, Turkov could see the small, crooked-backed figure of a man, his head wrapped in a piece of rabbit fur, fetching in a piece of wood for his fire. 'Well, of course, Comrade Major. We would welcome a visit from the great Inspector Pekkala. And you, too, of course. Goodbye. Yes. Goodbye.' Turkov hung up the phone, walked over to the window and looked out at Father Detlev who, by now, had retreated inside his one-room shack, pushing out the small pot-bellied pig who was his only real companion and who had taken advantage of the open door to make its way inside. Then Father Detlev shut the door behind him.

Turkov felt a moment of pity for the old priest. Visits from the outside world, even those that were well-intentioned, seldom did the inmates any good. In a world where a man's sanity was held together only by the rhythm of his daily routine, good news could do as much harm as bad.

During his time as minder of these ancient convicts, Turkov had become protective of their privacy. He had come to admire the dignity of their silence, since few of them ever spoke, at least to him. And when they died, it was Turkov who laid them out on their lumpy, pine-cone-stuffed mattresses, straightened their clothes and folded their hands on their chests before calling for the bodies to be taken away to an unmarked grave in the Karaganda bone pits.

*

Having set out at dawn on 11 February, Pekkala, Kirov and Zolkin drove until dark before stopping at an inn just outside the town of Krasnoye Baki. There was only one room available, with two small beds taking up much of the space. They had not been in residence long before discovering that the place was infested with fleas.

Pekkala, who had chosen to sleep on the floor, with no sheets or pillow except his coat rolled up under his head, remained untouched by the blood-sucking insects.

Zolkin, too, was also left alone, thanks to a strange ritual he performed just before turning in for the night.

He had removed a handful of stewed tea leaves from the

samovar laid out for them after their meal. Then, to the surprise of his travelling companions, he had packed the tea leaves in his mouth and chewed them to a pulp. After this, he took the Emka's repair kit from the boot of the car and removed the thermometer used for gauging radiator fluid temperature. He broke the end off the thermometer, spilling the teaspoon of mercury it contained into an old tin cup. As Kirov and Pekkala looked on in suspicion and amazement, he stirred the mercury into the tea leaves until the silver liquid had broken up into hundreds of tiny spheres, each one not much bigger than a grain of sand. In the last step of this strange procedure, Zolkin rolled the mixture into a large handkerchief, which he then tied around his neck. Turning to his companions, he smiled and held open his hands, like a man who had just performed a successful magic trick.

'And this will accomplish what exactly?' Kirov demanded scornfully.

'It wards off the fleas,' explained Zolkin. 'I could easily make one for you. Just find me another drop of mercury . . .'

'No, thank you,' Kirov answered flatly. 'There is enough bizarre behaviour around here with Pekkala sleeping on the floor. I've no intention of encouraging any more.'

'And you, Inspector?' asked Zolkin.

But Pekkala, lying stretched out on the floorboards, his boots still on and his hands folded serenely across his stomach, had already fallen asleep.

The next morning, Kirov was covered with red welts.

Zolkin, on the other hand, had none. Instead, lying all around him on the bed were dead fleas which, drawn by the smell of the tea, had bitten into the handkerchief, ingested the mercury, and perished.

Pekkala, having chosen the floor, was similarly left alone, either because of having chosen to sleep on the floor or, as Kirov suggested, because of some Finnish spell he had cast upon the Russian fleas.

'Next time, perhaps, Major,' said Zolkin cheerfully, as he untied the handkerchief from his neck and tucked it away in his pocket.

'Stay away from me, you hobgoblin!' growled Kirov, scratching at the bites, which dotted his chest and arms like the constellations of an unmapped universe.

From then on, even though the temperature dropped well below freezing at night, they slept in open country, avoiding the taverns altogether.

By sunset, they had reached the outskirts of Nagorskoye. With Kirov still itching from his flea bites, they pulled off the road and made camp not far from the Kobra River. They built a fire out of driftwood salvaged from the river bank and, after a meal of black bread, sausage and pickles, washed down with a bottle of kvass, they spread their blankets on the ground and were soon asleep.

Four days after leaving Moscow, the mud-splashed Emka pulled up outside the main gates of Karaganda Prison. The front grille, which had once been silver, now wore a pale shellac of Moscow highway mud, made up of thousands of spatters, fused and overlapping until they had formed into a virtual coral reef of grime. The lights had been similarly plastered. Several times a day, Zolkin was forced to scrape the glass lenses clean with a knife.

From a guard shack whose entrance was curtained with a piece of burlap sacking, a guard strolled out to meet them. He wore the dark blue uniform of a prison guard, with a white patent leather belt and silver buttons. His face, deeply marked by old acne scars, made him look as if he had been hewn out of pumice stone.

Kirov rolled down his dirt-splashed window and explained the reason for their visit.

'If you're looking for Father Detlev,' said the guard, 'you'll need to go around the back. That's where we keep the fossils.'

The section of the prison in which Father Detlev lived, along with several others of his vintage, was separated from the main compound by a narrow path that ran through a field where, in summer time, convicts grew beets and cabbages for the Karaganda kitchen. Barbed wire had been set up to keep the chickens and the pigs from rooting through the crops, but there was nothing to contain the prisoners.

Zolkin parked the Emka outside Warder Turkov's hut.

The warder's face appeared in the window and, a moment later, he emerged, huddled in his heavy coat. 'You must be the Inspector,' said Turkov.

Pekkala nodded in greeting.

On the other side, Kirov stumbled out, raised his hands above his head, stretched and groaned from the pain in his cramped legs.

'I will bring you straight to Father Detlev.' Turkov motioned for the two men to follow him. 'Your driver can wait in my house. There's fresh tea in the samovar.'

He led Pekkala and Kirov towards the jumble of huts, scattered among the leafless, crooked branches of the convicts' apple trees. 'Please forgive the lack of formality at this end of the compound,' he added.

'A prison without fences,' remarked Kirov.

'These men are not going to escape,' explained Turkov. 'There is nowhere for them to go. The world they left behind when they arrived at Karaganda no longer exists. We try to make life as easy as possible for them. I have brought Father Detlev seeds to make his garden, and watercolours for the paintings that he does from time to time.'

At that moment, Pekkala sensed he was being watched. A face, accordioned with wrinkles, peered from the doorway of a hut. As soon as the man realised that he'd been seen, he stepped back into the darkness and the door slid silently shut.

'Why has Father Detlev been here so long?' asked Kirov. 'I thought he would have been released years ago, since it was on the Tsar's orders that he came here in the first place. Back then, to be an enemy of the Romanovs was to be a friend of the Revolution.'

'You are forgetting, perhaps, that Detlev is also a man of the Church, an organisation not favoured by the Communist Party.'

'But the churches have been opened again, on the orders of Comrade Stalin!'

'True,' agreed Turkov, 'and if his only crime had been to worship God, he might have been a free man by now. But he is not only a priest. He is also a man who destroyed one of the Church's most sacred artefacts. So you see, Comrade Major, he made himself the enemy of both sides in this war of faith.' Turkov came to a stop outside a hut, whose door was made from pieces of old packing crates which had once held tins of cooking oil. The collage of wording, stencilled on the splintery wood, resembled a large and partially finished crossword puzzle. He rapped on the door and stood back. 'Father Detlev,' he called. 'Your visitor is here!'

There was a shuffling inside.

A moment later, the door swung open to reveal a small, bewildered-looking man, with weather-beaten cheeks and a haze of short grey hair protruding like splinters from his scalp. In spite of his age, he appeared strong and healthy. To greet the men, he raised one callused hand, its knuckles crooked with arthritis. In spite of the years since they had last seen each other, Detlev recognised Pekkala immediately. 'Inspector,' he said. 'You said we'd meet again and here we are!' Glancing at the bundle tucked under Pekkala's arm, the old priest knew at once what it contained. 'It seems I am to have more than one reunion today,' he remarked. 'Come inside, gentlemen. You've come a long way to hear my story, and I've waited a long time to tell it.'

While Turkov returned to his duties, Pekkala and Kirov entered the small hut, ducking as they passed through the doorway.

Inside the hut, it was dark and dry and warm. Dried herbs hung suspended from the rafters. As Kirov's head brushed past a bundle of shrivelled leaves, some of them crumbled on to his shoulder. As he swept them away with his fingertips, he breathed in the scent of sage grass.

Pekkala studied the paintings Detlev had made, using sheets of paper mounted on to wood cut from the spindly sides of packing crates. In one, Pekkala recognised the altar at the Church of the Resurrection. Several of the other paintings were of swans floating on what Pekkala identified as the Great Pond, near the Catherine Palace.

He remembered those swans. They came each spring and lingered until late in the summer. He had always been struck by their dignity, and their solemn detachment from the affairs of men, who carried on their lives of self-obsession all around them.

Each morning, for as long as the swans remained at Tsarskoye Selo, the Tsar would rise early for his usual breakfast of green tea and toast before making his way to the Great Pond. There, he would be met by the gardener, Liamin, who was in charge of the watercourses on the estate. Liamin would hand him a clean pair of gloves, along with a basket filled with bread crusts for the swans, which the Tsar had trained to eat out of his hands.

Pekkala was impressed at the amount of detail Detlev had recalled from his days on the Tsarskoye Selo Estate, especially since he had nothing but memory to go by, and given the primitive tools with which he had to work.

Father Detlev showed them to a bare table, and gestured at the only two chairs in the room. Detlev himself sat down on a small barrel, of the type used for storing grain.

Pekkala placed the bundle on the table and pushed it towards the old man.

'There's no need for me to see it again,' said Detlev. 'I glimpse the icon every time I close my eyes.'

'I have a few questions,' said Pekkala.

'You came here to find out the truth,' Detlev answered patiently, 'and I see no reason to keep that from you any longer.'

'Was this all your idea from the start?' asked Pekkala.

'My idea?' Detlev breathed out sharply through his nose. 'I would never have dared even to think it!'

'Then who came to you with the plan?'

'Rasputin!' exclaimed the priest.

'And when was this?'

'One Sunday afternoon, back in June of 1915. Just as I was leaving the church, a car pulled up at the kerb. Rasputin was behind the wheel. He called my name and beckoned to me.'

'Had you ever met him before?' asked Kirov.

Detlev shook his head. 'I'd seen him in the church from time to time, but we had never spoken until then. He said he had something important to discuss with me and asked if I would drive with him to meet a friend of his. At first, I told him no, but he insisted. "When you meet this person," he said, "you will know that it was wise to have done as I asked." I had only just begun my service at the church and I knew that Rasputin was someone of great influence. He may have been a stranger to me, but his reputation was not. In truth, I was afraid to refuse his request. So I got into that fancy car and went with him.'

'Where did he take you?' asked Kirov.

'We drove across the Alexander Park and stopped outside a little house on the far side of the estate. Before we even reached the door, it opened and a woman welcomed us in. I recognised her at once. It was Anna Vyroubova. I often saw her praying at the chapel. She led me into the front room and there, sitting on a chair with a blanket thrown over her knees, was the Tsarina Alexandra. At first, I was so shocked I could not even breathe. I had seen her at the church, of course, but we had never actually met. I was so flustered that I couldn't recall what I was supposed to do in her presence, so I dropped to my knees!'

*

'You know who I am,' said the Tsarina.

'Yes, Majesty,' whispered Detlev.

'And I know I can count on your loyalty to the Tsar.'

'Majesty, of course!' Only now did Detlev raise his head and look the Tsarina in the eye. He had no idea if this was permitted, but his curiosity overwhelmed him.

What he saw was a woman in a lavender dress with a necklace of pearls which formed three strands about her throat. The thing that struck him most about her were the eyes. They looked sad and strangely empty. Deep lines, carved by worry, had trenched themselves into the corners of her mouth and round her eyes.

As the Tsarina returned Detlev's gaze, her fingers tightened on the cane until the bone handle seemed to merge with her flesh. Then she turned and nodded to Vyroubova.

Vyroubova, who had been standing off to one side, reached behind a curtain and withdrew a small painting in a jewelled frame.

'The Shepherd!' gasped Detlev. 'What is it doing here?'

Before the Tsarina could answer, there was a loud popping sound from the kitchen.

'What was that?' she demanded angrily.

At that moment, Rasputin appeared from the kitchen, carrying a bottle of champagne and several glasses wedged between his fingers.

'That's a Veuve Cliquot 1910!' exclaimed Vyroubova. 'I was saving that for a special occasion.'

'Every day is special when you're me,' answered Rasputin. Then he glanced down at Detlev, who was still on his knees. 'Is that where she put you?' he asked the priest. 'Or is that where you put yourself?'

'Grigori!' scolded Vyroubova. 'Does your insolence have no boundaries at all?'

Rasputin fixed Vyroubova with a stare. 'I take it you won't be joining us for the champagne.'

'She's right, Grigori,' said the Empress, in a voice whose gentleness caught Detlev by surprise. 'Now is not the time. Take it away.'

Rasputin shrugged and walked back into the kitchen. A second later, they could hear the rustle of effervescence as he poured himself a glass.

Now the Tsarina turned her attention back to the man who knelt before her. 'You have been chosen to carry out a very important task, Father Detlev.'

'I am yours to command,' Detlev answered solemnly.

'The country is in danger, and God has chosen us to bring salvation.'

'But how?'

'In a few days,' explained the Tsarina, 'The Shepherd will be moved to the house of my dear friend Grigori.'

'And you wish for me to guard it?' asked Detlev, still confused.

'No,' Rasputin called from the kitchen, 'she wants you to steal it from me!'

'Why would I steal it?' stammered Detlev, struggling to comprehend.

'The only way to keep The Shepherd safe,' said the Tsarina, 'is for the world to believe it has been destroyed.'

'You want me to destroy it?'

'No.' Slowly the Tsarina shook her head. 'But I want you to say that you did.'

'Say to whom?'

Once more, it was Rasputin who answered. 'To the police,' he said, 'when they come to arrest you for the crime.'

'I don't understand!' protested Detlev. 'You would have me confess to a crime which I did not commit? Why not just hire a thief? Why give such a task to a priest?'

'Because a thief would not destroy what he had stolen,' replied the Tsarina. 'He would sell it to another thief. But a priest would not do this for money. He would steal the icon and destroy it, because that was what God had told him to do.'

'But God has not told me!'

'No,' said the Tsarina. 'I have. Now, Father Detlev, you may get up off your knees.'

Detlev climbed unsteadily to his feet. 'They'll throw me in jail for this,' he said.

'They certainly will,' she replied, 'but I'll see to it that you are freed again, just as quickly as I possibly can.'

'But what will become of the icon if all the world thinks it is gone?'

'It will be safe,' the Tsarina told him. 'More than that, you do not need to know.'

'Nobody looks for something that isn't there,' added Vyroubova, replacing the icon behind the curtain.

'And this will somehow save the country?' Detlev asked incredulously.

'God willing,' said the Tsarina.

Rasputin emerged from the kitchen, carrying a glass of champagne in each hand. One of these he handed to the priest. 'Drink up!' he commanded.

Detlev stared at the glass in his hand, as if for a moment he had forgotten how it came to be there.

'Do as he says,' commanded the Tsarina. *'It might be your last for a while.'*

Slowly, Detlev raised the glass to his mouth, wincing as the sharp, metallic-tasting bubbles crackled in his mouth.

*

'And that was the first time, and the last,' said Detlev, 'that I have ever tasted champagne.'

'Why do you think Rasputin chose you for this task?' asked Pekkala. He wondered if Grigori had simply spotted the priest as he drove past the church and made his decision on the spot to recruit Detlev into the scheme. If it had been anyone other than Rasputin, Pekkala would never have imagined such an impulsive decision, but his old friend had often acted entirely on instinct, and in doing so had walked a tightrope line between the genius that first drew the attention of the Tsarina and the recklessness that ultimately got him killed.

In answer to Pekkala's question, Detlev only shrugged. 'Perhaps,' said the priest, 'because he knew that I wouldn't dare refuse.'

'And how did Rasputin arrange for you to steal the icon?' asked Kirov.

'It was very simple,' replied Detlev. 'I was given a time to arrive at the house, when Rasputin himself would not be there. The door was unlocked, I walked in, and found the icon lying in an open suitcase on the table in the front room. By then, the frame had already been removed. I closed the suitcase and took it with me down the stairs.'

'What happened then?' asked Pekkala. 'Where did you hide the icon?'

'I didn't,' answered Detlev. 'I walked to the Potsuleyev Bridge, as I had been told to do and there I met a man who took the suitcase from me.'

'Can you describe this man?'

'He was tall and imposing, with a face that belonged in a nightmare. He looked as if he had been summoned from the grave.'

Pekkala thought back to the man who had attacked him with a butcher's knife. 'Had you seen him before?' he asked.

'Never,' answered Detlev, 'and thankfully never again.'

'Did he say anything to you?'

'Yes,' replied Detlev. 'He said that when the police asked me what I had done with the icon, I should tell them to look in the pavilion on the island of the Lamskie pond on the Tsarskoye Selo estate. And that, you will recall, Inspector, is exactly what I told you when we spoke at Okhrana headquarters all those years ago.'

Pekkala recalled how, after receiving that information from Detlev, he had rowed across the pond to the pavilion. There he had discovered the charred remains of a frame which had once been inlaid with intricate silver filigree and semi-precious stones. Of the icon itself, nothing but ashes remained.

'What did you do then?' asked Kirov.

'I returned to the church, knelt before the altar and prayed. One hour later, the police arrived. There was no trial. I never saw a judge. Within a week, I had been sent here to Karaganda, and I have been here ever since.'

'When did you realise that the Tsarina wasn't going to re-lease you, after all?'

'In 1919, when I heard that she was dead. And even then I hoped that someone might be sent to rescue me. But no one ever did.'

'Why did you not say something?' demanded Kirov.

'Say what?' laughed Detlev. 'That, on the orders of the Tsarina, I had not destroyed the icon, after all, but that I still had no idea where it was? The Tsarina would surely have denied it and who would have taken my word over hers? I am sorry that I lied to you, Inspector. At the time, I didn't feel as if I had a choice.'

'You paid for that lie long ago,' said Pekkala, 'and I will see to it that you are released.'

'Thank you,' said Father Detlev, 'but I would prefer to stay where I am.'

'In prison?' Kirov asked, bewildered. 'For a crime you didn't commit?'

'There was a time when I dreamed of seeing the Church of the Resurrection one last time,' said Detlev.

Pekkala did not have the heart to tell the priest that the church had been destroyed in a battle that took place on the estate, back in the autumn of 1941.

'In recent years, however,' continued Detlev, 'I have come to believe that there is nowhere else but here for me now. The truth is, I am closer to God in this garden, which I made with my own hands, than I ever was in any church.'

Pekkala thanked him for his time and the two men stood up to leave.

'Aren't you curious about where we found the icon?' asked Kirov, as he gathered the bundle from the table.

'Beside a corpse, I imagine,' said Detlev.

'How did you know that?' asked Pekkala.

Detlev smiled at him. 'Because everyone who touches that seems to end up dead before their time.'

As Detlev shook hands with the Inspector, he felt a twinge of guilt, like a pinched nerve in his spine. He had told Pekkala his story, as he promised, but he had not told him all of it. He thought back to that evening, when he and Rasputin had driven back across the estate after the meeting with the Tsarina, the drunken Siberian crashing through the gears of the beautiful car.

Suddenly, Rasputin pulled off the road as if he had lost control of the vehicle.

Detlev cried out and covered his face, convinced they were about to crash.

But there was no sickly thud of engine parts against the nearby tree, nor the glittering spray of shattered glass. There was only the sound of Rasputin, laughing quietly at the sight of the priest, whose arms remained wrapped about his head.

Slowly, Detlev lowered his hands. 'What's happening? Why have we stopped?'

'So that there can be no doubt in your mind about the reason I chose you for this task, Father Detlev.'

'What do you mean?' asked the priest.

'I am referring to a certain file, one with your name on it, safely tucked away, at least for now, within the offices of the Tsar's Secret Police.'

Detlev's mouth fell open. 'That part of my life is over and done with! I made a new start. I am a priest now!'

'Of course,' Rasputin lifted one hand in a gesture of conciliation, 'and we would hate to see any obstacle appear in this new and admirable path on which you find yourself. But a man's past can come back to haunt him, if he is not careful with the present.'

'In other words,' said Detlev, his face reddening, 'I'm going to prison if I do as you ask, and I'll go there as well if I don't.'

'It's true you're bound for a jail cell. There's nothing you can do about that, but your stay there can be long or brief. The choice is entirely yours, Father Detlev.'

For a moment, Detlev did not speak. 'Then it appears I have no choice at all.'

'Now you understand!' Rasputin slapped him on the back.

'I never thought that someone as exalted as the Tsarina would stoop so low as to blackmail a servant of God.'

'She's not blackmailing you. I am!' Rasputin grinned at the priest's naivety. 'Besides, do you honestly believe that the Tsarina needs your police file as an excuse to throw you in prison? File or no file, she could have you put away for life,' he said, snapping his fingers in Detlev's face, 'as fast as that.'

'Why have you dragged me into this?' demanded the priest, a note of pleading in his voice. 'Surely there are others guilty of far worse deeds than mine, whose secrets you can drag from the shadows?'

'It wasn't the fact that you had committed crimes which brought you to my attention,' explained Rasputin. 'It's the specific nature of those crimes.'

In the silence that followed, Detlev found it difficult to breathe.

'Are you beginning to understand me, Father Detlev?'

'I am,' he answered quietly. 'You need me to go back to work.'

'Precisely!' boomed the Siberian. He started up the car, and pulled out on to the road again. 'Just follow my instructions,' he told the priest, 'and this will all be over soon.'

'And when the truth comes out,' asked Detlev, 'as it surely must some day? What then?'

Rasputin laughed. 'There is no truth in Russia! Only rumours backed up with the threat of violence.'

Now, as Detlev watched Pekkala and Kirov make their way among the leafless apple trees towards the mud-splashed car that would take them back to Moscow, he began, very quietly, to laugh. 'You were wrong, Siberian,' he muttered. 'There is truth in this place, after all.'

*

The three men drove back towards Moscow, with Zolkin singing loudly as he swerved around the potholes in the road. Kirov and Pekkala remained silent, lost in thought.

As Pekkala mulled over his conversation with the priest, he kept returning to the moment when Detlev had described handing over the icon to the pale-faced man. If they were ever to trace the path of the icon from the time of its disappearance to the day it was uncovered in the crypt, they would have to find the solution to a riddle which Detlev himself had been unable to solve – what happened to the stranger on the Potsuleyev Bridge?

If, at that moment, Pekkala could have travelled back through time to a lonely, snow-bound road in the winter of 1922, he would have learned the answer to his question.

2 January 1922

Near the village of Markha, west of the city of Irkutsk, Siberia

The stranger was running down the middle of the road. His half-frozen feet splashed in the thick slush which the Siberians call *schoom*. In spite of the cold, his face was red with exertion and his lungs whistled with every gasping breath he took.

Following him along the otherwise deserted road was a black car, its wipers sweeping jerkily across the windscreen, clearing the fat flakes of snow which drifted down on to the glass.

The man stumbled. He sprawled face down, sending up a spray of icy water, then scrambled to his feet and kept on running.

The car maintained its speed just behind him, making no attempt to overtake the man or block his path. On one side of the road was forest, waist deep in drifts of snow. On the other side, just visible through a screen of trees, a frozen lake spread out towards the horizon.

The stranger's pace began to falter. His arms flailed like broken wings. The rhythmic puffing of condensed air from his shattered lungs rose like a Morse-code signal endlessly repeated into the sky. Just when it seemed that the running man could go no further, he swerved and threw himself at the tall bank of ploughed snow on the side of the road. He clambered over the dirty, hard-packed chunks of ice and grit and rolled down the other side. A moment later, he was up again and heading for the lake.

The car's brakes squealed as it came to a stop. The rear door opened and a passenger climbed out. He wore the close-fitting brownish-olive uniform of an officer in the Bolshevik Secret Police, known as the Cheka. He was of medium height, with thin legs tucked into knee-length boots, narrow shoulders and a face so frighteningly gaunt that, when his eyes were closed, he more closely resembled a corpse laid out for a wake than someone whose heart was still beating. Leaving the door open, he set off after the fugitive.

The Cheka officer moved in slow, loping strides towards the lake, his left hand clutching a peculiar wooden holster attached to his belt, to stop it from bouncing against his thigh.

The stranger had already reached the ice, which was covered by a layer of ankle-deep snow. Half blind with fear, he headed for the jagged silhouette of pine trees on the far shore, where the sunset was a smear of red against the clouds. As he ran towards the centre of the lake, he could hear the dry, splintering sound of the ice giving way beneath his feet. Even though his instincts screamed at him to stop, he kept on going, knowing there was nowhere else to go but onward.

For a while, the Cheka officer kept up the pace, but when he began to hear the same sound of cracking ice beneath him, he came to a panicky halt, as if poised at the edge of a cliff.

The only sounds then, reaching across the terrible white silence of that landscape, were the footsteps of the running man and the hollow scraping of his breath.

For a brief moment, it appeared as if the Cheka officer

had decided to let his prisoner escape. Then he unbuckled his belt and slid off the bulky wooden holster. Opening the top, he removed a broom-handled Mauser pistol. With movements slowed by freezing fingers, he fitted the butt of the pistol into a locking mechanism located at the forward end of the holster. Tucking the stock into his shoulder, he took aim, drew three deep breaths and on the third breath paused and squeezed the trigger.

The snap of the bullet echoed across the lake.

The spent brass cartridge spun up into the air and then fell, disappearing as the hot brass melted through the snow.

The Cheka officer squinted through the haze of cordite smoke. For a second, he thought he had missed. But then the man slowed and stopped. He bent until his hands were resting on his knees and finally collapsed into the snow.

The officer buckled up his belt and, with the gun still in his hand, took one hesitant step towards the man he had just shot.

'Commander Dzerzhinsky!' shouted a voice.

The gunman turned and looked back at the road. There, by the edge of the lake, stood his driver and bodyguard, an ex-bare-knuckle boxer named Pevsner.

'It's not worth it, Commander,' Pevsner called out. 'The ice is too thin and the man is obviously finished.'

'How can you be sure?' replied Dzerzhinsky, his voice travelling cleanly through the winter stillness.

'If the bullet did not kill him,' said Pevsner, 'the cold most certainly will.'

Dzerzhinsky stared doubtfully at the still form of his victim. He took aim with the gun again, but then thought better of it. 'Not worth another bullet,' he muttered to himself, then turned and headed back across the ice, replacing the gun inside its hollow wooden stock.

'That's the last of them,' Dzerzhinsky remarked to Pevsner as he climbed into the car. Before he drew his legs in, he tapped his boot heels together, dislodging clumps of snow that had gathered on the soles. The sharp sound echoed through the empty forest, carried away by the cold wind blowing through the treetops.

'What was his name?' asked the driver.

'Kohl,' answered Dzerzhinsky. 'Stefan Kohl. One of those Volga River Germans we told to go home at the start of the war. Seems like this one didn't get the message.' He hawked and spat, as if to say the words had left a bad taste in his mouth. Then he slammed the door shut. 'Let's get out of here,' he said, 'before we freeze to death as well.'

With a series of turns, some of which threatened to strand it in the snow banks, the car headed back in the direction from which it had come. After a while, the headlights came on and their beams carved a path through the frost-glistening air.

As the Emka rattled back towards Moscow, Kirov finally gave voice to the thing which plagued both of their minds. 'We'll never find out who that stranger was,' he said. 'Everyone who might have known – the Tsar, the Tsarina, Rasputin – they're all dead.'

'Not quite everyone,' replied Pekkala.

'Then who?' asked Kirov.

'Vyroubova,' he said. 'Anna Alexandrovna Vyroubova.'

'But she fled the country years ago. Who knows where she is hiding now?'

'I do,' answered Pekkala. 'Finding her is not the hard part, Major Kirov. It's getting her to talk that will be difficult. For that, I'll need to pay a visit to the country of my birth.'

Not long after this, Pekkala found himself in a two-seater Polikarpov Po-2 biplane as it droned through the morning mist, barely sixty feet above the ground, near the Russo-Finnish border east of the town of Lappeenranta.

The plane was piloted by a frail and serious-looking woman named Marina Popova. Even in the plane, she wore a skirt along with clunky black boots that came up almost to her knees and a *gymnastiorka* tunic festooned with medals.

Popova was on loan from a squadron of women pilots who

specialised in bombing German front-line positions at night. For this, they had been equipped with hopelessly outdated planes, so slow and ponderous that they were normally reserved for crop dusting.

The fact that the Polikarpov's top speed was slower than the stalling speed of German planes sent out to intercept them meant that the Po-2s were actually very difficult for the enemy to shoot down. Added to this was the pilots' tactic of cutting their engines as they neared the German lines, so that they glided in over their targets, with only the sound of the wind whistling through their wing struts. This eerie noise had earned them the name of 'Night Witches'.

'No parachutes?' Pekkala had asked, as he climbed into the forward of the two cockpits. The pilot and the passenger sat in separate compartments, each one open to the air, rather than sitting side by side.

'There's no point,' replied Popova. 'We fly so low that the chute would never open in time.'

'Exactly how low will we be travelling?' asked Pekkala, as he tried and failed to hide his consternation.

The answer to this soon became apparent as Pekkala stared out through a pair of fur-trimmed goggles at the haze of the propeller only an arm's length in front of him and the tops of the pine trees so close to the fixed wheels of the Polikarpov that they seemed to be bouncing along the roof of the forest.

Just over the Russian side of the border, the plane landed in a forest clearing which had been paved with a corduroy road of felled trees. With his spine shaken by the landing, Pekkala emerged from the cockpit and stood back while the Polikarpov taxied about, revving its engine for take-off. Soon it had vanished into the clouds and Pekkala found himself alone.

But his solitude did not last long.

A man soon appeared at the far end of the clearing. He was tall and thickly bearded, and his dirty skin glistened as if it had been smeared with motor oil. Slowly, he raised one hand.

Pekkala raised his own hand in reply. A guide had been arranged for him through the Bureau of Special Operations in Moscow, but he had no idea whom to expect, and wasn't even sure if this was the right person.

The man did not come out to meet Pekkala. Instead, he stepped backwards into the shadows and waited.

Pekkala set off towards him, treading carefully over the uneven ground.

At last he reached the cover of the trees. Face to face with the man, Pekkala was surprised to discover that the stranger wore his clothes inside out.

Noticing the look of confusion on Pekkala's face, the man explained. 'When you get where you are going, you don't want to look like a man who's been wandering in the woods.'

Seeing the wisdom in this, Pekkala stripped down to his underclothes, pulled his trousers and his coat inside out and dressed himself in the fashion of his guide.

When this strange ritual had finally been completed, the man introduced himself. 'My name is Hokkanen,' said the man. 'I deserted from the Finnish Army in the winter of 1940. Now I am an errand boy for the Bureau of Special Operations. One day, I know, I will outlive my usefulness. Whenever I am summoned to this clearing, I wonder if they've sent someone to kill me.'

'Not this time,' replied Pekkala.

Hokkanen nodded. 'Try to keep up,' he said, 'and tread quietly if you want to stay alive.'

For several hours, the two men headed west, skirting the edge of a great swamp, where thickets of frozen bulrushes, each with its own skullcap of snow, swayed and rattled in the frost-glittering air.

Pekkala marvelled at how little sound Hokkanen made as he travelled through the forest. He moved with a strange and cautious tread, placing the tips of his toes upon the earth before allowing the rest of his foot to make contact with the ground.

Eventually, they came to a long, straight, empty road.

'We have crossed the border now,' said Hokkanen. 'This is as far as I go.'

Reaching into his pocket, Pekkala pulled out a small leather bag containing gold coins and tossed it to the guide. Hokkanen tucked it away in his shirt without examining the contents.

'Aren't you going to count it?' asked Pekkala.

'If I don't show up to lead you back to the airfield,' he replied, 'you'll know that it wasn't enough.' Then he pointed to the south. 'That way is Lappeenranta. I will see you here again in three days' time. If you're late, I'll leave without you.' Then he turned and walked back among the trees, moving with his careful, deer-like steps until he had faded away among the bony ranks of birches.

Finding himself alone again, the first thing Pekkala did was to put his clothes back on the right way around.

It had been a long time since he had last set foot in Finland. Even though the trees on one side of the border looked much the same as the trees upon the other, nevertheless, Pekkala felt in his chest the strange, gyroscopic balance of knowing he'd returned to the place where he was from. In spite of that, he knew he could not stay. The course of his life had steered him to a different land, and had given him purpose there and he knew that what a person does, not where they do it, is the thing which makes them who they are. One day, perhaps, Pekkala would return for good, but that day had not yet come. For now, in many ways, he was more of a stranger in this place than if he'd never been here at all.

That evening, at the Lappeenranta railyard, Pekkala stowed away on a freight train bound for Helsinki. The following morning, he woke to find that the train had reached the city. Climbing down from the wagon, he pulled a straight-edge razor from his coat, rubbed a handful of snow across his face and shaved. Then he made his way to the house of Anna Vyroubova.

Vyroubova's escape from the Bolsheviks had been nothing short of miraculous. After her arrest by soldiers of the Provisional Government, she was eventually released, only to be arrested again after the Bolsheviks had taken over. She managed to slip away from her guard while being transported through the streets of Petrograd to Kronstadt Prison, where she would, almost certainly, have been shot. For more than a year, she eluded the Cheka by living with Romanov sympathisers. Some of her hiding places were little more than huts out in the forest. Eventually, in the winter of 1920, she was taken by sledge to Finland, across the frozen waters of the Baltic.

It was many years before Pekkala learned what had become of Anna Vyroubova and even though the two of them had rarely seen eye to eye during their days among Romanovs, he was glad to know she had survived. Almost everyone else from that small circle had been hunted to extinction by Dzerzhinsky and his Cheka.

After receiving permission to settle in Finland, which had only recently declared its independence from Russia, Vyroubova had taken the vows of an orthodox nun, a move calculated to separate herself from her past and, with luck, to avoid a bullet from one of Stalin's numerous assassins.

Now she owned a small, white house with navy-blue shutters, located in the suburbs of Helsinki. Due to the injuries Vyroubova had sustained in the train crash before the Revolution, which had left her partially crippled, she had been allowed to live in her own place, instead of at a convent, and whatever duties her new station might have required of her seemed to have been largely overlooked by the Church.

For a while, Pekkala lingered at a bus stop across the road, studying the building, to see if it was under observation, or being guarded. But no one came or went, and he saw nothing to indicate that anyone was keeping an eye upon the place.

Satisfied, he crossed the road and knocked upon the door.

A lace curtain flicked in a downstairs window, but Pekkala had placed himself where he knew he could not be seen until the door had actually been opened.

There was a sound of two locks being unfastened, and then the door slid open a crack. Vyroubova's plump, moon-shaped face peered out into the street.

'Anna,' Pekkala said quietly.

For a second, she only stared at him uncomprehendingly. Then a look of astonishment flashed in her eyes as she realised who it was. 'You!' she spat, and tried to slam the door.

Pekkala jammed his foot in the way. 'I only want to talk,' he explained.

'I have nothing to say!' shouted Vyroubova, and she fled back into her house.

Pekkala followed her in. 'Anna, if you'll just let me explain.'

Vyroubova reached the dresser in the living room, snatched up a letter opener and brandished it at him. 'Have you come to kill me? Is that why you are here, Pekkala?'

'Of course not,' he replied. 'What possible reason would I have for doing that?'

'I don't know, but that doesn't mean you haven't got one.'

'I have come a long way,' said Pekkala, 'and at considerable risk, considering that Finland and Russia are still at war, to ask for your help with a matter which involves some of our mutual friends.'

'Our mutual friends are dead!' spat Vyroubova.

'But their reputations are not,' answered Pekkala, 'and what I have to say concerns not only theirs but yours, as well. Anna, *The Shepherd* has been found.'

Until that moment, Vyroubova had continued to brandish her letter opener at Pekkala. But now she hesitated. 'Where?' she asked.

'In the coffin of a priest in Germany. I'm trying to find out how it got there.'

With a grumble of resignation, Vyroubova tossed the letter opener back on to the dresser, whose black-lacquered surface had been inlaid with chips of abalone shell arranged into bouquets of flowers. 'If you want to find out what happened to the icon,' she muttered as she hobbled over to a chair padded with a well-worn cushion, 'why don't you ask the man who took it?'

'I have already spoken to Father Detlev,' answered Pekkala. 'I found him in the Karaganda Prison, where he has spent most of his life because of this.'

'What happened to Detlev is regrettable.' Vyroubova sighed. 'But that was never a part of the plan. The Tsarina was going to have him released, but in the end, there was no time. Everything happened so quickly in those first days of the Revolution.'

'Father Detlev explained what the Tsarina told him to do. What I came here to find out is why.'

'Because she wanted peace!' shouted Vyroubova. 'For herself and for her country. By 1915, the Tsarina had reached the conclusion that Russia could never defeat the combined forces of Germany and Austria-Hungary. The only hope for our country, she told me, was for Russia to make peace. And the sooner it happened, she believed, the better our chances for making that peace on our own terms.'

'Did the Tsar know about this?'

'No!' snorted Vyroubova. 'And that was the problem. He could not know. Even to speak of such things amounted to treason. The Tsar had taken an oath to fight on as long as a single enemy soldier remained on Russian soil. By the following year, he had taken over command of the entire military. If word leaked out that his own wife had been colluding with the enemy, it would only have confirmed the rumours which were already circulating through the Russian court – that she, a German by birth, was more sympathetic to her own people than she was to the people of Russia.'

'It would have spelled the end of everything,' agreed Pekkala.

'Exactly!' And with that single word of agreement, the anger seemed to lessen in her voice. It was as if the burden of this secret, which had knotted around Vyroubova's heart like the strangling roots of a vine, was finally beginning to unravel.

'So what did the Tsarina do?' asked Pekkala.

'She decided to send a secret delegation to meet with representatives of the German government.'

'Who were the members of this delegation?'

'Lutukin,' replied Vyroubova, 'and Briulov.'

The faces of those two politicians glimmered into focus in Pekkala's mind. Neither had survived the Revolution. Lutukin was dragged from his car by mutinous Cossacks and then run through with his own sabre, which he carried with him when he toured the streets of Petrograd. Briulov, after being fired by the Tsar from his post as Minister of Education, had joined an international pacifist group, based in Sweden. In 1919, he was convicted of treason by a Bolshevik tribunal. Sentenced to twenty years in the Gulags, he died while working on the White Sea Canal, and his body, along with those of thousands of other slave labourers, was buried in the cement walls of the canal. 'Only those two?' asked Pekkala.

'No,' answered Vyroubova. 'There was also a pair of military officers. One was General Yagelsky, and the other was Naval Commodore Asikritov.'

Pekkala was surprised to hear the names, since neither had, at least publicly, shown any reluctance to wage war. Yagelsky had been with General Samsonov at Tannenberg and Asikritov had served under Admiral Kolchak in the Tsar's Pacific Fleet at Vladivostok. These men, too, were dead. Yagelsky committed suicide when guards of Kerensky's Provisional Government

169

came to his house to arrest him in 1917. Asikritov, one of the top-ranking officers at Kronstadt, an island just across the river from Petrograd, was killed by his own chauffeur on the same day the Cossacks put to death the sabre-wielding Minister Lutukin.

'And how did the Tsarina make contact with the Germans?'

'Through her uncle, the Grand Duke of Hesse. He guaranteed their safety, provided that they could be delivered across the border. He also assembled members of the German government and military, who might listen to the Russian peace proposal.'

'But how did she propose to deliver the Russian emissaries without alerting the Tsar, or anyone else, for that matter?'

'They had to be smuggled in.'

'By whom?' asked Pekkala, thinking of his own journey from Moscow to Helsinki and the shadowy Hokkanen who had led him through the forest. Such guides were not impossible to find, but these men and women usually operated under the protection of one and sometimes both governments simultaneously. No border could ever be completely secured, even in wartime, and the shifting boundaries between mortal enemies were never more than porous screens, through which brave travellers might pass, provided they could find someone to show them the way.

'I don't know who smuggled them across the border. What I do know is that they demanded a great deal in payment.'

'I am not surprised,' remarked Pekkala, 'given the risks they were taking, but surely the amount would not have been hard to come by for the Tsarina. We are talking about the one of the richest families in the world, after all, at least at the time.'

'Normally, the money would not have been an issue,' agreed Vyroubova. 'Romanov bank accounts held more than enough to meet the demands of the guides, but to withdraw funds from these accounts, especially such a large amount, would not have gone unnoticed by the Tsar.'

Pekkala knew she was telling the truth. The Tsar kept a very close eye on his personal finances. He met once a month with his financial adviser to discuss the family budget, with which he was notoriously frugal. If the Tsarina had made even a modest withdrawal, questions would have been asked.

'But the smugglers had to be paid,' continued Vyroubova, 'which is how we come to *The Shepherd*. That icon was the price they demanded.'

'I find that hard to believe,' said Pekkala, 'given the importance she placed on its powers.'

'Which only goes to show that perhaps you did not know her as well as you thought. Yes, she gave them the icon. I think she would have given more than that if it meant saving the lives of thousands of soldiers on the battlefield, German and Russian alike. If her plan had worked . . .' Her voice trailed off.

'What happened, Anna? Why did it go wrong?'

'The delegations never even met,' she explained. 'On the way there, our emissaries first had to travel through territory which was held by the Austro-Hungarian Army. And that is as far as they got. They made it through several checkpoints, but eventually had to turn back.'

'Because they were discovered?'

'No, because the area through which they were travelling came under Russian attack. So you see, Pekkala, it all came to nothing. *The Shepherd* might as well have been burned, after all, instead of just given away.'

'Surely these guides, whoever they were, must have known that they could never make a profit from the icon. They could never sell it, and they would have been discovered if they tried. *The Shepherd* was too well known.'

Vyroubova shrugged. 'I don't know what they were thinking. The Tsarina didn't tell me anything about them and she warned me not to ask. It was for my own good, she said, and I believed her.'

'How did she find them in the first place?'

'That I *do* know!' she laughed. 'They came on the recommendation of our dear departed friend, Rasputin. He arranged the whole thing, even the theft of the icon from his house.'

'And Father Detlev?'

'Chosen by Rasputin himself to carry out the robbery.'

'Did Grigori honestly think that the negotiations would work?'

'Probably not,' answered Vyroubova, 'but he knew that once the Tsarina's mind was set upon a course, she would throw her whole life into it, no matter what the cost. I think he was trying to protect her, so that when the plan failed, her good intentions would not recoil upon her head, and the heads of the Tsar and their children, as they surely would have done if news of the mission came out. The loss of one icon, precious as it may be, was a small price to pay for the lives of the people Grigori had grown to love. That's why he chose people who knew how to keep their mouths shut. Whoever the Tsarina gave the icon to, they never breathed a word about it, at least not to me or anyone I knew. If you ask me, you're lucky you got one word out of Father Detlev, even after all this time.'

'For what it's worth,' said Pekkala, 'I think it did him good to talk. I hope it does some good for you as well.'

Vyroubova set the tip of her cane upon the ground and rose unsteadily to her feet. 'Maybe it will, in time,' she told him. 'It has taken me years to chase away the ghosts of the past, but they never stay away for long. All it needs is a word, or a sound or a smell, or,' she jerked her chin at him, 'the sight of a familiar face, and they all come howling back into my mind.'

'You are not the only one with ghosts,' Pekkala told her.

'I did not doubt that for a second.' In an unfamiliar moment of kindness, she reached out and touched his hand. 'Take heart, Pekkala! Maybe one day we'll wake up and find they're gone for good.'

Pekkala smiled. 'Perhaps,' he said, 'but I doubt it.'

'If the truth be told,' replied Vyroubova, gently releasing his hand, 'so do I.'

25 February 1945

Karaganda Prison

'A package has come for you, Father!' Clutching a cardboard box, Prison Warder First Class Turkov opened the gate to Detlev's garden. With the toe of his boot, he nudged aside the priest's pot-bellied pig, who had emerged from its straw-padded lean-to in order to see if there was anything to eat.

Detlev had been taking a nap, as he did most afternoons after his lunch. He appeared in the doorway, blinking the sleep from his eyes and his face crumpled like a piece of old brown paper.

'This doesn't happen every day,' remarked Turkov as he placed the box into Detlev's outstretched hands.

'Not any day,' Detlev corrected him, 'and I see it hasn't been opened for inspection.'

Turkov brushed aside the comment. 'There's nothing to worry about. We already know who it's from.'

'We do?'

'Of course. Inspector Pekkala has sent it. Look here. It has a Moscow postmark. That's where Pekkala lives, and who else do you know from Moscow?'

Detlev peered at the blurred black ovals which had covered the postage stamps. 'But why would he have sent me this?'

'I'm sure it's just Pekkala's way of saying thank you for your help with the investigation. Whatever it is, I expect it's something nice.' Turkov sounded as happy as if he had received the package himself.

'Probably,' said Detlev, and there seemed to be the faintest trace of annoyance in his voice.

'Well, aren't you going to open it?' asked Turkov, smiling expectantly.

'All in good time,' answered Detlev. Then he turned and walked back into his house and closed the door.

'Well I . . .' Turkov mumbled as the smile faded slowly from his face. 'I suppose I'll be going then,' he announced to the door.

Father Detlev watched him depart, peering through a crack in the door. He had always resented Turkov's nosiness, even if his curiosity never seemed to contain any particular malice. In fact, it struck Father Detlev that he had been singled out by Turkov for better than average treatment. If their situations had been different, Detlev felt they might even have become friends. But he had learned in his years as a convict that the relationship between a prisoner and his guard could never be based on anything more than mutual mistrust. Turkov's enquiries about Detlev's health, his willingness to linger and converse, even the occasional present, such as a much-coveted sewing needle and thread, or an extra loaf of the dark *paika* bread given out to each prisoner as part of the daily rations – all these things only served to make Detlev more suspicious about Turkov's motives.

But there was another reason why he did not want to open the package in front of Turkov. He did not want to share the surprise of what it contained. There were, as a rule, no surprises in his life. Even the monthly surprise inspections did not surprise him any more and he wanted this to belong to him alone.

Detlev turned back to the box, which was waiting on his kitchen table. He did not open it at first, but smoothed his hands over the paper wrapping. He admired the stamps, some depicting Lenin and Stalin, their profiles placed side by side, as if they were almost the same person. Others showed battle scenes, in which Red Army soldiers bayoneted barely human shapes beneath a red sky emblazoned with the hammer and the sickle.

The pig, whose name was Tolstyak, nudged open the door and trotted over to Father Detlev.

'I know what you're thinking,' Detlev told the pig.

Tolstyak, who would have been just as happy to eat the box as anything it might contain, stared longingly at the package.

Detlev tore open the paper wrapping, then prised apart the flaps of the cardboard box. At first, the inside appeared to be filled entirely with straw. Detlev sank his hand into the dry, blond stalks and fished about until his fingers closed upon an object. He lifted it out, scattering straw on the floor, which the pig immediately investigated with his flat, twitching nose.

It was a small metal bottle, about the length of Detlev's hand, sealed with a cork which had been coated with red wax. On the bottle was a brightly coloured paper label, showing the Virgin Mary set against an orange sunset, and two people kneeling before her with crutches laid upon the ground beside them. The writing on the bottle was not in the Russian alphabet, but Detlev could tell that it was in several languages. He could make out French, German and finally English, of which he spoke a little. And what he deciphered were the words 'Lourdes Holy Water'.

Detlev gasped. He shook the bottle and heard its contents

slosh about inside. 'Thank you, Inspector,' he whispered. 'Thank you. Thank you.'

He considered not opening the bottle and instead keeping it safe upon the shelf until the day might come when its powers would be needed. But then he laughed to himself at such foolishness. I am almost seventy years old, he thought. I have spent more than half my life in Karaganda Prison. There is no better time than now.

With his thumbnail, Father Detlev carved away the wax around the cork, watching it crumble on to the table. After mouthing a silent prayer of gratitude, he uncorked the bottle, and poured its contents over his head.

The liquid smelled of flowers, reminding Detlev a little of rosewater, with which his mother used to scent her pocket handkerchiefs. No sooner had this thought entered his head than he began to feel dizzy. And then nauseous. He put the bottle down upon the table. His hands began to tremble. All around him, it grew suddenly dark, as if a storm had swept in from the forest. His breathing became laboured and he tried to sit down, but misjudged the location of the chair and fell upon the floor.

Convulsions racked the old man's frame as spasming muscles writhed beneath his skin. A foamy white fluid, like frogspawn, poured from his mouth and his nose. His pupils had contracted into pinpricks. The last thing he saw was the nose of the pig, sniffing at his face.

For several minutes, Father Detlev's body twitched uncontrollably, as if it were being subjected to violent electrical charges. Then, at last, he lay still. In his lower legs, a bluish haze appeared beneath the skin. The haze spread through his limbs, until his whole body had turned a smoky, lavender colour.

Beside him lay Tolstyak the pig, as dead as its owner, pieces of half-chewed straw bristling from its mouth.

*

'Inspector,' said Kirov, holding the phone out towards him. 'A call has come in from Karaganda.'

Pekkala looked up from his desk, where he was writing a report on his visit to Vyroubova, from which he had only just returned.

'The guard there wants to know if you sent a package to Father Detlev.'

'No,' answered Pekkala. 'Why?'

Kirov pressed the phone back to his ear. 'He says no. Why do you ask?'

Pekkala was watching Kirov, trying to figure out the meaning of this call. He saw a shadow pass across the major's face, and he knew that the news was not good.

Kirov replaced the receiver. For a moment, he just stared at his desk.

'What is it?' asked Pekkala.

'Father Detlev is dead.'

Pekkala set down his pen. 'When did this happen?'

'Yesterday.'

'And how did he die?'

'The guard didn't want to tell me over the phone.'

'Why not?'

Kirov shook his head. 'All he told me was that we'd better come and see for ourselves.'

'Again?' asked Zolkin. He stooped over the bonnet of the Emka, the sleeves of his shirt rolled up and braces stretched tight across his shoulders. In his hand, he held a cloth with which he had been waxing the car.

At his driver's urging, Kirov had rented a small garage for the Emka just across the road from their office. At first, the major had refused, saying that the Emka could continue to live in the alleyway outside their building, just as it had always done. But on their next trip to the Kremlin, Zolkin took a detour through the city, and Kirov could not help but notice the cars, many of them Emkas, that had been stripped by gangs of thieves. On some cars even the wheels had been taken, leaving the vehicles balanced on blocks of wood brought along by the thieves for that purpose. Zolkin did not have to say a word. By the end of that day, Kirov had rented the garage.

It had a rolling steel door which padlocked at the base, and a single light bulb hanging from the ceiling inside. There was no window. The walls were painted concrete and the ceiling had been constructed from wood so old that the marks of an adze could be seen where some long-dead carpenter had trimmed the boards. Although it was spartan, even by the standards of Pekkala, Zolkin was content to spend his time there. The rusty, oil-dripping parts which he had scrounged from various junkyards on the outskirts of the city had been installed inside the engine and even Pekkala, who had previously paid little attention to the quality of their transport, remarked that the car was running more smoothly than it had ever done before. Kirov, who had previously been in charge of the car, remarked grumpily that it seemed a remarkable coincidence that Zolkin would have known the exact location of so many of the city's pillaged Emkas, and wondered if they owed their upgraded performance to some of those other vehicles.

'You can't be serious about driving all the way back to Karaganda!' protested Zolkin, pausing to wipe the sweat from his forehead. 'I've just finished cleaning the car. Look at how it shines!' He gestured pitifully at the gleaming radiator grille. 'It took me two days to scrape away the mud!'

'It can't be helped,' Pekkala told him gently.

Zolkin sighed and shook his head. 'When do we leave, Inspector?'

'Immediately,' said Kirov, and as he spoke, he noticed, on the otherwise bare walls, a heavy sailcloth flap hanging by two iron rings from an iron hook embedded in the concrete wall. 'What is that thing?' he asked.

'Oh, that!' Zolkin squinted at the canvas, as if he had just noticed it himself. 'Well, to tell you the truth, Major, that is my bed.'

'Your bed?' Kirov echoed, his voice rising in disbelief.

'It's a hammock,' explained Zolkin, as he lifted one of the rings, stretched it over to the other wall and replaced it on a second hook. Now they could see it clearly. The ends of the canvas had been fitted with strings, attached by brass grommets and woven together to form a mesh which came together around the anchoring ring. To illustrate, Zolkin hopped up into the hammock, rolling his body into the envelope of dirty white cloth. Then he grinned down at the two men.

'But why are you sleeping in here?' demanded Kirov? 'I found you a place at the Lubyanka barracks.'

'With all due respect, Major,' said Zolkin, 'it's hard to get a good night's sleep at Lubyanka.'

'Why?' asked Kirov. 'Is it too noisy?'

'No,' replied Zolkin, 'it's the silence that keeps me awake.'

*

When the Emka pulled up once again before the gates of Karaganda, it was in even worse condition than after its previous trip. All trace of Zolkin's hand-polished wax finish had been obliterated in a pointillist spray of multi-coloured filth. Having been ordered by Kirov to stop his complaining, Zolkin had begun speaking to himself in his native Ukrainian dialect, but after the windscreen was cracked by a stray pebble thrown up from the wheels of a passing army truck, the driver had lapsed into such a menacing silence that both Kirov and Pekkala felt obliged to engage him in conversation, since he now seemed on the verge of total madness.

While Zolkin was left to contemplate his misfortune, Warder Turkov escorted Kirov and Pekkala to the prison morgue.

It was a single-storey building just behind the prison hospital, which doubled as a place where services were held for the dead, as well as a crematorium, its underground vent pipe emerging in the forest just beyond the prison wire. Having risen into the air, the cremation ash sometimes blew back over the prison, covering everything with a fine greyish-white powder, known to the inmates as 'dead man's snow'.

On their way, Turkov explained about the package, and why he had assumed it was a gift from Pekkala. He struggled to describe what he had found in Detlev's hut when making his rounds the following morning.

'I knocked on the door and there was no answer,' said Turkov, still clearly upset by what he had witnessed. 'I knew that Father Detlev sometimes slept in late, so I was about to walk on and leave the old man in peace when I smelled something peculiar. It reminded me of freshly cut grass. I opened the door and there he was. Him and his pot-bellied pig.'

'They were both dead?' asked Kirov.

'Oh, yes,' confirmed Turkov. 'And then I started to feel ill.'

'It is a natural response,' Pekkala tried to reassure him.

'That's not what I mean, Inspector. The smell, whatever it was. That's what made me feel ill. By the time I arrived at the prison hospital, I could barely walk. My vision was blurred. But the doctor gave me a shot,' Turkov continued, 'and in an hour or two, I was fine again.'

'Was there any sign of violence on Detlev's body?' Pekkala asked the prison guard.

'Not that I could see,' replied Turkov.

By now, they had passed through the double steel doors of the morgue and were in a low-ceilinged hallway. To the left was a small room filled with metal chairs, where funerals were held for the dead inmates. Beyond, through another steel door, was the mortuary itself.

'I'll leave you here,' said Turkov. 'I have seen what you're about to see, and once is more than enough.'

Inside the mortuary, they were met by a slim, dignified man wearing steel-rimmed spectacles and an apron made of brick-red, rubberised cloth over his suit, along with a pair of gloves, made from the same material as the apron, which came up almost to his elbows. He introduced himself as Dr Tuxen. 'I hope you both have strong stomachs,' he said.

With those words, he turned and pulled the handle of a large metal drawer, one of several which were set into the wall. The drawer slid out, revealing a body draped with a white cloth. Grasping the sheet with both hands, he carefully folded it back, disclosing the head, shoulders and stomach of the dead man.

In spite of the doctor's warning, both men flinched at the sight of what had happened to the priest.

The skin of the corpse was a vivid bluish grey. Detlev's lips had turned almost black and his swollen tongue lay wedged between yellowed teeth. A silver crucifix, attached by a leather cord around his neck, gleamed in the morgue's pale electric light. A huge Y-shaped scar criss-crossed his chest where it had been opened for autopsy, the interior organs examined and the chest cavity closed up again.

'What did this?' asked Pekkala.

'Poison,' replied Tuxen, 'although which one I'm not entirely certain. It was not ingested as food. I can tell you that for certain. The manner of death bears a strong resemblance to exposure to lethal gases of the type used during the last war.'

'Then shouldn't we be wearing gas masks?' Kirov asked nervously.

'There is no need to worry, Comrade Major,' said the doctor. 'The body and the area where it was found have been sprayed with a solution of sodium hydroxide. Fortunately, we have such chemicals on hand for cleaning out the drains in this prison. The sodium hydroxide neutralised the chemicals which killed Father Detlev.'

'How was the poison delivered?' asked Pekkala.

'In this,' replied Dr Tuxen, holding up the small, grey metal flask, whose label identified it as holy water from Lourdes. 'It appears to have entered his bloodstream through direct contact with his skin.'

'Was anyone else affected?' asked Pekkala.

'Only the warder who found him. Luckily for Turkov, by the time he showed up the vapour released from the liquid had largely dissipated. I was able to treat him with an injection of atropine, which we use here during surgery for normalising a patient's heart rate. The warder's exposure was very slight, and I am confident that he will make a full recovery.'

'You say this is one of the gases used during the war?' asked Kirov.

'I said it resembled one,' replied the doctor, 'but what killed Father Detlev is unlike anything I've seen before. I was an army doctor during the war and treated, or attempted to treat, many cases of gas poisoning. Chlorine, for example, is primarily a choking agent. It is inhaled, which then causes the kind of frothing at the mouth you see here, but with chlorine, there is a specific tarnishing effect on anything silver and, as you can see, the crucifix around his neck, which is made of silver, remains bright. Phosgene, too, produces many of the same symptoms, but the effects are delayed by several hours. Although it would almost certainly have proved fatal in the end, Detlev should have been alive when the warder came to check on him. In addition, I have run a chemical analysis of the fluid in the lungs, which indicates strong traces of ethanol and phosphorus, neither of which are components of chlorine or phosgene.'

'What about mustard gas?' asked Pekkala.

Dr Tuxen shook his head. 'I thought of that, but the effects of mustard are also delayed, even more so than with phosgene.

In addition, those who have been exposed to mustard gas show blistering of the skin, which is not the case here. This man appears to have died almost instantly, leading me to believe that whatever killed him attacked his nervous system, as opposed to the mucous membranes of his lungs and eyes, which is a characteristic of the other compounds. In addition to the ethanol and phosphorus, I have detected traces of sodium and chlorine, the combination of which sets it apart from any of the lethal gases of the Great War. What we are dealing with here is something new. New to me, at any rate.'

'Do you still have the box in which it was mailed to him?' asked Kirov.

Dr Tuxen nodded towards the counter.

In spite of the doctor's confidence that all of the chemicals had been neutralised, Kirov still didn't dare touch anything. 'This was mailed from Office 24 in Moscow,' he remarked as he examined the box. 'I can make out the postmarks.'

'Office 24 is just down the street from NKVD headquarters,' said Pekkala.

'Perhaps that's why Turkov believed the package came from you,' replied the doctor.

'But who would want to poison this old man?' asked Kirov.

'Wherever it came from,' said Pekkala, 'it looks as if we have a bigger problem on our hands than the murder of a single individual.'

'I am forced to agree,' said the doctor. 'If whoever made it has been able to mass produce the compound, it could wipe out an entire city in a matter of minutes if it was properly delivered to its target and in great enough concentration.'

'In that case,' said Pekkala, 'we should return to Moscow at once and report our findings to the Kremlin.'

'You had better take these with you,' said Tuxen, holding out two syringes. 'They are filled with atropine, and you may need them if you're going after the person who did this to Father Detlev.'

'Exactly how are we to use it?' asked Kirov.

'If you come into contact with this substance, or if you are even in its presence, you must immediately administer the full dose contained in one of these syringes.'

'You mean, I just stick myself in the arm with it?' Kirov winced at the sight of the long, capped needles.

'Not in the arm, Major.' Tuxen rested a finger against Kirov's chest. 'You must inject yourself in the heart. That is why the needles are so long.'

While Kirov stared queasily at the needles, Pekkala reached over and took them from the doctor's hand.

'There is one other thing,' said Dr Tuxen. 'It may have nothing to do with this man's murder, but I think it's something you should know about.' Taking up the ends of the sheet that still covered the lower half of Father Detlev's body, Dr Tuxen removed the cloth completely.

Pekkala breathed in sharply when he saw what had been done to Father Detlev. The priest had been castrated. His organs had been completely removed. All that remained of his manhood was a small hole in the flesh, surrounded by a white haze of scar tissue.

'In the war,' said Dr Tuxen, 'I treated men who had been wounded in the groin. In a number of cases, it became necessary to perform surgery not unlike what you see here. But in the case of this man, I can find no evidence of any injury which would have necessitated such radical amputation. The wound is old. If I had to guess, I'd say it healed up decades ago.' He covered up the body once again.

'Are they the result of some kind of torture?' Kirov wondered aloud.

'I don't believe so,' answered Tuxen. 'This is the work of a surgeon, or at least someone acquainted with performing the procedure. Whoever did this intended that Father Detlev should survive, and with a minimum of damage to the rest of his body. With no other obvious signs of trauma, I am left with the impression that Father Detlev submitted to this operation willingly, although why on earth a man would agree to such a thing is beyond me. As the doctor here, I've treated many men who went through torture, and in spite of all the terrible things I have seen, not one of them resembled this.'

'Was it mentioned in his prison file?' asked Pekkala.

'Yes,' replied Tuxen, 'although the record was filled out long before I ever came to Karaganda and judging from the dust, no one had touched the file for years.'

'And you've never had cause to examine him before?'

'I treated him for colds and other minor ailments, but nothing that required a full examination. Bear in mind, gentlemen, this is a prison hospital and not some private clinic. Given how many people I must care for, and what few medicines I have to cure the sick, a man is lucky if he receives any treatment at all. Whatever his reasons, Father Detlev kept them to himself.'

'Why would someone murder that old man?' asked Kirov as the two men left the mortuary building.

'To answer that,' replied Pekkala, 'we will first have to learn who created the weapon that killed him.'

15 May 1944

German High Command Headquarters, Rastenburg, East Prussia

As the armoured Mercedes, model 770k, passed through the third and final checkpoint of the Wolf's Lair compound, each one of which was protected by a fence of electrified wire, Professor Otto Meinhardt looked out at a row of simple wooden huts, surrounded by several massive concrete bunkers, all of them camouflaged with amoeba-shaped splotches of paint, and he wondered if this was going to be his last day on earth.

Meinhardt was a solidly built man with a wide forehead and hair parted severely down one side. His deep-set eyes and expressionless mouth gave little away of what was going on inside his head.

Some fifteen hours before, the professor had been abruptly summoned from the IG Farben research facility in Leverkeusen, south of Cologne, where he conducted research into the application of chemical compounds for military use. The men who came to fetch Meinhardt identified themselves as members of the SD, or Sicherheitsdienst; the Intelligence branch of the SS, headquartered in the Berlin suburb of Zossen. They gave no explanation as to why he had been summoned, by whom or where he was being taken. He was not allowed to pack a bag, or even to call his family to tell them he would be late for dinner. The SD men, who wore civilian clothes, bundled him into a car and drove him to an airstrip near the town of Bad Godesberg, where he was put aboard a Junkers Ju52 cargo plane and flown towards the east.

At Rastenburg airfield, the plane had not even finished taxiing before the black Mercedes pulled up beside it. It was only as Meinhardt descended from the Junkers and a man climbed out of the car, wearing a black-and-silver cuff title with the word Führerhauptquartier, indicating a member of Hitler's private staff, that he finally understood where he was going.

Since then, Meinhardt had been struggling to comprehend the reason for this virtual kidnapping. Although he was able not to show it, he was a nervous wreck and worried that he might faint at any moment.

The Mercedes pulled up outside the largest of the wooden buildings.

The car door was opened by a guard carrying a sub-machine gun.

Meinhardt climbed out, hurriedly buttoning his coat. Directed by the guard, he walked through the open front door of the building, passing a radio room on the left, and made his way down a narrow, low-ceilinged corridor to a conference room at the end of the hall.

As he entered the room, he caught sight of three men, all of whom he recognised immediately from their pictures in the papers and the newsreels. One was Albert Speer, Minister of Armaments and War Production. The second was Field Marshal Wilhelm Keitel, Supreme Commander of the

Wehrmacht, and the third – the only one Meinhardt had actually met before, although only briefly – was General Walter Scheiber, Head of Chemical Industries for the Reich.

Scheiber sprang to his feet. Then, seeing it was Meinhardt, he settled back into his chair. 'Oh, it's only you,' he sighed.

'Hurry up and sit down,' ordered Speer. 'You are late and he will be here any minute.'

'If I may ask, Herr Minister . . .' began Meinhardt.

'You may not!' snapped Keitel. It was cool in the room and Keitel still wore his greatcoat, its lapels faced with the crimson cloth of a general.

Meinhardt felt his bowels clench. He had just reached his chair when there was the soft rustle of footsteps, a side door opened and Adolf Hitler walked into the room.

He wore black wool trousers, sharply creased, and a white shirt with black tie and a double-breasted jacket of cara-mel-coloured cloth. He looked pale, and stooped as he approached the table, carrying a large leather-bound folder tucked under his right arm.

By now, all the men had risen to their feet, filling the room with the scrape and creak of chair legs shunted back across the bare wood floor.

Hitler made no acknowledgement of anyone in the room. It almost seemed as if he thought he was alone. He stood at the head of the table, placed the folder down and opened it. For the next few minutes, he studied the documents inside, his finger-tips balanced on the highly polished surface.

Without moving his head, Meinhardt rolled his eyes around and studied the men in the room. They all looked nervous, even Speer, and it occurred to Meinhardt that perhaps he wasn't the only one in the room who had no idea what he was doing there.

Finally, Hitler spoke. 'Sit,' he told them in a voice barely above a whisper.

There was another shuffling of chairs as the men took their places at the table.

'The purpose of this meeting,' he began, 'is to discuss Germany's readiness to begin poison-gas attacks upon the enemy and whether such attacks should be instigated by the German military or used only as a retaliatory gesture should the Allies use poison gas first.' Only then did he raise his head and look carefully at each man in turn until his gaze came to rest on Otto Meinhardt.

Meinhardt felt Hitler's stare playing like a searchlight across his face.

'You are the man from IG Farben,' said Hitler.

'Yes, mein Führer!' spluttered Meinhardt. He felt as if he ought to leap to his feet again, but managed to restrain himself.

'It is known to me that the Allies possess the agents phosgene, mustard and chlorine.'

'That is correct,' said Meinhardt.

'What I do not know,' continued Hitler, 'is whether they also have in their arsenal any of the new compounds you have invented.'

Instinctively, Meinhardt glanced across at General Scheiber. He had been expressly forbidden from even mentioning the existence of these compounds.

Scheiber's eyes grew round. His lips pressed together. He looked as if he might explode. 'Tell him!' he whispered urgently.

Meinhardt turned to face Hitler again. 'You are referring to tabun and sarin?'

'Yes,' replied Hitler. 'Tell me about these new weapons. What makes them different from the other gases that we currently have at our disposal?'

'As you know,' Meinhardt began, 'the chlorine, phosgene and mustard gases which both we and the Allies possess in significant quantities were all used extensively in the last war. In order to be effective, they must be inhaled or absorbed through the skin. The effect . . .'

'I know all about their effects!' Hitler interrupted angrily, and a sudden silence descended upon the room.

*

It was on 13 October 1918, near Werwicq, south of Ypres, in Belgium, that Corporal Hitler of the 16th Bavarian Reserve Regiment had been injured in a gas attack.

In a hastily dug foxhole, knees tucked up against his chin, he heard the gas shells falling. Unlike regular artillery shells, which exploded in geysers of black smoke, poppy-coloured fire, stone and mud, gas shells made a soft thump as they landed. He had pulled his gas mask from its fluted metal case and put it on, but the mask had been used many times before and he had neglected to replace the charcoal filter. The gas had seeped in and he felt it as a burning in his eyes. His lungs became outlined with pain and each breath felt as if he were swallowing embers. Through the foggy lenses of his gas mask, he watched the tombac silver disc in the centre of his belt buckle, emblazoned with a Bavarian crown and the words 'In Treue Fest', turning grey and then black as the metal reacted with the chlorine gas. In the distance, through the trees, he could just make out the white building known as the Domaine Dalle-Dumont, which had once served as the manor house on the estate where his regiment had dug in. All around him, men writhed coughing in their foxholes. One soldier ran past the corporal's dugout, clutching his throat with one hand. In his other hand, he held his gas mask, its rubberised fabric torn in haste and clumsiness. The corporal recognised the man. His name was Eisen, and he had only recently been posted to the regiment. His heavy, knee-length boots swished through the fallen leaves. The corporal watched him run until he reached the nearby road, the Rue de Linzelles. There, the man stopped and appeared to be looking around.

The corporal wondered what on earth he could be doing there. Did he imagine that help would come so soon? Or at all, in the middle of a gas attack? Help would not come, and even if it did, there would be nothing they could do. Eisen was as good as dead, and he probably knew it.

After a few seconds, the man staggered and fell. His legs moved back and forth, churning the dirt. And then he lay still.

Some hours later, when the gas attack had ended, the corporal saw trucks moving past on the road and men marching without their gas masks. Knowing that gas sometimes collected in the hollows of the ground, he tried to stand. Overcome with nauseating dizziness, he fell back over the edge of his foxhole. His eyes felt as if someone had rubbed salt into them.

Stretcher bearers were making their way through the woods. He could see the white arm bands with the red crosses. He tore off his mask and called out to them.

He was loaded on to a stretcher, then carried to the Rue de Linzelles, where an ambulance was waiting to take them. As the corporal was loaded on board, he glanced down at the road and saw the man who had collapsed during the gas attack. Eisen's skin had turned a jaundiced yellow and his eyes, the whites filled with blood, were wide open. He had been run over several times by trucks coming up and down the road and his body was almost completely flattened.

The corporal did not know how badly he himself had been gassed, and whether he had long to live. As the truck pulled away, heading for the Field Hospital, he glanced back at the remains of the corpse on the road. He felt no pity for the man. Instead, he considered him lucky. He had seen soldiers die in gas attacks before. He knew how long it took, and how painfully their lives were choked out of them. Better to be run over like a dog, he thought, than to cough up your lungs while you're strapped to a hospital bed, and he wondered if he would soon be filled with envy for his former comrade who'd been crushed on the Rue de Linzelles.

*

'What I was trying to explain,' Meinhardt said haltingly, 'was that while chlorine, mustard and phosgene must be inhaled or absorbed through the skin, and have a caustic effect upon the mucous membranes, tabun and sarin react directly with the body's nervous system, inhibiting the function of the enzyme acetylcholinesterase. This has the effect of preventing the function of muscles associated with breathing.'

'So the victims are asphyxiated.'

'Yes, and very quickly,' replied Meinhardt, 'sometimes in only a few minutes, depending on the level of exposure.'

'Is there a difference between tabun and sarin?' asked Hitler.

'In their effectiveness, yes,' answered Meinhardt. 'Sarin is approximately six times more efficient than tabun. Tabun does not vaporise at low temperatures. It also decomposes rapidly, whereas sarin has neither of these drawbacks.'

'And how were these nerve agents discovered?'

'By accident,' replied Meinhardt. 'In 1936, a chemist employed at IG Farben's research facility at Leverkeusen was attempting to produce a synthetic pesticide to destroy weevils in grain. In the course of his research, he discovered an organophosphate compound so toxic that even a tiny exposure left him so sick that he was unable to work for several weeks. The compound, which was initially designated Le-100, was far too poisonous to be marketed as an insecticide, but after the existence of Le-100 had been brought to the attention of the War Office, it was quickly determined that the substance had potential military applications.'

'And does it?' asked Hitler.

'Oh, yes!' replied Meinhardt. 'Extensive tests have been conducted.'

'What kind of tests?'

'Initially on rabbits—' began Meinhardt.

But Hitler cut him off. 'I am not gambling the survival of this country on rabbits!'

'Neither is IG Farben,' Meinhardt tried to reassure him. 'That is why volunteers from the Natzweiler Concentration Camp were exposed to the nerve agent.'

'Volunteers?' asked Hitler.

'They were promised that if they survived the experiments, they would be allowed to go free.'

'And were there any survivors?'

Meinhardt shook his head. 'The results were quite conclusive.'

'This project has a curious name,' said Hitler. 'Sartaman. What does it mean?'

'It is an acronym,' replied Meinhardt, 'from the names of the three compounds we were researching at the time.'

'Three?' Hitler narrowed his eyes. 'But you have only mentioned two.'

'That is correct. Sarin and tabun became the focus of our study after the third compound, known as soman, proved to be unstable. It was most unfortunate, because we had also discovered that soman was many times more lethal than either of the first two compounds.'

'Unstable.' Hitler repeated the word. 'How unstable?'

'We were not able to contain it in the laboratory, resulting in the deaths of half a dozen very valuable technicians. After that, we turned our energies to developing the more reliable compounds.'

'Are you are confident that the Allies have absolutely no idea of the existence of tabun or sarin?'

Once more, Meinhardt glanced across at General Scheiber.

'He is not asking the questions!' snapped Hitler. 'Do you have an answer for me or not?'

Meinhardt cleared his throat. 'Scientific papers were published in the 1930s concerning chemicals involved in nerve-agent production, but this was at a time when it was assumed that such compounds would only be used as insecticides.'

'And who published these papers?'

'We did,' answered Meinhardt. 'Most of them, anyway.'

'And the others?'

'A certain Professor Arbusov of the Soviet School of Organo-phosphorous Chemistry reported on his work in reactionary sequences which are part of the production of sarin. But that was years ago, and we have no evidence to suggest that the Soviets pursued any military applications of the compound.'

'Neither do you have evidence to the contrary.'

Meinhardt paused. 'That is correct.'

'So what you are telling me, in essence, is that the Allies could have developed their own versions of tabun and sarin.'

Suddenly a new voice entered the conversation. It was Speer. For the past few minutes, he had been nervously tapping a pen upon a leather briefcase lying on the table in front of him. 'It is irrelevant,' he announced, 'whether the Russians or the Americans or the British have this weapon.'

For several seconds, Hitler studied his Minister of Armaments, as if trying to decide whether to take offence at the abruptness of his remark. But he seemed to think better of it, and only asked, 'How so?'

'If we deploy one of these compounds against them,' replied Speer, 'no matter how devastating the result, it will only be a matter of time before their scientists have collected samples from the battlefield, brought them back to their chemical warfare facilities and replicated the synthesis.'

'Time,' said Hitler. 'How much time?' He looked across at General Scheiber. 'What do you think? A year? Six months?'

Scheiber breathed out sharply through his nose. 'Something like that.'

'And what do you say to that, Speer?' asked Hitler.

'Two weeks,' Speer replied flatly.

'That is impossible!' shouted General Scheiber, slapping his palm hard against the tabletop.

But Speer was in no mood to back down. 'If I gave Professor Meinhardt a sample today, I am confident that he could have a chemical breakdown ready for me, as well as a synthesis chart, in ten days.'

General Scheiber glared at him.

'Well, Scheiber?' demanded Hitler. 'Is my Minister of Armaments lying to me?'

Scheiber's jaw muscles clenched. He looked as if he was tied to his chair. 'Possibly not,' he muttered.

'With a fully operational facility,' continued Speer, 'the likes of which the Allies are known to possess, they could begin production in under two weeks. So you see, whatever damage we could do to our enemies with this new weapon, would be visited upon us tenfold, and any strategic advantage we had gained would quickly be reversed. So it is settled.' Hitler closed the file laid out before him. Then, without another word, he turned and walked out of the room.

There was a moment of silence.

'I don't understand,' Meinhardt said quietly. 'What is settled? What will happen to the Sartaman Project?'

General Keitel, who had said almost nothing up to this point, breathed out sharply through his nose. 'Nothing,' he answered. 'Nothing will happen. Does he have to spell it out for you?'

One by one, the men rose to their feet.

Meinhardt wondered how he was ever going to get home again, or if he was going home at all.

As if in answer to the question, General Scheiber walked up to him. 'You ride with me,' he said. It did not sound like a request.

The two men left the building and climbed into a waiting Opel staff car. They sat side by side in the back seat. Neither man spoke as they progressed through the various checkpoints until at last they reached the open road again. It was only when they were several kilometres beyond the Rastenburg compound that Scheiber ordered his driver to pull over.

By now, they were on a long, straight, well-paved track, with thick pine forest growing on either side.

'Out!' Scheiber barked at the professor.

It occurred to Meinhardt that perhaps Scheiber intended for him to walk the rest of the way back to Leverkeusen.

But Scheiber climbed out with him.

'With me!' snapped Scheiber. Followed by Meinhardt, the general strode ahead of the car for a minute, so as to be out of the driver's range of hearing. Then he stopped in the middle of the road.

For a moment, there was only the sound of the wind blowing through the tops of the pine trees.

Then General Scheiber spoke. 'Do you realise, Professor, that you have just singlehandedly destroyed the entire chemical weapons programme? Do you have any idea how much money you have cost us? And why didn't you explain to the Führer that we are still attempting to stabilise the soman compound? That might have bought us some time.'

'I didn't tell him that,' said Meinhardt, 'because I am not

going to risk another catastrophe like the one that killed half a dozen of our research assistants!'

It seemed, for a moment, that Scheiber was ready to continue the argument indefinitely. But then the fight seemed to go out of him suddenly, and he let out a long, whistling sigh. 'Fine,' he said. 'Get back to Leverkeusen. Transfer existing stocks of sarin and tabun to the Citadel Armoury at Spandau. Order all production and development to cease immediately. Cancel the Sartaman Project.'

28 February 1945

22 Pitnikov Street, Moscow

Alexander Mikhailovich Kratky, a representative of the People's Court, third class, stepped out of his office after a long day of reading depositions. As he turned to lock the door behind him, he heard someone moving about on the floor above, where Inspector Pekkala kept an office, along with his colleague Major Kirov from the shadowy Bureau of Special Operations.

In spite of the fact that they had been working just one floor apart for a number of years, it was only recently that Kratky had actually encountered the Emerald Eye.

To meet the great Inspector was both the fulfilment of a dream for Kratky, and at the same time completely terrifying. This was, after all, a man so steeped in legend that there were still people who, when Kratky confided to them that he worked in the same building as Pekkala, refused not only to believe that it was true but went on to claim that Pekkala was only a figment of the Tsar's imagination; some mythic creature conjured into being in order to terrify his enemies and perpetuated for that same reason by none other than Comrade Stalin.

For a while, Pekkala had proved to be so elusive that even Kratky had begun to doubt the Inspector's existence. Many times, when he heard footsteps on the landing outside his office, he had rushed to the door and flung it open, only to find himself face to face with Mrs Vedenskaya the cleaning lady, or the tall and rosy-cheeked Major Kirov, who appeared, at least on the surface, a most unlikely colleague for someone as lethal as Pekkala.

On the day he actually met Pekkala, Kratky had been so preoccupied with some important paperwork which had gone missing that, as he left his office, he barely noticed the sound of heavy footsteps coming down the stairs from the fifth floor. Withdrawing the key from the lock, he turned to see a tall figure in a heavy, thigh-length coat step down on to the landing. Even though Kratky didn't know what Pekkala looked like, since no pictures of the man were ever published, he had no doubt that this must be the Emerald Eye.

'Good evening,' said Pekkala. He stood head and shoulders taller than the lawyer.

Kratky spluttered out a greeting.

'You work here, don't you?' asked Pekkala.

The words seemed to bounce off Kratky's face like dried peas. 'I do,' he answered breathlessly, as if confessing to a crime.

For a moment, the two men stood awkwardly at the top of the staircase, waiting to see who would go first.

'Perhaps,' said Pekkala, 'we should both walk down together.'

This they achieved, although there was not really enough room for two men walking side by side.

At first, Kratky had no idea what to say. He had often wondered when and if he would ever cross paths with the Inspector, and he had composed dozens of questions for when that moment came. But now that it had arrived, Kratky's mind became a thrumming emptiness and he could not recall any of the things he'd planned to talk about.

Pekkala, meanwhile, seemed quite content to say nothing at all.

'The food,' Kratky stammered out at last.

Pekkala glanced across at him. 'What food?' he asked.

'The Friday food. The food on Friday.' Even as Kratky struggled to give shape to his thoughts, his mouth filled with saliva at the thought of the wonderful smells of cooking that filled the hallways at the end of every working week. This ritual had been going on for years, but who did the cooking and why had remained a mystery to Kratky.

'That's Major Kirov's tradition,' replied Pekkala.

'Comrade Kirov cooks the food?' Kratky could not believe what he was hearing.

'Oh, yes,' Pekkala assured him. 'The major is an excellent cook. If you are hungry on some Friday afternoon, you should come up. Kirov always makes a little extra.'

Kratky nodded thanks and the two men parted company.

Ever since then, at quitting time on Fridays, Kratky would try to summon the nerve to go upstairs and join the meal, instead of making his way home to the cramped apartment where he lived with his aunt and ageing parents.

And yet, at the last moment, his courage had always failed him. At least, until today. What made things different was the news he'd just received that he was being transferred to an office in far-away Ulyanovsk. If Kratky did not go, the chance would never come again and he knew he would always regret it, even if no one believed him when he told the story afterwards.

There are moments in a person's life when the things he has

achieved, some of which are so small that they seem beyond all reckonable calculation, suddenly come together and he can glimpse, in that rare moment, the triumphs and the failures that have made him who he truly is. For Kratky, this was one of those times, and in that instant he became the master of his fears. Standing first on one leg and then on the other, he rubbed the toes of his shoes against the backs of his calves to polish them up. Then he began to climb the stairs.

The smell of food had not yet drifted down the stairs. Kratky was glad to arrive before the cooking began, because he had brought with him a small bottle of Georgian Mukuzani wine, saved since before the war broke out, with the idea that they could drink it as an aperitif as the meal was being prepared.

The door to Pekkala's office was open.

Kratky stopped at the doorway, cleared his throat to announce his presence and said, 'Hello?'

There was no reply. The room seemed to be empty.

'It's lawyer Kratky from downstairs,' he announced, and, hesitantly, he stuck his head into the room. 'I come by invitation!' added the lawyer, with a formality which seemed to him appropriate for the occasion.

What happened next took place so quickly that the lawyer barely understood the meaning of events.

Kratky saw a large shadow stretch across the floor, and he perceived that it was the shadow of a person. He turned to look and saw, for a fraction of a second, a tall man standing just to the right of the door.

He did not have time to study the stranger's face. In the next instant, he felt something like an electric shock, which seemed to travel from his chin down to his feet and back again. He raised his hand to his throat and, to his terrified amazement, his fingers slipped into a gaping hole which had suddenly appeared in his neck. Kratky heard a roaring in his ears, as if he had been cast into a fast-flowing river. He tried to hold his breath but there was none to hold. The river seemed to flow right through him, its current dragging him down. Soon he was deep beneath the surface and, even in his confusion, it was clear to him that he was never coming back. The last thought Lawyer Kratky had in this world was that he wished he could have told someone about the day he summoned up the courage to have dinner with the great Inspector Pekkala.

8 March 1945

Moscow

Returning from their second trip to Karaganda, Pekkala and Kirov discovered that their office on Pitnikov Street had been sealed off as a crime scene. Multiple strips of red cloth tape were pinned across the doorway, making the place look as it had been wrapped inside a spiderweb.

Kirov called the city police, and it was some time before they were able to gain access to the room.

'The investigation is ongoing,' said the officer who arrived to let them in. He was a young, honest-looking man, tall and thin and freckled, with a shock of short-cropped ginger hair. 'It may still be a few days before you can move back in.'

'This was a robbery, I assume,' said Pekkala.

'I'll let you be the judge of that,' replied the officer, 'but we have been focusing primarily upon the murder.'

'Murder?' asked Kirov, and as he spoke the blood drained from his face. They had arrived such a short time ago that there had not yet been time for him to see Elizaveta. 'Who was murdered?' he shouted. 'For God's sake, tell me!'

The officer pulled out a notebook, and glanced at one of the pages. 'A man named Kratky. Lived downstairs.'

Kirov's breath trailed out. 'I thought . . .'

'What was Kratky doing up here?' asked Pekkala.

'We thought he might be checking on the place, since you've been out of town.'

Kirov shook his head. 'No such arrangement was made.'

'How did he die?' asked Pekkala.

'Had his throat cut,' answered the officer, as he removed the tape, wrapping it carefully around the knuckles of one hand, like a boxer preparing for a fight. Then he opened the door. 'See for yourself,' he said, pointing to a large blood-stain on the floor.

The office had been ransacked. The drawers of the desks had been pulled out and the desks themselves turned over. Books had been swept from the shelf and floorboards prised up in the corners of the room. Even the walls had been gashed open with a knife.

'He must have heard the intruder,' suggested Kirov, 'and come up to see who it was.'

The officer nodded. 'That's probably it.'

'If you'll let us look around,' said Pekkala, 'we should be able to tell you if anything's been taken.'

The officer waved his hand into the room. 'Be my guest, Inspector. I'll wait out here for you.'

'Someone must have been looking for the icon,' Kirov murmured to Pekkala, keeping his voice low so that the officer would not hear. 'Whoever broke in here and killed the lawyer must be the same person who mailed that poison.'

Pekkala continued Kirov's line of thought. 'He knew we would return to Karaganda to investigate Detlev's murder. Then, when we were gone, he'd have no trouble breaking in to steal the icon. The only thing he didn't factor in was that we'd have it with us.'

The two men returned to the hallway.

'Well?' asked the officer.

'Nothing has been taken,' said Pekkala.

The officer looked into the room and shook his head. 'Just some thief trying his luck. The lawyer must have caught him by surprise before he had a chance to rob the place. I'll file my report this evening, Inspector. You should have your office back by tomorrow. Before then,' he smiled sympathetically, 'you might want to find something to cover up that bloodstain on the floor.'

*

'Let me get this straight,' Stalin glared through narrowed eyes at his two visitors. Late-afternoon sunlight filtered in beneath the thick red curtains, which had remained drawn across the windows of Stalin's study. 'I send you to find out what happened to an icon and you return to me with stories of a chemical weapon?'

'That is correct,' said Pekkala.

'And have you identified this substance?' demanded Stalin.

'Samples have been sent to Professor Arbusov at the School of Organophosphorous Chemistry in Sosnogorsk,' explained Kirov. 'You should have the results in a couple of days.'

As Stalin considered this new development, he smoothed out his thick moustache with his thumb and index finger. 'And you believe that the killing of this priest and the break-in at your office might have been carried out by the same person, in order to steal back the icon?'

'That is correct,' answered Pekkala, 'although we have yet to figure out how he came to know that we are in possession of *The Shepherd*.'

'Whoever he is,' said Stalin, 'I doubt we've seen the last of him. I'll send some men to keep an eye on your office, as well as your apartments. In the meantime, find out who would value this old relic so much that they would be prepared to kill for it. *The Shepherd* led this murderer to you. Now let's see if it can lead you back to him. But be quick,' warned Stalin. 'If whoever made this weapon decides to test its full potential, we will need a greater miracle than any icon can provide.'

16 May 1944

Leverkeusen, Germany

Emil Kohl, elder son of Pastor Viktor Kohl and now a professor of organic chemistry at the IG Farben factory, arrived for work only to discover that the door to his laboratory had been padlocked.

After having been dismissed from his studies at the University of Kiev back in 1914, and expelled from Russia along with his family and the other Volga German inhabitants of Rosenheim, Emil had enrolled at the University of Tübingen, where he continued his studies, eventually graduating with a doctorate in science. Even before Emil's graduation, his talents had come to the attention of IG Farben. With his doctoral certificate in hand, Emil immediately travelled to Leverkeusen, where he began his research into industrial pesticides. It was during the process of this research that he stumbled upon the lethal organophosphate compounds which, together, formed the basis of the Sartaman Project.

Baffled by the sight of the padlock on his laboratory door, Emil was directed by a nervous-looking research assistant to a conference room down the hall. There, he found programme director Otto Meinhardt sitting at the large table where their weekly meetings took place. The director looked tired and dishevelled. He had not slept since his unscheduled trip to

Rastenburg and had come straight from the airfield to the factory in order to deliver the news directly to Professor Kohl. Emil's erratic and explosive temper made him notoriously difficult to work with. Since an amount of soman had leaked into a sealed chamber in his laboratory the month before, killing the six research assistants present in the room, all of his remaining colleagues had asked for reassignment. The fact that these requests had been refused, compelling them to continue to work under Professor Kohl, was the only reason that research into stabilising soman had been able to continue at all.

'Sit down,' said Meinhardt. 'I have something to tell you.'

Emil felt his stomach lurch. 'Has there been another accident?' he asked.

Meinhardt shook his head. 'It's over,' he said quietly.

'I don't understand.'

'The Sartaman Project has been terminated.'

Emil laughed. 'Don't be ridiculous! General Scheiber himself gave the order for it to proceed. You may outrank me, Professor Meinhardt, but unless I am mistaken, they haven't made you a general yet.'

'You're right. I don't outrank Scheiber, but Adolf Hitler does.'

The self-satisfied smile vanished from Emil's face. 'What?' he whispered.

'Hitler has cancelled the project. I heard this from him personally, not twenty-four hours ago,' explained Meinhardt. 'If it were my decision, Professor Kohl, you know that this would not be happening.'

Emil said nothing.

'Look,' said Meinhardt, 'I know how you must feel. Believe

me when I say that this is the last thing on earth I wanted to do. But we are only players in this game. We do not make the rules, do we?' He laughed softly at his own attempt at humour, then glanced up at the professor, hoping for some trace of empathy.

But Emil just stared at him.

'Well,' said Meinhardt, looking around the room, as if following the path of a fly. 'We should begin the process of dismantling the Sartaman laboratory. You'll have all the help you need. You'll keep your job, of course. We'll find something else for you to do.'

Emil made no acknowledgement of this. He simply turned and walked out of the room. The truth was, Emil had already passed through the various stages of shock and rage which Meinhardt had expected of him at the meeting and had reached the conclusion that this was part of an elaborate plan, not to destroy his work but only to give the illusion of its destruction.

Ever since Emil began the Sartaman Project, measures had been put in place to conceal the true nature of his work. Soon after the war broke out, IG Farben had learned that some of their most secret information was being passed on to the Russians. In spite of a thorough investigation, which was carried out with the help of Director Meinhardt, the source of the leak was never discovered. As a countermeasure, fabricated documents were prepared, indicating that the Sartaman project was concerned, not with chemical weapons but rather with solvents used in the refining of coal. The bogus reports were then leaked to various low-ranking assistants, with the expectation that some of the information would filter through them to the enemy. Another tactic employed by IG Farben was to place boxes labelled with the names of chemicals that would support the development of coal solvents for pick-up by the municipal waste management at Leverkeusen. Since these garbage collectors were mostly conscripted labourers from France, some of whom were almost certainly working for the Resistance, it was assumed that details of the contents of these boxes would soon be in the hands of Allied intelligence.

This staged meeting between himself and Meinhardt was, Emil felt certain, just another level of this brilliant subterfuge. My conversation with Meinhardt was only a part of the ruse, he told himself. The office is probably bugged and Meinhardt must have known that his words were being transmitted at that very moment through the secret wireless sets of an enemy agent. That explained his nervousness.

Emil did not believe for one moment that Hitler would actually cancel the programme. After the defeats at Stalingrad and Kursk, he knew that Germany could not hope to defeat Russia in a duel of conventional weapons. Only the most drastic and innovative measures could ensure a victory for National Socialism. The obvious solution was the Sartaman Project, and soman in particular. Emil was absolutely certain about that, and he was equally sure that Hitler felt the same way. So why would Hitler pretend to cancel his chemical weapons research? Kohl had the answer for that, too. Word of soman's existence must already have spread to the Allied High Command. Hitler, in his wisdom, had seen beyond this temporary setback. By appearing to shelve the programme, Hitler would put the enemy off-guard, thereby maximising the effects of the chemical weapon when soman was finally deployed upon the battlefield. There was still much to be done.

Meinhardt would undoubtedly have informed Hitler of so-man's lack of stability, but it was a problem Emil knew he could fix, if only he had time to work on it. Although Hitler could not say so, Emil knew that it was the Führer's intention that he should continue his research, until such time as the soman had been perfected and its use on the battlefield was required.

Such is the genius of our leader, thought Emil, and I will not betray his faith in me.

In the days ahead, as his laboratory was systematically pulled to pieces, Emil carefully inventoried each part as it was stored away in splintery crates, the fragile silver-lined glass beakers, pipettes and syringes nestled in beds of fresh hay. Then, when his assistants had gone home, Emil opened the crates and removed those components he felt were necessary for continuing his research, replacing them with other obscure and seldom-used pieces of equipment from the massive store-rooms at IG Farben.

In the basement of his house, only a short bicycle ride from the Leverkeusen facility, Emil reassembled a miniature labor-atory. The tools needed for stabilising the compound were far fewer than had been required at the outset of his research and he had no further need of whiny research assistants. From now on, he would handle things on his own.

When Meinhardt reassigned him to a department special-ising in industrial pesticides, with a focus on producing a less caustic powder for the removal of head lice, Emil did not com-plain. By day, he carried out his duties at Leverkeusen and, by night, he worked in his basement. Meanwhile, Allied bombing raids intensified. The nearby city of Cologne was reduced to rubble. Italy surrendered, and then joined forces with its former enemy. In addition, the Red Army was steadily reclaiming the territory it had lost in 1941.

All this time, Emil waited for the call he knew was coming, which would tell him that he and his creation were needed once again.

He waited a very long time.

8 March 1945

Moscow

'Who in this world values an icon enough to commit murder in order to get his hands on it?' Kirov asked Pekkala as they walked out of the Kremlin after their meeting with Stalin.

'I have an old friend who might be able to answer that,' replied Pekkala. 'He works at the Institute of Religion and Atheism in Leningrad. At least, he used to. I haven't seen or heard from him since the city was besieged back in 1941.'

'Then how do you know if he is even still alive?' asked Kirov.

'I don't,' answered Pekkala.

While Kirov returned home to his wife with the unwelcome news that they would now be guarded around the clock, Pekkala climbed aboard a cargo plane loaded with medical supplies bound for Leningrad.

Arriving at an airfield constructed by the German army during their encirclement of the city, which had lasted more than two years and cost the lives of over two million Russian civilians, Pekkala hopped a ride into town. The truck dropped him off on the Nevsky Prospekt. From there, it was only a short walk to the Institute, located in the former Cathedral of Kazan.

He walked across what had once been a green expanse of lawn and was now only a cratered sea of mud. Two long colonnades that extended from the building seemed to Pekkala like the arms of a giant, slowly enveloping him as he approached.

The original blue dome of the cathedral had been painted grey so as not to attract the attention of bombers raiding the city during the siege, and tents of hessian netting, interwoven with scraps of cloth, still obscured the building's profile from above.

At the Institute, Pekkala soon found the man he was looking for.

Anton Antokolvsky, Director of the Museum, was a frail-looking man with sloping shoulders, a little round chin and eyes so startlingly blue that they seemed like the eyes of a doll. Before the Revolution, Antokolvsky had worked as a teacher of religious studies at the small Tsarskoye Selo school, established by the Tsar for the education of children whose parents worked on the royal estate. It seemed a strange twist of fate for a teacher of religion to have ended up as director of a museum devoted to atheism, but Antokolvsky was not the first person he had known to survive the Revolution by transforming themselves into the inverted image of what they'd been before.

It had been years since they'd last met, but Antokolvsky had not forgotten his old friend, and the two men shook hands as they stood in what had once been the nave of the cathedral.

Pekkala had not visited the building since it had been converted into the Institute of Religion and Atheism back in 1932. The last time he'd set foot in here, the place was still a church. The Institute, with its garish posters mocking the existence of an afterlife and illustrated Bibles placed open under glass like the cracked chests of autopsy cadavers, only seemed to show

how the Russian people had traded one faith, one god and one promise of salvation for another. Beneath this veil of cynicism, however, the building still held all the silent dignity of the purpose for which it had originally been built.

'What brings you here?' Antokolvsky wondered aloud. 'Glad as I am to see you, Inspector, this does not seem the kind of place to take your fancy.'

After explaining that *The Shepherd* had been found – a fact which astonished Antokolvsky – Pekkala went on to what he had seen at Karaganda, including the horrific scars on the priest.

'It sounds like he might have been Skoptsy,' remarked Antokolvsky, when Pekkala had finished the story.

'Who?' asked Pekkala.

'Not who,' answered Antokolvsky. 'What. The Skoptsy were a sect which became active in the Orel region during the second half of the eighteenth century. During the early 1700s,' he explained, 'Peter the Great instituted a number of reforms of the Orthodox Church. These changes, which might appear to you or me to be so slight as to be almost irrelevant, such as whether to cross yourself with three fingers or only two, nevertheless created a division between those who were prepared to accept the revisions and those who were not. The people who clung to their traditions became known as the Old Believers. Many of them retreated to the forests of Siberia, rather than submit to the Tsar's will. But the Tsar pursued them, even into the most remote regions of Siberia, and whole villages were slaughtered, all over a few quibbles in the way that people prayed to God.'

'Did all of them perish?' asked Pekkala.

'No,' replied Antokolvsky. 'No matter how many soldiers he sent across the Taiga, Tsar Peter could not find them all. Instead, he declared that, since the Old Believers had fled to Siberia, they should from that moment on consider themselves to be exiled there forever. When Catherine the Great came to the throne, the persecution of the Old Believers was set aside and, in 1905, on the orders of Nicholas II, they were officially freed from their exile. By then, many of the Old Believers had splintered into different groups, as alien to each other as they were to the people who had consigned them to the wilderness. Eventually, some of the survivors began to make their way back into Russian society, although often in secret because, although they were no longer persecuted by the state, they remained outcasts from Russian society, who considered them to be radicals, who had twisted the meaning of the Church in order to suit their own corrupted vision of the world. People were both suspicious and afraid of them, and sometimes with good reason. Among these groups of outcasts were the Khlysty, the Molokans, the Dykobars, but none were as controversial as the Skoptsy.'

'And you say that Father Detlev was a Skoptsy?'

'I say he might have been,' answered Antokolvsky, 'given what you've told me, Inspector. The Skoptsy surfaced during the late 1700s, in a time of great terror and uncertainty in Russia. A plague had swept through Moscow, killing tens of thousands, and the revolt by Pugachev had been ruthlessly suppressed, killing thousands more. The Skoptsy, under their leader Kondratii Selivanov, believed that these were signs of a fast-approaching Day of Judgement, in which only those who stood on the right hand of God would be saved, leaving everyone else to be cast down into Hell.'

'That sounds like the story of *The Shepherd*,' remarked Pekkala.

'Certainly!' exclaimed Antokolvsky. 'The Skoptsy considered that icon to be humanity's most sacred conduit to God and themselves as the lambs of God, whose sacrifice would purify the world. In imitation of this, and to prove the intensity of their faith, the Skoptsy sought to cleanse themselves with their own blood. Their goal was absolute spiritual purity, casting out the beast within themselves, which could be attained only through ritual castration. Within the Skoptsy, there were two levels of commitment. The first was known as the Minor Seal, and involved only partial removal. The second, known as the Major Seal, is what this Father Detlev had endured.'

'So was it only men . . . ?' began Pekkala.

'Oh, no,' Antokolvsky interrupted. 'The women, too, were subjected to the ritual, sometimes along with their children, if they had any at the time they joined the sect.'

Pekkala let his breath trail out, trying to keep his mind clear of the horror these self-scarred people brought into his mind. There had been times, during the course of investigations, when he had, even against his will, formed a certain empathy for even the most savage of deeds, but what these Skoptsy had done to each other in the name of worship was beyond his ability to grasp. 'Surely,' he whispered, 'they could not have kept this secret.'

'That is correct,' said Antokolvsky. 'Unlike the Khlysty or the Molokans, who bear no outward signs of their religion, the mutilations carried out by the Skoptsy often caused changes in their complexions and their facial structures.'

'What kind of changes?' asked Pekkala.

'It was said that their eyes became glassy and lifeless, and that their skin grew unnaturally soft and pale.'

'Like wax,' said Pekkala, remembering the face of the man who had attacked him with the butcher's knife in the alley behind the Gosciny Dvor. 'But Father Detlev's complexion was not unusual.'

'It all depends on when the operation was performed,' explained Antokolvsky. 'If the individual had already reached adulthood by the time the ritual was performed, the side effects were not as noticeable. Whatever the outward signs, the extremity of their methods could not stay hidden forever, and even the more tolerant views of Catherine the Great could not support such acts of mutilation. On Catherine's orders, the Holy Synod of the Orthodox Church conducted an inquiry and it was determined that the Skoptsy were not criminal, only misguided. The Church believed that these people had, by castrating themselves, doomed their own faith to extinction. As a result, only the leaders of the movement were punished, with floggings and exile to Siberia.'

'And Catherine the Great thought that would be the end of them?' asked Pekkala.

'She did, but she was wrong. The Skoptsy order clung to life for another hundred years, until they were finally run to ground by the Bolsheviks. It is said that Dzerzhinsky himself killed the last of them, back in the winter of 1922, but judging from this priest you found, they may not have been extinct, after all.'

The two men stepped out into the shelter of the colonnade.

'I was surprised to learn,' said Pekkala, 'that a former man of God was working here.'

Antokolvsky smiled. 'Between you and me, old friend, my faith is still alive and well.'

'So the Skoptsy are not the only ones to have gone into hiding.'

'We all wear masks, Inspector, and what better place for me to wear my own than here in this temple of the unbelievers? The existence of the Institute is the only reason they have not torn this cathedral to the ground. You and I may never live to see it, but this place will be a church again some day. You mark my words, Inspector.'

'Does it not worry you,' asked Pekkala, 'that those who might come here to pray will never realise which side you fought for?'

'If the price of my faith is to be damned by the very people whose church I helped to save, then I am prepared to pay it. I think you'll find the same was true for Father Detlev.'

'But how did Rasputin know where to find him?' Pekkala wondered aloud. 'Unless perhaps their meeting was only a coincidence.'

'I doubt that very much,' replied Antokolvsky. 'Rasputin was well known to have had dealings with the Khlysty, a sect closely allied to the Skoptsy.'

Pekkala knew about these accusations, which had first been levelled at Rasputin by Sofia Tyutcheva, a governess to the daughters of the Tsar. Although Rasputin denied membership of the cult, he could not deny his dealings with its adherents, nor the fact that many of his own teachings echoed the Khlysty beliefs.

'The Khlysty,' continued Antokolvsky, 'were outlawed, just like their Skoptsy cousins. There is no doubt that members of these groups often turned to each other for mutual support. Knowing the Skoptsy's obsession with *The Shepherd*, Rasputin could easily have used it to broker a deal between them and the Tsarina.'

'But why choose them?' asked Pekkala.

'What better guides across the murky frontiers of that war,' replied Antokolvsky, 'than those who had spent centuries living in the shadows, especially when they could be bought with something other than money?'

'And why would they have murdered Father Detlev, as it now seems increasingly likely that they did? Why kill such a harmless old man who was, after all, one of their own?'

'Remember you are dealing with people for whom secrecy has been the only guarantee of survival. Detlev told you his story. Unwittingly or not, he put you on the trail that led you here. That may have been enough to seal his fate.'

'And mine, as well, perhaps,' added Pekkala, 'if I don't find the man who killed him.'

'Be careful,' warned Antokolvsky. 'The Skoptsy creed is written in blood.'

'That is a lesson I have already been taught,' said Pekkala, tracing a finger across the old scar on his forehead.

11 March 1945

Karaganda Prison

Warder First Class Turkov selected a brass key from the dozens he kept on a large iron ring. Inserting the key into a battered metal door, he stepped into a musty, darkened room and locked himself inside.

Feeling around in the blackness, he located the light switch. Three powerful bulbs crackled into life, illuminating the dreary chamber. The room had a tall ceiling and no windows. It had once been the power plant, whose massive, wood-fired boiler heated the entire prison, but the camp's engineers had replaced it with a number of smaller boilers and wood stoves, which heated separate buildings at Karaganda.

Although the room still smelled of smoke and engine oil, the place had been converted, a number of years ago, into a place of execution.

A large grid-iron scaffold had been erected in the centre of the room. A narrow staircase climbed up to a platform roughly three times the height of a man above the ground. On the platform was a bar from which the noose would be suspended. There was also a large lever, reaching up from the base of the platform to the height of a man's waist. At the moment of execution, the bar would be pulled back, opening a trapdoor through which the prisoner would fall to his death.

The prison only carried out about three executions a year, for punishments such as killing a fellow inmate, grievous injury to a guard, or a third attempt at escape. The executioner, Carl Levitsky, a precise and humourless man with a bald head and bushy grey eyebrows, took a solemn pride in his profession.

At first, Turkov had kept his distance from Levitsky, convinced that only the most twisted of minds could follow such a calling.

As time passed, however, Turkov began to appreciate the skill and precision that the executioner brought to his work. The night before a man was to be hanged, Levitsky would come to the isolation cell where the condemned was fed his last meal. Sliding back a peephole in the door, he would judge the man's weight and height and only then would he construct the noose. Levitsky's aim was to cause a minimum of suffering to those whom he dispatched from this world. For this, he had compiled charts showing exactly how far a man had to fall in order to cleanly sever the third vertebra, killing the condemned man instantly. If the rope was too long, the drop could sever the man's head from his body. Too short, and a man could take minutes to die.

As Turkov watched the executioner go about his work, he came to understand that Levitsky's attention to detail served to cause a minimum of suffering to those he dispatched from this world and his original revulsion for the man transformed into a kind of awe.

Levitsky knew nothing of this, because Turkov rarely spoke to him. In the beginning, Turkov had been too disgusted to make the man's acquaintance and now he was simply too humbled.

It was required that a warder be present beside Levitsky when the executions were carried out, to assist in unbolting the floor if the drop handle should ever fail. The bolts could be drawn back very quickly, but it was a two-man job and, although the drop handle had never failed, Levitsky insisted on the presence of a warder at his side, just in case.

The role of executioner's assistant was not a popular one at Karaganda, mostly because executions took place on the stroke of midnight, but Turkov often volunteered for the job.

His fellow guards considered him a morbid follower of death, but Turkov never saw it that way. To him, it was a privilege to watch such a master at work.

A hanging had been scheduled for that night, and this time the Chief Warder had not even asked for volunteers. He had simply appointed Turkov.

The man due to be hanged was an embezzler named Klebnikov. The money he had stolen from the State Tobacco Monopoly was never recovered. Klebnikov claimed that it had all been gambled away, but from the first day he arrived at Karaganda, rumours began to circulate that the embezzler Klebnikov had hidden it somewhere. Some prisoners became fixated on the idea that he still had access to a fortune. With petty bribes, they attempted to draw his secret out of him, and when that did not work, they tried to frighten him into giving it up. Eventually, inevitably as far as Turkov was concerned, the death threats began to emerge. Fearing for his life, Klebnikov decided to act first. With a knife fashioned out of a tiny triangle of metal from a used tin can, which was then fitted into the wooden stem of a broken toothbrush, Klebnikov murdered a fellow prisoner by jamming the blade into the man's throat and severing the carotid artery. His pleas of self-defence were met with stony silence by the members of the prison tribunal, and a date of execution was set.

As Levitsky's assistant, Turkov's job was to arrive before the execution, make sure that everything was in order, and test that the drop door was functioning correctly. It was now 11.15 p.m.

Turkov made his way up the metal stairs to the scaffold platform.

The rope was already in place, fitted to an iron ring attached to a bar above his head. Turkov paused to admire the craftsmanship of the noose, its lower edge fitted with a piece of leather, so that the rough hemp did not cut into the dead man's skin.

It was very quiet.

Turkov stepped on to the drop door, his hands trembling at the thought that it might give way suddenly and send him falling to the floor, which would certainly break both his legs.

The bow of the noose hung directly in front of his face. Next to him was the metal lever for releasing the drop door, the paint worn from its handle.

Turkov leaned forward, resting the underside of his chin upon the leather padding.

This is the last thing they see, he thought, before the hood goes on. He remembered the way the black cloth billowed as the person gasped for breath, and the medicinal smell of the alcohol the prisoner had been given to drink just before he entered the execution chamber. The prisoner would be handed a green enamelled tin mug, of the type in use in every government-run institution in the country. It was filled with what appeared to be vodka, and indeed about a third of the drink was vodka, but the rest of it was some concoction of

Levitsky's own invention, containing rubbing alcohol, embalming fluid and surgical anaesthetic. The effect on the prisoner was stupefying. By the time they reached the stairs, some of the condemned had to be carried to the rope.

Some thought it was a cruel joke to play upon a man, to serve him such a revolting cocktail as his traditional last drink.

As far as Turkov was concerned, however, it was yet another sign of Levitsky's humanity. He wondered if they ever knew, these men condemned to death, how lucky they were to be shepherded out of existence by such a compassionate soul.

Turkov settled the noose around his neck.

'So this is how it feels,' he muttered to himself, and he felt a sudden urge to ease his conscience of the burden it had carried for so long. It is secrets that weigh a man down, he thought, when the time comes to rise up from his shackling of bones.

For Turkov, there was only one.

When he was five years old, his father had joined the Skoptsy, and submitted to the full measure of castration as a gesture of his faith. The Skoptsy priest had then re-sharpened his knife in preparation for doing the same thing to the son. But the father had refused, saying that the boy could decide in his own time what path he intended to follow.

The stigma of completeness followed Turkov through his youth and into manhood. He was on the verge of being thrown out of the Skoptsy when a delegation of elders approached him with an offer of salvation. He could forgo the operation, they said, and remain among the chosen on the condition that he became a warder at the Karaganda Prison.

A man was there, they explained. One of their own. And this man needed a protector.

'What crime has he committed?' asked Turkov.

'None at all,' they told him. 'In fact, this man, a certain Father Detlev, has been sent to Karaganda as a test of his own faith.'

'I don't understand,' said Turkov.

'You don't need to,' they replied, and went on to explain that Turkov would, as a warder at the prison, keep watch over Father Detlev, until such time, and it might only be a matter of months, as he would be released.

'And this is all you want of me?' he asked.

'Just see that no harm comes to him,' they told Turkov, 'for as long as he stays behind bars. You cannot tell him who you are. He must not know you're watching over him. Then they gave him an address in Moscow, of someone he had never heard of before, named Anatoly Argamak, and told him to write to Argamak if anything out of the ordinary occurred.

Turkov applied to become a member of the prison staff and was accepted. He never knew what bribe, blackmail or debt had cleared his path, but he was soon on his way to Karaganda.

And he had been there ever since.

Months turned into years, and Detlev was never released. Turkov, whose anger at the course his life had taken initially found its voice in the daily brutality which made him a legend at the prison, began, in time, to realise that this was not a place to which he had been sentenced like the convicts. This was, in fact, exactly where he belonged.

A thousand times, Turkov almost blurted out the truth to Father Detlev, but in the end he kept his peace. Better to live in the lie, he told himself. It made life easier to bear.

In all that time, he heard nothing from the men who had

sent him to Karaganda, or from anyone else among the Skoptsy. Once, back in the 1920s, he had overheard a conversation between two of the senior guards about the numerous sects, the Skoptsy among them, that had been hunted down by agents of Internal Security and exterminated. But there was nothing in the papers about it, and Turkov did not dare to ask the guards about their sources, for fear of giving himself away. He began to wonder if he and Father Detlev might be the last of their kind. Even though Turkov could not understand why the old priest seemed to resent the many small kindnesses he had been shown over the years, still the guard felt a sacred bond with Detlev and he never wavered in his task of making sure that no harm came to him.

On the same day Inspector Pekkala and the major from Special Operations visited the prison, Turkov sat down and wrote to Anatoly Argamak in Moscow, informing him of the Inspector's visit. It was the first time he had ever written. Until that day, there had never been anything worth mentioning. The address was so old by now that he wondered if anyone would even be there to read it on the other end, but he still paid the extra money to have it sent by priority mail.

When it became clear that Father Detlev had been killed by the contents of the package sent from Moscow, and that the package had not come from Pekkala, as he had first believed, Turkov realised that his letter must indeed have been read and the reply had cost Detlev his life.

For this, Turkov blamed only himself. After years of watching over the old man, he had inadvertently set in motion the events which caused his death. The fact that he had not known what he was doing offered him no consolation, and he guessed that it would not be long before Inspector Pekkala realised that someone at the prison had tipped off the outside world about his visit.

What justice should a man choose for himself, wondered Turkov, when he knows that if he hesitates, the world will choose it for him?

A little over half an hour later, when the embezzler Klebnikov was led, kicking and spitting, into the place of execution, the small procession of guards, condemned and executioner stopped in their tracks and stared in amazement at the body of Warder First Class Turkov, his third vertebra neatly severed, hanging from the leather-bound rope.

12 March 1945

22 Pitnikov Street, Moscow

By the time Pekkala returned from Leningrad, the police had allowed Kirov back into their office and Elizaveta had found a carpet to cover up the bloodstain on the floor.

While Kirov fired up the samovar, sprinkling into it some of his last, precious reserves of pine-smoked tea, Pekkala told them what he had learned in his talk with Antokolvsky. 'The first thing we need to do,' he explained, 'is to find out about Cheka operations against the Skoptsy. Dzerzhinsky believed that they had been wiped out but, as we now know, that appears to be far from the truth.' Turning to Elizaveta, he asked, 'Do you think you can find us Dzerzhinsky's report at the Lubyanka record office?'

'You won't find it at Lubyanka,' she answered.

'Why not?' asked Kirov.

'Cheka files were moved to Archive 17 years ago,' continued Elizaveta. 'That's where you'd find them now. But what you're looking for are not ordinary Cheka files. Cases handled personally by Dzerzhinsky were kept among his private documents. Access to those requires special clearance. The Archive director himself must apply to the Kremlin for permission to release them. It could take weeks, or months.'

'We don't have time for that,' muttered Pekkala. 'We are

looking for a murderer who seems to know a great deal more about us than we presently know about him. We need those files from the Archive and we need them now.'

'Archive 17,' Kirov groaned and let his head fall back against the tired stuffing of his chair. 'Even if that's where they are, good luck trying to find them! Ever since Vosnovsky took over, it has been impossible to get anything out of that place.'

After the death of its previous director at the hands of one of Stalin's own assassins, control of the Archive had been handed to a small and energetic man named Alexander Vosnovsky.

Before the Revolution, Vosnovsky had served as a railway conductor on the short carriage line between Petrograd and the Tsar's estate at Tsarskoye Selo. In his immaculate blue uniform, with its double row of silver buttons, each one emblazoned with the double-headed eagle of the Romanovs, Vosnovsky had been the ruler of this tiny and efficient universe. He would stride back and forth between the two carriages that made up the train singing loudly and passionately from his favourite operas. Mussorgsky. Tchaikovsky. Rimsky-Korsakov. He seemed to know them all and he sang them so well that there were people who travelled on that train simply to hear the man perform.

At stations along the way, Vosnovsky would step down on to the platform, haul a large watch from his vest pocket and wait for the precise second before blowing two short blasts on a nickel-plated whistle. He would then produce a small red flag, which he would raise above his head to show the conductor he could depart. Then he would bring the flag down with a sharp, jerking motion, the fabric snapping smartly as it descended.

Vosnovsky tolerated no delays. Old ladies tottering into the station at the last minute, and old men gimping on bunioned feet, in spite of all their pleading, would be left in a cloud of steam as they hobbled out on to the platform.

There had been many late nights when Pekkala had fallen asleep while riding the train back from Petrograd to his cottage at Tsarskoye Selo. Vosnovsky was always there. He never seemed to take a day off. For a man who appeared to have so little patience for the failings of the human race, it was with surprising gentleness that he would rest his hand upon Pekkala's shoulder, shaking him awake when it was time for the Inspector to depart.

The Revolution swept away Vosnovsky's career. All that remained of those days was his watch, which he still carried on its heavy chain, but the former conductor had lost none of his bearing, and still carried himself as proudly as he had ever done before. There was a certain symmetry between his old life and the new one he had found for himself as the sole living inhabitant of Archive 17. He had quickly established himself as nearly impossible to work with. Anyone arriving at the Archive without the necessary authorisations, of which there seemed to be an infinite and ever-changing variety, was sent packing regardless of their rank. The cruel harmony Vosnovsky had achieved in the clockwork running of the railroad belonged here, too, in this place devoted to the cold undreaming logic of the archivist.

'You must be the one to go to Vosnovsky, Inspector,' pleaded Kirov. 'You're a friend from the old days, after all.'

'I would not call us friends,' replied Pekkala, 'but I think Vosnovsky can be persuaded to help us, with or without the necessary clearance.'

'Then you will go?' Kirov asked hopefully.

'No,' Pekkala answered flatly.

Kirov threw up his hands. 'Then what hope is there of getting to Dzerzhinsky's private files?'

'Our hope,' answered Pekkala, nodded to Elizaveta, 'is sitting over there.'

Kirov turned and stared at his wife. 'I hadn't thought of that,' he said.

'Me?' gasped Elizaveta. 'Oh, no, please don't send me. What possible sway could I have with that horrible little man?'

'The swaying of your hips, perhaps,' replied Kirov. 'I think that's what Pekkala has in mind.'

'I only meant . . .' began Pekkala.

'Yes,' she interrupted indignantly. 'What exactly do you mean?'

Pekkala shrugged and rolled his eyes.

Now Elizaveta turned to Kirov. 'Aren't you going to say anything? You can't really expect me to go in there and deal with Vosnovsky simply because I'm a woman.'

'Better you than me,' replied Kirov.

'Fine!' snapped Elizaveta as she rose to her feet. 'I'll go, but you will owe me for this.' She looked from one man to the other. 'Both of you!'

*

The door to Archive 17 was a huge sheet of metal, painted battleship grey and scarred with strange dimpled impressions, like the skim on a cup of boiled milk. There was no window in the door; only a steel plate which slid back and forth like the gap through which food was passed to a prisoner in his cell.

Elizaveta knocked, but her fist made almost no sound against the steel. She tried again, and with the same effect. Why couldn't they have a bell? she wondered as she stood back and looked at the building, hoping to see some sign of life behind its windows. But the windows were so high up, well above her head, that there was no hope of spotting anyone. It looked dark inside, and there was no sign of any light.

Elizaveta puffed out a sigh and was about to turn and head for home when she thought about what her husband would say if she came home empty-handed. And Pekkala. What would he say? Probably nothing, she thought, and that would make it even worse.

Then she noticed several large stones lying in the cobbled street outside the archive building. There were no stones anywhere else, and it took her a moment to realise that these rocks were the explanation for the unusual dents made in the door. People, like herself, who had failed to make themselves heard with their pounding on the door had instead pelted the metal with these rocks in order to attract attention.

Elizaveta felt a moment of solidarity with those anonymous visitors who had gone before her as she picked up a stone, marched over to the door and began to hammer against it.

Before she had a chance to really get to work, the door opened a crack, and a small, fierce-looking man with a thick black moustache peered at her from the darkness.

It was the infamous Vosnovsky. 'I could have you arrested for that,' said the little man.

'By all means do!' exclaimed the woman. 'And may I suggest

you put through your call to my husband, Major Kirov of Special Operations.'

'Titles don't scare me,' muttered Vosnovsky.

'Then call Pekkala,' she told him, 'and talk to him instead!'

Vosnovsky blinked, as if she had just blown dust into his face. 'You know the Inspector?'

'He is the one who sent me here.' Elizaveta felt vaguely disgusted with herself to be dropping the name of a man whose presence she could barely tolerate, and yet it was also curiously satisfying to see that it produced an effect.

'And am I correct,' Vosnovsky asked, a note of hesitation in his voice, 'that Pekkala still works only on the direct orders of Comrade Stalin?'

Elizaveta only smiled by way of answer.

'What is it you want?' inquired Vosnovsky.

Elizaveta handed over the file request, which had been correctly filled out on NKVD stationery and was countersigned, in arterial-red ink, by Sergeant Lyudmila Gatkina, Elizaveta's superior at the Lubyanka records office.

'Dzerzhinsky's private files!' exclaimed Vosnovsky. 'Well, it's a good thing you have come with such impeccable credentials. Otherwise I would have sent you packing!' With those words, he stood aside to let her pass.

The first thing Elizaveta saw when she walked into the building was a huge, bronze hand, held palm up as if waiting for giant raindrops. As her eyes grew accustomed to the gloom, she saw more pieces of statuary, scattered about among rows of filing cabinets. Headless men in tall riding boots. A horse, saddled but without a rider. A bare-headed man, down on one knee, his hands clasped together in prayer.

Vosnovsky stopped beside a tall, black filing cabinet. After a few minutes of combing through the files it contained, he removed an envelope, its edges frayed and faded. 'Here it is,' he told her. 'Dzerzhinsky's operation against the Skoptsy. I don't think anyone has looked at this since it was filed away in 1922.' He carried it over to a table, withdrew the documents one by one and laid them out, overlapping like the blades of a lady's fan.

Together, they began to go through the file.

Elizaveta soon found what she was looking for. She held up the fragile piece of paper, which had been written in Dzerzhinsky's own hand.

'According to the Cheka leader,' she said, 'the last Skoptsy to be liquidated was a man named Stefan Kohl. It says here that he came from one of the German families that immigrated to the Volga region in the 1770s. When the Great War broke out, the Kohl family was deported to the village of Ahlborn in Germany, but their youngest child, Stefan, did not go with them. Against the wishes of his parents, Kohl joined a Skoptsy pilgrim who was returning to his home in Siberia.'

'And what became of him?' asked Vosnovsky.

Elizaveta paused while she read. 'Several years later, he turned up in a village called Markha, a settlement founded by the Skoptsy when they were first exiled to the wilderness, back in the 1700s. Dzerzhinsky states here that Kohl was the leader of a group of men who ambushed a carload of Cheka agents who were on their way to Markha, hacking them to death with axes. By the time the Cheka office in Irkutsk learned of the massacre, Kohl and the others who had taken part in the attacks had already fled. That's why Dzerzhinsky took over his case. Avenging those deaths became a personal matter for him. One by one, he tracked them down until only Stefan Kohl remained.' A moment of silence followed as Elizaveta attempted to decipher a paragraph of Dzerzhinsky's spidery handwriting. 'Subject shot while attempting to escape across lake. Body not recovered. Returned to Kazan. File closed.'

17 June 1921

Markha, Siberia

News of the Cheka's approach reached the Skoptsy village only a few hours before the agents were due to arrive.

In the minds of the inhabitants, there could be only one reason for this visit – the whereabouts of their sacred icon had somehow reached the ears of Bolsheviks.

In the deal arranged by Rasputin, the Skoptsy had agreed to transport a delegation of Russian dignitaries to a secret meeting with their German counterparts, in order to begin preliminary peace negotiations between the two countries. After living for generations as outcasts from society, there was scarcely a back road in the country that the Skoptsy did not know. In exchange, the Tsarina Alexandra agreed to relinquish *The Shepherd*.

Obtaining the icon had long been a dream of the Skoptsy, and Rasputin had guessed correctly that there was nothing they would not do to get their hands on it.

For the task of smuggling these men through the battle lines, the Skoptsy elders chose a newcomer among their ranks: a man who spoke both Russian and German and was equally at home in either culture.

His name was Stefan Kohl.

In July of 1915, he set out in a carriage through the Austrian lines, bearing his cargo of Russian diplomats and generals. Even though the dignitaries ordered him to turn back before they reached their destination, the Tsarina held up her end of the bargain. At a rendezvous on the Potsuleyev Bridge in Petrograd, Stefan received the icon from Father Detlev, another Skoptsy whom Rasputin had involved in the plot. Before he had a chance to leave the city, however, Stefan received word from Rasputin that the Tsar's personal investigator, the Emerald Eye, was already in pursuit of the lost icon.

Fearing that he would never make it out of Petrograd with Pekkala on his trail, Stefan followed the Emerald Eye and attacked him in the alley behind the Gosciny Dvor, nearly losing his life in the process. That same day, he boarded the Siberian Express train, eventually reaching Markha, the last remaining Skoptsy settlement, where he delivered the icon to the elders of the village.

To many of these elders, it had been a mistake to bargain with Rasputin for possession of the icon, however much they wished to possess it. The Tsarina's plan to make the world believe that *The Shepherd* had been destroyed could not last forever. Sooner or later, blame would fall upon the Skoptsy for the icon's disappearance. Now, with Cheka agents on their way from Irkutsk, it seemed as if their worst fears were coming true.

A council was hurriedly called by the leader of the village, a jowly man named Istvan Kor, to decide what might be done to save the icon. The meeting soon deteriorated into a loud and bitter argument. Some were for leaving it where it was now, hidden in a secret chamber dug deep into the permafrost beneath their own church here in Markha. Others voted to destroy the icon, knowing that the Bolsheviks had already begun selling the country's priceless relics at auction houses in London, New York and Paris, in order to bankroll their revolution. Better to have it vanish from the earth, they said, than for it to hang as a trophy on some banker's parlour wall.

'Or we could stop them!' shouted Stefan Kohl.

His voice plunged them all into silence.

The old men turned to glare at him.

Kohl stood with his back against the wall of the dimly lit room where the meeting was being held, defiantly returning their stares.

If it had been anyone else speaking that way before the elders, he would have been silenced with an angry shout. But they respected Kohl. Or rather, they feared him. He was famous for his physical strength. It was known that he could kill a horse with a single punch, and could butcher a steer to pieces in a matter of minutes with the long knife he always carried with him.

'Yes, you could stop them, perhaps,' said a man in a heavy wool coat. His name was Nikolai Latkin. He was one of the oldest members of the settlement, and spent his whole life in terror of the world beyond the boundaries of his village. 'But what about the ones who come after?' he demanded. 'And the ones who come after that? You know they will keep coming until we have been banished from the earth.'

'Then are we to live on bended knees forever?' shouted Kohl, looking from one man to the next.

'Before God, yes,' replied Lutukin.

'And everyone else, so it seems,' Kohl snapped back.

Now another man spoke up. His name was Pavel Zelenin. He had deep-set eyes and a wild crop of hair which bunched

242

at the side of his head, like the leafy branches of a tree which had grown on a windy hill. Twenty years before, he had given up his practice as an accountant in Rostov and headed east to seek a better life among the Skoptsy. Arriving at the village to plead his case, Zelenin had omitted to inform the elders that his exit from Rostov had been precipitated by the discovery that he was about to be investigated for tax evasion. Secretly, he worried that this visit from the Cheka might have nothing to do with the icon but was, in fact, to arrest him for his crimes. In his paranoia, Zelenin suspected that there were people in this room who knew of his past, and who would gladly sacrifice him to the Cheka in order to save their own skins. 'Why should we listen to you?' he asked Stefan Kohl, hoping to steer attention away from himself. 'You have only been here seven years. You are practically a stranger among us.'

Kohl turned and fixed Zelenin with a stare. 'And in those seven years, I have done more for this village than you have done in twenty. I have earned my place here and the right to speak my mind to men like you, Zelenin.'

'What you have said is true,' said Anatoli Bolotov, the pilgrim who had brought Stefan to Markha. In the years since his return, he had gone blind and his eyes were like the meat of hard-boiled eggs. 'We may soon need to choose between the icon and our lives,' continued Bolotov. 'For centuries, the Skoptsy have survived without the presence of *The Shepherd* among us, but what use is the icon to the Skoptsy if none of us are here to worship it?'

This was not the first time Kohl's volatile nature brought him into conflict with the elders and Bolotov had spoken out in his defence. In return, Kohl had shown the old man many kindnesses, even fashioning for him a walking stick, with a top made from the polished ball of a deer's femur bone. Although he never said so, there were times when Bolotov wondered if he had made the right choice bringing Stefan Kohl to Markha. Originally, he had hoped to bring new life and energy into this last outpost of their faith. Instead, he realised now, he had unwittingly welcomed into their midst a man who would never submit to the random acts of violence which had always been dealt out to the Skoptsy when outsiders came knocking at their doors. In his willingness to trade outrage for outrage, regardless of how outnumbered he was, Stefan Kohl had failed to grasp one of the absolute truths behind the Skoptsy faith – that they could not win this fight to which they had been challenged by the world. The best they could do was survive it.

Through all of this, Istvan Kor had said nothing at all. Now, at last, he spoke. 'There is no need for blood,' he told the gathering. Then, turning to Kohl, he said, 'Go to the road beyond the village. Take whatever men you need. Cut down some trees and block the way. That will stop the Cheka for a while. It is already late in the day. They will not spend the night out here alone and they will not continue on foot. They will have to turn back and by the time they return, if they return at all, we will have made the right decision, instead of one come to in haste.'

Kohl did not wait for the approval of the others. He dashed from the room, rounded up a dozen of his friends and set out in a cart. An hour's ride from the village there was a sharp bend in the road where a small, plank bridge crossed a stream known locally as Beggar's Brook. Here, they stopped. Kohl and his men piled off the wagon, axes in their hands, ready to fashion a barricade and then retreat back to the town.

But before the first tree had even fallen, they heard the sound of an approaching car.

It was the men of the Cheka, riding in a battered Opel saloon which had once belonged to the Ekaterinburg merchant named Ipatiev, in the basement of whose house the Romanovs had been shot and stabbed to death.

After hours of nothing but forest, and still some distance from the village, the six Cheka men were stunned to find a group of men clustered in the road. The driver, moving at speed around the sharp bend, lost control of the car, which swerved and rolled upside down into the weed-choked stream. The four passengers who survived the crash jumped out, some with blood streaming down their faces from the shattered windscreen glass. These men drew their weapons and began firing wildly at the strangers. Two Skoptsy men fell dead.

For Kohl, the axe still in his hand, there was now no choice about what had to be done. In the ensuing fight the remaining Cheka agents were massacred.

The following morning, a second detachment of Cheka arrived at Beggar's Brook and discovered the Opel saloon still upside down in the stream. It had not rained in the night and the road was still splashed with blood from the fighting of the day before. The bodies were gone, hastily buried in shallow graves not a stone's throw from the road. The Cheka did not wait around to search for them. Instead, they sped back to their headquarters in Irkutsk and reported their findings to Dzerzhinsky. The Cheka leader immediately declared war upon the Skoptsy, and personally set out to punish those who were responsible for the deaths of his agents.

By then, Kohl and the other men who had taken part in

the massacre were already fleeing for their lives. Pursued by the Cheka, some lasted only weeks, hauled from carts and river barges on which they'd begged for transport. These men were executed on the spot, and the ears were cut from their heads as the proof of their deaths, a ritual which Dzerzhinsky himself practised on those whom he had liquidated.

Others reached the cities of Tobolsk, Tyumen and Zlatoust, where the Skoptsy had always been met with suspicion. One by one, they were betrayed to informants, who collected rewards for their capture.

By January of 1922, only Stefan Kohl was left.

Returning to the office on Pitnikov Street from her visit to Archive 17, Elizaveta found her husband and Pekkala leaning up against the window, each of them armed with a pair of binoculars and peering down into the street. Their elbows rested on the windowsill, its multicoloured layers of paint chipped away in many places so that it resembled a map of a different world.

'What about that one?' asked Kirov.

'That's one of Stalin's people,' exclaimed Pekkala. 'He's been watching this place for the past two days.'

'That one then! I've seen him before.'

'That's your driver Zolkin!' Pekkala scolded the major. 'Have you even got those things in focus?'

Leaving their binoculars upon the windowsill, the two men slumped down in their chairs.

'He must have known that he would only get one chance to steal back the icon,' said Pekkala, rubbing his tired eyes.

'In which case,' added Kirov, 'he must be far from here by now.'

'But where did he go?' Pekkala wondered aloud.

'I think I can help you with that,' said Elizaveta. Neither of the men had heard her coming up the stairs and now they turned, startled by her presence.

'Did you make it to the Archive?' asked Kirov.

'I did,' she told him, 'and what is more, I found Comrade Vosnovsky quite cooperative once I told him who had sent me.'

Kirov rose up from his chair and embraced her. 'My darling, you are as talented as you are beautiful!'

'I told you she could do it,' Pekkala announced with satisfaction. 'I never doubted for a second.'

In spite of Elizaveta's frequent and bewildered irritation with this man, she felt herself blushing with pride at Pekkala's faith in her success.

Now she told them what she had learned. 'The Skoptsy were wiped out, at least according to Dzerzhinsky. I saw it written in his own hand. And the last of them was Stefan Kohl, whose family was deported to a village called Ahlborn in Germany just before the outbreak of the war in 1914.'

'Ahlborn!' said Pekkala. 'That's where they found the icon.'

'Well, whoever brought it there,' said Kirov, 'it couldn't have been Stefan Kohl. According to Dzerzhinsky, he died out in Siberia.'

'But what if Dzerzhinsky was wrong?' asked Pekkala, and as he spoke, he turned to Elizaveta. 'Was Kohl's body ever recovered?'

'As a matter of fact, it was not,' she admitted.

'Then maybe Kohl is alive, after all,' said Kirov. 'But how could Dzerzhinsky have made such a mistake?'

2 January 1922

Near the village of Markha, Siberia

The bullet fired from Dzerzhinsky's broom-handle Mauser smashed into Stefan's right shoulder blade, throwing him face down into the thin layer of snow which covered the half-frozen lake.

He felt the cold on his face, but there was no pain – only a blurred, thrumming sensation as he drifted into shock.

Feebly, he tried to get up, but his arms wouldn't work. Turning his head to one side so he could breathe, he gazed with dream-like detachment out across the lake, towards the grey-brown haze of trees on the horizon. Some time later, he heard a car door slam and then the sound of its motor as Dzerzhinsky sped away up the road, bound for Cheka headquarters in Irkutsk.

In the time that followed – whether it was seconds, minutes or hours, Stefan had no idea – the profound silence of that winter's evening settled on him. A terrible emptiness yawned open in his mind as he realised that the world was already moving on without him, relentless and uncaring. So this is what death feels like, thought Stefan; to understand how little you really matter to the universe.

The next thing he knew, he was lying on his back, looking up at the stars. He was choking. His throat felt as if it was on fire. He sat up and retched and, in that moment, he realised that he wasn't alone.

An old woman squatted in the snow beside him. The shawl which she had pulled about her face was crusted with ice from the freezing condensation of her breath.

She held something out towards his face. 'Again!' she said, and a metal cup clinked against his teeth.

The fire blazed again inside his throat and now he tasted it – homemade alcohol of the type known as *samahonka*, flavoured with the buds of birch trees gathered in the summertime.

Once, more, he retched.

'Keep it down, damn you!' the old woman commanded. 'It's no use poured out in the snow.'

She tried to pour another dose into Stefan's mouth.

He pushed her hand away. 'Enough,' he gasped.

'Good!' said the woman. 'At least you can talk. Now, can you walk or do we have to drag you off the ice?'

'We?' he asked.

As if in answer to his question, a dog appeared from behind him. It was a huge Malamute and wore the rawhide leather traces of a sledge. The wolf-like animal panted in his face and then slapped him across the mouth with its warm and slimy tongue.

He knew this animal. Its name was Demetrius, and it belonged to Yuliya Belyakina, the ancient woman who crouched before him now. She lived at the edge of the Samarsk Lake, which was one of many tributaries of the mighty Lena River. Beyond it, almost hidden in the forest, lay the settlement of Markha.

By the time Dzerzhinsky caught up with Kohl, he had been on the run for many months. After learning the fate of the others who had been with him that day they attacked the Cheka agents, Kohl returned to Markha, gambling that this was the one place where no one would expect him to go.

Unknown to Stefan, he had been spotted as he passed through Irkutsk, on his way into the wilderness which surrounded the old Skoptsy village, and it was Dzerzhinsky himself who drove out to settle the score. Only an hour's walk from the settlement, the Cheka leader caught up with the young Volga German.

Yuliya Belyakina, the Skoptsy woman who found Kohl half frozen on the lake, had never lived in Markha. Her husband had once kept pigs, which supplied the village with fresh meat. When he died, Belyakina sold the pigs and stayed on at the remote dwelling, preferring to remain separate from the community, yet still a member of it.

Belyakina had been out checking her rabbit traps when she heard a shot echo across the lake. She waited until it was dark, and the temperature had dropped below freezing, before venturing out on to the ice to investigate the reason for the gunfire.

When she came across Stefan, lying face down in the snow, he was the first person she had seen in months.

She heaved the injured man on to her sledge, which had been cut by her late husband from a single piece of wood. Then, with the help of her dog, she hauled Kohl back to her cabin.

That night, with a pair of long-nosed pliers normally reserved for removing fish hooks from the gullets of the pike and perch she caught in the lake, Belyakina pulled the bullet from Stefan's shoulder.

At the time, Stefan was still suffering from hypothermia and so dazed that he was barely aware of what took place. 'I must get to the village,' he told Belyakina. 'I must tell them what happened.'

'They know,' she replied, swabbing his head with a damp cloth. 'Go when you are feeling better.'

'Perhaps you're right,' he said.

Slowly, his wounds began to heal. In time, the nightmares faded. The only thing that never left him was that peculiar sensation of emptiness, which he had felt when he was lying in the snow. It was as if, for a moment, a curtain had been drawn back and he had glimpsed something normally too vast and horrifying to be held within the scaffolding of human thought – the terrible obliviousness of the universe to the fate of everything contained within it.

The spring thaw came, and with it the season of mud. The ice in the rivers broke up with a sound like cannon fire. Birds began to reappear. The world turned green again.

'Come with me,' Belyakina said one day. 'It is time that we went to the village.'

Stefan followed her along a series of winding trails until they arrived at Markha.

And suddenly Stefan understood why Belyakina had been in no hurry to bring him to the village.

Markha was gone.

The place had been burned to the ground. Only blackened chimneys remained, like sentinels guarding the places where the houses had once stood.

'I couldn't tell you,' explained Belyakina, 'not until you were strong enough, and then I knew you'd have to see it for yourself.'

It was three days after the murder of the Cheka men that soldiers had arrived from Irkutsk, bringing with them half a dozen trucks, and orders to obliterate the village. The elderly were shot. The animals were shot. Anyone who showed resistance was also shot. Shouting through a bull horn, an officer ordered the survivors to climb aboard the vehicles while, one by one, the houses were set on fire. While the town burned, barrel loads of salt were scattered on the small and tidy plots where cucumbers, turnips, beets and potatoes had been planted. Before they left, the soldiers heaped the bodies of the dead into a pile and burned them, too.

Belyakina's house, being at some distance from the village and hidden away among the trees, was not discovered. She had stood in her doorway, watching flames light up the evening sky and, later, she heard the trucks departing.

Belyakina waited until the sky above the village was no longer darkened by smoke. Then she went into the village, carrying a shovel, and buried the fire-splintered bones of the dead among the dust of ash and salt.

Within a week, those who had been taken prisoner were sent to labour in the goldmines at Kolyma, where life expectancy was less than one month. Some lasted longer than that, but eventually all of them perished.

Speechless, Stefan wandered among the ruins. In a heap of charred timbers, he found the remains of the walking stick he had made for Bolotov after the old man went blind. As he surveyed the destruction, he felt a rage building in his mind which he knew he would never be able to control.

He walked back to where Belyakina waited for him on the dead and salted earth.

'What has become of the icon?' he asked. Until that day, he had thought it was still safely hidden in the church at Markha.

Beluyakina did not speak, but only reached out and took hold of his arm.

In silence, they walked back to her house.

When they arrived, Belyakina went over to her bed, knelt down and pulled from under it a flat, rectangular object wrapped in cloth. 'On the day you left to block the road, Istvan Kor came here and gave this to me for safekeeping.'

'And you hid it under your bed?' Stefan asked incredulously. 'Did you really think it would be safe there?'

'You've been in this house for weeks and never thought to look,' replied Belyakina.

'Thank God the Cheka didn't find it!' exclaimed Stefan.

'As it turns out,' said the woman, 'they weren't even looking for the icon.'

The news stunned him. 'Then why were they coming to Markha?'

'To investigate rumours of grain hoarding.'

'Do you mean to say that all of this could have been avoided?'

'Perhaps.' The old woman shrugged. 'But who knows? They might have found it anyway. What's done is done.'

'And what do you intend to do with *The Shepherd*?' asked Stefan. 'Are you just going to put it back under your bed?'

'No,' she answered, handing him the icon. 'I am giving it to you.'

It had been a long time since Stefan had set eyes on *The Shepherd*. Now, as he carefully removed the cloth, the bright blues and greens and whites of the painting seemed to jump from the flat surface and to shimmer in the air, illuminated by the dim glow of the fat-burning lamps Belyakina used to light the cabin.

'What you hold in your hands,' said Belyakina, 'is all that remains of our world. If *The Shepherd* is destroyed, then so are we. From this moment on, whether you like it or not, you are the keeper of our faith.'

'I will be more than that,' he told her. 'I'll make the people of this country pay for what they did to us.'

'Be patient,' cautioned Belyakina. 'Now is not the time for vengeance. When that day comes, you will know it. In the meantime, you must leave this place. Soon the roads will be passable again. Hunters will come to the woods and fishermen to the lake. It is only a matter of time before one of them spots you and the Cheka learn that you aren't dead after all. Go, and take *The Shepherd* with you.'

'But where?' asked Stefan. 'There's no one left out there who I can turn to.'

'There may still be someone,' said Belyakina. She tottered on stiff legs to the window and removed an old book from its resting place upon the sill. It was a cookbook, with a publication date of 1890. The lettering that had been stamped upon its cover had all but faded away, leaving only a faint glint of the embossing, like a sprinkle of gold dust. Belyakina shook the book upside down, and a piece of paper fell out. Written on one side was a recipe for baked carp.

'Light that candle,' she told Stefan, nodding at a stump of wax upon her bedside table.

Stefan did as he was told.

Belyakina held the sheet above the candle, so that the glow

of the flame showed as a yellow ball through the paper. As the seconds passed, a curious brown stain began to slither across the back of the page, as if worms were crawling through it from the other side.

'There,' said Belyakina, handing him the document. 'That is where you're going.'

Stefan took the page, still warm from the candle, and saw, in the brown letters, the name of a man, Anatoly Argamak, and an address somewhere in Moscow.

'How did you do this?' asked Stefan. 'How did these letters appear?'

'It is an ink made from a mixture of alum powder and vinegar,' she explained, 'which is used for pickling fruits and vegetables. Copies of all our sacred prayers were written down this way, in books too insignificant for men like the Cheka, or the Okhrana before them, to examine. Of course, no one imagined that they would burn the whole village to the ground.'

'And who is this man Argamak?' asked Stefan.

'One of us.'

'There is a Skoptsy commune in Moscow?'

She laughed at him. 'If that were true, it wouldn't be there long. No, Argamak lives on his own and when you meet him, you'll know why. In the past, members of our faith who were wanted by the law could go to him and he would take them in. If anyone can help you now, it's Argamak.' Then she fetched out a handful of coins from a hole in her mattress. 'You may as well have these. They're no use to me any more.'

'But Moscow?' argued Stefan. 'That city is crawling with Bolshevik agents! It won't take five minutes for them to spot me.'

'They won't be looking for you,' answered Belyakina. 'As far as they're concerned, you're lying at the bottom of a lake.'

The next day, pulling a cart which had belonged to Belyakina's husband, Stefan set off towards the west. One week later, he arrived on the outskirts of Irkutsk, where he bought a horse with the money Belyakina had given him.

In the months ahead, when Stefan's money ran out, he would hire himself out as a butcher, the only trade he knew, until he had earned enough to move on.

One thing Stefan learned in his travels was that the less people knew about the world, the more certain they were that they alone deserved dominion over it. He learned to hide his true identity, far away inside himself, and to become, at least on the surface, precisely what people expected him to be. Like a wandering magician, he mastered the art of concealment. He wore a constantly changing mask which caused people to remark, even at their first meeting with him, that it was as if they'd always known him.

Sometimes, when Stefan found himself alone, out on the steppe near Penza, or resting in a field of young sunflowers on the road to Arzamas, or camped out in the bulrushes on the banks of the River Bug, he would take the icon from its hiding place beneath the seat of his cart and stare and stare at it until the colours and the figures seemed to flow together into something that was not of this earth.

On 30 October 1922, six months after setting out from Markha, Stefan finally arrived in Moscow.

There, he found Argamak working as a gravedigger at the Kalitnikowska Cemetery, not far from Lenin Station.

Argamak was a short, moon-bellied man with a bull neck

and fleshy lips. He wore mud-plastered boots and coarse wool trousers patched with leather at the seat and on the knees. His grey shirt, on which the dried sweat showed as hazy blooms of salt, had come untucked. He gave the impression of a man so disgusted with mankind that he could barely acknowledge his own membership among the human race, and so preferred to live among the dead.

Argamak stood by himself in the middle of the cemetery, surrounded by headstones in various states of disrepair. He was in the process of filling in a grave when Stefan approached him, cap in hand, and asked for a moment of his time.

'What do you want?' demanded Argamak, as Stefan stood before him in the rags of his worn-out clothes. 'Only the dead are welcome in my cemetery.'

'I am from the settlement at Markha,'

'Never heard of it,' snapped Argamak.

'I am one of your brothers,' said Stefan.

'I have no brothers,' replied Argamak, 'only a sister and she is uglier even than you!'

Having come all this distance, only to be turned away by the very man he'd come to find, Stefan felt his last reserves of energy crumbling away. 'Belyakina,' he whispered, 'what have you done to me?' He turned to leave, but he had only gone a few paces before Argamak spoke to him again.

'Did you say Belyakina?'

Stefan turned. 'I did. Yuliya Belyakina sent me here.'

Argamak leaned on his shovel, its blade sinking into the freshly dug earth. 'Why should I believe a word you say?' he asked, but now his tone was more cautious than belligerent.

'I will show you,' replied Stefan.

He led Argamak to his cart, lifted the package out from under the seat and carefully unwrapped the picture.

Argamak gasped when *The Shepherd* slid into view. For a while, he only stared at the icon. Then he turned slowly to Stefan. 'Come with me,' he said quietly, as if afraid that even the graves might be listening.

He brought Stefan to a hut at the edge of the cemetery, where it bordered the Skotoprogonaya Road. Stefan tied up his horse behind the hut, against which pieces of old headstones, broken and indecipherable, leaned like huge extracted teeth.

Inside was a small, wood-burning stove, a few chairs and a table made from coffin planks.

Argamak put a fresh log in the stove, and gestured for Stefan to sit.

'Will I be safe here?' asked Stefan.

'Yes, but not for long,' replied Argamak. 'Where are you headed from here?'

'From here?' replied Stefan. 'But this was my destination!'

Argamak slowly shook his head. 'I can shelter you for a day, two days maybe. But no more.' He gestured around the cramped space of the hut. 'This isn't a hotel, as you can see.'

'Then I am done for,' Stefan muttered.

'At times like this,' said Argamak, 'people should turn to their own flesh and blood.'

'My father disowned me when I became a Skoptsy,' Stefan remarked flatly. 'As far as he's concerned, I no longer exist.'

'And you have heard from your family recently?'

'Well, no . . .' admitted Stefan.

'Then how do you know they have not been regretting what happened between you ever since the day you left their house?'

'I don't know. Not exactly.'

'Then you don't know at all!' growled Argamak. 'Whatever happens in a family, no child is ever forgotten by the ones who gave them life.'

'Are you saying I should throw myself on their mercy?'

'I am asking if you think you have a choice.'

'It is a long way to travel on nothing more than faith.'

'Faith got you this far, didn't it?' asked Argamak. 'And as for how you'll get there, I think I can help you a little.' He walked over to one of the bare wooden beams which formed the ceiling, reached up and fetched something down. It was a small leather bag, which he tossed into Stefan's lap.

Stefan emptied out the bag into his hand, and a dozen rings tumbled into his palm. Most of them were gold. Some had diamonds fitted on them, others a mixture of rubies, emeralds and sapphires. 'Where did these come from?'

'From people who don't need them any more,' replied Argamak.

It took Stefan a moment to understand the meaning of his words. 'You mean you stole these from the dead before you buried them?'

'The dead do not care how they are dressed,' said Argamak. 'It is the sentimentality of the living that slid those rings on the fingers of their loved ones. And once they said goodbye, that chapter of their life was closed. The rings had served their purpose. What use are they to anyone if they are buried in the ground? You may not like where I got them, but ask yourself if you can afford to turn your back on what you know you will need to survive.'

'Very well,' Stefan said quietly, as he poured the rings back into the bag. He spent that night lying on a horse blanket in front of the iron stove. He listened to the soft roar of the logs as they burned in the grate, and the wheezy breaths of Argamak, who slept in a camp bed nearby.

The next morning, when he woke, Argamak had already left for work. A slice of cheese, hardened and glassy at the corners, lay on a piece of black bread on the stove, along with a lukewarm cup of tea.

Stefan ate the food, put on his coat and went out to his wagon.

By the end of that day, he had crossed the Moskva River, passed through the Zamoskvorechye district south of the city and moved out into the countryside beyond. All through that autumn, Stefan travelled west. He never stayed long in one place but pushed on, as restless as the wind. He had no idea what to expect when he reached Ahlborn. He wasn't even sure if his family still lived there and, even if they did, he had no way of knowing if they would welcome him or turn him away once again.

On a freezing January morning in 1923, Stefan Kohl crossed into Germany.

One week later he had almost reached the village of Ahlborn when his cart broke down in a snowstorm.

A passing rider stopped to help. Beneath the man's black winter coat, he wore the habit of a Lutheran pastor.

It was his father, Viktor Kohl, returning from a visit to a local parishioner who had been too sick to come to church.

For a moment, the two men just stood and faced each other, the snow falling thickly around them.

As the seconds passed, and the cold worked its way beneath

the layers of his clothing, Stefan began to wonder what madness had driven him to travel so far when part of him had always known how little chance there was of finding refuge.

But then the father spread his arms and embraced his son, whom he had thought he'd never see again. The guilt of having driven out his youngest child had never left him. He had even made a pilgrimage to Lourdes, to beg the Virgin for the return of his son, returning with a single bottle of holy water, which he kept in anticipation that his prayers might one day be heard. Now, as his son stood before him, the father saw the workings of a miracle in giving him a chance to set things right.

There, in the middle of that storm, the two men made their peace. They agreed never to speak of the things that had driven them apart. From this moment onwards, Kohl knew that the harmony between them would be balanced on the lie of his silence.

He learned that his mother had died soon after their arrival in Ahlborn, never having recovered from the trauma of being evicted from her home and then transported like livestock to a country she had never known except in stories passed down over the generations.

Stefan also learned that there would be no mending of the rift between him and his brother. When Emil, now living far away in Leverkeusen and busy with his work at IG Farben, received word from his father that Stefan had returned he could scarcely believe that his brother had their father's blessing to remain in Ahlborn. As far as Emil was concerned, it was Stefan's departure, and not the shock of deportation, that had caused their mother's untimely death.

In pleading letters, Viktor Kohl begged Emil to return and

reconcile with his brother. Anxiously, he awaited a response from Tübingen, but no letters ever came. Viktor Kohl had traded one son for another and, in his own mind, he had no one to blame but himself.

Stefan found employment as a butcher. In addition, he dug graves, repaired the leaking roof and tended to his father's ailing health. Both men worked hard to make up for the time they had lost.

Weeks became months, which carried over into years, and there were times when it seemed to Stefan Kohl as if he had always been there, in Ahlborn, and the life he'd lived before held no more substance than the gauzy fabric of a dream.

But the scars of Skoptsy ritual would always remind him of the truth.

From time to time, Kohl would check the icon's hiding place, tucked away among the rafters of his house. He did not know where else to keep the painting and he worried constantly about its safety. Crouched in the attic, he would unwrap the oilcloth covering, stare by candlelight at the image of the Shepherd, and remember how it had felt to be standing in the ruins of Markha. Then the rage which never slept would fill his mind again. Belyakina had warned him to be patient. The time would come for vengeance.

Back in the office on Pitnikov Street, Kirov and Pekkala were planning their next move.

Having learned from Elizaveta that Stefan Kohl might still be alive, they now realised who they were up against. For the first time, they held the advantage, and they knew they would have to act quickly if they were to have any hope of keeping it.

'Are you suggesting,' asked Kirov, 'that we travel all the way to Ahlborn, simply because that's where the icon was located?'

'I believe we'll find Stefan Kohl there,' replied Pekkala.

'But why?'

'Because that's where he thinks we will go.'

'You mean he *wants* us to find him?'

'Yes,' answered Pekkala, 'because he knows that we still have the icon, and we know that he has come into possession of a chemical weapon which, at all costs, we must prevent him from using again.'

'Even if it means giving up the icon?'

'Yes,' said Pekkala. 'Sacred though it may be, it is not worth another human life, let alone the thousands it might cost if we hold on to it.'

'And you think that Stefan Kohl will be prepared to make a trade?'

'I think he would do anything to get the icon back.'

'If that is true,' said Elizaveta, 'then why doesn't he simply show up at our door?'

'Because, having tried and failed to steal it, Kohl has lost the advantage of surprise. If Kohl shows his face again in Moscow, he will find himself surrounded and with no means of escape. He will never get out of Moscow alive. I think he has gone back to Ahlborn, because it is the only chance he has left to meet us on his own terms.'

'You mean he can set a trap for us,' said Kirov. 'Surely you don't expect us to walk right into it?'

'As long as we still have *The Shepherd*, we are safe.'

'You sound as if you believe in the mystical powers of that icon, after all,' remarked Elizaveta.

'There's nothing mystical about it,' answered Pekkala. 'If he tries to harm us, he might destroy the icon in the process. That's not a risk he's going to take.'

Kirov saw there was no arguing with Pekkala's logic. 'I'll call the Kremlin and let Stalin know about Kohl,' he said as he picked up the telephone. 'I'll also see if Poskrebychev can arrange for transport to Ahlborn. That place must be pretty close to the front line by now. I assume you'll want to leave right away, Inspector.'

'We should have left hours ago,' replied Pekkala.

A few minutes later, Kirov hung up the phone. 'Poskrebychev says that the Fascists have established a defensive line twenty kilometres to the west of Ahlborn. As of now, there are no reports of enemy troops in the vicinity, but the area is still patrolled by German fighter planes, which have shot down several Russian aircraft. This means that we will have to go by road. Poskrebychev has arranged for military transport to take us there, so Zolkin will have to sit this one out.'

'And the agents Stalin posted outside our building?' asked Pekkala.

'They are being withdrawn as we speak,' replied Kirov. 'Comrade Stalin wants to see us before we leave,' he added. 'The Boss has some news and, according to Poskrebychev, we are not going to like it.'

Down at Zolkin's garage, Kirov told their driver that he would be staying home.

In spite of his earlier complaints about the condition of the Emka, Zolkin took the news hard. 'But what am I to do while you are gone?'

'Look after Elizaveta,' answered Kirov. 'You'll do that, won't you, Zolkin?'

At first, Zolkin seemed too surprised to speak, but he quickly returned to his senses. 'Why, of course!' stammered the driver. 'I'll guard her with my life, Comrade Major.'

Kirov slapped him gently on the shoulder. 'I expected nothing less.'

While they waited for the transport to arrive, Pekkala remembered that he had left something behind. Excusing himself, he made his way up the five flights of stairs. Back in the office, he walked over to the mantelpiece, where he had placed the atropine given to him by Dr Tuxen at the Karaganda morgue. Carefully, he tucked the bulky syringes into his pocket. Although Pekkala hoped they'd never have to use the antidote he knew that sooner or later, for radicals like Stefan Kohl, dying made more sense than living. If the Skoptsy chose to make a martyr of himself, he and Kirov might well be the ones he chose to take with him to oblivion.

Shortly afterwards, a Russian Army GAZ-67 staff car arrived to pick up Kirov and Pekkala, and the two men were driven to the Kremlin for their meeting with Stalin.

'The results are back from the laboratory at Sosnogorsk,' he told them. 'I'm afraid the news is worse than we thought. What killed the prisoner Detlev is a substance they have never seen before. They're calling it,' Stalin snatched up the report and read from it directly, ' "an organophosphate compound of profound toxicity". According to them, this stuff is many times more lethal than any of the poison gases used during the last war.'

'Do they have any idea where it might have come from?'

Stalin shook his head. 'To our knowledge, the only company engaged in work on organophosphates was IG Farben, in Germany. Fortunately, we have an informant at the laboratory; a man named Otto Meinhardt, who has been keeping us informed of their work. Thanks to Meinhardt, in spite of IG Farben's attempts to conceal their true intentions behind a bogus programme for developing coal solvents, we learned that they were, in fact, engaged in the production of chemical weapons. At least they were until Hitler gave the order to cancel the project, which was code-named Sartaman. It was shut down last year and Meinhardt saw to it personally that the Sartaman laboratory was dismantled, the samples destroyed or quarantined and all development terminated. According to Meinhardt, the weapon which killed Detlev should not exist. It was known as soman, but it was never put into production because IG Farben was never able to stabilise it.'

'So what we must conclude,' continued Pekkala, 'is that

somebody managed to stabilise the compound after all.' Stalin slumped back in his chair. 'That appears to be the case.'

'But if not by IG Farben then by whom?' asked Kirov.

'According to Meinhardt, the only person who might have been able to stabilise the compound is the scientist who created it.'

'And who is that?' asked Pekkala.

'Professor Emil Kohl.'

'Kohl?' repeated Kirov.

'I thought that might sound familiar to you,' remarked Stalin. 'It did not become significant until we learned from you today that the man you might be looking for in connection with the icon has the same last name. We immediately contacted Meinhardt to find out if there was any connection. He confirmed that the two men are, in fact, brothers although Meinhardt says they have been bitter enemies ever since Stefan joined the Skoptsy.'

'And where is Professor Kohl now?' asked Pekkala.

'We don't know,' Stalin confessed. 'Emil Kohl has disappeared, and we must assume that he is in possession of the weapon he invented. That's how his brother got hold of it.'

'The two of them must be working together,' said Pekkala. 'The question is why, since, by all accounts, they hate each other.'

'War forges strange alliances,' said Stalin, 'and whatever the reason for this one, you must find a way to stop the Kohl brothers. Together, they have formed a lethal alliance. One of those men has a Doomsday prophecy and the other has a weapon that could make it a reality.'

One morning in January of 1945, Professor Emil Kohl received two letters. Both were postmarked Ahlborn, dated two weeks apart and written by different people.

The first was from his father, saying that he had been taken ill and once more pleading for a visit from his older son.

The second letter, this one written by Stefan, was an announcement of the death of Viktor Kohl and the date set for his burial. There was no request for Emil to attend, Stefan having assumed that it was hopeless even to ask.

So it caught the younger brother by surprise when, on the day of the funeral, Emil showed up at his door.

'I am not here for you,' were the first words out of Emil's mouth.

Even though the brothers had grown apart with the passage of time, they had also grown more similar in appearance. Their thinning hair had been cropped short and both men looked rounder in the chest. Once-prominent cheekbones were now hidden by the fullness of their age. In addition, each brother had independently adopted the curious habit of not looking directly at a person when speaking to them.

But if it caught either one by surprise to come face to face with this blurred reflection of himself, he made no mention of it.

Although Emil and Stefan stood side by side at the service, neither one talked to the other. They sang, they knelt, they prayed and they shook hands with a long line of parishioners, but it was as if each man stood alone. It had become a test of wills, to see who could cling longest to the silence that enveloped them. Only after they had accompanied their father's coffin down into the crypt did they finally begin to talk.

It was Stefan who spoke first. 'I can't undo what's done,' he said.

Without a moment's hesitation, Emil rounded on his brother. 'No you can't!' he shouted, 'and even if you spent the rest of your life begging for forgiveness, the pain you've caused could never be undone.'

'I will not apologise,' said Stefan. 'I have nothing to apologise for, least of all to you.'

'Nothing?' Emil demanded angrily, his voice echoing about the crypt, where the new pine of their father's coffin seemed to glow in the light of the paraffin lanterns used to light the space. 'You left me to clean up the mess you made of this family when you wandered off to join that monstrous cult. Even back at school in Krasnoyar, the pressure was on me to live up to our parents' expectations. You had it easy. They expected nothing from you.'

Stefan tried to reason with his brother. 'There's no point in blaming each other for the different ways in which our parents treated us. They are gone now. All we have left is each other, and if we could just sit down and talk . . .'

'You would not want to hear the things I have to say,' Emil interrupted.

'Maybe not,' replied Stefan, 'but I would rather hear them

now than get to the end of my life knowing we might have come to terms and chose instead to wallow in our pride.'

'It's too late,' said Emil.

'No!' Stefan told him. 'As long as we draw breath, it will never be too late, and I will always be here to help you if I can.'

That evening, the brothers walked the two kilometres to the railway station in the nearby town of Kottonforst. In the cool evening air, they stood on the platform and shared a cigarette. The burning tip glowed poppy red as each man inhaled the smoke, before passing it back to the other.

Before long, the train arrived, belching steam and clanking to a stop.

Two soldiers, home on leave, disembarked. One had made his way from Italy, still wearing the faded sandy-olive cuff title of his service in the Afrika Korps. Another man, bundled in the grey leather coat of a U-boat commander, wandered back and forth along the platform, softly calling the name of his wife.

'Remember what I said,' said Stefan, as his brother climbed aboard the train.

That night, fearing an imminent Soviet assault upon the town, German troops arrived in Ahlborn and ordered the villagers to evacuate. Those who could not walk were piled on to trucks. The rest escaped on foot. Before he joined the stream of refugees, Stefan Kohl returned to the crypt, prised open his father's coffin and placed the icon, still wrapped in its protective cloth, between the dead man's hands. It was the only place where he felt sure that the *The Shepherd* would be safe. 'You owe me that much,' Stefan whispered to his father's corpse, before he nailed the coffin shut again.

Only a few days after returning to the laboratory in his house at Leverkeusen, Emil completed his work on stabilising the soman compound.

All this time, Emil had been waiting for a call, perhaps from Hitler himself, informing him that he was needed. Now he began to realise that the call was never going to come, that he had been the victim of a hoax, and that this hoax had been his own invention. The dismantling of the IG Farben lab had not been a ruse after all. Hitler had never intended for him to keep the Sartaman Project alive, and the fact that he had done so, in spite of a direct order from the highest authority in the Reich, would virtually guarantee him a death sentence, if ever his work was discovered.

Emil's mind see-sawed between the fear that he might, at any time, find himself under arrest, and the dismay that the true potential of his discoveries had not been appreciated, after all.

This left him with very few options. He could go to Meinhardt, explain his mistake and hope that they showed him some mercy. Or he could destroy all the work he had done on his own and hope no one ever found out.

Neither one of these seemed very promising.

It wasn't long before a third option took shape, one that would allow him not only to save his own life but the Sartaman Project as well.

His own country had turned its back on him. That much seemed perfectly clear. And their ignorance would cost them dearly.

The only course of action now, Emil decided, was to turn himself over to the Allies. There, he had no doubt, his achievements would be properly recognised.

The only question was how.

Before the war, Emil had kept in touch with numerous chemists in the Soviet Union. He had been a part of several international organisations and had served on committees with men and women whom, thanks to the bungling of politicians, he was now forced to consider enemies. But he had never thought of them that way. Theirs was a community of science, not of political ideals and national boundaries. In spite of this, the war had severed their lines of communication and Emil had no way of getting in touch with them.

What he needed was someone familiar with Russian culture, who spoke the language and had travelled widely there. Such a person could re-establish contact with his former colleagues. Once they learned what he had to offer, they would surely waste no time bringing him across the lines.

Where could he locate such a person? He did not even know where to begin. But the more Emil thought about it, the more he came to realise that the answer to this dilemma was his own brother.

Stefan had said he would always be there to help. This would be his chance to prove it.

He immediately applied for two weeks' leave from IG Farben, where his continued employment was little more than a charade, and set out for Ahlborn, carrying a rucksack filled with clothes and a briefcase containing three vials of soman, each one contained within a silver-lined glass tube and sealed with a spring-loaded cap.

His leave had been readily granted by Meinhardt, who seemed quite happy to know that Kohl would not be glooming around the laboratory and performing tasks which, both men knew, were next to useless in light of Germany's current situation.

Knowing that Meinhardt would be in no hurry to have him return, Kohl reckoned that it would be at least a week after his leave ended before Meinhardt sent someone to find him. It would then take the authorities a further couple of weeks to track him to his brother's house in Ahlborn, by which time, with luck, he would already be gone.

On the morning of 4 February 1945, having reached the nearby town of Kottonforst by train, Emil managed to find a place on a cart belonging to a farmer heading in the direction of Ahlborn.

The farmer regarded Emil suspiciously, and seemed to take particular offence at the neatness and good repair of the professor's clothes. The man's own wardrobe included wooden clogs and a loosely woven sack coat with two large patch pockets on the front, each one of which was crammed with objects useful to the man, such as a pipe with a well-chewed stem and a pack of Skat cards. There was also a piece of paper with some phrases written down for him in Russian by a Soviet prisoner he had employed on his farm until, finally acknowledging that the war was lost for Germany, and anticipating the imminent arrival of the Red Army, had allowed the man to escape, but not before instructing the prisoner to write down the words for 'I am a friend', 'Long live Comrade Stalin' and 'Don't shoot. I surrender.' The prisoner, who had been half-starved by the farmer and made to live in a chicken coop, dutifully wrote down 'I hate all Russians', 'Death to Comrade Stalin' and 'Go ahead and shoot me you bastard' before slipping away from captivity.

'You can ride in the back,' the man said to Professor Kohl, and then to emphasise his lack of want for company, he spat on the plank next to him, where Emil might otherwise have sat.

With his suitcase on his lap, Kohl jostled on a pile of mouldy-smelling hay until they reached a crossroads in the woods. A signpost which had once pointed the way to Ahlborn had been snapped in half by retreating German soldiers, in a desperate attempt to lead the Red Army astray in any way they could.

'That way,' said the man, nodding down one of the roads.

Emil thanked him and climbed down off the cart.

'You are not from Ahlborn,' said the man.

'No,' admitted Kohl.

'Then why go?'

'I have family there.'

'Not any more, you don't,' the man told him. 'The Army took them all away. The Reds are coming, or haven't you heard? The only people left in Ahlborn now are either dead or those who are insane enough to have returned to their homes.'

Kohl nodded. 'That just about sums up my relatives,' he said.

'Suit yourself,' grunted the farmer.

Soon afterwards, Emil arrived at the outskirts of the village. There was little damage to be seen and the solidly built houses and small shops which lined Ahlborn's only street were all more or less intact. Some of the buildings had holes in their roofs. A few of the doors had been kicked in. As Emil made his way towards Stefan's house on the other side of town, he held his breath while he stepped around the rotting remains of a dead cow, its bones showing through the tightly drawn black-and-white hide. He was startled to see the dark hulk of a Russian tank parked in a muddy lane, but a second glance at its peeled paint and bare metal, already beginning to rust into a pinkish fuzz, told him the tank had burned out and been abandoned.

He passed the church where the service for his father had been held. This building showed more damage than any of the others he had seen so far. Of the few artillery shells which had landed in Ahlborn, only this one had done any real harm. The roof tiles of the church hung crooked like a set of rotten teeth. All along the front of the church, the stained-glass windows were smashed in and the lead bands which had held each piece of glass in place sagged like the wet strands of a spiderweb. Through the open door, Emil could see titled pews and hymn books strewn about.

At that moment, Emil was startled to hear a voice coming from somewhere inside the church where his father was buried. Someone had cried out, not in fear, it seemed to Emil, but in sadness and exasperation. Curious, he walked to the entrance of the church. The smell of old sandalwood incense, sunk into the walls from centuries of use, mingled with the damp odour of the charred roof beams.

'Hello?' he called into the dark.

There was a rustling noise, and then the swishing sound of footfalls on stone steps. Someone appeared from a doorway beside the altar, which Emil knew led to the crypt. He remembered helping Stefan to carry his father's coffin down the narrow staircase to the airless little chamber where the bones of other priests lay in their brittle wooden boxes. Even before Emil could discern the features of the man's face, he recognised from the silhouette that it was his brother. 'Stefan?' he called.

Stefan stopped in his tracks.

He had arrived in town only an hour before. When he learned that the Soviet onslaught had failed to materialise and that fighting in the village had been limited to a few small skirmishes between reconnaissance groups on both sides, he had slipped away from the tide of refugees, stolen a rickety bicycle and ridden back to Ahlborn. The first thing he did was to go straight to the church. Ever since leaving the village, he had been tormented by the thought that the icon might have been destroyed in the skirmishes. His first glimpse of the church, with its windows stoved in and door smashed open, seemed to confirm his worst fears. He raced into the building and shoved aside the splintered furniture, until he reached the door which led down to the crypt. In spite of the damage to the interior, at least the building was intact, and he took this as a hopeful sign that the icon might be safe, after all. It never occurred to him that the icon might have been removed from its hiding place. His only fear was that the crypt might have been engulfed in flames, or that its ceiling had collapsed. It was not until he had lit the oil lamp hanging on the wall that the possibility of theft occurred to him. As he stood among the splintered fragments of his father's coffin, staring down at the brittle, frost-gloved hands of Viktor Kohl, Stefan realised the icon had been stolen. He could not understand why this coffin was the only one that had been opened. It was as if the thieves had known exactly what they were looking for.

A part of him still refused to believe it. He began to prise the lids from the other coffins, in case, perhaps, he had placed the icon in the wrong one. One by one, he tipped out bodies and skeletons on to the floor, until he was wading through bones and the air was filled with a sweet and sickly-smelling dust which made the oil lamp sputter and clogged his lungs until he could barely breathe.

The Shepherd was gone.

Stefan Kohl dropped to his knees, pressed his filthy hands against his face and wept. It was the first time in his life that he had ever been completely without hope. Even lying on the frozen lake, and all around him the snow stained pink with his own blood, the certainty of death had brought with it the comfort of finality. Now he felt neither alive nor dead, but trapped someplace in between. He remembered the words of Belyakina – *If* The Shepherd *is destroyed, then so are we.* He had lived with that nightmare ever since, knowing that he alone bore the burden of its safekeeping. And he had failed. There was no chance of finding it again, or so it seemed to him just then, nor was there any possibility of learning who had taken it. From what he had heard, both German and Russian troops had entered the town since he had left. The icon could just as easily have been taken by one side as another. By now, *The Shepherd* could be a thousand kilometres away in any direction. Even if the icon did show up, some day far into the future, it would doubtless be so heavily guarded that acquiring it again would be impossible. These thoughts raked through his stomach, as if his guts were being sliced with razor blades.

At that moment, he noticed the leather jacket lying heaped in the corner, with a Red Army pass book sticking out of one pocket, and several battered campaign medals pinned to the chest.

Climbing stiffly to his feet, Stefan went over to the jacket and lifted it off the floor. The medals pinned to its chest clunked together with a dull sound. He removed the pass book and saw that it belonged to Antonin Proskuryakov, a captain in the 4th Guards' Kantemirovskaya Armoured Division. There was also a set of papers, granting Proskuryakov three weeks' leave at the time and permission to travel by whatever means he could acquire to his home in the city of Noginsk.

For a brief moment, the possibility that he might find this man flickered to life in Stefan's mind, but just as suddenly it died away again. The jacket was no guarantee that this Proskuryakov had discovered the icon. In all likelihood the man is dead, thought Stefan. Why else would he have left his jacket, his medals and all his papers behind?

You could spend the rest of your life searching for the thief, Stefan thought to himself, and have nothing to show for it at the end. He just had to face the fact that there was nothing to be done.

Stefan let the heavy coat slip from his grasp. After replacing his father's remains in his coffin, he picked up the lamp and turned to leave, kicking his way through remaining hollow skulls and crooked hoops of pelvic bones until he reached the stairs. Each step he took towards daylight seemed to hammer home the certainty of his loss. A long, deep moan escaped his lips. It was a sound he'd never heard before, as if the dead had snatched his breath away and now were calling out to him with his own voice.

He had almost reached the top of the stairs when he saw a figure standing in the doorway to the church. It looked like Emil, although Stefan could not fathom why his brother would be here. After their last meeting, Stefan had never expected to see him again. I must be mistaken, he thought, or else hallucinating, but the closer he came to the man, the more certain he was that the person waiting for him in the doorway was indeed his older brother. It was Emil who spoke first. 'The last time we met, you told me you would always be here to help.'

'Yes.' Stefan nodded, still confused.

'Well, brother,' Emil said, 'I need it now.'

The two men left the ruins of the church and made their way towards Stefan's house. Emil explained his situation.

As Stefan listened to his older brother, a plan of his own began to emerge which, if it worked, might save them both from ruin. Stefan said nothing of the icon. He had never trusted anyone with that secret and he wasn't about to start now.

That night, over a meal of smoked pork and pickled eggs, Stefan agreed to cross the border into Russia and to make contact with scientists at the chemical research facility in Sosnogorsk. For this, Emil provided him with the address of a professor named Arbusov, whom he had known before the war, as well as a vial of the soman, which would serve as his credentials to the Soviets.

To guard against the possibility that it might be found in a search, Emil transferred the liquid into a metal flask, once owned by his father, which had contained holy water brought back from a pilgrimage to Lourdes.

Stefan promised to return as quickly as he could and the two men agreed that Emil should wait here at the house.

The following morning, Emil saw him to the door. 'I'm sorry,' he told his brother.

Stefan looked surprised. It was the first apology he had ever received from his brother and he didn't even know what it was for.

'I can't pretend to understand the choices you have made,' explained Emil, 'but I see now that I should, at least, have tried.'

Carrying the identity papers of Antonin Proskuryakov, which he had retrieved along with the captain's medal-festooned jacket from the crypt, Stefan Kohl set out towards Moscow. Later that day, he flagged down a cart driven by a Russian Army private named Elias Matorin, who was too struck by the sight of Stefan's awards to notice that the officer wore a muddy pair of civilian trousers.

Matorin was a gentle, wistful-looking man with callused hands from years of riding horses and fingers made crooked by arthritis. Before the Revolution, he had served as one of the guards at the Winter Palace. Because of their burgundy-red tunics and gold sashes, they had been known as the Gilded Regiment. On that day in October of 1917, when the palace was stormed by revolutionary soldiers, Matorin had barely escaped with his life. He travelled far from Petrograd and, when he married ten years later, even his wife did not know about his past. Matorin lived quietly and, until the war broke out, he had been a chef at a tavern on the road between Salavat and Kumertau, down near the border of Kazakhstan. In spite of his age, Matorin had been called up in the spring of 1942 and had worked in an army field kitchen ever since.

When he stopped to pick up the captain, Matorin had been returning from the front line with six empty soup urns.

It was an hour's ride back to the field kitchen and Matorin was glad of the company.

The cart rattled along over the empty road and the two men sat side by side, squinting in the jungly sunlight coming down through the overhanging branches of the trees.

When Stefan said that he was heading home on leave, Matorin got tears in his eyes. He had never been granted a furlough and he missed his wife. Matorin wondered how she was getting on without him, and he worried she was getting on just fine. 'I would like very much to go home,' he told the officer.

Stefan put his arm around Matorin's shoulder. 'You will,' he said, and then he knifed the old man through the heart, so savagely that the blade came out through his back. Matorin fell back among the empty soup urns. The reins slipped from his grasp. Feeling the traces go slack, the horses shambled to a stop. Stefan dragged Matorin into the woods, stripped the body and put on the old man's clothes, after washing the blood from his tunic in a stream. Matorin's threadbare *gymnastiorka* bore no rank or insignia, which was common among front-line troops. Lastly, Stefan put on the leather jacket and buttoned it up to the throat. There was no time to bury the body, which lay spread-eagled on its back, the dappled shadows playing across Matorin's dingy undergarments.

As Stefan climbed back on to the cart, he noticed an old Nagant revolver tucked under the seat. Its narrow, curved handle had been thickly wrapped with black cloth electrical tape. Matorin had done this because, with his arthritic hands, he had been unable to grip the gun properly. Stefan checked that the Nagant was loaded, spun the chamber and then tucked the gun into his pocket.

Even with the horse and cart, his journey to Moscow took longer than he had expected. The roads were jammed with military traffic and many checkpoints had been set up along the way. Some of these he was able to detour around. At others, he took his chances, using the papers which had been issued to

Captain Proskuryakov. Stefan's luck changed when he reached a railhead near the city of Brasovo. By then, it was already 17 February. A train had just pulled in, carrying wounded from the front. Abandoning the cart, he showed his papers to a doctor on the train and explained that he was trying to get home on leave. Impressed by the captain's Order of the Red Banner medal, the doctor allowed him to climb aboard.

On 19 February 1945 Stefan Kohl finally reached Moscow. Arriving at the Saratovsky Station on the southern outskirts of Moscow, he crossed the Moskva River on the Krasnocholsk Bridge. From there, he made his way to the Taganskaya Square and followed the long Taganskaya Boulevard until he found the cemetery.

He was looking for Argamak, the Skoptsy gravedigger he had met when he passed through the city years before.

Stefan had no doubt that when Soviet authorities learned of his brother's work at IG Farben, they would leap at the chance to acquire the skills of such a valuable scientist. Emil's idea had simply been to trade his skills for a place in the Russian scientific community, but Stefan also saw an opportunity for himself.

Discovery of *The Shepherd* would quickly reach the ears of Joseph Stalin and the icon would soon find its way to Moscow. All Stefan had to do was make it a condition of Emil's transfer to the Soviets that they deliver the icon to him first. The Communists would not hesitate to exchange what to them was a worthless relic of a failed religion for a weapon of such devastating power.

But first he had to get their attention. For that, Stefan needed a place to lie low until he could broker the deal.

There was only one person whom he knew he could turn to for help, and that was Argamak.

At the edge of the cemetery, Stefan found the gravedigger's hut, looking much the same as it had done before, with its heaps of firewood outside and damaged tombstones propped against the wall.

But the man he found inside, dozing in the bed, was not Argamak.

'He died two years ago,' explained the man, blinking the sleep from his eyes. He pulled his suspenders up over a shirt almost as dirty as the one Argamak had worn, and lit the samovar for tea. 'My name is Bersin. I took his place. Were you a friend of his?'

'Yes,' Stefan answered in a daze. He knew that he should have taken it into account, but Argamak had seemed so indestructible that this news of his death still managed to catch him by surprise.

'Funny you should come looking for him now,' said Beresin. 'A letter just arrived for him.' He nodded to an envelope, which had been pinned to one of the bare planks that made up the wall of the hut. 'You might as well have it. It's no good to him and it's no good to me, either, since I never learned to read.'

Stefan took the letter from the wall. He sat down by the stove and read the words of Prison Warder First Class Feodor Turkov, describing the visit of Inspector Pekkala and his assistant, Major Kirov of the Bureau of Special Operations.

'I was told to notify you if ever something happened,' wrote Turkov. 'I hope this piece of news is worth reporting, as there has been no other since I came to Karaganda years ago.'

As Turkov went on to describe how the icon of *The*

Shepherd was now in the hands of Inspector Pekkala, Stefan knew he'd have to change his calculations.

The day after his arrival in the city, Stefan mailed the bottle, with its cheerful depiction of Lourdes, to Father Detlev's address. He knew from his brother's descriptions exactly what kind of a death awaited the old priest. But he didn't care. Detlev had committed the unforgivable sin of aiding those who sought to put an end to the Skoptsy faith. For men like that, thought Stefan, no manner of ending was too cruel.

When Pekkala learned of Detlev's murder, it would not take the Inspector long to grasp that somebody out there wanted the icon back, nor to understand what could be offered in return. It would then be a simple matter of making contact with Pekkala, and making clear the terms of his proposal.

Knowing that it would take several days for the package to reach Karaganda, Stefan decided to keep Pekkala's office under observation until then. It was not hard to learn the great Inspector's whereabouts. He accomplished this by striding into NKVD headquarters and announcing to the clerk at the front desk that he had an urgent message for the Inspector, direct from General Voroshilov at the front, which had to be delivered at once. Cowed by the mention of the general, and intimidated by the array of battered medals on this dirt-spattered 'Frontovik', the clerk hurriedly wrote out the address of Pekkala's office and handed it over.

*

Right about the time when Stefan knew that the soman would have reached the priest, Pekkala abruptly departed from

Moscow, bound, presumably, for Karaganda. This caught Stefan completely by surprise. It was a long, hard journey to the prison and Stefan had assumed that Pekkala would simply receive a report about what had happened to Father Detlev, rather than need to examine the murder scene first-hand.

With Pekkala out of the city, Stefan saw his chance to break into the Inspector's Pitnikov street office and steal the icon now, rather than wade through the dangerous business of a negotiation. By the time Pekkala returned, Stefan and the icon could be far away from Moscow. After that, a message mailed to the Inspector, giving Emil's whereabouts and explaining his brother's intention to defect, would accomplish the rest of what he had set out to achieve.

But it all went terribly wrong. Not only did Stefan fail to locate the icon, but he was forced to kill a man named Kratky who appeared at the office after he had broken in. Kratky's body was discovered and the place was soon crawling with police. Stefan knew that he had squandered his advantage, but he couldn't leave Moscow yet, not without the icon. He had come too far to turn back now.

Stefan broke into a ground-floor apartment across the road from Pekkala's building. It was a dingy little dwelling, accessed through a door halfway down a narrow alleyway. The tenant was a former pilot named Felix Ivanchenko, who had broken his back in crash landing a Sturmovik the year before. Although he made a partial recovery, Ivanchenko was discharged from the service and left to subsist on a meagre pension. This basement was the only thing he could afford.

When Ivanchenko returned from spending the afternoon at the library, where he often whiled away the afternoons, reading through old periodicals, Stefan grabbed him as he walked through the door. One look at Stefan, and Ivanchenko was in no doubt about what would become of him. He made no attempt to resist.

In the split second before Stefan killed Ivanchenko with a single, massive blow to the bridge of his nose, he saw in the doomed man's expression a look which could have passed for gratitude.

That night, Stefan prised up the flimsy wooden floorboards in the kitchen to the soft, powdery dirt which lay beneath. There, he dug a shallow grave and buried the man before replacing the boards and tapping the nails back in place with the heel of his boot.

As soon as the police departed, he imagined in a day or two, and Pekkala had returned from Karaganda, he would approach Pekkala directly, kidnapping the man if necessary, and deliver his terms for handing over Emil and the soman.

In the meantime, Stefan settled down to wait, subsisting off a case of tinned sardines which was the only food Ivanchenko had in his cupboard. From the front window of the apartment, he could keep an eye upon the building across the street, where Pekkala kept his office.

While Pekkala underestimated Stefan's tenacity, believing that surely the Skoptsy assassin would have chosen to flee the city after Kratky's murder, Stefan, too, had miscalculated the Kremlin's response.

When Pekkala arrived back from his journey to Karaganda, along with the Special Operations major who travelled with him, Stefan was alarmed to see the regular police replaced by plainclothes agents, who kept Pekkala's building under 24-hour surveillance, although they failed to conduct a house-to-house search, which might have resulted in Stefan's capture.

Stefan was trapped. If he tried to leave the apartment, the agents would spot him at once. All he could do was draw upon his last reserves of patience, and bide his time until Stalin called off his watchdogs.

On the afternoon of 12 March, by which time Stefan had been hiding in the apartment for more than a week, the plain-clothes agents suddenly departed. Hidden from view by the thick lace curtain which covered the window, Stefan watched the men slip away as quietly as they had appeared. Now, at last, he could get out of this wretched cave, which had been his home far longer than he had anticipated.

All he had to do now, he thought, was to wait for Pekkala to leave the building at the end of the day. Then he could follow the Inspector to wherever the man lived and there, at gunpoint, if necessary, he could deliver his ultimatum to Pekkala. As long as Emil remained safely hidden in Ahlborn, the threat of the soman's devastating potential would ensure Stefan's safety.

Instead, he was astonished to see a Red Army staff car pull up in front of 22 Pitnikov Street, followed moments later by the Inspector himself, who emerged from the building along with the tall, skinny major from Special Operations, and a wo-man who appeared to be either the major's wife or his fiancée, judging from the way they spoke to each other. After a short conversation with Pekkala's driver, in which Stefan distinctly overheard the word 'Ahlborn', Pekkala and the major climbed into the staff car and were driven away, leaving the driver and the woman behind.

Having heard the word 'Ahlborn' and witnessing this sudden departure, Stefan panicked. In his mind, there could only be one reason for this sudden turn of events – Pekkala had somehow discovered where Emil was hiding, and they must now be on their way to apprehend him. Stefan knew that if he did not get there first, and warn his brother, he would have nothing left with which to bargain for the icon.

In that moment, a desperate idea occurred to him. He stuffed a few cans of sardines into his pockets. Then, slinging his heavy jacket over his arm, Stefan tucked his butcher's knife beneath the heavy folds of leather and, for the first time in almost a week, stepped out into the alleyway.

*

Zolkin and Elizaveta watched the Red Army staff car, bearing Kirov and Pekkala to the Kremlin for their meeting with Stalin, as it reached the end of Pitnikov Street, turned the corner and was gone.

Now they found themselves awkwardly alone together.

'I've never had a bodyguard before,' said Elizaveta, trying to make conversation.

'And I have never been one,' Zolkin replied earnestly.

'But you look like a bodyguard to me.'

Zolkin wore army breeches, tucked into tall black boots, and over an olive cotton shirt he had on a waistcoat of civilian manufacture, which he usually wore under a heavy double-breasted canvas jacket normally reserved for the crews of armoured vehicles. But it was a warm day and Zolkin had left the coat hanging on a nail inside the garage.

'Appearances count for a lot in your new line of work,' she said encouragingly.

It was true, his thickly muscled arms and bear-like shoulders did much to conceal the gentleness of his nature.

'Then let us set off on our first mission together,' announced the sergeant.

'And what is that?' asked Elizaveta.

'To bring you home!'

Zolkin fished a bundle of keys from his pocket and jangled them in his hand. 'I'll just pull the car out,' he said.

'There's no need for that,' said Elizaveta. 'It's only a five-minute walk.'

Zolkin paused, the keys still clutched in his hand. 'Walk?'

'Unless that is somehow beneath you,' replied Elizaveta.

'It's just that, once you've been a driver, going anywhere on foot just seems a waste of time. Are you sure you wouldn't like to get there more quickly? The Emka is ready to go!' He made a hopeful gesture towards the garage.

'No,' Elizaveta told him flatly. 'Now close that place up and come with me.'

With a groan of resignation, Zolkin set his shoulder to the heavy wooden door, which rolled across the front of the garage. It fastened with a huge bronze padlock, the key for which was on the bundle which Zolkin carried with him everywhere.

Turning the corner of Pitnikov Street, they set off down Trubnaya Street. Zolkin plodded along behind Elizaveta, looking like a scolded dog.

After a while, Elizaveta stopped and turned. 'Are you going to drag your heels all the way there?'

'It just seems proper,' Zolkin said defensively. 'I am your bodyguard, after all.'

Elizaveta rolled her eyes. 'For goodness' sake, Zolkin, stop fussing and walk here beside me!'

Zolkin did as he was told and they continued for a while without speaking.

As people passed them on the street, Elizaveta noticed how others moved aside to let them pass, readily giving ground before the imposing bulk of Zolkin. Zolkin himself seemed completely unaware of the deference they showed to him.

It was rarely the case that anyone stepped aside for Elizaveta, as she was neither tall nor imposing. Even with her husband, the effect wasn't quite the same. If people did give ground to him, it usually seemed to be because of his uniform, rather than his physical presence. Elizaveta couldn't help enjoying this new and powerful sensation, even if it was for all the wrong reasons.

Zolkin still hadn't said a word.

'What is on your mind?' Elizaveta asked at last.

'I was thinking,' Zolkin replied eventually, 'that since you probably won't be wanting the car at all, I might as well just drain the oil and remove the battery while your husband and the Inspector are away.'

'Then we wouldn't be able to go on the picnic,' said Elizaveta.

'What picnic?' asked the driver.

'The one I have planned for tomorrow.' The thought had only just occurred to her, but it already seemed like a good idea. 'I have two friends where I work, in the records office on the fourth floor of Lubyanka. One is Corporal Koroleva and the other, whom I would like you to meet, is Sergeant Gatkina.'

'What's she like?' asked Zolkin.

'Oh, you'll see,' she answered vaguely. In truth, Sergeant Gatkina was no great beauty. Elizaveta knew of lotteries, down on the third and second floors, for when and if Gatkina ever smiled. She chain-smoked rough *machorka* cigarettes from dawn to dusk, which had given her a voice as gravelly as a tiger's, if such an animal had ever spoken Russian. Her hair was a thicket of grey brambly curls and the colour of her eyes was unknown to almost everyone, so fiercely did she squint at the world. As if that were not enough, she had a habit of stubbing out her cigarettes as if breaking the neck of some small animal that had strayed into her clutches.

This fearsome reputation had served to ward off even the most determined of suitors.

Gatkina may have given the impression that she was content to keep the world at arm's length, but in truth she was lonely – terribly lonely – and would gladly have put away the armour of her gruffness if someone could be found to remove it.

That someone could be Zolkin, thought Elizaveta. He would not be deterred by the things which drove others away. It was Zolkin's sheer obliviousness that gave her hope. In the past, she had even considered Pekkala as a possible partner for the sergeant. But she quickly abandoned the idea. No matter how lonely Gatkina might be, it would be simply cruel to inflict upon her the eccentricities of the Inspector. What could you say about a man who prefers to sleep on the floor? Elizaveta wondered to herself, and who, according to her husband, cried out in his sleep in his strange and guttural native tongue, as if he was pursued by wolves across the landscape of his dreams? No, thought Elizaveta. I will spare my beloved and misunderstood boss the impossible task of loving a man like Pekkala.

It was true Zolkin did have some unusual habits of his own. After all, he lived in a garage and spent his nights in a hammock, hanging from the ceiling like a silkworm in a cocoon. But those were matters of practicality, she persuaded herself, not facets of the man's true nature.

'Where will we go on this picnic?' asked Zolkin, his mood brightening at the thought. 'What will we have to eat?'

This isn't about food! Elizaveta wanted to yell in his ear. This is about love! But she simply shrugged and said, 'Let's let Sergeant Gatkina decide.'

By now, they had turned off Trubnaya Street and were walking along Pushkarev Street. It was much quieter here and, except for a few passers-by, they had the pavement to themselves.

One man emerged from an alleyway, carrying a brown leather coat over his arm, and walked in their direction. He was tall and muscular, much like Zolkin himself, and Elizaveta found herself wondering which one of them would give way to the other. She became so curious about it that she even stepped a little to the side, forcing Zolkin into the man's path, so that one of them would have to step out into the street in order to get by. She felt a little wicked to be conducting such an experiment, but no harm would be done, after all.

Other than this man, the street was empty.

As the stranger approached, he cast a glance at Elizaveta.

Elizaveta caught his eye. Defiantly, and to her own surprise, she returned his stare, a thing she would never have done if she were on her own.

Zolkin was paying no attention. Instead, he was carrying on about the food he would like for the picnic.

Just when it seemed as if the two men would collide, the other man stepped out into the road.

A faint, but satisfied smile crept across Elizaveta's lips.

In that moment, the man appeared to stumble. Perhaps he had caught his foot amongst the cobblestones which lined the gutter.

Elizaveta felt a sudden stab of guilt, knowing she had caused this little incident.

The man tipped to the side and his coat, which had been neatly folded over his arm, wafted up in Zolkin's face.

The driver shied away, eyes closed and lips pressed tight together.

Elizaveta saw a flash of silver, which she took to be sunlight off a cufflink of the stranger's.

Then the man regained his footing and Elizaveta sighed with relief, glad that he had not ended up sprawled in the street on her account.

She walked on a couple of paces. Then, conscious that Zolkin was no longer beside her, she turned. Her first thought was that Zolkin had stopped to have a word with the stranger, but what she saw when she turned made her face go numb with fear.

Zolkin stood on the pavement, one hand held against his neck. Blood was squirting from between his fingers. His face bore an expression of complete surprise.

'What happened?' she gasped.

Slowly, Zolkin dropped to his knees and, with his one free hand, groped across the pavement until he sat down with his back against the wall of a house.

The stranger crouched down in front of Zolkin, reached into the driver's waistcoat pocket and removed his set of keys and fuel-ration booklet. Then he stood and walked calmly towards Elizaveta, one hand held out as if to comfort her. His face was ghostly pale, like flesh preserved in formaldehyde.

A wave of terror swept across her mind. 'What happened?' she asked again, but even as she spoke, she saw the man slide a long butcher's knife back into the folds of his coat.

Elizaveta tried to cry out, but she found that she could barely speak, and there was no one else around.

Then the stranger laid her out with a single punch, the way he had learned to drop horses, focusing his power a hand's breadth beyond the place where he knew that his fist would connect. He had never hit a woman before and even though he could easily have killed her, he was careful not to do so. So little of his strength went into knocking her out that it almost felt gentle to him. He caught her as she tumbled to the ground. Leaving the driver to bleed to death, he bundled the woman into the boot of the Emka and set off towards Ahlborn, determined to arrive before Pekkala.

*

Meanwhile, in Stefan's plainly furnished house in Ahlborn, Emil Kohl paced like a cat in a cage. His nerves were strained to breaking point. He had been there for over a month and, although he had anticipated that it would take some time for Stefan to make contact with Professor Arbusov, his Soviet counterpart in the field of organophosphate chemistry, he had not imagined ever having to wait this long.

Ever since his brother had left for Russia, Emil's mind had been plagued with doubts.

He wondered if Stefan had been arrested, or even killed, or if by accident or out of curiosity he had opened the vial of soman, in which case he would have died on the spot, taking with him anyone who happened to be standing nearby. There was a third possibility, which was that Stefan had simply abandoned him to his fate. As the days wore on, this last option began to seem increasingly likely.

Emil cursed himself for having placed his faith in his younger brother. The more he thought about it, the more insane it seemed that he should have trusted him at all.

It was cold in the house. Even a small fire would have made a difference, but Stefan had warned him against lighting one, since the smoke would let people know he was there. His brother had left him with plenty of food, but almost all of it was meat. The man was a butcher, after all. The meat had been smoked with a variety of woods – oak, maple and alder – and hung in blackened strips from racks in the kitchen. The smell of it, which Emil had initially found pleasant, if a little overpowering, had now suffused into his clothes, his hair and his skin. He tasted the smoke every time he took a breath, and its stench had become nauseating.

The day after Stefan left for Moscow, Emil had been woken by the ear-splitting roar of engines. As his eyes snapped open, his first thought was that a tank was coming through the wall. He screamed, tipped himself on to the floor and crawled under the bed, just as six Messerschmitt 262 jet fighters screeched past at treetop level, heading east on their morning patrol. The whole house shook. The windows rippled as if the glass had turned to water. The vibration was still shuddering in his bones as he slithered out from beneath the bed and rushed to the window, just in time to see the planes pass out of sight, leaving behind oil-black trails of exhaust. He had heard about the new jet planes and recognised their Jumo engines from classified documents he had seen from a project designed to produce synthetic fuel. There was also the sound they made; not the buzz-saw hum of a propeller plane, but something that sounded to Professor Kohl more like a hive full of angry bees. There had been much talk, not only at IG Farben but in the press as well, of secret new 'revenge' weapons soon to be unleashed upon the Allies, which would turn the tide of the war. From the first mention of these *Vergeltungswaffen*, Professor Kohl had assumed that the Sartaman Project would feature prominently in this new arsenal of destruction. But now the fading rumble of the 262s seemed to drive home the fact that he, and his inventions, had been left out of the Führer's grand equation.

The planes returned a little over an hour later and this time Emil got a better look at their grey, shark-like silhouettes, the black German crosses almost hidden among blooms of camouflage paint, like giant, sooty fingerprints.

Two hours later, they flew past again and a third time before the sun went down, causing the house to tremble as if caught in the grip of an earthquake.

These regularly scheduled tremors became a daily fixture in Emil's existence. He grew to anticipate them, becoming more and more agitated as the time for their arrival drew near. And if they were late, even by a few minutes, he found himself with his nose pressed to the window, peering up through the trees to catch a glimpse of them as they flew past.

This, combined with inactivity and loneliness, was driving Kohl close to distraction, but still he did not dare go outside.

As the days passed, and the time allotted for his leave expired, Emil began to dwell upon the fact that his absence would, by now, have been reported. The disappearance of an IG Farben chemist, particularly one with his level of expertise and having been involved in such delicate work, would not be a matter for the bumbling municipal police. The matter would be handed over to the Secret State Police. It was only a matter of time before the Gestapo came knocking at his door and once they got their hands on him, all chance of escape would be lost.

I can't just sit here waiting to be arrested, thought Emil, staring out of the window at the dirt road lined with pine trees, which was his only view from the front of the house. From the back, all he could see was a small overgrown yard, filled with firewood and bordered by a tall stockade fence.

Weighing his options for the hundredth time, it became clear that there was only one possible course of action open to him now. He would return to Leverkeusen, hand over the briefcase containing the vials and confess what he had done. Of course, he would leave out the part about handing his brother a vial of soman, but if the Russians turned up with soman at some later date, he could rightly point out that they, too, had been looking into organophosphate compounds before the war and must have stumbled upon the same formula by themselves.

If the authorities asked him where he had gone, he would simply tell them he had travelled to his brother's house and had been unable to get back because of the fighting. The lie was both simple and plausible and, as for the chemical weapons, the only thing he had really done was to stabilise a pre-existing compound, thereby making it not only easier to transport but easier to neutralise as well. Yes, he had disobeyed an order, but he had done so with the best of intentions. It was simply a mis-understanding, and, at least the way he planned to tell it, no harm had been done.

The more Emil thought about it, the better his chances seemed. There was bound to be some kind of disciplinary ac-tion, but nothing too serious, he now convinced himself.

Soon, Emil's apprehensions had been swept aside. The way forward seemed clear. All he had to do was get back to Leverkeusen. It was now 18 March. He imagined he could be home again by the 20th, provided that he left immediately. The nearest station was about five kilometres to the west, in the town of Kottonforst. Travelling on foot, which appeared to be his only option, he knew he could be there in an hour or so. There was only one train a day at Kottonforst, which passed through the town at two o'clock each afternoon. It was only 9 a.m. now, which meant he had more than enough time.

Having dawdled away his time over the past few weeks, Emil now began to move at a feverish pace, packing his ruck-sack with clothes, wrapping some smoked meat in a handker-chief for a meal and filling a canteen with water from the pump in the garden. Once this was done, he still had four and a half hours before the train arrived.

Better, thought Emil, to arrive on time, rather than be seen hanging about the station for hours. That is bound to look sus-picious. He decided to head out at eleven.

Satisfied with his plan, Emil found himself once more at a loose end. Shuddering with the cold that had permeated every corner of this unheated house, it occurred to him that he could light a fire now. By the time anybody thought to check on the smoke, he would be gone, and at least he would have spent his last couple of hours getting warm, in preparation for the long journey ahead.

He made a fire in the iron stove, laying out splinters of kindling and crumpled pieces of newspaper. When these were burning, he placed a log on top and sat back, the stove door open, holding his hands out towards the spitting yellow flames.

At last, when the warmth had finally returned to the marrow of his bones, Emil kicked the stove door shut, put his rucksack on his back, picked up his suitcase and headed out through the door.

The road was long and deserted, and Emil whistled to keep himself company. The tune he whistled was called the 'Erikamarsch'. He couldn't remember all the lyrics but they were something about a little flower growing on the heath among a hundred thousand other flowers. He had often heard the soldiers singing it as they marched along his street earlier in the war, and for a moment, he remembered how it had felt when the armies of his country seemed unstoppable, and victory, both in the east and the west, had seemed so obvious a conclusion that no one even thought to doubt it. Then a weight settled in Emil's chest as his thoughts returned to the present and he remembered that the soldiers never sang any more when they went marching by his house.

18 March 1945

Ahlborn

Six days after leaving Moscow, Stefan Kohl reached home.

He was completely exhausted. For this last stretch of the journey, he had driven more than twenty hours straight, stopping only for fuel and fresh water. He had made better time than expected, since many of the roads leading west, far from being the quagmires of mud he had anticipated, had recently been shored up by the Red Army's Corps of Engineers. At fuel depots along the way, he had simply handed over the required number of fuel coupons and taken what he needed. Seeing his uniform and the Special Operations licence plate on the Emka, the depot operators had never given Zolkin's identification book more than a passing glance, and sometimes didn't ask for it at all.

At no point did he spot the GAZ-67 staff car which had driven Pekkala from Moscow. With its 54-horsepower engine, it was considerably more powerful than the tired old Emka, and Stefan assumed that they must be far ahead of him.

Elizaveta had soon regained consciousness, and Stefan was obliged to tie her hands and legs with rope, as well as put a gag in her mouth. He also covered her with a wool blanket, which he had found draped over the back seat of the car. The first time he tried to give her water, she screamed when he removed the gag, so he put the gag back in and didn't give her anything. The next time he stopped, six hours later, she no longer screamed when he gave her something to drink, and he also gave her some of the tinned sardines he had been saving for himself.

From then on, they maintained an uneasy truce. Several times a day, on deserted stretches of road, he would stop the car and let her out for a few minutes at a time.

'I know who you are,' she told him. 'I know what you are looking for and, even as we speak, my husband and Pekkala are on their way to give you what you want. If you hurt me, the deal will be off and, I assure you, that will be the least of your troubles.'

Kohl smiled faintly. 'I have no intention of hurting you,' he replied. 'I need you very much alive.'

'Why not just let me go?' she demanded. 'This has nothing to do with me!'

'Think of yourself as insurance,' he answered, then put the gag in place, closed the boot and got back on the road. Having reached Ahlborn at last, Stefan drove the dirt-crusted Emka through the tall grass around the back of his house, so that it could not be seen from the road. Cutting the engine, he let his head sink forward on to the steering wheel. He then pulled the Nagant revolver from his coat pocket, climbed out of the car and let himself into the house. 'Emil!' he called out, but even as he spoke, he could sense the place was empty. There was a hollow stillness in the air, like the emptiness which hovered around animals just after he had butchered them.

A quick inspection of the house confirmed that there was no sign of a struggle. He stepped out through the front door and walked a short distance down the road that led towards the centre of the village. Aside from his own, there were no recent tyre tracks, but he did catch sight of a single line of footsteps, leading away from the house. He knew they must belong to Emil, but why he had left was a mystery. At that moment, from the direction of Ahlborn, he heard the sound of a car engine.

I'm too late, thought Stefan. Pekkala has found my brother, and now they're heading back across the border.

At that moment, a noise like distant thunder reached his ears. Stefan looked up into the cloudless sky. The ground began to shake beneath his feet and, a second later, he flinched as six planes flew past, flying so low that he felt the heat of their engines. Before he was even fully aware of what had happened, the aircraft were already gone. The power of those winged monsters seemed to him less like inventions of man and more like the riders of the Apocalypse, galloping past on their hollow-eyed horses.

Then, above the clamour of the planes, Stefan heard the hammering pulse of heavy-weapons fire. It took him a second to realise that one of the planes must have been firing at a target on the ground.

Stefan dashed back to the Emka, opened the boot and hauled out his prisoner. 'You had better pray it's not too late,' he said through clenched teeth as he gripped Elizaveta's arm. With the young woman stumbling along beside him, he set off at a run towards the centre of the town.

*

The sound Kohl had heard was not that of Pekkala leaving Ahlborn. In fact, he and Kirov had only just arrived. Their car had got stuck behind a column of supply vehicles just outside Bryansk and, later, outside Kalinkovichi, they had arrived at a fuel depot, only to discover that soldiers of Marshal Zhukov's 1st Belorussian Front had requisitioned every drop of fuel. They were forced to detour to the north, following directions to another fuel depot, where they were able to fill their tank.

Their driver was a gaunt-faced Mongolian named Narmandak, who had been forcibly recruited into the Red Army after straying across the border in search of lost sheep from his herd. They had taught him to drive and then shipped him off to Moscow, where he had ended up at the army motor pool. When he received the call to collect Kirov and Pekkala from outside their office, there had been no explanation of how far they would be travelling. He was simply told to take the two men wherever they wanted to go. Such vague instructions were not uncommon, and usually involved driving generals around to various bars and brothels in the city. Narmandak had prepared himself for a long night of sitting in some polished lend-lease Buick from America outside whatever back-alley club these two men chose to visit. He was surprised, therefore, when his motor pool requisition orders specified a GAZ-67. This was a serious machine, with big, chunky tyres, and none of the well-sprung creature comforts to be found in the cars normally given to those who found themselves in Stalin's favour.

Major Kirov had simply told him to head west along the Moscow highway. Narmandak had not left the Moscow city limits in over a year and he had never been west of Mozhaysk, only a few hours' drive from the city.

By the end of that day, as the GAZ bumped along over the wide and unpaved road, Narmandak was further from his home than he had ever been before. The thought unnerved him, and he kept returning to that day when he had strayed from his home in the bare and rocky foothills of Altan Bulak, in search of that lost flock of sheep. He shared his shepherding duties with a dim-witted cousin named Batu. Under the shadow of a stone, Narmandak had fallen asleep in the heat of the day, while Batu stood guard. But Batu had also nodded off and, when they awoke, more than ten sheep were missing. Leaving Batu to guard the remainder of the flock, Narmandak followed their tracks to a stream, where he came across some men who were watering their horses and trying unsuccessfully to catch taimen, a breed of salmon native to Mongolia, with their bare hands in the shallow, fast-running water. By the time Narmandak found them, they were all completely soaked and had nothing to show for their efforts but fish scales stuck to their palms from the taimen which had slipped through their fingers. It turned out that they were Mongolian cavalry in the service of the Soviet Union, who had been sent into this wasteland to find volunteers for military service. Narmandak had not volunteered. In fact, as soon as the men had revealed the purpose of their mission, he had turned around and run the other way. But they soon caught up with him. They whipped him with a quirt, with chips of bones threaded on to the leather tassels. Then they tied him hand and foot, threw him over a saddle and returned to their barracks, a four-day journey away.

He wondered about those sheep. What had become of them? Had Batu searched for him when he failed to return? Had he seen the hoof-prints in the sand down by the stream and sounded the alarm? Did they think he had been carried off by demons? Why, in all the time since then, had they not come for him, or even sent word to ask if he was well?

These questions creaked and clattered in his mind, as when wind blows through the ice-covered branches of a tree and, as a result, he found it hard to concentrate upon the conversations of these two men, from which he hoped to learn their destination.

By the third day of driving, Narmandak was exhausted. Even though he had been given plenty of food and a place to sleep every night, the vast distances they covered across what was to him a flat and dreary landscape sapped all of his strength away.

On the morning of the fourth day, it rained and the going was slow, but by the afternoon the sun had come out, making the air heavy and soft. As they raced along the road towards the city of Shepetovka, Narmandak found himself mesmerised by the slate rooftops of the houses, which shone in the misty air, like scales scraped from a fish. This made him think of those taimen that the cavalrymen had been chasing through the stream that day and how, if they had been a little kinder to him, he could have shown them how to actually catch the fish. And it suddenly occurred to him why no one had come looking for him since his kidnapping by those horsemen. It was Batu. After all, it was his fault that the sheep got away and he would have done anything to avoid taking the blame. Instead of telling people what really happened, he probably spun some web of lies to make it seem as if he, Narmandak, had stolen the sheep and fled. It all seemed so clear to him now, and he swore that if he ever made it back to Altan Bulak . . .

Narmandak heard a rustling sound. Then he opened his eyes.

They were in the middle of a field. The GAZ had stalled out

and it was perfectly quiet, except for the faint rustle of a breeze through the steppe grass.

He realised he had fallen asleep.

There was no ditch at the side of the road along this stretch of highway or they would have gone straight into it. Instead of that, the car had just veered off into the field, moving more and more slowly until the engine finally quit.

Glancing hesitantly in the rear-view mirror, the first thing he saw was Major Kirov, who lay snoozing with his head thrown back and mouth open. Narmandak breathed a sigh of relief, and wondered if he might even be able to get them back on to the road without his passengers being the wiser. But then, in the corner of the mirror, he noticed a shiny brown eye, with what appeared to be a glint of silver winking from the black depths of the pupil.

Inspector Pekkala was awake. 'This road is long and dreary,' he remarked.

Narmandak only nodded in reply.

'Easy for a man to fall asleep while driving such a road,' said Pekkala.

Narmandak let out a whistling sigh.

'I'm guessing you're not from around here,' remarked the Inspector.

'Altan Bulak,' replied the driver. 'In Mongolia.'

'I know where it is,' said Pekkala, 'and I expect you miss the mountains.'

'Who doesn't miss the place which he calls home?'

Pekkala leaned forward and slapped him gently on the shoulder. 'Until you leave it, though, you cannot really know where you come from.'

Narmandak had never thought of it that way before and suddenly the distance between himself and those bare foothills, and the familiar tinny jangling of sheep bells and the constant rolling thunder of the water coming out of the mountains did not seem so painfully far.

Narmandak switched on the engine and they drove back to the road.

Major Kirov knew nothing of this. He continued to nap, snuffling contentedly as the GAZ sped off towards Shepetovka.

The next morning, having spent the night in an unlocked cell at the police barracks, Narmandak's eyes fluttered open and he was surprised to see, from the colour of sunlight through the barred window above his head, that it was already quite late in the morning. He pulled on his boots and walked down the corridor to the guardroom, expecting to find Major Kirov and the Inspector ready to depart. But all Narmandak found was a solitary policeman sitting at a desk, drinking tea from a green enamel mug.

'Where are they?' he asked.

'Gone,' replied the policeman.

'Gone?' gasped Narmandak.

'Some time ago, in fact.'

Narmandak went to the door and looked out into the street. 'Are they coming back?' he asked.

'Didn't say anything about it,' answered the policeman. 'They left you something, though.' With the heel of his boot, he shunted a crumpled brown paper bag across the desktop so that it was within Narmandak's reach.

Narmandak opened the bag. Inside was a bar of chocolate,

a packet of cigarettes and a set of transfer papers back to Altan Bulak.

Meanwhile, several hours' drive to the west, Major Kirov sat behind the wheel. Unused to the pedals, he had crashed the gears several times, filling the air with the zipping, nerve-wrenching noise of metal cogs grinding together. 'Why the hell did you send him to Mongolia?' he demanded.

'That's where he lives,' answered Pekkala.

'He was our driver!'

'But Mongolia is where he belongs. Besides, you'll get the hang of it.'

Kirov crashed the gears again.

'Eventually,' added Pekkala.

Two days later, knowing they were close to their destination, Kirov pulled over at the outskirts of the village in order to consult his map. The quality of the roads had improved since they'd crossed the German border but all signposts had been ripped up, which made navigating complicated.

While Kirov unfolded the map, trying to find their location as the large, creased sheet of paper flapped like a banner in the breeze, Pekkala stood in the middle of the road, hands tucked behind his back, looking out across the deserted countryside. Neat wooden fences criss-crossed the fields, and farmsteads dotted the horizon, each one enclosed by high stone walls so that only the upper floors and rooftops were visible, in marked contrast to the thatched barns and whitewashed houses of the Russian farms.

'According to this,' said Kirov, squinting at the map, 'Ahlborn should be the next village we come to.' Receiving no reply from Pekkala, he glanced towards the Inspector.

Pekkala's attention was fixed upon the horizon.

'Inspector?' asked Kirov.

'What the hell is that?' asked Pekkala.

Following the Inspector's gaze, Kirov saw what appeared to be a line of smoky, black smudges on the pale blue horizon. 'I don't know,' he replied. 'It's curious.'

Then they heard a sound; a deep, throaty roar, faint at first but rapidly growing in volume. It seemed to come from everywhere at once.

'Well, that's very curious indeed,' remarked Kirov.

Pekkala was still watching the horizon. Suddenly, he turned to the major. 'Run,' he said.

'What?'

'Run!' shouted Pekkala.

Kirov let go of the map, which wafted away across the road.

As the two men sprinted for cover, Kirov still had no idea what he was running from.

By now the sound had become deafening.

Pekkala threw himself into a weed-choked ditch, landing in a dusty clump of black-eyed susans, just as the lead plane opened fire with its 30mm cannons on the GAZ-67.

The pilot had spotted the vehicle, parked out in the open and its outline clearly visible, only two seconds before. He was closing so quickly on his target that he barely had time to aim as he pressed the red fire button on his control stick. The plane shuddered as the four cannons opened up and he saw tall puffs of dirt converging upon the Soviet Army vehicle. And then he was past it, with no idea if he had done any damage at all. He made a mental note to check if the vehicle was still there when they returned from their sortie.

Back in the ditch, Pekkala flinched at the drumming of the cannon fire accompanied by the clank-clank-clank of rounds striking the GAZ. At the same moment, he glimpsed the flickering shadows of the planes passing overhead.

It was several seconds more before he dared to raise his head.

The first thing Pekkala saw was fluid pouring from beneath the engine of their car. One of the tyres had burst and the bonnet of the vehicle was filled with so many jagged holes that it reminded him of a cheese grater.

On the other side of the road, Kirov crawled out of the ditch. 'What kind of planes were those?' he asked, as he disentangled himself from a garland of purple-flowered vetch. 'I've never seen anything move so quickly in my life!'

'Or do so much damage in so short a space of time,' added Pekkala, as he joined Kirov up on the road.

The two men stood before the car, wearing identical frowns.

The air filled with the sweet smell of radiator fluid which had soaked into the dirt.

Kirov unfastened the bonnet latch and lifted the perforated sheet of metal to inspect the engine. When he saw what had been done, he groaned.

One of the cannon rounds, each one of which was as big as a man's thumb, had gone through the side of the radiator, torn a gash across its entire length and then exited through the other side. Another round had punctured the manifold, leaving a hole the size of a man's fist, through which both men could see the pistons, still glistening with oil, and now as gnarled and crooked as the fingers of a witch. Even those bullets which had not struck vital parts of the engine had shredded the body of the vehicle, ricocheting from one panel through another so that it appeared to Kirov as if the car had been assaulted by some axe-wielding psychopath. 'It's hopeless,' he muttered.

'We'll have a hell of a long walk back to Moscow,' agreed Pekkala.

'The icon!' said Kirov.

Pekkala breathed in sharply.

In all the chaos, they had forgotten about it.

Pekkala went around to the metal storage bin behind the back seat. A round had passed clean through the steel, but there was no telling what damage it had done to the contents. Holding his breath, Pekkala undid the two clasps which held the lid in place. Slowly, he lifted it up. The oilcloth bundle, although it had been showered with tiny fragments of paint and metal, was undamaged. He lifted out the package and tucked it under his arm. 'How far did you say it was to the village?'

'It should be just beyond those trees,' replied Kirov.

'Well,' said Pekkala, 'it's time we stretched our legs.'

As they set off towards Ahlborn, Kirov glanced back at the car. The GAZ had been a considerable improvement over the contemptible old Emka and he had grown fond of it over the past few days. Now, with its front tyres blown, the once rugged-looking machine slumped awkwardly forward in a way that reminded Kirov of an elephant named Maximus, which had been one of the star attractions at the Moscow zoo and was killed in an air raid on the city back in the winter of 1941.

Soon afterwards, they entered the village.

Here, Pekkala paused. Until this point, he had carried the icon hidden under his coat, but it was too dangerous to carry it with them any further. The icon would need to be hidden, although somewhere close enough that an exchange could be made if things went according to plan.

'What is it, Inspector?' asked Kirov.

'Walk on a hundred paces,' he said, 'and wait for me there, in the street.' With those words, Pekkala dashed back among the houses, behind which he came across a narrow alley, bordered on either side by tall wooden fences. He moved along the alley, until he reached the church's north transept. There, a side door hung lopsided on its broken hinges. After looking around to make sure he had not been seen, Pekkala entered the building.

The church had been damaged by a combination of fire, which had scorched the ante-chapel but had failed to spread into the nave, and blast from a mortar that had landed in the churchyard, leaving a chest-deep crater, now partially filled with rainwater. He heard the purring trill of pigeons in the shattered rafters and the mutter of wind through broken stained-glass windows which spilled their brightly coloured shades of blue, red and yellow on to the warped boards of the floor below.

He proceeded to the altar, now occupied only by a bare wooden table pushed against the far wall, the adornments having been hidden away before the town was evacuated. After placing the icon on the table, Pekkala ducked out through the same side door and emerged into the street, where Kirov was waiting for him.

The major's gaze was fixed on something up the road.

Following Kirov's line of sight, Pekkala noticed a solitary figure standing in the middle of the road.

'Is that him?' whispered Kirov.

'I can't tell,' answered Pekkala. 'He's still too far away.'

As if by compelled by some unspoken command, they began to walk towards the stranger.

*

Emil watched the two men approaching from the east.

After leaving Stefan's house, he was hurrying along the road through town when he heard the planes fly past. Glancing at his watch, he noted that they were right on time today. By now, he had grown used to the sound of those engines, but the sound of gunfire caused him to stop in his tracks.

The only people he had seen were the few civilians who had accompanied him on his cart ride into town, and they had all come from the west. But the planes had been shooting at something on the other side of town.

His first thought was to hurry on towards the railway station, but after a few steps he paused. It could be Stefan, he thought. Maybe he has come back after all. Cautiously, he turned around. I'll wait, he told himself. Just for a few minutes. Just so that I can be sure.

Now he squinted at the approaching figures. One of them, wearing a short, double-breasted coat and corduroy trousers, was a civilian. But the other man's silhouette was clearly military, and not German military, either. From the blousy rising breeches and the way he wore his tunic like an untucked shirt, Emil knew he was looking at a Russian.

Neither of them was his brother.

His mind had turned into a hornet's nest of calculations as he tried to gauge the situation. Are they looking for me? he wondered. Did Stefan get a message through to the scientists at Sosnogorsk? Maybe that civilian is one of them. Have they come to bring me back with them?

Whatever the answer, it was too late now to run.

They were close enough now that Emil could see their faces.

He set down his briefcase and slowly raised one hand in greeting. 'By any chance,' he called to them, 'are you looking for Professor Emil Kohl?'

'Indeed we are,' answered the civilian, 'and also his brother, Stefan.'

'Did he send you here to find me?' Emil asked.

'In a manner of speaking,' answered Pekkala.

Kohl lifted the briefcase. 'It's all here, as promised.' Fumbling with the brass catches, he lifted the lid and removed one of the two remaining spring-loaded metal canisters. He held it up for them to see, his hands trembling. 'The crown jewel of Sartaman Project, along with its creator!' Then he hurriedly returned the vial to its blue velvet nest inside the briefcase.

'What about your brother?' asked the civilian.

'I don't know,' Emil admitted. 'He left here weeks ago and I haven't seen him since. I thought you . . .'

His voice was silenced by a gunshot.

Emil's legs collapsed beneath him. A jet of blood as long as a man's arm sprayed from his shattered skull. The briefcase fell from his hands.

As Pekkala and Kirov drew their weapons, they searched the houses for any sign of movement, but all they could see were their own blurred reflections in those windows not blinkered by the wooden shutters.

At that moment, a stranger appeared from a gap between

two houses, smoke still leaking from the barrel of the old Nagant revolver in his grasp. He stood at the very edge of the narrow alleyway, but still in full view of the men. It was Stefan Kohl.

Even after all these years, Pekkala remembered that face. He lined Stefan up in his gunsight.

Kirov did the same.

Stefan made no attempt to raise his pistol, as if he knew that he had nothing to fear from the two men, in spite of the weapons they had aimed at him. 'Why did you kill him?' asked Pekkala, nodding at the crumpled body of Emil Kohl.

'He betrayed me.'

'He thought you were trying to save him,' said Pekkala.

'What I'm saving is far more important,' answered Stefan. 'I warned you long ago to stay away from me, Inspector. How much more blood must we shed before you will finally listen?'

'None,' replied Pekkala, 'including yours if you walk away now.'

'Not without *The Shepherd*.'

'It is only a matter of time,' said Pekkala, 'before Russian scientists have reproduced the compound you used to murder Father Detlev. All you have is the contents of that briefcase, and I will shoot you dead before you lay a hand on them. You must face the fact that you have nothing left to bargain with.'

'That is where you're wrong, Inspector.' Reaching back into the shadows of the alley, he hauled out his prisoner.

To the horror of Kirov and Pekkala, they saw it was Elizaveta.

With one hand knotted in her hair, Stefan dragged her out into the street. A shout went up from Kirov. Without thinking, he lunged towards his wife.

'Stop if you want her to live!' bellowed Stefan.

The words cut through the blindness of Kirov's rage and he skittered to a halt, his face red, and breathing hard. 'If you have harmed her . . .' he growled.

'I have no wish to hurt her, Major Kirov, but I will not leave this place without *The Shepherd*.' He pressed the barrel of the Nagant against the back of Elizaveta's skull and tightened his grip in her hair, causing the young woman to gasp with pain. 'Now, what is it to be?'

Pekkala's mind reeled as he attempted to calculate the situation, but he soon reached the inevitable conclusion. He would not see the value of that icon measured out in human blood, least of all hers. 'Let her go,' he told Stefan. 'I placed *The Shepherd* on the altar table in the church. All you have to do is go and get it.'

'Why should I trust you?' demanded Stefan.

'Because I have given you no reason to do otherwise,' replied Pekkala.

Stefan paused as Pekkala's words sank in. 'Very well,' he said at last, 'but empty your guns before I leave.' He jerked his chin at Kirov. 'And him too.'

Pekkala unfastened the top break of the Webley, causing the barrel to tilt forward. He ejected the bullets, and they fell to the ground. Then Pekkala held up the gun, so that Kohl could see daylight through the empty cylinders.

But Kirov seemed frozen in place, his Tokarev still aimed at the Skoptsy.

'Do as he says,' ordered Pekkala.

A moment passed. Kirov's arm trembled, as if his body was at war with itself. Then he pressed a button near the trigger guard, slid out the magazine and threw it away to the other side of the street. 'Now let her go,' he commanded.

Kohl released his grip on the woman and pushed her to the ground, but before he turned to run, he took aim at the briefcase which contained the vials of soman and fired. The case jumped as if it had suddenly come to life. A slab of its leather side flew off. He fired once more and the brass latch was ripped from its mounting more and the lid sprang open. Another round smashed through the blue velvet protecting the glass and silver vials. Again and again, Stefan pulled the trigger of the Nagant until all of its chambers were empty.

Elizaveta had been climbing to her feet in the moment that Kohl opened fire. Hearing the whip-crack of bullets, she threw herself back down, covering her head with her hands.

Kohl's third shot had ploughed through the mangled briefcase, shattering the vials and spraying their contents into the air.

A single droplet landed on Elizaveta's wrist, so tiny that she did not even feel it. She stood, but then immediately began to stagger. Her eyes rolled back into her head and she fell in a heap.

Pekkala knew immediately what must have happened and he reached for the two syringes of atropine in his coat pocket.

Kirov, standing right beside Pekkala, had also grasped the situation. To help Elizaveta meant the possibility of being exposed to the soman, and there was only enough antidote for two people. 'What should I do?' he gasped.

'Kohl,' was all Pekkala said.

Without another word, Kirov spun on his heel and sprinted towards the church and, as he ran, he removed the spare magazine from his Tokarev holster and fitted it into the pistol.

By the time Pekkala reached Elizaveta, she was already beginning to choke. Her hands had twisted into claws and a slick of white foam seeped from the corner of her mouth. He knelt down beside her, twisted off the cap of the metal container and slid out the syringe. Then he tore away the buttons of her shirt at the same time as he clamped his teeth over the Bakelite needle protector, pulled it off and spat it away. He placed his hand directly over her heart and felt for a gap between her ribs. Then he forced the needle home, pressing hard to drive it in between her ribs.

For a moment, which seemed to Pekkala to last forever, it seemed as if the drug had no effect.

Then suddenly, she gasped and sat upright, her eyes wide and terrified.

Grabbing her under the arms, Pekkala dragged her away from the contaminated ground. They had reached the other side of the street before he let her go again. As Pekkala watched her lying there, too weak to stand and retching as she tried to clear her lungs, he wondered if the atropine had saved her life or was only prolonging her agony.

At that moment, he began to feel dizzy. A darkness seemed to crowd in from the corners of his mind and he realised he was struggling to breathe. He looked down and saw that the material of his trousers was wet where he had been kneeling in the street. Then he knew that some of the liquid must have soaked through the heavy corduroy. Fumbling with the second atropine container, he removed the syringe and began struggling with the buttons of his coat and then his waistcoat. By then, he could not breathe at all and his vision was so blurred that he began to suffer vertigo. He staggered back against the wall of a house, and tried to jam the needle into his chest, only to realise that the cap was still on. He pulled it off, exposing the needle at last and rammed it in between his ribs, feeling it scrape against bone. Then, with the last of his strength, he pushed the plunger, watching the liquid vanish into his heart. With the needle still between his ribs, he slid down against the wall and blacked out.

He had no idea how long he was unconscious. It may only have been a couple of seconds. The first thing he saw when his eyes opened was Elizaveta.

She was lying on her side, with her arm hooked under her head as a pillow. She looked exhausted, but he could see that she was breathing normally.

Pekkala turned away and spat. As he did this, he caught sight of the syringe, which was still jutting from between his ribs. He grasped the tube and pulled it out. It slipped from his fingers and fell with a clatter on the road.

Then he reached into his pocket and pulled out the old stag-handled knife which he always carried with him. Opening the blade, Pekkala heard the reassuring click of its locking mechanism and he then proceeded to cut away the cloth around his knees where the soman had soaked in.

'What are you doing?' asked Elizaveta. She was sitting up now and watching him with a baffled look on her face.

'Ruining a perfectly good pair of trousers,' answered Pekkala, as he carved through the thick brown corduroy.

In that moment, they were startled by the sound of a shot, quickly followed by two more, and then silence.

Stefan Kohl had reached the church. He entered through the open door beside the north transept and quickly made his way to the altar. On the table lay a bundle, wrapped in the same oil-cloth he had used when he placed it in his father's coffin for safekeeping.

His first thought was simply to take it and run, but now he paused. He had to be sure. They might have tried to trick him, after all. Carefully, he unwrapped the bundle and the bright blues and greens of the icon seemed to jump out of the darkness of that tattered piece of cloth. There could be no mistaking the painting he had carried with him twice across the length of Russia. This frail and brittle panel had become the substance of his life. With *The Shepherd* in his hands again, Stefan felt as if some vital part of him had been restored. Once more, he was the keeper of his faith. Clutching the icon to his chest, he stepped out into the churchyard. A long journey lay ahead of him, he knew, and where it would take him, he had no idea. All he knew was that it must be far away from here.

He did not see Kirov until it was already too late.

The major stepped out from behind one of the stone buttresses of the church, appearing so suddenly in front of Stefan that the two men actually collided.

Kirov did not hesitate.

The bullet passed through the icon, smashed through Stefan's chest and left a hole the size of a man's fist as it exited through his back.

Kohl stepped back abruptly, a startled look on his face.

Kirov fired two more rounds before Stefan's legs gave out from under him.

Stefan lay on his back. Through dimming sight he looked up at the sky. He could smell smoke; sweet like church incense and through the sputter of his failing senses he perceived that the Shepherd had come to life and stood before him now, casting a shadow on his face and filling him with warmth as what he believed could only be his soul was lifted from the ruins of his body. Stefan thought about the night he had stood in the rain, speaking to the man he had pulled from the ditch on the road to Krasnoyar, and how his mind had been so plagued with doubt about choosing the course his life would take. How he wished he could go back to that moment in time and reassure his younger self that everything the pilgrim had told him was the truth. There is no doubt, he thought. 'No doubt at all,' he whispered.

'What?' Kirov looked down pitilessly upon the man he had just shot. 'What are you saying?'

Kohl breathed out in a long, rattling sigh.

Then Kirov knew that there would be no answer to his question. Coughing, he stepped back from the tatters of smoke rising from the dead man's chest. The muzzle flash of the Tokarev had ignited highly flammable paint, setting fire to the ancient wooden panel and causing Stefan's blood to crackle and blacken as it boiled.

Kirov holstered his gun and went back to find Elizaveta. He caught up with her and Pekkala as they were walking down the street. They both moved slowly and unsteadily, as if old age had suddenly crept up on them.

Kirov ran up to his wife and embraced her.

Pekkala, his pale knees poking from the ragged holes in his trousers, waited patiently, until at last they stood back from each other. 'Did you find him?' he asked Kirov.

Kirov nodded.

'Where is he now?' demanded the Inspector.

'Lying in the churchyard,' Kirov replied.

'And the icon?'

Reluctantly, Kirov explained what had happened. 'It was only a painting, after all,' he added with a kind of hopeless optimism.

For a moment, Pekkala said nothing. Then finally he spoke. 'You may be right about that, Major,' he said, much to Kirov's surprise.

From the distance came the rumble and clank of approaching Soviet tanks.

'Perhaps the offensive has begun,' remarked Elizaveta.

'If we start walking now,' said Pekkala, 'we'll run into them before they reach the town. We can warn them about the so-man and they will take the necessary steps to decontaminate the area.'

'And after that?' asked Kirov. 'Those planes destroyed our vehicle. How are we supposed to make it back to Moscow?'

For the first time since Kohl had kidnapped her off the street, Elizaveta smiled. 'Come with me, gentlemen,' she said. 'An old friend of yours is waiting.'

One hour later, with Kirov behind the wheel of the Emka, they encountered a Red Army reconnaissance squad making its way cautiously towards Ahlborn. After flagging down the lead armoured car of the squad, Pekkala informed the commander about the briefcase. Then they carried on towards Moscow, passing dozens of tanks and trucks, all of them loaded with soldiers, making their way steadily westwards.

By then, Elizaveta had told the men the story of her capture, and what had become of Sergeant Zolkin.

'But he was alive when you saw him last,' said Pekkala.

'Yes,' she replied, 'but . . .'

Pekkala cut her off. 'Then there is still room for hope,' he said.

'I should never have left you in Moscow,' Kirov told Elizaveta.

'And I should never have allowed you to leave.'

'Allowed me?' One eyebrow raised, he glanced at his wife in the rear-view mirror. 'Is that so, Corporal?'

'It is, Major Kirov,' she replied.

'This time I think she outranks you,' agreed Pekkala.

24 March 1945

Moscow

At the Sklivassovsky Hospital, they found Zolkin alive, although with twenty stitches in his neck. As soon as they entered the room, he climbed out of bed and embraced each one in turn. Although he was under orders not to speak, and could manage no more than a whisper, he immediately inquired about the Emka, which he had last seen driving off with Stefan Kohl behind the wheel.

He took Elizaveta's hand in both of his. 'I suppose you will no longer need me as your bodyguard,' he croaked.

'Luckily for both of us, that's true,' she replied.

Then a nurse arrived and ordered him back into bed.

Kirov and Pekkala left Elizaveta at the hospital, to make sure that she was suffering no ill effects from her exposure to the chemical weapon.

'But what about you?' she asked Pekkala.

'I'll be back,' he told her, 'but first your husband and I have some business to take care of.'

'Where are we going?'

'To see if your theory is correct.'

'Theory?' asked Kirov, following him down the corridor. 'What theory?'

26 March 1945

Gorokhovaya Ulitsa, Leningrad

In what had once been the courtyard of Rasputin's apartment building, the mangled wreckage of a Soviet 37mm anti-aircraft gun still aimed its useless barrel at the sky. An artillery round had landed in the street outside, blown through the brick wall of the courtyard and demolished the steel gun-carriage used to transport the gun. The gun itself bore the scars of multiple shrapnel strikes and the rubber tyres, which had been painted a camouflage green, were now warped and deflated and the paint had crackled so that it resembled the skin of a reptile. It appeared that the gun had simply been abandoned, along with the ground floor of the building, which had also been ruined in the blast.

Pekkala stood in the courtyard, shielding his eyes with one hand as he squinted up to the floor on which Rasputin had lived.

'I still don't understand what we're doing here,' said Kirov.

Pekkala lowered his hand and turned to the major. 'Testing your theory,' he said.

'I wish you would tell me what this damned theory of mine is!' shouted Kirov.

They entered the building through the gaping hole in the masonry which had once held an ornate front door, complete with frosted glass engraved with a French-influenced pattern of twined ivy leaves that had once been all the rage in this city. Then Pekkala began to climb the stairs.

Kirov followed, grudgingly.

When the two men reached Rasputin's old apartment, Pekkala paused and looked around. The landing on which he stood had not seen a coat of paint in many years. The loose panes of the window looking out over the courtyard rattled in the breeze. It was not that things had looked that much better in Rasputin's day. The Siberian had never paid attention to the up-keep of the various houses where he stayed as a guest of wealthy benefactors. That duty had usually fallen to the Tsarina herself, who had been known to send in teams of decorators to recarpet floors, replace every article of furniture, even down to the cutlery, and repaint the walls in her favourite shade of mauve.

That colour, which Pekkala loathed because it reminded him of the boiled liver he had been forced to eat as a child, had returned many times to his mind over the past few days as he recalled the occasion when he came to visit Rasputin after the theft of the icon. The walls had just been painted. When he remarked upon the fact to Rasputin, he had received the answer that the Tsarina had ordered it to be done out of reverence for the icon. And he had thought no more about it. Until now.

Pekkala rapped his knuckles on the door.

'Who's there?' called the nervous voice of a man standing on the other side, so close that the shadow of his feet showed on the floor.

'Special Operations,' said Pekkala.

'Special Operations?' echoed the man. 'What did they send you for?'

Kirov turned to Pekkala and shrugged. Then he faced the door again. 'Are you going to open up or not?'

There was a rattling of chains and the clunk of a deadbolt sliding back. The door swung wide, revealing a short, elderly man with a fuzz of grey hair and startled-looking blue eyes, which gave him the appearance of a baby bird that had been ousted from its nest. He wore a thick, long-sleeved undershirt tucked into high-waisted black trousers that were held up by a pair of white braces. He had no shoes on, and his bare feet looked small and vulnerable. 'My name is Gleb Kutsov,' said the man, pronouncing his name in a way that sounded almost like a sneeze, 'and I would have taken care of it. All I needed was a little more time.'

'What is he talking about?' whispered Kirov.

Pekkala stepped into the room and was surprised to see Rasputin's old leather couch still sitting in the corner. But that, other than the layout of the room, was the only remaining trace of the Siberian. The walls, no longer mauve, had been covered over in paper of a chiffon-yellow colour decorated with a repeating pattern of tiny red flowers. In the place where the icon had been, however briefly, hung a small reprint of Leonid Kotliarov's portrait of a miner named Alexei Stakhanov, who had come to symbolise the ideal Soviet worker. In the picture, Stakhanov was chipping away at a coalface with a large pneumatic drill. He wore clothes almost as dark as the coalface itself and his features were illuminated by some impossible light source.

'Like I said,' repeated the man, 'there was no need to call on Special Operations for a matter as simple as paying the rent!'

'Is that why you think we are here?' asked Pekkala.

'Well, isn't it?' replied the man. 'Let me tell you something about this so-called landlord.'

Pekkala raised his hand, opening his fingers slowly, like a magician revealing the disappearance of a coin.

The man fell immediately silent.

'I am not here about the rent,' Pekkala said quietly.

'Then what on earth . . . ?' Kutsov paused as he followed Pekkala's gaze to the painting of Stakhanov. 'The print?' he asked. 'Is there something wrong with it? Has the artist fallen out of favour? Because if he has, I swear to you, comrades, I knew nothing about it!' Kutsov began to breathe heavily. 'I never really liked it, to be honest. A friend gave it to me, and a friend no longer, I should say!' He all but lunged at the wall, removed the painting from its supporting nail and handed it to Major Kirov. 'Take it!' he commanded, turning his head away as if he could not even bear to see the painting any longer. 'Make it go away! I never want to see it again.'

Pekkala stepped up to the blank wall. 'Was this nail here when you moved in?' he asked.

'Yes, I think so.'

'And when did you move in?'

'I've been here since 1923. The place had been empty for several years when I arrived.'

Pekkala reached over and tapped against the wall. 'It's not very thick.'

'It's just a board, I think,' said Kutsov, staring at the space as if to find some meaning in its blankness.

'I am sorry to do this,' said Pekkala, and with those words, he removed the lock knife from his pocket, opened the blade and rammed the tip into the wall.

Kutsov gasped, as if the metal had pierced his own flesh.

Without letting the blade sink in too deeply, Pekkala dragged the knife down the wall, and then across and then dragged it back up again, creating a U-shaped scar in the thin plaster board. Then, his teeth clenched with the effort, he worked the knife across the top until a rectangular cut had been made. He then put the knife away and, with one sharp strike from the heel of his palm, knocked the piece loose. It fell back into the space behind the wall and dropped away.

And then the three men stared in amazement at the picture which met their eyes. It was *The Shepherd*, its bright colours obscured by a fine layer of plaster dust.

Pekkala leaned forward and, as if extinguishing a candle, blew away the powder.

'I know that painting,' said Kutsov. 'But I thought . . .'

'So did we all,' replied Pekkala.

Slowly Kutsov sank to his knees. 'Do you mean to tell me that this has been hanging in my house the whole time I've been living here?'

'That appears to be the case,' said Kirov, as he reached in through the gap and carefully removed the icon.

Pekkala rested his hand upon Kutsov's shoulder. 'Someone will come to fix the damage,' he said.

When the two men walked out of the room, Kutsov was still fixated upon the crater in his wall, as if at any moment, more treasures might tumble from the dusty gloom.

'How did you know?' asked Kirov, as they walked down to the street.

'Back in Ahlborn,' said Pekkala, 'when you told me it was

just a painting, I remembered that I'd heard those words before.'

'From whom?'

'Rasputin,' answered Pekkala. 'On the day the icon was reported stolen, I came to this house and he told me to abandon my search. He warned me how dangerous it would be if I continued the investigation. Grigori was right, but he was trying to tell me something else as well. When he said it was only a painting, I thought that sounded strange coming from a man as devout as Rasputin. What I didn't understand until you spoke those words again was that he meant it literally.'

'Then the thing Stefan Kohl was chasing all this time . . .'

'Was a forgery, and, whoever did the work,' said Pekkala, 'the Tsarina must have known about it, as well as where the original was stashed. After all, she was the one who ordered the wall to be painted, which must have been to cover up the damage they had caused when hiding it.'

'Why leave it at Rasputin's?' asked Kirov.

'Because that is the one place she thought no one would look,' replied Pekkala. 'And when the people of Russia had finally resigned themselves to the fact that *The Shepherd* was gone, the Tsarina would spirit it back to its hiding place in their own Church of the Resurrection. You see, Kirov, although she believed in its power, she never had any intention of sharing that power with the world.'

'But the forgery was perfect,' remarked Kirov. 'Even Semykin, the Kremlin's own authenticator, was convinced. Is there no way to find out who painted it?'

'Under different circumstances, I would probably say no,' Pekkala told him. 'A forger this accomplished would be well acquainted in the art of covering his tracks. However, the same is not always true of his employers and, in this case, I think I might know where to find the answer.'

28 March 1945

Moscow

Outside the battered metal door of Archive 17, Pekkala stood in the rain.

He had knocked several times, but there was no response. And yet he could see through the transom windows at the top of the wall, that the lights were on inside. Someone was there, and he knew that someone was Vosnovsky.

He turned up the collar of his coat as a cold breeze swept along the empty street, ripping the puddles like stucco.

With a low growl, he stepped up to the door and pounded on it once again.

Nothing.

'Vosnovsky!' he shouted. 'Open this wretched door!'

But his only reply was the wind, moaning through the broken windows of the abandoned warehouse across the street.

Pekkala paced out into the road, picked up one of the stones which had previously been hurled at the archive and prepared to pitch it at the door. But then he thought better of it and dropped the stone. Instead, he breathed in deeply and began to sing.

He belted out a piece from Rimsky-Korsakov's *Legend of the Invisible City of Kitezh and the Maiden Fevroniya*, in which a woman who is lost in the wilderness of the Kerzhenskii woods dreams that she has awoken in paradise. In February of 1907, Pekkala had accompanied the Tsar to the opera's premiere at the Mariinsky Theatre in St Petersburg. He did not want to go but the Tsar had insisted.

'Pekkala, my wonderful savage,' said the Tsar, 'it is time we civilised you just a little.'

It was Pekkala's first time at the opera. Although his seat was too small, the music too loud for his taste and he felt over-whelmed to be packed in with so many people, he did enjoy the evening, even in spite of himself.

The song of the Kerzhenskii woods had tattooed itself into Pekkala's mind, as the songs from his childhood had done, and he sang it as best he could, which was not particularly well.

The reason Pekkala bothered at all was that he had suddenly remembered the way Vosnovsky, in his previous incarnation as conductor on the Imperial Russian Railway line between Petersburg and Tsarskoye Selo, had sung operas while marching up and down the aisle of the rattly little train of which he was inordinately proud.

Pekkala had not been yowling long before the door to the Archive suddenly flew open and there stood Vosnovsky, eyes wide in astonishment. 'Rimsky-Korsakov!' he shouted.

'Actually,' said Pekkala, 'it's me.'

'Good God!' exclaimed Vosnovsky. 'Don't stand there in the rain. Come in!'

Inside the Archive building, Vosnovsky spread his arms to take in the hundreds of filing cabinets. 'Just say a name, In-spector!'

'Detlev,' answered Pekkala. 'If he's in here, he should be in one of the old Okhrana files.'

Vosnovsky turned sharply and strode away down one of the cabinet-lined avenues. 'Okhrana!' he said. And then he said it again, and again, and before long he was singing the word in a voice that echoed through the rafters of the Archive.

Once more, Pekkala recalled the proud conductor of the Petrograd-to-Tsarskoye train line, a double row of silver buttons shining on his dark blue tunic, bellowing out arias as he strode up and down the aisles of the carriage.

Then Vosnovsky came to an abrupt halt. 'Here!' he announced. 'D. Detlev.' He slid out one of the file drawers and walked his fingers across the brittle, dog-eared ranks of files. Smartly, he yanked out an envelope and was just about to hand it to Pekkala when the satisfied expression on his face suddenly faltered. The envelope rose and fell as he weighed in in his hand. 'There's something wrong,' he said.

'It's empty,' remarked Pekkala.

'Why, yes,' agreed Vosnovsky. 'It almost sounds as if you knew already.'

Pekkala nodded wearily. 'I thought there was a chance that the contents might have found their way home.'

Confused, Vosnovsky looked back into the crammed contents of the file drawer. 'Well, Inspector, unless you know who might have taken it, I'm afraid there is very little chance . . .'

Vosnovsky's words snagged like a fish hook in Pekkala's brain. 'We could try the Blue File,' he said.

Vosnovsky turned to him, startled. 'The Blue File!' he echoed in a whisper. 'No one has asked to see that in a very long time, and if the request were coming from anyone other than you, Inspector, I can assure you that request would be denied.'

The Blue File was one of the most secret collections of documents in all of Russia. It had been compiled by the Tsar, and contained lists of agents whose identities had never been revealed. Code names were used, and the names of the men to which they had been assigned were known only to the Tsar himself. These included not only top-level Okhrana operatives on special missions for the Tsar, but also spies who had been tasked to infiltrate their own secret service, as well as to perform other duties the Tsar considered too sensitive to reveal even to his closest and most trusted confidants.

After the Tsar and his family had been banished from Tsarskoye Selo, beginning the long journey which would ultimately end with their murders in the far-away city of Ekaterinburg, the file was discovered in a secret compartment of a desk in the Tsar's study by agents of the newly formed Bolshevik Secret Service. It became known as the Blue File because all entries had been made in blue pencil in the Tsar's own hand.

Rather than simply remove the file, the entire desk had been transported from Tsarskoye Selo in the hopes that, contained somewhere within this finely constructed piece of furniture, there might exist some other document, in which the real names of the agents might be found. But no book decoding the names had ever been discovered. If such a thing had even existed, it was likely that the Tsar had simply burned it before his departure, leaving the unsolved riddle of the file to torment those who had toppled him from power.

Even though the Tsar's Secret Service, the Okhrana, was gone forever, and the men who once worked for the Tsar had either fled the country or were dead, access to the Blue File was still restricted only to those who had been granted the express permission of Stalin. The reason for this was not so much to protect what the Blue File contained, but to keep hidden its very existence. The very fact that such a file had been created might have led people to wonder if there might be another such file, one kept in Stalin's own hand, and hidden away from the world. Stalin knew, as did the Tsar before him, that the best secret was not one whose answer was kept hidden by the strongest lock and key. The best secret was one which nobody knew existed.

'Did the Tsar make you aware of Detlev's code name?'

'No,' admitted Pekkala.

'Or even that he was on special assignment for the Romanovs?'

Pekkala shook his head.

Vosnovsky regarded him solemnly. 'Then why . . . ?' he began.

Pekkala fixed him with a stare.

Vosnovsky's mouth snapped shut. Motioning for Pekkala to follow, he made his way down the aisles of cabinets until he came to a locked door. The door was made of metal, painted in the same grey colour as the walls, and was as solidly constructed as the door that led out to the street. The only difference was that it had no handle, only a lock, which meant that it had not only to be unlocked from the outside, but that anyone entering was then expected to lock themselves in. Rummaging in his pocket, Vosnovsky produced a large bundle of keys and fiddled with it for some time before he found what he was looking for. Then he slid the key into the lock. With a heavy clunk, the deadbolt slid back and the door slid open with a groan of its seldom-used hinges.

The desk was the only piece of furniture in the room, which had no windows or ventilation. It appeared to have been some kind of storage room, or else a workplace deliberately set aside from the main floor in the days when the Archive had been a foundry.

Vosnovsky walked around to the back of the desk, crouched down and slid out a large compartment which contained the file. He lifted it up on to the desk. The file comprised thousands of pages, each particular set of documents separated by a small tab containing the code word by which the individual agent was known. As Pekkala squinted at the tidy collection of manila folders, each one marked with the code names of agents likely long since dead or living far away in carefully maintained obscurity – Angel Wing, Aldebaran, Balalaika, Carousel – he recognised the Tsar's handwriting, and even the faint blue colour of the pencil which the Tsar had also used to make margin notes in the sheaves of documents supplied to him each week by his parliament, the Duma. Suddenly, Pekkala paused. There, jammed in between Carousel and another agent, code-named Dromedary, he saw a crumpled collection of pages, with no folder or anything to mark the agent's name. He lifted them out and placed them on the desk.

It was the contents of Detlev's Okhrana file, clearly showing his arrest in June of 1910, incarceration in the fortress of Peter and Paul and then his release only one month later. But it was the reason for his arrest that caught Pekkala's attention. In a raid on a guesthouse suspected of being the residence of a bomb maker named Kachalov, municipal police had come across a man, later identified as Detlev, in the act of creating a forgery. But this was not just any forgery. It was a study of a figure contained within Titian's *Burial of Saint Sebastian*, one of the most famous paintings in the Tsar's private collection. Although Titian produced many detailed studies of characters he later incorporated into his masterpieces, almost none were known to have survived. Upon interrogation, Detlev confessed that he was working for an art dealer named Kramer, who owned a well-known gallery in St Petersburg and who had furnished the Tsar with several paintings over the years. Well aware that a previously undiscovered canvas relating to the *Burial of Saint Sebastian* would prove irresistible to the Tsar, Kramer had commissioned the forgery, intending to make a small fortune off the sale. Having learned of Detlev's arrest, Kramer left the country before police could track him down. But Detlev was sentenced to hard labour for a term of no less than twenty-five years, a length of time few prisoners survived. And then, quite suddenly, and only a few weeks later. Detlev found himself a free man, by order of the Tsar. There was no mention in the Okhrana report as to why the Tsar had ordered his release, but there, at the bottom of the page, faintly written in the Tsar's own hand, Pekkala found the answer. It was a list of other paintings forged by Detlev. Among them, he saw *Communion of the Elders* by Crespi, and Rosa's *Court Musician*, which he knew had been part of the Romanovs' extensive art collection. As far as Pekkala knew, the true provenance of these paintings had never been revealed. According to the rest of the world, these paintings were all original. The only person left in Russia who knew the truth was Detlev. Having got word to the Tsar that the forgeries were part of his collection, Detlev had done what few men had ever been able to accomplish – he had struck a deal with Nicholas II. Detlev had traded his silence for freedom. In doing so, he had taken an extraordinary risk. The safest way to ensure a man's silence was to have him put to death, something the Tsar could have accomplished easily, quietly and efficiently. If word had leaked out that the Tsar had paid such mighty sums for paintings that were worthless, it would not only have made him a laughing stock but would have cast his entire collection into doubt. So why keep the forger alive? The Romanovs must have seen that a man with such extraordinary skills might come in handy some day. In the meantime, the Tsar had kept him close at hand, as a priest in the Church of the Resurrection on his own estate. Detlev might have believed that he had put his past behind him, thanks to the benevolence of the Tsar, but the day had come when his old skills were needed again. With access to the original, something almost never granted to a forger, Detlev had created a near perfect copy. It was this forgery that Stefan Kohl had received that day on the Potsuleyev Bridge and which, years later, the Skoptsy had died trying to protect.

Pekkala thought back to the day when, with the stitches from his knife wound still new and painful on his forehead, he had gone to the Alexander Palace, to make his report to the Tsar. He recalled how the Tsar's fingers had drummed across the top of his desk, this same desk on which Pekkala's knuckles rested now. If Pekkala could only have reached into the drawer, he would have found the missing contents of Detlev's criminal record, recently removed from Okhrana headquarters, perhaps by one of those same agents whose code names were listed in the file which lay before Pekkala now.

Whether or not it had been the Tsar's idea, or that of the Tsarina, to begin secret peace negotiations with his enemies, the Tsar had nevertheless been drawn into it. To pay the Skoptsy's asking price, he had played his role in the deception. And worse than that, the Tsar had stopped his own investigator from finding out the truth.

Vosnovsky's eyes grew rounder and rounder as Pekkala told him the story.

Afterwards, Pekkala wrote down the list of paintings in his notebook and Vosnovsky returned Detlev's record to the Tsar's secret file before placing it back inside the drawer.

Then the two men left the room, locking the door shut behind them.

They were walking back towards the entrance when suddenly Vosnovsky stopped and turned. 'But the original,' he asked, taking hold of Pekkala's arm. 'Who has the original now?'

*

'Ha!' Stalin boomed exultantly, grasping the icon with both hands and raising it above his head. 'I knew it!'

Kirov and Pekkala stood before him, wincing as Stalin brandished the work of art.

'I knew that first one you brought in here was a fake,' Stalin told them. 'I've got the knack, you see. The *instinct*!' He put the icon on his desk and wagged his finger at the shepherd in the painting, as if to scold the white-robed man for hiding all these years. 'That's why I said I didn't like the other one. It was a forgery. I told you so.'

Pekkala raised his eyebrows.

This did not go unnoticed by Stalin. 'Not in so many words,

perhaps,' he explained. 'I implied it. I insinuated. In matters of art, you cannot be so literal, Pekkala! The major was here. He knows what I'm talking about.' Stalin cast a threatening glance at Kirov. 'Don't you, Major?' he asked.

'Indeed, Comrade Stalin!' exclaimed Kirov, coming to attention.

Stalin turned back to Pekkala. 'There you are, you see. But there's no reason to feel ashamed, Inspector. The gifts of the gods are not handed out equally. It's just something I have and you don't.'

'Yet another miracle,' whispered Pekkala.

'Miracles!' Stalin grumbled. 'There's no such thing.'

'And what of the soman?' asked Kirov, anxious to change the subject.

'Chemical weapons specialists were sent to Ahlborn,' replied Stalin, 'where they collected samples from the broken vials which had belonged to Professor Kohl. These have now been safely stored away at our laboratory in Sosnogorsk, which is where they are likely to remain. Even our enemies seem to have grasped the madness of unleashing such a weapon on the battlefield.' As Stalin talked, his voice trailed off and his gaze returned to the icon. 'I think I might keep this for a while,' he said. 'I might even put it up on the wall next to my Repin.' He gestured towards the painting of the young lovers standing at the edge of the Neva River on a stormy winter's day. An expression of longing passed across his face as he stared at the couple, frozen in perpetual exhilaration.

Pekkala and Kirov stood there in silence for a while.

Finally, Pekkala spoke. 'Will there be anything else, Comrade Stalin?'

Stalin breathed in sharply, as if woken from a trance. He seemed surprised to find the two men standing there. 'Go now,' he told them gruffly. 'You'll be needed again soon enough.'

Kirov and Pekkala made their way out of the office, passing by a flustered-looking Poskrebychev, who had not heard them coming and was now pretending to fiddle with the dials on his intercom.

As they strode along the marble-floored hallway, Pekkala glanced across at Kirov. 'Indeed, Comrade Stalin!' he muttered, mimicking the shrill obedience of Kirov's voice back at him.

'What else was I supposed to say?' replied Kirov.

Pekkala did not reply. He reached into a pocket for his notebook, then tore out a page and handed it to Kirov.

'What's this?' asked the major.

'A list of Detlev's forgeries,' replied Pekkala. 'Do any of them look familiar?'

Kirov searched the list. He was not expert in matters of art and most of the titles were just mysteries to him. But one of them he did recognise. '*What Freedom!*' he said, and then he glanced at the Inspector. 'Isn't that the one by Repin?'

'Yes,' replied Pekkala. 'And it is hanging on the wall of Stalin's office.'

23 April 1945

Seelow Heights, Germany, 50 kilometres from Berlin

Pulled over at the side of the main east–west highway, known as Reichsstrasse Number 1, blue-grey diesel smoke coughed from the exhaust pipes of Captain Proskuryakov's new tank. It was a Model 76F, the latest in a long line of T34s that had rolled off the assembly line of the Uralmash factory in Sverdlovsk only two weeks before. Now the steel turret hatch clanked open and Captain Proskuryakov, resplendent in his new leather jacket, climbed up from the commander's seat below. 'Will you get a move on!' he bellowed at his driver, Sergeant Ovchinikov, struggling to make himself heard over the constant roar of machinery which passed them on the road. There were tanks and trucks and armoured cars, all of them loaded with men and supplies.

'Almost done!' replied Ovchinikov, who was crouched beside the turret, hobnailed boots balanced upon the engine grille.

'I swear to you, if this war ends before we reach Berlin . . .' Proskuryakov did not finish his sentence, but only shook one black-gloved fist at the sergeant. 'You can always tell when a man's luck has run out,' he added with a growl. 'You can see it in their eyes, and I'm starting to see it in yours!'

'There!' said Ovchinikov. 'Finished!' He scrambled over to

the driver's hatch and lowered himself inside.

A moment later, the engine slammed into gear and two fresh geysers of exhaust smoke belched into the sky. The wide, segmented tracks churned against the earth and Proskuryakov's tank turned out on to the road, joining the mass of vehicles streaming relentlessly towards the west.

As the T34 gathered speed, wet paint from letters daubed by Ovchinikov upon the turret began to merge, trickling into each other and forming a strangely beautiful pattern in which, before long, the word *Pastukh* – 'The Shepherd' – had merged into invisibility.

Acknowledgements

The author would like to thank the following for their help and encouragement:

At Faber: Walter Donohue, Katherine Armstrong, Will Atkinson, Miles Poynton, Neal Price, Simon Burke, Sophie Portas, Katie Hall, Hannah Griffiths, Angus Cargill and Alex Kirby.

At Opus: Glenn Young and Kay Radtke.

At Juicy Orange: Mark Robohm and Lauren Ruggeri.

At RCW: Deborah Rogers, Cara Jones, Gill Coleridge, Matthew Turner and Ruth McIntosh.

My Baker Street Irregulars: Richard Lloyd, Bill McMann and Charles Barber, Professor of Early Christian and Byzantine Art at Princeton University.

And in the Western Mountains: My friend and guide Bob Foster.